最啟發人心的
英文得獎
感言

Inspirational
Award
Speeches

"It always seems impossible until it's d
-Nelson Mandel

CONTENTS

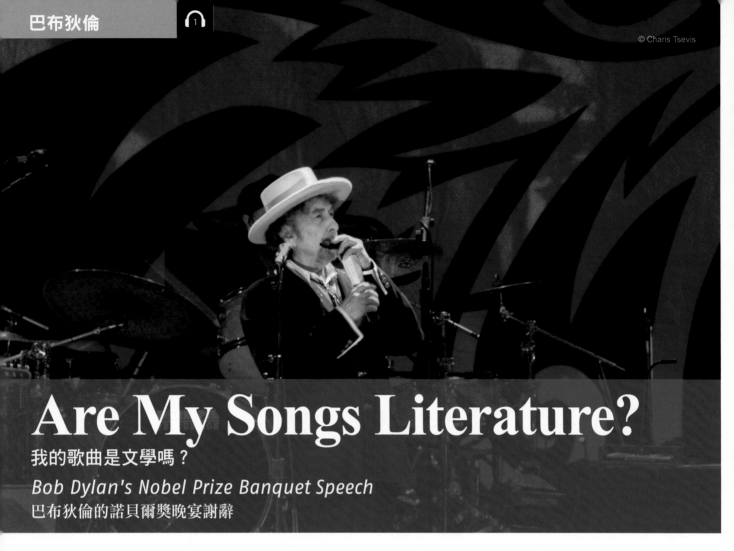

© Charis Tsevis

Are My Songs Literature?

我的歌曲是文學嗎？

Bob Dylan's Nobel Prize Banquet Speech
巴布狄倫的諾貝爾獎晚宴謝辭

Good evening, everyone. I [1)]**extend** my warmest [2)]**greetings** to the members of the LG Swedish Academy and to all of the other [3)]**distinguished** guests in [4)]**attendance** tonight.

各位晚安，我要向今晚出席的瑞典學院成員，以及其他出席貴賓致上最熱誠的問候。

 Standing Among Giants
站在巨人中

I'm sorry I can't be with you in person, but please know that I am most definitely with you in spirit and honored to be receiving such a [5)]**prestigious** prize. Being awarded the Nobel Prize for Literature is something I never could have imagined or seen coming. From an early age, I've been familiar with and reading and [6)]**absorbing** the works of those who were [7)]**deemed** [8)]**worthy** of such a [9)]**distinction**: LG Kipling, Shaw, Thomas Mann, Pearl Buck, Albert Camus, Hemingway. These giants of literature whose works are taught in the schoolroom, housed in libraries around the world and spoken of in [10)]**reverent** tones have always made a deep [11)]**impression**. GM That I now join the names on such a list is truly LG beyond words.

VOCABULARY

1) **extend** [ɪk`stɛnd] (v.) 致上，給予
We extend our apologies for any inconvenience caused.

2) **greeting** [`gritɪŋ] (n.) 賀詞，問候
Robert couldn't make it, but he sends his greetings.

3) **distinguished** [dɪ`stɪŋgwɪʃt] (a.) 高貴的，卓越的，著名的
The general retired after a distinguished career in the army.

4) **attendance** [ə`tɛndəns] (n.) 參與，在場
The concert set a new attendance record.

5) **prestigious** [prɛs`tɪdʒəs] (a.) 著名的，有名望的
The novel won several prestigious awards.

6) **absorb** [əb`sɔrb] (v.) 汲取（知識）
It's easier for children to absorb a new language.

抱歉我無法親自到場，但請理解我的精神絕對與各位同在，且很榮幸能獲得這項享譽盛名的獎。獲得諾貝爾文學獎是我從來不敢想像或預期的事。我從小就熟讀並汲取配得上這項殊榮的大師作品：吉卜林、蕭伯納、湯瑪斯曼、賽珍珠、卡繆、海明威。這幾位文學鉅子的作品不論是在學校裡教授、收藏在全世界的圖書館中，或帶著恭敬語氣引述時，總是能讓人留下深刻印象。能與這些名字並列得獎名單，真是無法用言語形容。

I don't know if these men and women ever thought of the Nobel honor for themselves, but I suppose that anyone writing a book, or a poem, or a play anywhere in the world might harbor that secret dream deep down inside. It's probably buried so deep that they don't even know it's there.

我不知道他們是否曾想過會獲得諾貝爾獎的殊榮，但我想世上任何寫書、創作詩詞或劇本的人可能內心都深藏著這個祕密夢想。大概因為藏得太深，連自己都未察覺。

Against All Odds
排除萬難

If someone had ever told me that I had the ¹²⁾**slightest** chance of winning the Nobel Prize, I would have to think that I'd have about the same ¹³⁾**odds** as standing on the moon. In fact, during the year I was born and for a few years after, there wasn't anyone in the world who was considered good enough to win this Nobel Prize. So, I recognize that I am in very rare company, to say the least.

若有人曾告訴我，我有那一絲機率能贏得諾貝爾獎，我會認為那個機率就跟站在月球上一樣渺茫。事實上，在我出生那年和後幾年間，世上沒有人被認為有資格獲得諾貝爾獎。所以我至少可以說，我了解自己屬於一個非常難能可貴的群體。

諾貝爾文學獎歷年桂冠得主

Rudyard Kipling
吉卜林（1865~1936），英國作家，1907 年諾貝爾文學獎得主，最知名的作品為《叢林奇譚》The Jungle Book。

© rook76 / Shutterstock.com

George Bernard Shaw
蕭伯納（1856~1950），出生於愛爾蘭都柏林，1925 年諾貝爾文學獎得主，最知名的作品是《賣花女》Pygmalion（後來拍成電影《窈窕淑女》My Fair Lady）。

© catwalker / Shutterstock.com

Pearl S. Buck
賽珍珠（1892~1973），在中國長大的美國作家，1932 年獲得普利茲小說獎（Pulitzer Prize），1938 年獲得諾貝爾文學獎，是目前唯一同時獲普利茲獎和諾貝爾獎的女性作家，最知名作品為小說《大地》The Good Earth。

© Andrey Lobachev / Shutterstock.com

Thomas Mann
湯瑪斯曼（1875~1955），德國作家，1929 年以《布登勃洛克家族：一個家族的衰落》Buddenbrooks: Verfall einer Familie 一書獲得諾貝爾文學獎。

© rook76 / Shutterstock.com

Albert Camus
卡繆（1913~1960），法國小說家、劇作家、哲學家。1957 年以《異鄉人》L'Étranger 獲得諾貝爾文學獎。

© neftali / Shutterstock.com

Bob Dylan 巴布狄倫

1941 年生於美國明尼蘇達州，原名 Robert Allen Zimmerman，因喜愛英國詩人 Dylan Thomas，大學期間一次登台時自稱為 Bob Dylan。成名於 60 年代的 Bob Dylan 許多作品都被視為反戰、民權運動的代表。他的樂風從早期的民謠、藍調，到後來結合搖滾，乃至於英倫民謠，經常搭配吉他、口琴、鍵盤樂器表演。除了創作音樂，Bob Dylan 也是造詣深厚的畫家，而他最深入人心的，還是他所作的歌詞。

© www.flickr.com/photos/

---

7) **deem** [dim] (v.) 認為，視作，斷定
The protest was deemed to be illegal.

8) **worthy** [ˋwɚðɪ] (a.) 值得的，配得上的
Few politicians are worthy of people's trust.

9) **distinction** [dɪˋstɪŋkʃən] (n.) 殊榮，榮譽，特殊之處
The school's faculty has won many distinctions.

10) **reverent** [ˋrɛvərənt] (a.) 恭敬的，虔誠的
A reverent crowd gathered in the church.

11) **impression** [ɪmˋprɛʃən] (n.) 印象
What was your impression of Jennifer's boyfriend?

12) **slight** [slaɪt] (a.) 輕微的，微不足道的
Timothy walks with a slight limp.

13) **odds** [ɑdz] (n.) 機率，可能性
The odds of getting struck by lightning are very low.

Shakespeare the Dramatis
劇作家莎士比亞

© Yuri Turkov / Shutterstock.com

I was out on the road when I received this surprising news, and it took me more than a few minutes to properly [1)]**process** it. I began to think about William Shakespeare, the great [2)]**literary** figure. I would [3)]**reckon** he thought of himself as a [4)]**dramatist**. The thought that he was writing literature couldn't have entered his head. His words were written for the stage. Meant to be spoken not read. When he was writing *Hamlet*, I'm sure he was thinking about a lot of different things: "Who're the right actors for these roles?" "How should this be staged?" "Do I really want to set this in Denmark?" His creative vision and ambitions were no doubt at the [5)]**forefront** of his mind, but there were also more [6)]**mundane** matters to consider and deal with. "Is the [7)]**financing** in place?" "Are there enough good seats for my [8)]**patrons**?" "Where am I going to get a human [9)]**skull**?" I would bet that the farthest thing from Shakespeare's mind was the question "Is this literature?"

我接到這驚喜的消息時，我正在巡迴演出，我花了不只幾分鐘時間才消化這消息。我開始想到偉大的文學名人威廉莎士比亞。我猜他會自稱為劇作家，他應該沒想過自己是在寫文學作品。他的文字是為舞台劇而寫，是為了讓人說出口而寫，不是為了讓人閱讀。他在寫《哈姆雷特》時，我相信他有很多不同的想法：「哪些演員適合這些角色？」「要如何搬上舞台？」「背景真的要設在丹麥嗎？」他的創意願景和野心無疑是他腦海中最優先考慮的事，但他也有一些世俗雜事要考慮和處理。「資金到位了嗎？」「給贊助人的好座位夠嗎？」「我到哪裡去找骷髏頭？」我敢說莎士比亞不會去想這個問題：「這算是文學作品嗎？」

Dreaming Big
胸懷大志

When I started writing songs as a teenager, and even as I started to achieve some [10)]**renown** for my abilities, my [11)]**aspirations** for these songs only went so far. I thought they could be heard in coffee houses or bars, maybe later in places like Carnegie Hall, the London [12)]**Palladium**. If I was really dreaming big, maybe I could imagine getting to make a record and then hearing my songs on the radio. That was really the big prize in my mind. Making records and hearing your songs on the radio meant that you were reaching a big audience and that you might get to keep doing what you had set out to do.

我從青少年時期開始寫歌，我憑藉自己的能力博得一些名聲時，對這些歌的志向也不過如此。我認為可以在咖啡廳或酒吧演唱，或許日後有機會在卡內基音樂廳、倫敦帕拉丁劇院之類的地方演奏。我若真有遠大的志向，也許可以想像一下有機會灌唱片，在廣播上聽

VOCABULARY

1) **process** [ˈprɑsɛs] (v.) 消化、理解（資訊、事情等）
It took Anne years to process her husband's death.

2) **literary** [ˈlɪtəˌrɛri] (a.) 文學的，文藝的
The novel has been praised by literary critics.

3) **reckon** [ˈrɛkən] (v.) 認為，視…為
I reckon it's going to rain today.

4) **dramatist** [ˈdræmətɪst] (n.) 劇作家
Henrik Ibsen is my favorite dramatist.

5) **forefront** [ˈforˌfrʌnt] (n.) 最前面，最前列
Apple products are at the forefront of technology.

6) **mundane** [mʌnˈden] (a.) 世俗的，普通的，平凡的
He wasn't interested in the mundane concerns of everyday life.

7) **financing** [ˈfaɪˌnænsɪŋ] (n.) 籌措（的）資金，提供（的）資金
It was difficult for businesses to obtain financing during the recession.

到我的歌。那已經是我心中的大獎。灌唱片和在廣播上聽到你的歌，表示你會有廣大聽眾，這樣你才有機會繼續照自己的初衷往前走。

Well, I've been doing what I set out to do for a long time, now. I've made dozens of records and played thousands of concerts all around the world. But it's my songs that are at the [13]**vital** center of almost everything I do. They seem to have found a place in the lives of many people throughout many different cultures and I'm [14]**grateful** for that.

到現在我一直按自己的初衷走了一段很長的時間。我灌了數十張唱片，在世界各地演出數千場演唱會。但我的歌曲才是我所做的每件事的重心，許多不同文化的許多人都為這些歌曲找到它們的意義，我為此感激不盡。

巴布狄倫經典作品

Blowing' in the Wind 在風中飄送

How many roads must a man walk down
一個人必須向前邁進多遠
Before you call him a man?
才能稱他是個男子漢
Yes, and how many seas must a white dove sail
白鴿必須飛越幾重大洋
Before she sleeps in the sand?
才能在沙地上安歇
Yes, and how many times must the cannonballs fly
砲彈必須凌空飛越幾次
Before they're forever banned?
才能永遠被禁止
The answer, my friend, is blowin' in the wind
這些答案啊，朋友們，就在風中飄送
The answer is blowin' in the wind
答案就在風中飄送

The Times They Are A-changin' 變革的時代

Come senators, congressmen
注意了，參、眾議員
Please heed the call
請留意人民的聲音
Don't stand in the doorway
不要擋住門口
Don't block up the hall
不要封鎖走廊
For he that gets hurt
凡阻撓者
Will be he who has stalled
必將嚐到惡果
There's a battle outside and it is ragin'
外面戰聲隆隆、硝煙四起
It'll soon shake your windows and rattle your walls
很快就要搖撼你的窗戶和牆壁
For the times they are a-changin'
變革的時代已經到來

A Hard Rain's A-gonna Fall 大雨將至

I saw a newborn baby with wild wolves all around it
我看見新生兒被野狼圍繞
I saw a highway of diamonds with nobody on it
我看見鑽石公路空無一人
I saw a black branch with blood that kept drippin'
我看見暗黑樹枝正在滴血
I saw a room full of men with their hammers a-bleedin'
我看見滿屋的人手持淌血的鎚
I saw a white ladder all covered with water
我看見白色的梯子浸在水中
I saw ten thousand talkers whose tongues were all broken
我看見大眾噤口不敢言
I saw guns and sharp swords in the hands of young children
我看見孩子手持槍枝利劍
And it's a hard, and it's a hard, it's a hard, it's a hard
一場大雨啊一場大雨
And it's a hard rain's a-gonna fall
一場大雨將至

© www.flickr.com/photos/83883735@N00/

8) **patron** [ˈpetrən] (n.) （藝術家的）贊助人，資助者
The billionaire is a well-known patron of the arts.

9) **skull** [skʌl] (n.) 頭骨，頭顱
The skull protects the brain from injury.

10) **renown** [rɪˈnaʊn] (n.) 名聲，聲望
The scientist achieved great renown for his discoveries.

11) **aspiration** [ˌæspəˈreʃən] (n.) 渴望達到的目的
Heather's aspiration is to become a doctor and save lives.

12) **palladium** [pəˈlediəm] (n.) 希臘守護神像（常作為音樂廳、劇院等的名字）
I hear La Bohème is playing at the Palladium.

13) **vital** [ˈvaɪtl̩] (a.) 極為重要的，不可缺少的
Foreign trade is vital to Taiwan's economy.

14) **grateful** [ˈgretfəl] (a.) 感謝的，感激的
We felt grateful to be alive after the earthquake.

A World unto Themselves
各自的世界

But there's one thing I must say. As a [1]**performer** I've played for 50,000 people and I've played for 50 people and I can tell you that it is harder to play for 50 people. 50,000 people have a [2]**singular** [3]**persona**, not so with 50. Each person has an individual, separate identity, a world [4]**unto** themselves. They can [5]**perceive** things more clearly. Your honesty and how it relates to the depth of your talent is tried. The fact that the LG Nobel committee is so small is not LG lost on me.

但有一件事我必須說。身為表演者，我為五萬人表演過，也為五十人表演過，我可以說為五十人表演更難。五萬人可以看成是單一個體，但五十人就不一樣了。每個人都是個體、不同的身分，他們有各自的世界。他們對事物的感知更清楚。你的真誠，以及真誠與才華深度之間的關係都會受到考驗。諾貝爾委員會的人數這麼少這一事實，我不會等閒視之。

Bob Dylan 與民歌手 Joan Baez 於美國民權運動盛會 March on Washington 上演唱，攝於 1963 年 8 月 28 日。

But, like Shakespeare, I too am often [6]**occupied** with the [7]**pursuit** of my creative [8]**endeavors** and dealing with all [9]**aspects** of life's mundane matters. "Who are the best musicians for these songs?" "Am I recording in the right studio?" "Is this song in the right key?" Some things never change, even in 400 years.

但就像莎士比亞，我也經常汲汲營營於創作，同時要處理生活上各方面的世俗雜物。「這些歌最適合哪些樂手？」「我的錄音室找對了嗎？」「這首歌的調子正確嗎？」有些事就算過了四百年也從沒改變。

Not once have I ever had the time to ask myself, "Are my songs literature?" So, I do thank the Swedish Academy, both for taking the time to consider that very question, and, [10]**ultimately**, for providing such a wonderful answer. My best wishes to you all.

我從來沒有時間問自己：「我的歌是文學嗎？」所以，我非常感謝瑞典學院，不但花時間考慮這個問題，最後還提供如此美妙的答案。祝福各位。

" People seldom do what they believe in. They do what is convenient, then repent.

大家很少秉持信念做事，只會因循苟且，接著懺悔。

巴布狄倫談人性

VOCABULARY 6

1) **performer** [pɚˋfɔrmɚ] (n.) 表演者，演奏者
The audience clapped when the performers walked onto the stage.

2) **singular** [ˋsɪŋgjəlɚ] (a.) 單一的，獨特的，非凡的
The singular form of "mice" is "mouse."

3) **persona** [pɚˋsonə] (n.) 角色，個性，身份
The salesman has a friendly and outgoing persona.

4) **unto** [ˋʌntu] (prep.)（古、詩）對於
Do unto others as you would have them do unto you.

5) **perceive** [pɚˋsiv] (v.) 感覺，理解
The man's words were perceived as a threat.

6) **occupy** [ˋakjə͵paɪ] (v.) 忙著（做某事）
After retiring, Betty kept herself occupied with charity work.

7) **pursuit** [pɚˋsut] (n.) 追求，從事
Tom is diligent in the pursuit of his goals.

8) **endeavor** [ɪnˋdɛvɚ] (n.) 努力，力圖
I hope you succeed in all your endeavors.

9) **aspect** [ˋæspɛkt] (n.) 方面
We must consider the various aspects of the problem.

10) **ultimately** [ˋʌltəmɪtlɪ] (adv.) 最後，總而言之
Stress can ultimately lead to heart disease.

Swedish Academy 瑞典學院與 Nobel committee 諾貝爾委員會

諾貝爾獎的提名及遴選過程嚴謹且冗長，世界各地的提名資料會在每年初送進各項目的提名單位：

文學獎 → Swedish Academy（瑞典學會）

物理、化學、經濟獎 → Royal Swedish Academy of Science（瑞典皇家科學院）

醫學獎 → Nobel Assembly at the Karolinska Institute（卡羅琳學院諾貝爾大會，位於瑞典斯德哥爾摩）

和平獎 → Norwegian Nobel Committee（挪威諾貝爾委員會，位於挪威奧斯陸）。

© Vladimir Mucibabic / Shutterstock.com
位於瑞典斯德哥爾摩的瑞典學院暨諾貝爾博物館

提名單位確定資格後，將入圍者資料送交各項目的 Nobel committee（諾貝爾委員會），接近年底時集會討論，最後由提名單位宣布得獎名單，並於 12 月 10 日（紀念諾貝爾逝世）頒獎。

beyond words 無法用言語表達

這個片語用來形容「難以言表」，讓人不知道要說什麼才好。

A: What did you say when your husband told you he was leaving you?
妳先生說要離開妳時，妳怎麼回應？

B: Nothing. I was shocked beyond words.
完全無言。我驚訝到說不出話來。

名詞子句作主詞

Bob Dylan 的這句話：That I now join the names on such a list is truly beyond words. 其實是由以下兩個句子組成：

(1) I now join the names on such a list.
(2) It is truly beyond words.

當你要將兩個獨立的句子組成一個句子，將第一個句子放在第二句話的主詞時：I now join the names on such a list is truly beyond words.

看起來是不是不太對勁？因為這句話出現了兩個動詞，而造成文法上的錯誤。因此，當一個句子要作為另一個句子的主詞時，第一個句子前面需要加上 that 形成名詞子句，that 不能省略。

例 **That Peter lies makes Mom angry.**
彼得說謊讓媽媽很生氣。

to say the least 輕描淡寫

the least 是「最少」的意思。這句話接在一句話後面，用來強調「這樣說已經很客氣了」。

A: Your parents invited your ex for Thanksgiving?
妳爸媽邀妳的前男友一起參加感恩節聚餐？

B: Yeah. It's gonna be awkward, to say the least.
對啊。一定尷尬死了，不誇張。

也可以用來回應他人的意見，表示完全同意對方的說法。

A: he professor's lecture today was so boring.
那位教授今天的課好無聊。

B: To say the least!
就是說啊！

in place 準備就緒

字面上是「到位」的意思，表示所需事物已經準備好。

A: Is everything in place for the meeting this afternoon?
今天下午的會議都準備就緒了嗎？

B: Almost. I just have to set up the projector.
差不多了。我只剩要把投影機架好就行了。

Carnegie Hall 卡內基音樂廳

位於紐約曼哈頓，由美國鋼鐵大王安得魯卡內基（Andrew Carnegie）捐款建造，建築構造及音響設備均為世界一流，是當今古典音樂及流行音樂的最高殿堂。

© DW labs Incorporated / Shutterstock.com

set out to (do sth.) 著手（達成目標）

這個片語表示帶著特定的目標採取行動。

A: What was the purpose of their research project?
他們這次的研究專案目的為何？

B: They set out to find a cure for cancer, but discovered something completely different.
他們原本想要尋找治療癌症的方法，但發現了完全不相關的東西。

lost on (sb.) 無法體會

表示無法欣賞、體會，一般用在抽象的事物，如一種想法、概念。

A: I didn't get that joke that Allan told.
我聽不懂艾倫說的笑話。

B: Me neither. It was totally lost on me.
我也不懂。我聽不出哪裡好笑。

唱片銷量超過一億張的 Bob Dylan 獲獎無數，為表彰他的歌詞對美國文化產生的影響，普立茲獎於 2008 年頒發特別貢獻獎，2012 年由美國總統歐巴馬頒發總統自由勳章。2016 年，Bob Dylan 獲得諾貝爾文學獎，本文 Are My Songs Literature?（我的歌曲是文學嗎？）節錄自當晚由美國駐瑞典大使代為宣讀的得獎演說。

© Rena Schild / Shutterstock.com

Writing Is a Lonely Life

寫作是孤獨的

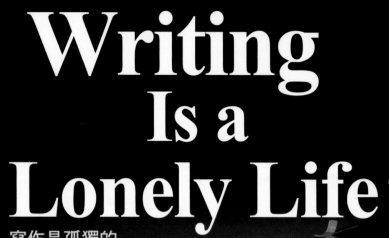

Ernest Hemingway's Nobel Prize Banquet Speech
海明威的諾貝爾獎晚宴謝辭

海明威為《戰地鐘聲》*For Whom the Bell Tolls*
第一版書封拍攝的照片。1939 年攝於愛達荷州。

© Photographer: Lloyd Arnold

Having no facility for speech-making and no command of [1]**oratory** nor any [2]**domination** of [3]**rhetoric**, I wish to thank the [4]**administrators** of the generosity of Alfred Nobel for this Prize.

不具演說才能、無法滔滔雄辯,又不善辭令的我,想謝謝慷慨的諾貝爾獎委員會頒給我這個獎。

No writer who knows 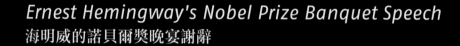 the great writers who did not receive the Prize can accept it other than with [5]**humility**. There is no need to list these

VOCABULARY

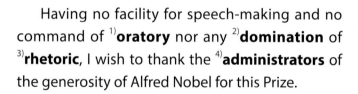

1) **oratory** [ˋɔrəˏtori] (n.) 演講術,雄辯
Winston Churchill was a master of oratory.

2) **domination** [ˏdɑməˋneʃən] (n.) 精通,掌握,支配
China's domination of table tennis is now being challenged.

3) **rhetoric** [ˋrɛtərɪk] (n.) 修辭,辯才,辭令
The professor is an expert on political rhetoric.

4) **administrator** [ədˋmɪnəˏstretə] (n.) 管理人,行政官員
Jeffrey works as a college administrator.

5) **humility** [hjuˋmɪləti] (n.) 謙卑
Kevin doesn't have the humility to admit when he's wrong.

6) **discernible** [dɪˋsɝnəbəl] (a.) 可識別的
The river's water quality has shown discernible improvement.

writers. Everyone here may make his own list according to his knowledge and his conscience.

在知悉有偉大作家尚未獲獎的情況下，沒有作家不抱持謙卑的心來領這座獎座。這些作家的名單沒有列出的必要。這裡每個人都可以依照自己的知識和良心列出自己的名單。

It would be impossible for me to ask the ambassador of my country to read a speech in which a writer said all of the things which are in his heart. Things may not be immediately [6]**discernible** in what a man writes, and in this sometimes he is fortunate; but eventually they are quite clear and by these and the degree of [7]**alchemy** that he possesses he will endure or be forgotten.

我不可能要求我國的駐外大使幫一位作家唸出心中所有想說的話。一個人所寫文字的意涵或許不是當下都能立即解讀，這有時對他而言也是種幸運；但最終都會浮現，並依照他們點石成金的程度流芳百世或被遺忘。

He Does His Work Alone
他獨自寫作

Writing, **LG** at its best, is a lonely life. Organizations for writers [8]**palliate** the writer's loneliness but I doubt if they improve his writing.

> **"** An intelligent man is sometimes forced to be drunk to spend time with his fools.
>
> 一個聰明人有時不得不醉，否則無法與蠢才共處。
>
> *海明威談醉酒*

> **"** I wake up in the morning and my mind starts making sentences, and I have to get rid of them fast—talk them or write them down.
>
> 我一早醒來，腦中開始浮現句子，我必須設法擺脫──不是說出來，就是寫下來。
>
> *海明威談寫作*

He grows in public [9]**stature** as he [10]**sheds** his loneliness and often his work [11]**deteriorates**. For he does his work alone and if he is a good enough writer he must face [12]**eternity**, or the lack of it, each day.

寫作狀態最好的時候，就是孤獨的。作家組織可以減輕作家的孤獨感，但我懷疑是否能增進作家的寫作功力。隨著聲望提升，作家不再感到孤獨，但作品往往會退步。獨自工作的作家，如果是夠好的作家，一定要面對無止盡的永恆，或沒有永恆，日復一日。

Ernest Hemingway
海明威

歐尼斯特海明威（1899~1961）不只是影響美國二十世紀文壇的偉大小說家，也是一名記者。他的一生參與兩次世界大戰及西班牙內戰，行跡遍及歐洲、非洲、南美洲甚至中國，既能拿筆寫作、又能出海釣魚、拿槍打獵的強烈形象，深深影響後世。

© Charlesimage / Shutterstock.com

---

7) **alchemy** [ˈælkəmi] (n.) 錬金術，神奇力量
The chef is famous for his alchemy in the kitchen.

8) **palliate** [ˈpælɪˌet] (v.) 緩和，減輕
The patient was given medicine to palliate his symptoms.

9) **stature** [ˈstætʃə] (n.) 聲望，地位
William Faulkner is a novelist of great stature.

10) **shed** [ʃɛd] (v.) 甩掉，擺脫
Karen wants to shed a few pounds before swimsuit season.

11) **deteriorate** [dɪˈtɪrɪəˌret] (v.) 退化，惡化
Rainy weather causes roads to deteriorate rapidly.

12) **eternity** [ɪˈtɜnəti] (n.) 永遠，（似乎）無止盡的時間
It seems like an eternity since we've seen each other.

2　Each Book a New Beginning
每本書都是新的開始

For a true writer each book should be a new beginning where he tries again for something that is beyond [1]**attainment**. He should always try for something GM that has never been done or that others have tried and failed. Then sometimes, with great luck, he will succeed.

對真正的作家來說，每本書都應該是新的開始，他要再次努力去追求難以企及的造詣。他應該一直嘗試從未寫過，或其他人試過但失敗的東西。然後有時，運氣很好的話，他就會成功。

How simple the writing of literature would be if it were only necessary to write in another way what has been well written. It is because we have had such great writers in the past that a writer is driven far out past where he can go, out to where no one can help him.

> 66 The most painful thing is losing yourself in the process of loving someone too much, and forgetting that you are special too.
>
> 最痛苦的莫過於愛得太深失去自我，而忘了自己其實也很特別。
>
> 　　　海明威談愛情

> 66 There is nothing to writing. All you do is sit down at a typewriter and bleed.
>
> 寫作之道無他。只要坐在打字機前嘔心瀝血。
>
> 　　　海明威談寫作

假如已完成的佳作只要換個方式再寫一次即可，文學寫作就簡單多了。由於過去已有那麼偉大的作家，為了超越前人，有作家把自己逼出極限，到了孤絕無援的境地。

I have spoken too long for a writer. A writer should write what he has to say and not speak it. Again I thank you.

以作家來說，我說得太久了。作家應該寫下想說的話，而不是用說的。再次謝謝大家。

© phortun / Shutterstock.com

© phortun / Shutterstock.com

（上圖）古巴哈瓦那的 El Floridita 餐廳。海明威於 1939~1960 年旅居古巴，並完成《老人與海》，這裡是海明威時常光顧的地方。

（左圖）餐廳內有海明威雕像，旁邊是一杯他在這間餐廳最愛點的雞尾酒 daiquiri，他偏愛的配方被流傳下來，被稱作 Papa Doble，Papa（老爹）是古巴人對海明威的暱稱，doble 是西班牙文的 double（雙份）。

VOCABULARY 🎧 10

1) **attainment** [əˋtenmənt] (n.) 達到，獲得，成就
   Bonuses are based on the attainment of sales targets.

14

Language Guide

海明威心目中更該得諾貝爾的作家

1954 年 10 月，海明威獲知得到諾貝爾文學獎時表現非常謙遜，他向媒體表示該得獎的是以下這幾位作家：

© rook76 / Shutterstock.com

Isak Dinesen 在肯亞奈洛比的住處，現為凱倫白列森博物館（Museum of Karen Blixen）。

Carl Sandburg

© YANGCHAO / Shutterstock.com

卡爾桑德堡（1878~1967）美國詩人、作家，以其混合街頭口語、為勞苦大眾發聲的樸質詩作（*Chicago*、*Fog* 為最重要的兩首詩），及他為亞伯拉罕林肯（Abraham Lincoln）所寫的傳記聞名。一生獲得三次普立茲文學獎。

Isak Dinesen

伊莎克丹尼森（1885~1962）為丹麥作家凱倫白列森（Karen Blixen）的筆名，最為世人熟知的是以其自傳改編拍攝的奧斯卡最佳電影《遠離非洲》*Out of Africa*；另一部名作《芭比的盛宴》*Babette's Feast* 也被改拍為電影，獲得奧斯卡最佳外語片。

© www.flickr.com/photos/136879256@N02/

丹尼森一生與諾貝爾有緣無份，多次被提名、1959 年甚至都已被宣布獲獎，卻在最後一刻被更換名單。

Bernard Berenson

伯納德貝倫森（1865~1959）是美國歷史學家，專精文藝復興時期藝術史。

Bernard Berenson 於 1955 年參訪義大利羅馬博爾蓋塞美術館。

Grammar Master

關係代名詞 that 的使用時機（1）

多數時候，關係代名詞 that 可以和 which 或 who 代換，但是本句 He should always try for something that has never been done or that others have tried and failed. 中的關代 that，就不可以用 which 替換，以下整理關係代名詞 that 的使用時機：

1. 先行詞是有限定意味的名詞： 如序數詞（the first, second...）、最高級、the only、the very、the last 之後。

例 **Cheating is the last thing that I would do.**
作弊是我最不願意做的事情。

例 **The original Star Wars movie is the only one that I like.**
星際大戰最初的電影版本是我唯一喜歡的版本。

2. 先行詞是不定代名詞： 如 all, everything, something 等，本句就屬於此類。

例 **Everything that comes out of his mouth is a lie.**
他說出的每句話都是謊言。

3. 當先行詞有人又有物： 或是性質不同時，統一用 that。

例 **The people and places that I visited left me with lasting memories.**
我遇到的人跟去過的地方都給我難以忘懷的回憶。

4. 同個句子中已經出現一次 which 或 who，為避免重複時：

例 **Which is the car that overtaken us?**
超我們車的是哪台車？

at its best 在最佳狀態下

這裡的 best 是名詞，表示「最好的狀態，最大限度」，如同字面上的意思「在其最好的狀態下」，表示某件事物將本身的能力發揮到淋漓盡致。這個片語一般用於書寫，口語不太使用。

The article is an example of journalism at its best.
這篇文章是新聞寫作的絕佳作品。

1952 年，海明威以畢生得意之作《老人與海》*The Old Man and the Sea* 獲得普立茲獎之後，二度前往非洲。此行災禍不斷，先是遭遇兩次墜機意外受傷，幾乎喪命；幾週內又遭叢林野火波及，全身多處燒傷，自此之後渾身傷病疼痛，原本就貪杯的海明威更是藉酒止痛。獲得諾貝爾獎時，他的健康狀況已無法讓他前往斯德哥爾摩，只能由美國大使代為宣讀本篇講稿。

© neftali / Shutterstock.com

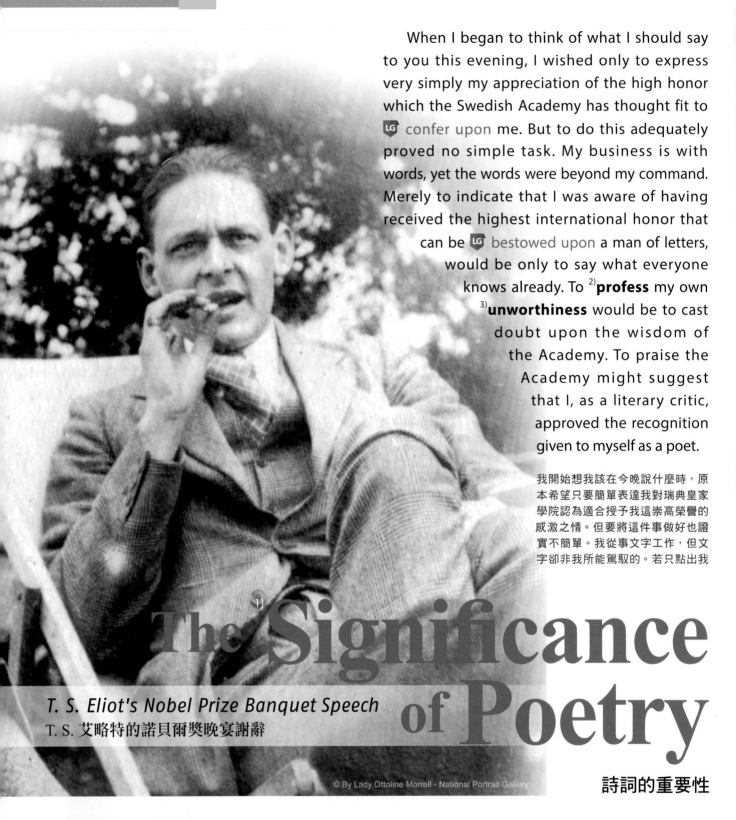

When I began to think of what I should say to you this evening, I wished only to express very simply my appreciation of the high honor which the Swedish Academy has thought fit to **LG** confer upon me. But to do this adequately proved no simple task. My business is with words, yet the words were beyond my command. Merely to indicate that I was aware of having received the highest international honor that can be **LG** bestowed upon a man of letters, would be only to say what everyone knows already. To ²⁾**profess** my own ³⁾**unworthiness** would be to cast doubt upon the wisdom of the Academy. To praise the Academy might suggest that I, as a literary critic, approved the recognition given to myself as a poet.

我開始想我該在今晚說什麼時，原本希望只要簡單表達我對瑞典皇家學院認為適合授予我這崇高榮譽的感激之情。但要將這件事做好也證實不簡單。我從事文字工作，但文字卻非我所能駕馭的。若只點出我

The Significance of Poetry

T. S. Eliot's Nobel Prize Banquet Speech
T. S. 艾略特的諾貝爾獎晚宴謝辭

© By Lady Ottoline Morrell - National Portrait Gallery

詩詞的重要性

VOCABULARY 🎧12

1) **significance** [sɪgˋnɪfɪkəns] (n.) 意義，重要性
The castle should be preserved because of its historical significance.

2) **profess** [preˋfɛs] (v.) 公開宣稱，自稱
The murder suspect continues to profess his innocence.

3) **unworthiness** [ʌnˋwɝðɪnəs] (n.) 不值得，無價值
After losing his job, Bob experienced feelings of shame and unworthiness.

4) **exaltation** [ˌɛgzɔlˋteʃən] (n.) 欣喜如狂，得意洋洋
Fans cheered in exultation after the winning touchdown.

5) **vanity** [ˋvænəti] (n.) 虛榮，自負
The star was criticized for his vanity and arrogance.

6) **flattery** [ˋflætəri] (n.) 奉承，討好
Sometimes flattery can get you what you want.

> The last temptation is the greatest treason: to do the right deed for the wrong reason.
>
> 最後的誘惑是最大的背叛：為了錯誤的原因做出對的事。
>
> *T.S. 艾略特談誘惑*

知道這是文學家所能獲得的最高國際榮譽，那等於只是說出大家早已知道的事。若自稱我配不上這個獎，那就等於質疑皇家科學院的智慧。讚揚皇家學院又好像是在暗指身為文學評論家的我同意了認可我是詩人的表彰。

All the Normal Emotions
所有的正常情緒

May I therefore ask that it be 🄻🄶 taken for granted that I experienced, on learning of this award to myself, all the normal emotions of [4]**exaltation** and [5]**vanity** that any human being might be expected to feel at such a moment, with enjoyment of the [6]**flattery**, and [7]**exasperation** at the inconvenience, of being turned overnight into a public figure? Were the Nobel Award similar in kind to any other award, and merely higher in degree, I might still try to find words of appreciation. But since it is different in kind from any other, the expression of one's feelings calls for resources which language cannot supply.

因此我能否請你們相信，得知領獎之後我確實體驗到了任何人類可能會感受到的欣喜、虛榮等所有正常情緒，加上享受被奉承，以及

因一夜間成為公眾人物而帶來不便的惱怒？若諾貝爾獎跟其他獎項類似，只是地位更高，那我可能仍要找出讚美的言詞。但既然這獎是如此與眾不同，那麼個人感受表達所需的能力是言語無法企及的。

I must therefore try to express myself in an indirect way, by putting before you my own [8]**interpretation** of the significance of the Nobel Prize in Literature. If this were simply the recognition of merit, or of the fact that an author's reputation has passed the [9]**boundaries** of his own country and his own language, we could say that hardly any one of us at any time is, more than others, 🄶🄼 worthy of being so distinguished.

因此我必須設法以迂迴的手法表達，用我自己的方式為各位詮釋諾貝爾文學獎的意義。這若只是對功績的肯定，或肯定作家的名聲已超越自己國家和語言的疆界，那我們可以說不論什麼時候，幾乎沒有誰比其他人更配得上這項獎。

T. S. Eliot T. S. 艾略特

Thomas Stearns Eliot （1888~1965）於 1948 年榮獲諾貝爾文學獎。他在美國出生長大，哈佛大學畢業後旅居英國並歸化英國籍。這位詩人對後世影響最深的，要算是他的詩作《荒原》 *The Waste Land*（1922年出版）。T.S. 艾略特不只是詩人，也是劇作家，而著名的音樂劇《貓》 *Cats* 則是安德魯洛伊韋伯改編自他的詩集《老負鼠的貓經》 *Old Possum's Book of Practical Cats*。

© Doc Searls

© Wikimedia Commons（Creator:littleT889）
T.S. 艾略特在密蘇里州的聖路易斯的老家。

© Wikimedia Commons（Creator:Midnightblueowl）
T.S. 艾略特的工作地點，位於英國倫敦。

---

7) **exasperation** [ɪɡˌzæspəˈreʃən] (n.) 惱怒，懊惱
We've all experienced the exasperation of holiday shopping.

8) **interpretation** [ɪnˌtɜprɪˈteʃən] (n.) 解釋，闡述
The judge didn't agree with the lawyer's interpretation of the law.

9) **boundary** [ˈbaʊndərɪ] (n.) 邊界，界限
The river forms a boundary between the two countries.

❝ I have measured out my life with coffee spoons.

我都用咖啡匙的數量衡量生命。

T.S. 艾略特談酗咖啡

An Act of Grace
給予恩賜

But I find in the Nobel Award something more and something different from such recognition.

It seems to me more the election of an individual, chosen from time to time from one nation or another, and selected by something like an act of grace, to fill a peculiar role and to become a peculiar symbol. A [1]**ceremony** takes place, by which a man is suddenly **LG** endowed with some function which he did not fill before. So the question is not whether he was worthy to be so **LG** singled out, but whether he can perform the function which you have assigned to him: the function of serving as a representative, so far as any man can be, of something of far greater importance than the value of what he himself has written.

但我認為諾貝爾獎不只是這種肯定，也有別於這種肯定。對我而言更像是挑選一個人，他偶然從諸國間被挑中，選出他來給予恩賜，以擔任一個獨特角色，成為獨特的象徵。並為此舉行一套儀式，被選中的人突然間被賦予一種任務，是他從未擔任過的。所以問題不

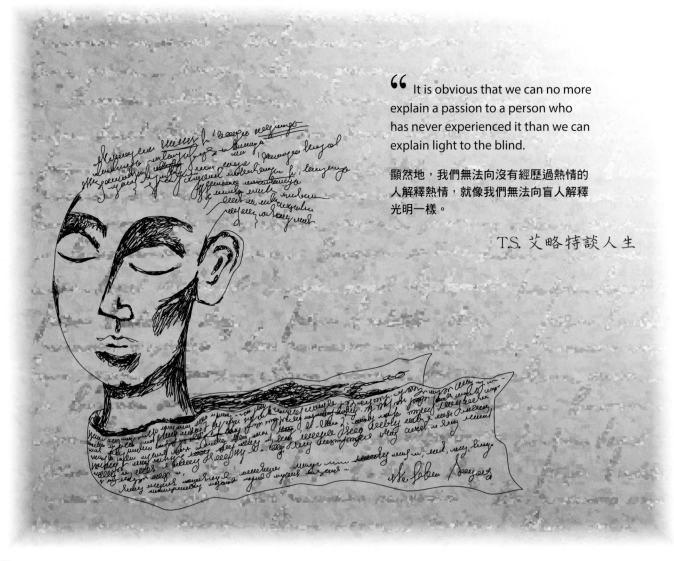

❝ It is obvious that we can no more explain a passion to a person who has never experienced it than we can explain light to the blind.

顯然地，我們無法向沒有經歷過熱情的人解釋熱情，就像我們無法向盲人解釋光明一樣。

T.S. 艾略特談人生

是他是否值得被選中，而是他是否能履行你所賦予他的任務：擔任一種代表的任務，假如說任何人做得到，代表某種比他自己所寫的文字更重要的東西。

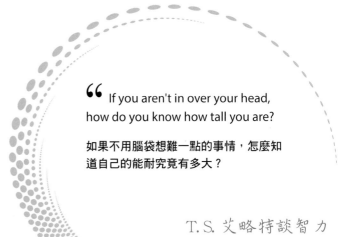

The Most Local of All the Arts
所有藝術中最具當地特色的

Poetry is usually considered the most local of all the arts. Painting, sculpture, [2]**architecture**, music, can be enjoyed by all who see or hear. But language, especially the language of poetry, is a different matter. Poetry, it might seem, separates peoples instead of uniting them. But on the other hand, we must remember, that while language constitutes a barrier, poetry itself gives us a reason for trying to overcome the barrier.

詩詞通常被認為是所有藝術中最具當地特色的。繪畫、雕塑、建築、音樂，只要是用眼睛看得到、耳朵聽得到的人都能欣賞。但語言，尤其是詩詞的語言，是另外一回事。詩詞似乎會讓人們疏遠，而不是讓人們團結。但另一方面，我們必須記住，雖然語言構成障礙，但詩詞本身給了我們努力克服障礙的理由。

欣賞屬於另一種語言的詩詞，就是欣賞並理解屬於那種語言的人，這種理解是我們無法用其他方式做到的。我們也可以思考一下歐洲的詩詞歷史，以及某種語言的詩詞對另一種語言會造成巨大影響。我們必須記住，每位重要詩人都欠其他語言的詩人巨大恩情。我們可以反思，每個國家和語言的詩詞若不由外國語言的詩詞來滋養，那麼詩詞將會衰落和滅亡。

To enjoy poetry belonging to another language is to enjoy an understanding of the people to whom that language belongs, an understanding we can get in no other way. We may think also of the history of poetry in Europe, and of the great influence that the poetry of one language can [3]**exert** on another. We must remember the [4]**immense** debt of every considerable poet to poets of other languages than his own. We may reflect that the poetry of every country and every language would decline and [5]**perish**, were it not [6]**nourished** by poetry in foreign tongues.

VOCABULARY 🎧 14

1) **ceremony** [ˈsɛrəˌmoni] (n.) 儀式，典禮
The wedding ceremony was held at a small church.

2) **architecture** [ˈɑrkɪˌtɛktʃə] (n.) 建築，建築學
The city of Aberdeen in Scotland is famous for its Gothic architecture.

3) **exert** [ɪɡˈzɝt] (v.) 發揮，施加
Some parents try to exert too much control over their children.

4) **immense** [ɪˈmɛns] (a.) 極大的，巨大的
The Sahara is an immense desert.

5) **perish** [ˈpɛrɪʃ] (v.) 死去，消滅
Dozens of people perished in the fire.

6) **nourish** [ˈnɝɪʃ] (v.) 滋養，培育
This natural lotion will help nourish your skin.

When a poet speaks to his own people, the voices of all the poets of other languages who have influenced him are speaking also. And at the same time, he himself is speaking to younger poets of other languages, and these poets will [1]**convey** something of his vision of life, and something of the spirit of his people, to their own. Partly through his influence on other poets, partly through translation, which must be also a kind of recreation of his poems by other poets, partly through readers of his language who are not themselves poets, the poet can contribute toward understanding between peoples.

> " Moving between the legs of tables and of chairs, rising or falling, grasping at kisses and toys, advancing boldly, sudden to take alarm, retreating to the corner of arm and knee, eager to be reassured, taking pleasure in the fragrant brilliance of the Christmas tree.
>
> 在桌腳和椅子間穿梭，攀高躍下，攫取親吻和玩具，大膽衝鋒，忽又驚疑，躲到臂彎和膝邊，渴望被人安撫，享受著耶誕樹的馨香燦爛。
>
> *T.S. 艾略特描寫歡度耶誕節的小孩*

當一位詩人跟自己的同胞對話時，影響過他的其他語言所有詩人也齊聲說話。同時他自己也正在和其他語言的年輕詩人說話，而這些詩人會傳遞他的生活願景，以及他人民的精神給他們自己的國民。一部分透過他對其他詩人的影響，一部分透過翻譯──這必定也是一種由其他詩人對他的詩詞的重新創造，一部分透過講他的語言但本身不是詩人的讀者，於是這位詩人得以對雙方人民的瞭解有所貢獻。

An Essential Understanding

必要的瞭解

In the work of every poet there will certainly be much that can only appeal to those who [2]**inhabit** the same region, or speak the same language, as the poet. But nevertheless, there is a meaning to the phrase "the poetry of Europe," and even to the word "poetry" the world over. I think that in poetry, people of different countries and different languages—though it be apparently only through a small minority in any one country—acquire an understanding of each other which, however partial, is still essential.

在每位詩人的作品中，一定有不少只對住在同地區或說同一種語言的人有吸引力。不過，「歐洲的詩詞」這句話是有意義的，就算全世界的「詩」一詞也一樣。我認為在詩詞中，不同國家和語言的人──儘管在任何國家顯然只有少部分──能夠互相了解對方，而這樣的了解雖不完整但仍然是必要的。

And I take the award of the Nobel Prize in Literature, when it is given to a poet, to be primarily an [3]**assertion** of the [4]**supranational** value of poetry. To make that [5]**affirmation**, it is necessary from time to time to [6]**designate** a poet: and I stand before you, not 🆖 on my own merits, but as a symbol, for a time, of the significance of poetry.

諾貝爾文學獎授予一位詩人時，我認為這個舉動要是在宣示詩詞的超國家價值。為了如此斷言，有必要時不時指定一位詩人：站在你們面前的我，不是為了我自己的功績，而是暫時做個象徵，代表詩詞的重要性。

VOCABULARY 🎧16

1) **convey** [kən`ve] (v.) 傳遞，表達
My father had difficulty conveying his feelings.

2) **inhabit** [ɪn`hæbɪt] (v.) 棲息，居住
Thousands of penguins inhabit the island.

3) **assertion** [ə`sɝʃən] (n.) 主張，斷言。動詞為 **assert** [ə`sɝt]
I disagree with his assertion that women are bad drivers.

4) **supranational** [ˌsuprə`næʃənəl] (a.) 超越國家、民族的
The European Union is a supranational organization.

5) **affirmation** [ˌæfɚ`meʃən] (n.) 肯定，斷言。動詞為 **affirm** [ə`fɝm]
The film is an affirmation of the human spirit.

6) **designate** [`dɛzɪgˌnet] (v.) 指定，命名
The Grand Canyon was designated as a national park in 1919.

confer (upon / on) 授予（榮譽）

confer [kən`fɚ] 是「授予（學位等榮譽）」，尤指有正式儀式的，常見的句型是 confer sth. upon / on sb.。

A: Why is that star giving the commencement speech this year?
那個明星為什麼來發表今年的畢業演說？

B: Because our school's conferring an honorary degree on him.
因為本校授與他榮譽學位。

善於舞文弄墨的詩人在這篇演講稿中，還用了其他的片語表示授予（榮譽）：

- bestow (upon / on)：句型為 bestow sth. upon / on sb.

A: How did your ancestors acquire so much land?
你的祖先如何獲得這麼多土地？

B: It was bestowed on them by the king.
是國王賜給他們的。

外表很像，但用法不同的 worthy 與 worth

worth 與 worthy 兩者都是形容詞，意思相近長得很像，但是用法完全不同：

1. worth——當「值得的，夠格、足以…的」，後面接名詞時要與 of 連用，接動詞時要用不定詞 to V，不過接動詞的用法較不常見：

- **be worthy of + N.**
例 **I think every person is worthy of respect.**
我認為每個人都值得獲得尊重。

- **be worthy to + V.**
例 **It is worth to be mentioned.**
這個很值得一提。

2. worth——有兩種用法，一是直接加上金額，表示「價值多少錢的」；另一個是表達「值得…的」，加上名詞或動名詞 Ving：

- **be worth + 金錢「價值…（錢）的」**
例 **This painting is probably worth thousands of dollars.**
這幅畫價值數千元。

- **be worth + Ving/N.「值得…的」**
例 **Is the new Star Wars movie worth seeing?**
最新出的《星際大戰》電影值得看嗎？

- 另一個常見的 worth 片語：be worth it，指的是「某人或某事是值得的」
例 **The trail was steep, but the view from the top was worth it.**
這條山路很陡峭，但登頂的景色很值得。

- endow with：句型為 endow (sb. / sth.) with (sth.)

A: I think Michael would be a great catch.
我覺得麥可是很棒的對象。

B: Yeah. He's endowed with both brains and good looks.
是啊。老天給他腦袋，也給他容貌。

take for granted 視為理所當然

這個片語是在描述身在福中不知福的人，把發生在身上的好事，或對他好的人當作是應該的，我們就可以說他 take sth./sb. for granted。

A: Eric is really lucky to have a girlfriend like Martha.
艾瑞克真是好命，交到像瑪莎那樣的女朋友。

B: Yeah. I hope he never takes her for granted.
是啊。希望他千萬別把她當作理所當然的。

single out 使鶴立雞群，被孤立突顯出來

是指從一群人當中選出最優者，或是讓一個人顯得特別出色。

A: Why are you in such a good mood?
你為什麼心情這麼好？

B: The teacher singled out my paper for praise.
老師特別把我的報告拿出來讚美。

若用於負面的意思，則表示一個人被刻意孤立出來。

A: Why do you hate your manager so much?
你為什麼這麼討厭你的主管？

B: He always singles me out for criticism.
因為他總是故意針對我挑毛病。

on (sb.'s/sth.'s) (own) merits 靠（自己的）實力

merit 是「價值，優點，功勞」。這個片語用來表示一個人（得到成功）完全靠實力。

A: Is it true that Steven is the owner's son?
史蒂芬真的是老闆的兒子？

B: Yes, but he got the job on his own merits.
對，但他是靠實力得到這份工作。

得到堪稱人類文明最高獎項的諾貝爾獎，是至高無上的榮耀，不適合在得獎場合謙遜過頭不斷稱謝，卻又不能顯得志得意滿，T. S. 艾略特採取的策略——將自己視為「代領獎」者——表示自己是代表一個更大的群體（像是所有的詩人）來領獎。這種做法在後面的演說中還能看到。

倫敦一面牆上嵌了一塊磚，印有 T.S. 艾略特《荒原》詩句。

1) Nonviolence Is the Answer

非暴力才是問題的解答

Martin Luther King, Jr.'s Nobel Acceptance Speech
小馬丁路德金恩的諾貝爾獎得獎感言

I accept the Nobel Prize for Peace at a moment when 22 million Negroes of the United States of America are engaged in a creative battle to end the long night of racial 2)**injustice**. I accept this award on behalf of a civil rights movement which is moving with determination and a 3)**majestic** 4)**scorn** for risk and danger to establish a 5)**reign** of freedom and a rule of justice.

我在接受諾貝爾和平獎的這一刻，美國兩千兩百萬名黑人正在進行一場戰役，以結束種族不平等的長夜。我代表一場民權運動接受這個獎，這場運動正堅定不移地進行著，且對風險和危險不屑一顧，以建立一個自由和正義法則的時代。

Mindful of Injustice
意識到不公不義

I am 6)**mindful** that only yesterday in Birmingham, Alabama, our children, crying out for 7)**brotherhood**, were answered with fire hoses,

VOCABULARY 18

1) **nonviolence** [ˌnɑnˋvaɪələns] (n.) 非暴力
Gandhi believed nonviolence was the best way to achieve Indian independence.

2) **injustice** [ɪnˋdʒʌstɪs] (n.) 不公，不義
Native Americans have suffered many injustices.

3) **majestic** [məˋdʒɛstɪk] (a.) 雄偉的，莊嚴的，崇高的
Alaska is famous for its majestic scenery.

4) **scorn** [skɔrn] (n./v.) 輕蔑，藐視，不屑
I have nothing but scorn for his opinions.

5) **reign** [ren] (n.) 統治
The king's reign lasted for 30 years.

6) **mindful** [ˋmaɪndfəl] (a.) 注意的，留心的
Travelers should always be mindful of their surroundings.

7) **brotherhood** [ˋbrʌðəˏhʊd] (n.)
手足之情，四海一家的信念
Last Sunday, our pastor talked about the importance of brotherhood.

8) **snarl** [snɑrl] (v.) （狗）吠，咆哮
The dog snarled in warning as we approached.

9) **secure** [sɪˋkjʊr] (v.) 獲得，取得
Richard managed to secure a loan from the bank.

10) **worship** [ˋwɜʃɪp] (n./v.) 拜神，做禮拜
For Christians, Sunday is a day of worship.

11) **sanctuary** [ˋsæŋtʃuˏɛri] (n.) 避難（所），禁獵區
Many refugees sought sanctuary in neighboring countries.

12) **segregation** [ˏsɛɡrɪˋɡeʃən] (n.)
（種族）隔離
A law ending segregation in American schools was passed in 1954.

13) **debilitating** [dɪˋbɪləˏtetɪŋ] (a.)
使人衰弱的，削弱力量的
Diabetes is a debilitating disease.

[8)]**snarling** dogs and even death. I am mindful that only yesterday in Philadelphia, Mississippi, young people seeking to [9)]**secure** the right to vote were brutalized and murdered. And only yesterday more than 40 houses of [10)]**worship** in the State of Mississippi alone were bombed or burned because they offered a [11)]**sanctuary** to those who would not accept [12)]**segregation**. I am mindful that [13)]**debilitating** and [14)]**grinding** poverty [15)]**afflicts** my people and chains them to 🛡 the lowest rung of the economic ladder.

我意識到彷彿不過是昨日在阿拉巴馬州伯明罕為友愛疾呼的孩子，他們得到的回應是消防水柱、吠叫的狗，甚至死亡。我意識到彷彿不過是昨日在密西西比州費城，爭取投票權的年輕人遭到殘酷虐待和殺害。彷彿不過是昨日，單單在密西西比州就有四十多棟教堂遭到轟炸或燒毀，只因為他們為那些不接受種族隔離的人提供庇護。我意識到令人衰弱和難熬的貧困折磨著我的同胞，將他們拴在經濟階梯的最低階上。

Therefore, I must ask why this prize is awarded to a movement which is [16)]**beleaguered** and committed to [17)]**unrelenting** struggle; to a movement which has not won the very peace and

brotherhood which is the [18)]**essence** of the Nobel Prize. After [19)]**contemplation**, I conclude that this award which I receive on behalf of that movement is a [20)]**profound** recognition that nonviolence is 🛡 the answer to the [21)]**crucial** political and moral question of our time—the need for man to overcome [22)]**oppression** and violence without [23)]**resorting** to violence and oppression. Civilization and violence are [24)]**antithetical** concepts.

所以，我必須問，為什麼這個獎要授予一場陷入困境、掙扎不斷的運動；授予尚未贏得和平和友愛的運動，而和平和友愛正是諾貝爾獎的精髓。經過深思後，我的結論是，我代表這場運動獲得的這個獎，是在大大地表揚一件事，乃非暴力是我們這時代重要的政治和道德問題的解答，需要人類不訴諸暴力和壓迫，以戰勝壓迫和暴力。文明和暴力是對立的概念。

> 66 The time is always right to do what is right.
>
> 要做對的事，任何時間都是好時機。
>
> 金恩博士談時機

Martin Luther King, Jr.
小馬丁路德金恩

1929 年出生於喬治亞洲雅特蘭大，是美國最知名的民權領袖之一。他在浸信會牧師父親的影響下，於 1955 年獲得波士頓大學神學博士學位，回到美國南方，在阿拉巴馬州擔任牧師。金恩博士在民權運動最激烈、暴力事件頻繁的 60 年代，堅持推動非暴力抗爭，於 1964 年獲得諾貝爾和平獎。

33 USA

---

14) **grinding** [ˈɡraɪndɪŋ] (a.) 折磨人的，惱人的
The grinding boredom of prison life drives some people crazy.

15) **afflict** [əˈflɪkt] (v.) 折磨，使痛苦、苦惱
Many African countries are afflicted by malaria.

16) **beleaguered** [bɪˈligəd] (a.) 困難重重的，圍困的
The beleaguered company is in danger of going bankrupt.

17) **unrelenting** [ˌʌnrɪˈlɛntɪŋ] (a.)
接連不斷的，不緩和的，不退讓的
The heat and humidity was unrelenting.

18) **essence** [ˈɛsəns] (n.) 本質，精髓，要素
Change is the very essence of life.

19) **contemplation** [ˌkɑntəmˈpleʃən] (n.)
沈思，深思熟慮
After much contemplation, Pam decided to change careers.

20) **profound** [prəˈfaʊnd] (a.) 深刻的，深遠的
Pollution has profound effects on human health.

21) **crucial** [ˈkruʃəl] (a.) 重要的，關鍵的
This election is crucial to the country's future.

22) **oppression** [əˈprɛʃən] (n.) 壓迫，壓制
Every person has the right to freedom from oppression.

23) **resort (to)** [rɪˈzɔrt] (v.) 訴諸、憑藉（某種手段）
I had to resort to threats to get my money back.

24) **antithetical** [ˌæntɪˈθɛtɪkəl] (a.) 對立的
His religious beliefs are antithetical to mine.

A Powerful Moral Force
強大的道德力量

Negroes of the United States, following the people of India, have demonstrated that nonviolence is not [1)]**sterile** [2)]**passivity**, but a powerful moral force which makes for social [3)]**transformation**. Sooner or later, all the people of the world will have to discover a way to live together in peace, and [4)]**thereby** transform this [5)]**pending** [6)]**cosmic** [7)]**elegy** into a creative [8)]**psalm** of brotherhood. If this is to be achieved, man must [9)]**evolve** for all human conflict a method which rejects revenge, [10)]**aggression** and [11)]**retaliation**. The foundation of such a method is love.

美國的黑人，繼印度人民後，已證明非暴力不是消極的順從，而是強大的道德力量，能使社會轉型。這世界所有人民遲早必須找到和平共處的方式，繼而將這懸而未決的宇宙挽歌轉變成富有創意的友愛讚美詩。若要實現這點，人類必須把所有衝突發展出一種拒絕報復和侵略的方式。這種方式的基礎就是愛。

© Forty3Zero / Shutterstock.com

> 66 The ultimate measure of a man is not where he stands in moments of comfort and convenience, but where he stands at times of challenge and controversy.
>
> 最終要衡量一個人，不是看他在順境時如何，而是他在逆境下所採取的態度。
>
> 金恩博士談人的價值

The [12)]**tortuous** road which has led from LG Montgomery, Alabama to Oslo bears witness to this truth. This is a road over which millions of Negroes are traveling to find a new sense of dignity. This same road has opened for all Americans a new era of progress and hope. It has led to a new Civil Rights Bill, and it will, I am convinced, be widened and lengthened into a super highway of justice as Negro and white men in increasing numbers create [13)]**alliances** to overcome their common problems.

從阿拉巴馬州蒙哥馬利市通往奧斯陸的曲折之路見證這個道理。這是一條數百萬黑人踏上尋找新尊嚴的道路。這條道路同樣為所有美國人開啟進步和希望的新時代。這條路已促成新的民權法案，而且我相信這條路也將拓展成正義的超級高速公路，因為已有越來越多黑人和白人聯盟克服共同的問題。

I accept this award today with an [14)]**abiding** faith in America and an [15)]**audacious** faith in the

VOCABULARY 🎧 20

1) **sterile** [ˋstɛrəl] (a.) 無生氣的，冰冷無味的
Vicky left the bank because she hated working in such a sterile environment.

2) **passivity** [pæˋsɪvəti] (n.) 被動，消極，順從
The increasing passivity of voters is a threat to our democracy.

3) **transformation** [ˌtrænsfɚˋmeʃən] (n.) 變化，轉變，變形
The city has undergone a dramatic transformation in the past decade.

4) **thereby** [ðɛrˋbaɪ] (adv.) 因此，從而
Hybrid cars burn less gas, thereby reducing pollution.

5) **pending** [ˋpɛndɪŋ] (a.) 迫近的，即將發生的，懸而未決的
The residents of the small town were unaware of the pending disaster.

6) **cosmic** [ˋkɑzmɪk] (a.) 宇宙的
According to the Big Bang theory, the universe began with a cosmic explosion.

7) **elegy** [ˋɛlədʒi] (n.) 哀歌
Walt Whitman wrote an elegy for Abraham Lincoln.

8) **psalm** [sɑm] (n.) 讚美詩，聖歌
What's your favorite psalm in the Bible?

9) **evolve** [ɪˋvɑlv] (v.) 演變，演化，發展
Is it true that humans evolved from apes?

10) **aggression** [əˋgrɛʃən] (n.) 侵略（行動），侵犯（行為）
Dogs that show aggression toward people should be kept indoors.

11) **retaliation** [rɪˌtæliˋeʃən] (n.) 報復
The terrorist bombing was an act of retaliation against the government.

future of mankind. I refuse to accept [16]**despair** as the final response to the [17]**ambiguities** of history. I refuse to accept the idea that the "isness" of man's present nature makes him morally incapable of reaching up for the [18]**eternal** "oughtness" that forever confronts him. I refuse to accept the idea that man is mere flotsam and jetsam in the river of life, unable to influence the [19]**unfolding** events which surround him. I refuse to accept the view that mankind is so tragically bound to the starless midnight of [20]**racism** and war that the bright [21]**daybreak** of peace and brotherhood can never become a reality.

我今天憑藉對美國一貫堅定的信念，和對人類未來無比的信心接受這個獎。我拒絕視絕望為晦暗歷史的最後答案。我拒絕接受人類因本性難移而無法在道德上追求更高的終極理想。我拒絕接受將人類視為生命長河中隨波逐流的漂流物，無法對周圍情勢的演變發揮影響力。我拒絕接受將人類視作悲慘地困在種族歧視和爭戰的無星暗夜之中，以致和平及友愛的破曉光明永遠無法實現。

種族隔離法與民權運動

美國一直到第二次世界大戰結束，南方還以法律規定種族隔離（racial segregation），而北方也還普遍存在種族隔離現象。戰後十年間，美國黑人爭取平等自由的民權運動團體受到政府鎮壓，只能在法院進行鬥爭。由於美國法院偏袒種族主義，黑人轉向呼籲國際重視此問題。為改變美國在國際上的形象，美國最高法院於 1954 年做出「公立學校實行種族隔離教育是不平等的」之判決。

由於訴諸法律的進度太過緩慢，黑人不再寄望於修法，轉而靠自身的力量。1955 年，黑人女性帕克斯在阿拉巴馬州蒙哥馬利市（Montgomery）的公車上拒絕讓座給白人，因而被捕入獄。

當時還很年輕的馬丁路德金恩博士領導全城五萬黑人拒搭公車長達一年，迫使公車的種族隔離規定取消，開啟了美國黑人摧毀種族隔離制度的希望。

1957 年，馬丁路德金恩博士帶頭組成南方基督教領袖會議（Southern Christian Leadership Conference, SCLC），將民權運動推廣到美國南部的各個生活角落。1960 年，北卡羅萊納州格林斯伯勒市（Greensboro）有四位黑人大學生進入一間餐廳，遭到白人服務員斥離，四

民權運動人士帕克斯（Rosa Parks），攝於 1955 年，照片後方為金恩博士。

個大學生靜坐不動，此舉獲得美國南部廣大黑人學生響應，進而發展成大規模靜坐，最後有將近兩百個城市取消餐廳隔離制。

美國民權運動持續發燒，1961 年迫使南部各州取消州際公車上的種族隔離制。1963 年，金恩博士在南部種族隔離極嚴重的伯明罕組織示威遊行（Birmingham campaign），要求取消全市隔離制，示威群眾受到殘酷鎮壓。演說中提及警察放狗咬人、用水柱驅離的行為，就是在此次行動中發生。最後該市的種族隔離制全部取消。

民權運動勢力從此迅速擴大，8 月 28 日更集結二十五萬人向華府進軍（March on Washington，本書另一篇演説主講者 Bob Dylan 當時亦登台演唱聲援，金恩博士則在此發表了著名的「我有一個夢想」I Have a Dream 演説），同時部分黑人展開以暴制暴的鬥爭，終於在 1964 年迫使詹森總統（Lyndon Johnson）簽署《民權法案》Civil Rights Act。同年，金恩博士獲得諾貝爾和平獎。

© National Archives and Records Administration

金恩博士在向華府進軍活動上發表 I Have a Dream 演説。

---

12) **tortuous** [ˋtɔrtʃuəs] (a.) 彎曲的，迂迴的
A tortuous path was the only way through the mountains.

13) **alliance** [əˋlaɪəns] (n.) 聯盟，同盟，結盟
The two countries have formed a military alliance.

14) **abiding** [əˋbaɪdɪŋ] (a.) 不變的，持久的
Tom's country childhood gave him an abiding interest in nature.

15) **audacious** [ɔˋdeʃəs] (a.) 大膽的，無畏的
The general came up with an audacious plan to capture the city.

16) **despair** [dɪˋspɛr] (n.) 絕望
The destruction of the earthquake left the villagers in despair.

17) **ambiguity** [ˌæmbɪˋgjuətɪ] (n.) 模稜兩可，含糊
There was no ambiguity in the president's speech.

18) **eternal** [ɪˋtɜnəl] (a.) 永恆的，永久的，無休止的
Scientists are searching for the secret to eternal youth.

19) **unfolding** [ʌnˋfoldɪŋ] (a.)（逐步）展開、呈現、發展的
All the major papers covered the unfolding story.

20) **racism** [ˋresɪzəm] (n.) 種族主義，種族歧視
Racism is still a problem in many countries.

21) **daybreak** [ˋdeˌbrek] (n.) 黎明
The farmers get up at daybreak to work in the fields.

Hope for a Brighter Tomorrow
期待更美好的明天

I refuse to accept the ¹⁾**cynical** ²⁾**notion** that nation after nation must ³⁾**spiral** down a ⁴⁾**militaristic** stairway into the hell of ⁵⁾**thermonuclear** destruction. I believe that ⁶⁾**unarmed** truth and ⁷⁾**unconditional** love will [LG] have the final word in reality. This is why right temporarily defeated is stronger than evil ⁸⁾**triumphant**. I believe that even amid today's ⁹⁾**mortar** bursts and ¹⁰⁾**whining** bullets, there is still hope for a brighter tomorrow. I believe that wounded justice, lying ¹¹⁾**prostrate** on the blood-flowing streets of our nations, can be lifted from

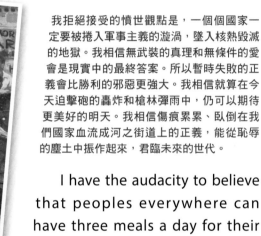

" In the end, we will remember not the words of our enemies, but the silence of our friends.

到頭來，我們不會記得敵人的攻訐，而是朋友的沈默。

金恩博士談沈默即背叛

this dust of shame to reign ¹²⁾**supreme** among the children of men.

© Forty3Zero / Shutterstock.com

我拒絕接受的憤世觀點是，一個個國家一定要被捲入軍事主義的漩渦，墜入核熱毀滅的地獄。我相信無武裝的真理和無條件的愛會是現實中的最終答案。所以暫時失敗的正義會比勝利的邪惡更強大。我相信就算在今天迫擊砲的轟炸和槍林彈雨中，仍可以期待更美好的明天。我相信傷痕累累、臥倒在我們國家血流成河之街道上的正義，能從恥辱的塵土中振作起來，君臨未來的世代。

I have the audacity to believe that peoples everywhere can have three meals a day for their bodies, education and culture for their minds, and dignity,

VOCABULARY 22

1) **cynical** [ˈsɪnɪkəl] (a.) 憤世嫉俗的，悲觀的
Voters are becoming more and more cynical about politics.

2) **notion** [ˈnoʃən] (n.) 概念，觀念，想法
I only have a vague notion of what Ryan does for a living.

3) **spiral** [ˈspaɪrəl] (v.) 螺旋形盤旋（上升或下降）
The weak dollar caused inflation to spiral upward.

4) **militaristic** [ˌmɪlɪtəˈrɪstɪk] (a.) 軍國主義的
Many world leaders are worried about North Korea's militaristic ambitions.

5) **thermonuclear** [ˌθɜmoˈnukliə] (a.) 核熱的
Experts believe Iran is capable of developing thermonuclear weapons.

6) **unarmed** [ʌnˈɑrmd] (a.) 沒有武裝的
The riot started when police shot an unarmed protester.

7) **unconditional** [ˌʌnkənˈdɪʃənəl] (a.) 無條件的
Japan agreed to unconditional surrender on August 10, 1945.

8) **triumphant** [traɪˈʌmfənt] (a.) 勝利的
The triumphant German army marched through the streets of Paris.

9) **mortar** [ˈmɔrtə] (n.) 迫擊炮
The military runway was destroyed by mortar fire.

10) **whine** [waɪn] (v.)（物體迅速飛過空中）嗖嗖響
Bullets whined all around the soldiers' heads.

11) **prostrate** [ˈprɑˌstret] (a.) 俯臥的，倒在地上的
The dead body was found in a prostrate position.

12) **supreme** [səˈprim] (a.) 頂級的，最高等的
The president is a man of supreme confidence.

equality and freedom for their spirits. I believe that what ¹³⁾**self-centered** men have torn down men other-centered can build up. I still believe that one day mankind will bow before the ¹⁴⁾**altars** of God and be crowned triumphant over war and ¹⁵⁾**bloodshed**, and nonviolent ¹⁶⁾**redemptive** good will ¹⁷⁾**proclaim** the rule of the land. "And the lion and the lamb shall lie down together and every man shall sit under his own vine and fig tree and none shall be afraid." I still believe that we shall overcome!

我大膽地相信，各地人民可以每天有三餐溫飽，有教育和文化充實心靈，有尊嚴、平等和自由滋養靈魂。我相信以自我為中心的人所破壞的事物，可以靠無私的人重建。我依然相信總有一天，人類會在上帝的祭壇前臣服，在戰爭和殺戮中加冕獲勝，非暴力的救贖善良將宣告統治天下。「獅子應與羔羊同臥，每個人應坐在自己的葡萄樹和無花果樹下，沒有人應該害怕。」（編註：出自聖經以賽亞書 11:6）我依然相信我們能戰勝！

This faith can give us courage to face the ¹⁸⁾**uncertainties** of the future. It will give our tired feet new strength as we continue our forward ¹⁹⁾**stride** toward the city of freedom. When our days become ²⁰⁾**dreary** with low-²¹⁾**hovering** clouds and our nights become darker than a thousand midnights, we will know that we are living in the creative ²²⁾**turmoil** of a genuine civilization struggling to be born.

這種信念能給我們勇氣面對未來的不確定性，並將為我們疲憊的雙腳帶來新的力量，讓我們繼續大步邁向自由之城。當我們遇到濃雲密佈的陰鬱日子，且夜晚比一千個午夜更黑暗時，我們會知道自己正處於真正文明因掙扎著誕生而引起的動盪中。

Today I come to Oslo as a ²³⁾**trustee**, inspired and with renewed dedication to humanity. I accept this prize on behalf of all men who love peace and brotherhood. I say I come as a trustee, for in the depths of my heart I am aware that this prize is much more than an honor to me personally.

今天我以受到啟發並決心對人道重新做出努力的受託人身分來到奧斯陸。我代表所有熱愛和平和友愛的人領獎。我說我是以受託人的身分前來，因為在我內心深處，我知道這個獎遠遠超過了我個人的榮耀。

13) **self-centered** [ˌsɛlf ˈsɛntəd] (a.) 自我中心的
Dave is far too self-centered to put himself in your shoes.

14) **altar** [ˈɔltə] (n.) 祭壇，供桌
The worshippers placed offerings on the altar.

15) **bloodshed** [ˈblʌdˌʃɛd] (n.) 流血，殺人
Peacekeeping troops were brought in to prevent further bloodshed.

16) **redemptive** [rɪˈdɛmptɪv] (a.) 救贖的
The Bible teaches about the redemptive power of suffering.

17) **proclaim** [prəˈklem] (v.) 聲稱，聲明，公佈
Brazil proclaimed its independence from Portugal in 1882.

18) **uncertainty** [ʌnˈsɝtənti] (n.) 不確定性，缺乏把握
There's still uncertainty about the time of the accident.

19) **stride** [straɪd] (n.) 大步，進步；(v.) 跨大步走
The scientists are making rapid strides in their research.

20) **dreary** [ˈdrɪəri] (a.) 沈悶的，乏味的
Rebecca left London because of the dreary weather.

21) **hover** [ˈhʌvə] (v.) 停懸，盤旋
An eagle hovered high in the sky.

22) **turmoil** [ˈtɝˌmɔɪl] (n.) 騷動，混亂
The country is entering a period of political turmoil.

23) **trustee** [trʌsˈti] (n.) （財產）受託管理人
The museum's board of trustees meets once a month.

Honoring Heroes of the Struggle
推崇奮鬥中的英雄

Every time I take a flight, I am always mindful of the many people who make a successful journey possible—the known pilots and the unknown ground crew. So you honor the [1]**dedicated** pilots of our struggle who have sat at the controls as the freedom movement [2]**soared** into orbit. You honor, once again, Chief Lutuli of South Africa, whose struggles with and for his people, are still met with the most brutal expression of man's [3]**inhumanity** to man. You honor the ground crew without whose labor and sacrifices the jet flights to freedom could never have left the earth.

每次我坐飛機時，總是注意到那些盡力造就成功旅程的許多功臣——看得到的機師和幕後的地勤人員。所以你們表揚的是推崇專心奮鬥的機師，在自由運動升空運行時，他們就坐在駕駛艙中。你們也再次表揚了南非的盧圖利酋長（編註：相關介紹請見「曼德拉諾貝爾獎得獎感言」），他為同胞所做的奮鬥，仍遭到人類相殘中最殘酷的對待。要推崇地勤，沒有他們付出的勞力和犧牲，航向自由的飛機是不可能飛離地表。

Most of these people will never make the headline and their names will not appear in *Who's Who*. Yet when years have rolled past and when the [4]**blazing** light of truth is focused on this marvelous age in which we live—men and women will know and children will be taught that we have a finer land, a better people, a more noble civilization—because these humble children of God were willing to suffer for [5]**righteousness'** sake.

這些人大部分的名字都不會登上頭條，也不會出現在名人錄。但在多年過去後，當真理的熾熱之光聚焦在我們生活的美妙時代時，不論男女都會知道、下一代也會被教導，我們的世界、人民之所以更美好，文明也更高尚，是因為上帝的謙卑子民願意為正義而受苦。

I think Alfred Nobel would know what I mean when I say that I accept this award in the spirit of a [6]**curator** of some precious [7]**heirloom** which he holds in trust for its true owners—all those to whom beauty is truth and truth beauty—and in whose eyes the beauty of genuine brotherhood and peace is more precious than diamonds or silver or gold.

我說我以珍貴傳家寶的監護人精神接受這個獎，我認為阿佛烈諾貝爾會明白我的意思，因為他也是為真正的所有者——那些認為美即是真、真即是美（編註：引用英國浪漫詩人濟慈的詩句）的人——保管這個獎。在這些人眼中，真正友愛與和平之美，遠比鑽石或金銀更珍貴。

© Forty3Zero / Shutterstock.com

---

1) **dedicated** [ˈdɛdɪˌketɪd] (a.) 專注的，投入的
   John is a dedicated and diligent student.

2) **soar** [sor] (v.) 往上飛升，高飛，翱翔
   The airplane soared above the clouds.

3) **inhumanity** [ˌɪnhjuˈmænəti] (n.) 殘忍，暴行
   The photographer's photos capture the inhumanity of war.

4) **blazing** [ˈblezɪŋ] (a.) 熾烈的，輝煌的
   Firefighters rushed to save the blazing building.

5) **righteousness** [ˈraɪtʃəsnɪs] (n.) 公正，正義
   We fully believe in the righteousness of our cause.

6) **curator** [ˈkjuretɚ] (n.) 管理者，館長
   Who is the curator of this art collection?

7) **heirloom** [ˈɛrˌlum] (n.) 相傳遺物，傳家寶
   The ring on Ellen's finger is a family heirloom.

African American 非裔美國人

African American 是美國人口中的黑人，是指從撒哈拉以南的非洲（Sub-Saharan Africa）移居美國的人民。從 16 世紀開始，非洲黑人被英國送去美國做奴隸。在美國獨立之後，這些黑人的奴隸身分並沒有被改變。19 世紀的南北戰爭，他們在名義上擺脫了奴隸的身分，卻沒有獲得真正的自由。終於到了 1950、60 年代，他們展開一連串的民權運動，認同自我，爭取平等，不再認為自己的膚色代表低等，因而提出 black people 和指美國黑奴後代的 **negro**（在西班牙語中意思為黑色）區分。後來為了更具有歷史含義，因此以 African American 表示移民美國的非洲人來稱呼他們。

on behalf of 代替某人

意思是「代替某人去做某件事」、「做某人的代表」。也可以說 in behalf of sb.、on / in sb.'s behalf、in sb.'s name。

· The producer accepted the award on behalf of the director.
＝ The producer accepted the award on the director's behalf.
那位製作人代替導演領獎。

A: Rob just called. He's sick and can't attend the meeting today.
　　羅伯剛剛打電話來。他生病了，今天無法參加會議。
B: Oh. Can you go on his behalf and report back to me?
　　喔。你能代表他去開會，再向我回報會議結果嗎？

the lowest rung of / on the ladder 最低階層

字面上的意思是「梯子最下面那根橫桿」，指最基層、最基本的單位、最低下的位階。

A: Were you given a management position when you joined the company?
　　你進入這家公司時，是被指派擔任主管的工作嗎？
B: No. I started out on the lowest rung of the ladder.
　　不是。我是從最基層幹起。

isness 和 oughtness

這兩個字都加上表示「性質、狀態」的字尾 –ness。is 是用於現在式的 be 動詞，isness 是指事物、局勢的「現狀」。ought 是用於表示應該或期望的助動詞，因此 oughtness 表示事物的「理想狀態」。

flotsam and jetsam 殘骸破片

flotsam 是指船隻解體的漂流物，或從船上漂出的垃圾，引申為「無價值的零碎雜物」及「遊民」。flotsam and jetsam 是取兩個押韻字連用，意思相同。

A: I think it's time to get rid of the flotsam and jetsam in the attic.
　　我覺得該把閣樓上的那堆雜物清一清了。
B: You're probably right—I'm sure it's becoming a fire hazard.
　　說的也是——恐怕會引發火災。

have the final word 有最後決定權

是指當發生爭執時，某個人能做出最後的裁決，平息爭議，引申為「有最後的決定權」。

A: Do you have anything else you want to say, Martin?
　　你還有意見想表達嗎，馬丁？
B: That's OK. I'll let you have the final word.
　　就這樣了。我讓你做結論。

介系詞 to 當所有格表示

英文裡有一類名詞的所有格，既不是加 of，也不是加 's，而是以介系詞 to 來表示，像這裡的 the answer to...「…的答案」，以下是更多的例子：

1 **the key to the door** 這扇門的鑰匙

2 **the secretary to the managing director** 總經理的秘書

3 **a right to the throne** 王位的繼承權

4 **a solution to a problem** 解決之道

5 **an approach to solving cases** 破案的方法

6 **access to the information** 獲取資訊的管道

在上面的例子裡，介系詞 to 所連接的兩個名詞之間有「屬於」的意義在裡面（如例子 1、2）。另一方面，以 to 連接的兩個名詞也可以用來表示「與…有關」（如例子 3~5）。值得注意的是，例子 5 中的介系詞 to 後面如果接動詞時，應改為動名詞的形式，即 solving。

金恩博士 1964 年底獲得諾貝爾獎之後，繼續前往極端種族主義的阿拉巴馬州塞爾馬市推動黑人選民登記運動，並於 1965 年 3 月冒著被恐嚇暗殺的風險發起另一次行動，向阿拉巴馬州首府蒙哥馬利市進軍。最後美國政府終於在全球輿論壓力下，於八月要求國會通過《選民登記法》。可惜美國南部的種族隔離制度與歧視尚未完全消弭，長期的紛擾反而挑起美國北部的種族歧視情緒。1968 年 3 月，金恩博士發起另一次「貧民進軍」（亦稱「窮人運動」），途經田納西州孟菲斯市（Memphis）時，不幸被種族主義分子槍殺。

© Steven Frame / Shutterstock.com

金恩博士遇夫人合葬的陵墓，位於喬治亞州亞特蘭大市的小馬丁路德金恩國家歷史園區（Martin Luther King, Jr. National Historic Site）。

Let a New Age Dawn

讓新時代大放曙光

"It always seems impossible until it's done."

-Nelson Mandela

Nelson Mandela's Nobel Prize Acceptance Speech
納爾遜曼德拉諾貝爾獎得獎感言

@COLOSSALMEDIA

I would like to take this opportunity to congratulate my [1]**compatriot** and fellow [2]**laureate**, State President F.W. de Klerk, on his receipt of this high honor. Together, we join two distinguished South Africans, the late 🛈 Chief Albert Lutuli and 🛈 His Grace Archbishop Desmond Tutu, to whose [3]**seminal** contributions to the peaceful struggle against the evil system of 🛈 apartheid you paid well-deserved tribute by awarding them the Nobel Peace Prize. It will not be [4]**presumptuous** of us if we also add, among our [5]**predecessors**, the name of another outstanding Nobel Peace Prize winner, the late Rev. Martin Luther King, Jr. He, too, [6]**grappled** with and died in the effort to make a contribution to the just solution of the same great issues of the day which we have had to face as South Africans.

我要藉此機會恭喜我的同胞和同為獲獎者的總統，弗雷德里克威廉戴克拉克，恭喜他接受這崇高榮譽。我們和兩位傑出的南非人一起加入諾貝爾獎得主的行列，他們是已故的艾伯特盧圖利酋長和戴斯蒙屠圖大主教，他們對於和平奮鬥，以及對抗種族隔離政策的邪惡

VOCABULARY 26

1) **compatriot** [kəm`petriet] (n.) 同胞，同一國人
The two compatriots will be competing in the Wimbledon singles final.

2) **laureate** [`lɔriət] (n.) 獲獎者，享有殊榮者
Our professor is a Nobel laureate in chemistry.

3) **seminal** [`sɛmənəl] (a.) 開創性的
The band's seminal second album has become a collector's item.

4) **presumptuous** [prɪ`zʌmptʃuəs] (a.) 冒昧的，放肆的
It was presumptuous of him to order for me at the restaurant.

5) **predecessor** [`prɛdɪˌsɛsɚ] (n.) 前任，先前之物
The new CEO had to deal with the problems left by his predecessor.

6) **grapple (with)** [`græpəl] (v.) 努力解決（問題），格鬥
The government continues to grapple with the problem of air pollution.

體制做出開創性貢獻，你們藉由頒發諾貝爾和平獎，表達了他們當之無愧的敬意。若再加上我們的前輩，應不至於冒昧，他也是傑出的諾貝爾獎得主，即已故的馬丁路德金恩牧師。他當時所努力對付的重大問題，並因此喪生，也是我們在南非面臨的問題。

We speak here of the challenge of the [7)]**dichotomies** of war and peace, violence and non-violence, racism and human dignity, oppression and [8)]**repression** and liberty and human rights, poverty and 📘 freedom from want. We stand here today as 📘 nothing more than a representative of the millions of our people who dared to rise up against a social system whose very essence is war, violence, racism, oppression, repression and the [9)]**impoverishment** of an entire people.

我們說的是戰爭與和平、暴力與非暴力、種族歧視和人類尊嚴、壓迫和鎮壓與自由和人權、貧困和免於匱乏的對立性挑戰。我們今天站在這裡，代表勇敢挺身對抗某個社會體制的數千萬人民，因為這個體制的本質是戰爭、暴力、種族歧視、壓迫、鎮壓和全民貧困。

An Injury to One Is an Injury to All
傷害一人等於傷害全體

I am also here today as a representative of the millions of people across the globe, the 📘 anti-apartheid movement, the governments and organizations that joined with us, not to fight against South Africa as a country or any of its peoples, but to oppose an [10)]**inhuman** system and 📘 sue for a speedy end to the apartheid crime against humanity. These countless human beings, both inside and outside our country, had the [11)]**nobility** of spirit to 📘 stand in the path of [12)]**tyranny** and injustice, without seeking selfish gain. They recognized that an injury to one is an injury to all and therefore acted together in defense of justice and a common human [13)]**decency**.

我今天在此也代表全球各地的數千萬人，代表反種族隔離運動，代表跟我們站在同一陣線的政府和組織，不是對抗南非這個國家或其任何種族，而是對抗非人道體制，並要求迅速終結有違人道的種族隔離罪行。這些數不清的人，包括國內外的人，都有高尚的情操，不為尋求私利，阻擋暴政和不公義。他們明白傷害一人等於傷害全體，因此一起挺身而出，捍衛正義和基本人類尊嚴。

© Alessia Pierdomenico / Shutterstock.com

Nelson Mandela
納爾遜曼德拉

1918 年生於南非川斯凱（Transkei），騰布族名為 Madiba。1940 年因率領學生罷課活動，被福特哈爾大學退學，1943 年加入非洲民族議會黨（ANC，African National Congress），隨後成立該黨的青年聯盟。受到甘地非暴力抗爭運動影響，曼德拉於 1950 年代致力於鞏固 ANC 反種族隔離政策，並與福特哈爾大學的同學奧利佛坦波（Oliver Tambo，南非第一家黑人法律事務所負責人）合作，為南非弱勢黑人提供免費法律諮詢。1956 年，曼德拉連同 150 位反政府領袖被控叛國遭到逮捕，四年後全部無罪釋放。

1960 年發生警察槍殺 69 名抗議者的夏普威爾屠殺（Sharpeville Massacre），曼德拉因此成立了 ANC 的軍事組織——民族之矛（Spear of the Nation），進行對抗政府的破壞行動，曼德拉因而被逮捕，1964 年被判無期徒刑。他雖然身體遭到監禁，但名聲開始在海外傳開，遭囚 28 年後，曼德拉於 1990 年獲釋，立即投入建立自由民主南非的工作，與當時的南非總統戴克拉克（F.W. de Klerk）共同規劃南非首次自由選舉，並於 1994 年成功當選南非總統，終於成功終結南非的種族隔離制度。兩人於 1993 年共同獲得諾貝爾和平獎。

© catwalker / Shutterstock.com

戴克拉克（右）於曼德拉當選南非總統後擔任其副手，1997 年由公職退休。

7) **dichotomy** [daɪ`kɑtəmi] (n.) 分裂，對立，對比
The book explores the dichotomy between Western and Asian culture.

8) **repression** [rɪ`prɛʃən] (n.) 壓制，鎮壓
Citizens marched in protest against government repression.

9) **impoverishment** [ɪm`pɑvərɪʃmənt] (n.) （使）貧困
The dictator was blamed for the impoverishment of his people.

10) **inhuman** [ɪn`hjumən] (a.) 無人性的，野蠻的
Prisoners in the camp suffered inhuman treatment.

11) **nobility** [no`bɪləti] (n.) 高貴，高尚，貴族
Nobles don't necessarily possess nobility of character.

12) **tyranny** [`tɪrəni] (n.) 暴政，專制，專橫
The people struggled bravely to free themselves from tyranny.

13) **decency** [`disənsi] (n.) 禮度，懂得情理
You should at least have the decency to apologize.

LG

Style 榮銜與尊稱

在位階森嚴的王室、政界、法界、軍隊等場合，提到領導與上級時必須加上尊稱。目前常見的王室稱謂如下：

His/Her Majesty
國王／女王陛下
（用於第二人稱則將 His/Her 改為 Your，以下同）

His/Her Highness
王子／公主殿下

His/Her Grace
公爵／公爵夫人

His/Her Excellency
閣下／閣下夫人

此外，英國及其他英語系國家也用 His Grace 尊稱天主教的總主教（archbishop，用作頭銜時字首大寫）。

圖片來源：Dutch National Archives, The Hague, Fotocollectie Algemeen Nederlands Persbureau (ANEFO), 1945-1989

Albert Lutuli 盧圖利

南非人盧圖利（1898~1967）領導南非黑人對抗白人政權，以非暴力手段反對種族隔離制度。1960 年獲頒諾貝爾和平獎。

apartheid 種族隔離政策

apartheid（讀作 [əˋpɑrtaɪt]）是南非（荷蘭）語（Afrikaans）「隔離」的意思，字典一般翻譯成「（南非的）種族隔離」。南非的白人政府於 1948 年到 1991 年實行種族隔離政策，後來經曼德拉的努力才將該政策廢止、並解除黨禁。apartheid 不僅僅是一種「政策」，這個字在一定程度上，代表了南非長久以來的社會狀態。然而，南非後期的白人政府卻總是避談這個字，強調他們是在發展一種基於民族自覺等概念的「多種族主義」multinationalism。

因受歐洲殖民歷史影響，南非白人過去一直是 dominant minority（居統治地位的少數族群），曼德拉講稿中提到 **white-minority rule**（少數白人族群統治）就是在講南非隔離下的那段歷史。白人以極不人道的通行法（pass laws）控制南非黑人，規定他們不得與白人同車，日落後不得滯留白人區，並逮捕監禁未持通行證就離開居住地的黑人。除此之外，群居法（Group Areas Act）將黑人活動區域限制在獨立黑人家邦（bantustan），使他們遠離政治核心。

A Great Step Forward 一大進步

© Tinseltown / Shutterstock.com

Desmond Tutu 戴斯蒙屠圖

1931 年生，他是南非聖公會首位非裔大主教，1980 年代致力於廢除種族隔離制度，也為愛滋病、兩性平權及貧窮問題發生。1984 年獲得諾貝爾和平獎。1995 年起領導真相與和解委員會（Truth and Reconciliation Commission）促成南非的轉型正義。

Because of their courage and [1]**persistence** for many years, we can, today, even set the dates when all humanity will join together to celebrate one of the outstanding human victories of our century. When that moment comes, we shall, together, rejoice in a common victory over racism, apartheid and LG white minority rule. That triumph will finally bring to a close a history of five hundred years of African [2]**colonization** that began with the establishment of the Portuguese empire. Thus, it will mark a great step forward in history and also serve as a common [3]**pledge** of the peoples of the world to fight racism, wherever it occurs and whatever [4]**guise** it assumes.

因為他們多年來的勇氣和堅持，我們今天甚至可以預見何時能看到全體人類一起慶祝我們這一世紀的大勝利。當那一刻到來時，我們將一起拋開種族主義、種族隔離和少數白人統治，一起歡慶。這一勝利最終將結束自葡萄牙帝國建立以來的五百年非洲殖民，因此這將是歷史上的一大進步，也是世界人民對抗種族主義的共同保證，不論是在哪裡出現，或以什麼假象呈現。

VOCABULARY 28

1) **persistence** [pəˋsɪstəns] (n.) 堅持，堅毅
Mark's persistence in asking for a raise was finally rewarded.

2) **colonization** [ˌkɑlənɪˋzeʃən] (n.) 殖民
I'm reading a book on the Dutch colonization of Indonesia.

3) **pledge** [plɛdʒ] (n./v.) 誓言，保證
The mayor kept his pledge to reduce air pollution.

4) **guise** [gaɪz] (n.) 偽裝，外觀，裝束
The man was accused of collecting money under the guise of charity.

5) **invaluable** [ɪnˋvæljəbəl] (a.) 非常有用，有價值的
The Internet is an invaluable tool for sharing information.

6) **collective** [kəˋlɛktɪv] (a.) 集體的，共同的
The event has become part of our country's collective memory.

7) **bowel** [ˋbauəl] (n.) 深處，內部
The tunnel descends into the bowels of the earth.

8) **tread** [trɛd] (v.) 踩踏，行走
Don't tread on the grass.

9) **vulnerable** [ˋvʌlnərəbəl] (a.) 易受傷害的
Your eyes are one of the most vulnerable parts of your body.

10) **torture** [ˋtɔrtʃə] (v.) 折磨
Many captured soldiers were tortured by the enemy.

11) **pang** [pæŋ] (n.) （肉體）痛苦，（精神）突然襲來的傷痛
I felt a pang of jealousy when I saw her with another man.

The Greatest of Our Treasures
最珍貴的寶藏

At the southern tip of the continent of Africa, a rich reward is in the making, an [5]**invaluable** gift is in preparation for those who suffered in the name of all humanity when they sacrificed everything— for liberty, peace, human dignity and human fulfillment. This reward will not be measured in money. Nor can it be reckoned in the [6]**collective** price of the rare metals and precious stones that rest in the [7]**bowels** of the African soil we [8]**tread** in the footsteps of our ancestors. It will and must be measured by the happiness and welfare of the children, at once the most [9]**vulnerable** citizens in any society and the greatest of our treasures.

在非洲大陸南端，為全體人類犧牲一切以爭取自由、和平、人類尊嚴和圓滿的人，有個豐富的獎賞和無價的禮物正在等著你們。這個獎賞無法用金錢衡量，也無法用埋藏在非洲土壤深處，踩在我們歷代祖先腳下的稀有金屬或珍貴寶石估計總價。那一定要用孩子的幸福和福祉來衡量，他們是社會中最脆弱的公民，也是我們最珍貴的寶藏。

The children must, at last, play in the open veld, no longer [10]**tortured** by the [11]**pangs** of hunger or [12]**ravaged** by disease or threatened with the [13]**scourge** of ignorance, [14]**molestation** and [15]**abuse**, and no longer required to engage in deeds whose [16]**gravity** [17]**exceeds** the demands of their tender years. In front of this distinguished audience, we commit the new South Africa to the [18]**relentless** pursuit of the purposes defined in the World [19]**Declaration** on the Survival, Protection and Development of Children.

孩子終於可以在開闊的大草原上玩耍，不再受飢餓折磨、或受疾病摧殘，或受無知、猥褻和虐待之患所威脅，也不再需要從事超越幼齡所能夠承受的危險。在尊貴的觀眾前，我們承諾為新南非持續追求世界兒童生存保護和發展宣言所確定的宗旨。

The reward of which we have spoken will and must also be measured by the happiness and welfare of the mothers and fathers of these children, who must walk the earth without fear of being robbed, killed for political or material profit, or spat upon because they are beggars. They too must be relieved of the heavy burden of despair which they carry in their hearts, born of hunger, [20]**homelessness** and [21]**unemployment**. The value of that gift to all who have suffered will and must be measured by the happiness and welfare of all the people of our country, who will have torn down the inhuman walls that divide them.

我們說到的獎賞也必將由這些孩子之父母親的幸福和福祉衡量，他們必須在這世上不會因為政治或物質利益而害怕被搶劫、殺害，或因為身為乞丐而遭唾棄。他們自己也曾經因為飢荒、無家可歸和無業而絕望，所以一定也很高興擺脫絕望的重擔。給所有受苦之人的禮物價值，必將由我們國家所有人民的幸福和福祉衡量，他們將拆除分裂他們的不人道之牆。

LG

veld 南非大草原

也拼做 veldt，這個字源自南非（荷蘭）語的 field，指分布於南非、史瓦濟蘭、辛巴威、納米比亞一帶的平坦大草原。這個地區因降雨量不大，零星暴雨多集中在夏季降下，加上每三到五年會發生週期性的大乾旱，因此樹木無法生長，造成一望無際的短草及灌木叢景觀。

---

12) **ravage** [ˈrævɪdʒ] (v.) 蹂躪，摧毀
The country was ravaged by years of war.

13) **scourge** [skɜrdʒ] (n.) 禍根，亂源
Gangs are a scourge on society.

14) **molestation** [ˌmoləsˈteʃən] (n.)
性騷擾，妨害
Child molestation carries a heavy penalty.

15) **abuse** [əˈbjus] (n.) 虐待，濫用（藥物，職權等）
The parents were accused of child abuse.

16) **gravity** [ˈgrævəti] (n.) 嚴重性，危險性
I don't think you appreciate the gravity of the situation.

17) **exceed** [ɪkˈsid] (v.) 超出，超過
The driver was found guilty of exceeding the speed limit.

17) **relentless** [rɪˈlɛntlɪs] (a.) 不懈的，堅韌的，不間斷的
Daniel is relentless pursuing his goals.

19) **declaration** [ˌdɛkləˈreʃən] (n.) 宣佈，宣告，聲明
The declaration of war was approved by Congress.

20) **homelessness** [ˈhomləsnəs] (n.)
無家可歸
The lack of affordable housing has led to a homelessness crisis.

21) **unemployment** [ˌʌnɪmˈplɔɪmənt] (n.)
失業
The government has promised to reduce unemployment.

Our Shared Reward
共享的獎賞

These great masses will have turned their backs on the grave insult to human dignity which described some as masters and others as servants, and transformed each into a [1]**predator** whose survival depended on the destruction of the other. The value of our shared reward will and must be measured by the joyful peace which will triumph, because the common humanity that bonds both black and white into one human race will have said to each one of us that we shall all live like the children of paradise.

廣大群眾將捨棄對人類尊嚴的嚴重侮辱，即是將一些人歸類為主人，另一些人歸類為奴僕，使每個人變成靠毀滅對方才能生存的掠奪者。我們共享的獎賞價值必將由歡樂的和平衡量，且和平必勝，因為將黑人和白人連接成同一人類的共同人性，都將告訴我們每一個人，我們將過著天堂之子的幸福生活。

Thus shall we live, because we will have created a society which recognizes that all people are born equal, with each [2]**entitled** in equal measure to life, liberty, prosperity, human rights and good [3]**governance**. Such a society should

南非公園保留種族隔離時期常見的椅子，
上面寫著「依法僅供白人使用」。

1) **predator** [ˋprɛdətə] (n.) 掠奪者，肉食性動物
Large predators are at the top of the food chain.

2) **entitle** [ɪnˋtaɪtəl] (v.) 給（某人）權力、資格（做某事）
All citizens are entitled to free medical treatment.

3) **governance** [ˋgʌvənəns] (n.) 統治，管理
Weak governance has contributed to the growth of terrorism.

4) **usurper** [juˋsɜpə] (n.) 僭取者，篡奪者
The throne was seized by a brutal usurper.

5) **ignoble** [ɪgˋnobəl] (a.) 不名譽的，可恥的
The man's ignoble behavior brought shame to his family.

6) **imposition** [͵ɪmpəˋzɪʃən] (n.) 實行，施加，強加
The President is considering the imposition of martial law.

never allow again that there should be prisoners of conscience nor that any person's human rights should be violated. Neither should it ever happen that once more the avenues to peaceful change are blocked by [4]**usurpers** who seek to take power away from the people in pursuit of their own, [5]**ignoble** purposes.

我們將過著這樣的生活，因為我們打造了一個認定人人生而平等的社會，人人都享有生活、自由、繁榮、人權和德政的平等標準。這種社會永遠都不應該允許良心犯的存在或任何違反人權的行為。另外不應該再次發生的，是和平改革之路又被篡奪者阻撓，他們為追求自己卑鄙的目的，企圖從人民手中奪走權力。

An Appeal to Burma's Rulers
對緬甸統治者的呼籲

In relation to these matters, we appeal to those who govern Burma that they release our fellow Nobel Peace Prize laureate, LG Aung San Suu Kyi, and LG engage her and those she represents in serious dialogue, for the benefit of all the people of Burma. We pray that those who have the power to do so will, without further delay, permit that she uses her talents and energies for the greater good of the people of her country and humanity LG as a whole.

鑒於這些事情，我們也呼籲緬甸政府釋放同為諾貝爾和平獎得主的翁山蘇姬，為了緬甸所有人民的福祉著想，請與她和她所代表的人民認真對話。我們祈禱有能力解決此事的人，刻不容緩地允許她用自己的才能和精力為她的國民和所有人類的最大利益服務。

Far from LG the rough and tumble of the politics of our own country, I would like to take this opportunity to join the Norwegian Nobel Committee and LG pay tribute to my joint laureate, Mr. F.W. de Klerk. He had the courage to admit that a terrible wrong had been done to our

Aung San Suu Kyi 翁山蘇姬

1945 年生於緬甸仰光，為緬甸獨立英雄翁山將軍之女，年輕時留學英國，1988 年為照顧生病的母親回到緬甸，因緣際會投入反抗軍政權運動，同年建立政黨「全國民主聯盟」，致力推行民主。她受到甘地非暴力理論影響，堅持不以暴力行動解決國內問題，隔年遭軍政府以煽動罪名軟禁，斷斷續續長達 20 年，期間遭逢英國籍的丈夫癌末，她為了怕離開緬甸之後將無法再次入境，只能忍痛放棄最後探視的機會。

翁山蘇姬於 1991 年獲得諾貝爾和平獎，2010 年獲釋。2015 年她所領導的全國民主聯盟贏得大選，她於隔年開始擔任國務資政，成為緬甸實際領導人，惟其縱容軍隊迫害羅興亞人（Rohingya，緬甸及孟加拉邊境的穆斯林民族），已有褫奪其諾貝爾和平獎得主身份的聲浪出現。

© 360b / Shutterstock.com

country and people through the [6]**imposition** of the system of apartheid. He had the [7]**foresight** to understand and accept that all the people of South Africa must through [8]**negotiations** and as equal participants in the process, together determine what they want to make of their future.

在此遠離我們國家顛簸坎坷的政治之處，我要藉這機會跟挪威諾貝爾委員會一起向同為得主的戴克拉克先生表達敬意。他有勇氣承認過去對我們國家和人民所做的可怕錯誤，即實行種族隔離制度。他有先見之明，理解並接受所有南非人民必須透過協商並平等參與整個過程，一起決定如何打造未來。

7) **foresight** [ˈfɔrˌsaɪt] (n.) 先見之明，遠見
I wish I'd had the foresight to invest in Apple a decade ago.

8) **negotiation** [nɪˌgoʃɪˈeʃən] (n.) 談判，協商
The company hired a lawyer to handle the contract negotiations.

南非開普敦（Cape Town）的種族隔離博物館（Apartheid Museum），入口處刻意分為「白人」、「非白人」兩處。

History Will Not Be Denied
歷史不容否認

But there are still some within our country who wrongly believe they can make a contribution to the cause of justice and peace by [1]**clinging to** the [2]**shibboleths** that have been proved to spell nothing but disaster. It remains our hope that these, too, will be blessed with sufficient reason to realize that history will not be denied and that the new society cannot be created by [3]**reproducing** the [4]**repugnant** past, however [5]**refined** or [6]**enticingly** repackaged.

但我國仍有一些人誤以為執著於過去的信念，可以為正義與和平的目標做出貢獻，儘管那已證明毫無用處，只會帶來災難。我們希望

曼德拉 2013 年 12 月 5 日於南非約翰尼斯堡（Johannesburg）過世，全球哀悼。
© Lenscap Photography / Shutterstock.com

VOCABULARY　32

1) **cling (to)** [klɪŋ] (v.) 墨守，緊握不放
Doris clings to the hope that her husband will come back to her.

2) **shibboleth** [ˈʃɪbəlɪθ] (n.) 過時的信念、習俗等
Old shibboleths must be abandoned before the country can modernize.

3) **reproduce** [ˌriprəˈdus] (v.) 複製，使重現，繁殖
The scientists were unable to reproduce the results of the experiment.

4) **repugnant** [rɪˈpʌgnənt] (a.) 可惡的，可憎的
I find his attitude toward women repugnant.

5) **refine** [rɪˈfaɪn] (v.) 使升華，使精練
The class helped me refine my writing style.

6) **enticingly** [ɪnˈtaɪsɪŋli] (adv.) 誘人地
The prices at the sale were enticingly low.

7) **patriotic** [ˌpetriˈɑtɪk] (a.) 愛國的
Many patriotic young men joined the army to fight in the war.

這些人將擁有充分的理性，以明白歷史不容否認，若一再重蹈過去的醜惡，只不過是改良或重新包裝迷人的外表，新社會就無法創造。

南非開普敦附近的羅賓島（Robben Island）監獄，是種族隔離時期關押政治犯的地點，曼德拉即在此服刑。

We would also like to take advantage of this occasion to pay tribute to the many formations of the democratic movement of our country, including the members of our [7]**Patriotic** Front, who have themselves played a central role in bringing our country as close to the democratic transformation as it is today. We are happy that many representatives of these formations, including people who have served or are serving in the "homeland" structures, came with us to Oslo. They too must share the [8]**accolade** which the Nobel Peace Prize confers.

我們也要藉這場合，向我們國家的許多民主運動組織致敬，包括愛國陣線，他們在我們國家現今即將完成的民主轉型扮演核心角色。這些組織的許多代表，包括曾在「家園」組織中服務或正在服務的人，很高興他們跟我們一起來奧斯陸。他們也應該一起分享諾貝爾和平獎授予的榮譽。

The Birth of a New World
新世界的誕生

We live with the hope that as she battles to remake herself, South Africa will be like a [9]**microcosm** of the new world that is striving

> 66 Courageous people do not fear forgiving, for the sake of peace.
>
> 為了和平，有勇氣的人不怕原諒。

曼德拉談原諒

to be born. This must be a world of democracy and respect for human rights, a world freed from the horrors of poverty, hunger, [10]**deprivation** and ignorance, relieved of the threat and the scourge of civil wars and [11]**external** aggression and unburdened of the great tragedy of millions forced to become refugees.

隨著南非為重塑自己而奮鬥時，我們真心希望她能像正在努力誕生之新世界的縮影。這一定要是一個民主和尊重人權的世界，一個擺脫恐怖的貧窮、飢餓、物資匱乏和無知的世界，免受內戰和外欺的威脅和苦難，並卸除數百萬人被迫成為難民的悲劇重擔。

A Living Example
活生生的例子

The processes in which South Africa and Southern Africa as a whole are engaged, [12]**beckon** and urge us all that we take this tide at the flood and make of this region a living example of what all people of conscience would like the world to be. We do not believe that this Nobel Peace Prize is intended as a [13]**commendation** for matters that have happened and passed. We hear the voices which say that it is an appeal from all those, throughout the universe, who sought an end to the system of apartheid.

南非和非洲南部正歷經的過程，正召喚並督促我們所有人，我們要趁著這波浪潮，讓這一區變成活生生的例子，即有良知的人希望世界是什麼樣子。我們不認為諾貝爾和平獎是為了表揚已經發生和過去的事情。我們聽到了一些聲音，那些聲音說，這是來自宇宙各界的訴求，尋求終結種族隔離體制。

8) **accolade** [ˋækəˏled] (n.) 稱讚，讚譽
The professor received many accolades for his research.

9) **microcosm** [ˋmaɪkrəˏkɑzəm] (n.) 縮影
Detroit is a microcosm of the problems facing American industry.

10) **deprivation** [ˏdɛprɪˋveʃən] (n.) 缺乏，貧乏，剝奪
Many accidents are the result of sleep deprivation.

11) **external** [ɪkˋstɜnəl] (a.) 外部的，外面的
The external walls of the house are painted yellow.

12) **beckon** [ˋbɛkən] (v.)（以手勢或點頭示意）召喚，吸引
Steve beckoned the waiter to ask for another glass of water.

13) **commendation** [ˏkɑmənˋdeʃən] (n.) 表揚，獎賞
The rescuers received commendation for their bravery.

> " Resentment is like drinking poison and then hoping it will kill your enemies.
>
> 心懷仇恨就像飲下毒汁，卻希望能因此殺死敵人。
>
> *曼德拉談仇恨*

We understand their call, that we devote what remains of our lives to the use of our country's unique and painful experience to demonstrate, in practice, that the normal condition for human existence is democracy, justice, peace, non-racism, non-sexism, prosperity for everybody, a healthy environment and equality and [1]**solidarity** among the peoples. Moved by that appeal and inspired by the [2]**eminence** you have [3]**thrust** upon us, we [4]**undertake** that we too will do what we can to contribute to the renewal of our world so that none should, in future, be described as the "[5]**wretched** of the earth."

我們瞭解他們的訴求，要我們奉獻餘生，運用我國獨特且痛苦的經驗來實際證明，人類生存的正常條件是享有民主、正義、和平、無種族歧視、無性別歧視、人人享有繁榮、健全的環境、人人享有平等和團結。受到這訴求的感動，也受到諸位重託於我們這份名聲的鼓舞，我們承諾也會盡力為世界的重建做出貢獻，如此未來不會有人被形容為「地球上的受苦者」。

Let it never be said by future generations that [6]**indifference**, [7]**cynicism** or selfishness made us fail to live up to the ideals of [8]**humanism** which the Nobel Peace Prize [9]**encapsulates**. Let the strivings of us all prove Martin Luther King, Jr. to have been correct when he said that humanity can no longer be tragically bound to the starless midnight of racism and war. Let the efforts of us all prove that he was not a mere dreamer when he spoke of the beauty of genuine brotherhood and peace being more precious than diamonds or silver or gold. Let a new age dawn!

不要讓後世說我們因為冷漠、憤世嫉俗或自私，而無法實現諾貝爾和平獎所象徵的人道主義理想。讓我們所有人努力證明小馬丁路德金恩所說的是正確的，即人類不能再悲慘地困在種族歧視和戰爭的無星黑夜中。用我們所有人的努力證明，在他說到真正的友愛與和平之美，比鑽石和金銀更珍貴時，不是癡人說夢。讓新時代大放曙光！

© SAPhotog / Shutterstock.com

為紀念曼德拉，南非在他 1962 年被捕的地點設立紀念雕像。

VOCABULARY 🎧 34

1) **solidarity** [ˌsɑləˈdɛrəti] (n.) 團結
People wore red ribbons to show solidarity with AIDS victims.

2) **eminence** [ˈɛmənəns] (n.) 卓越，顯赫，著名
The professor achieved eminence in the field of psychology.

3) **thrust** [θrʌst] (v.) 用力推
The boy thrust his hands into his pockets.

4) **undertake (to)** [ˌʌndɚˈtek] (v.) 答應，保證，承擔
The candidate will undertake to improve education if he is elected.

5) **wretched** [ˈrɛtʃɪd] (a.) 悲慘的，可憐的
Residents of the slum live wretched lives.

6) **indifference** [ɪnˈdɪfrəns] (n.) 漠不關心
One of the greatest threats to democracy may be indifference.

7) **cynicism** [ˈsɪnɪˌsɪzəm] (n.) 憤世嫉俗，犬儒主義
All the government scandals have caused widespread cynicism among voters.

8) **humanism** [ˈhjumənˌɪzəm] (n.) 人道主義，人文主義
In many places, religion is being replaced by humanism.

9) **encapsulate** [ɪnˈkæpsjəˌlet] (v.) 象徵，概述，作為縮影
It's difficult to encapsulate the war in a single documentary.

Language Guide

nothing more than 只不過是

這個片語用於強調「只不過是」，等於 only。

A: Don't you think Bill Clinton is a great man?
你不覺得比爾柯林頓這個人很偉大？

B: No. He's nothing more than a politician.
不。他只不過是個政客。

sue for 求償，籲請，懇求

sue 是「控告」，sue for 表示對人採取法律行動以求償。

A: Did you hear Rick is suing for custody of the kids?
你有聽說瑞克正在打官司爭孩子的監護權嗎？

B: No. I though he and his ex had agreed on joint custody.
沒。我以為他跟前妻協議共同監護。

也可引申為「呼籲請求」。

A: How did the First Sino-Japanese War end?
第一次中日戰爭是怎麼結束的？

B: The Qing government sued for peace in April 1895.
清朝於 1895 年 4 月求和。

stand in the path of... 阻擋，妨礙…

字面上的意思是「擋在路中間阻斷（某人的）去路」，也可以說 stand in the way of...、stand in one's way。

Grammar Master

「自由」有兩種：
freedom to 和
freedom from

英文有兩種表達自由的用法，一是 freedom to「追求…的自由」，如 freedom to express（表達意見的自由）。另一是 freedom from「免於…的自由」，如這裡的 freedom from want（免於匱乏的自由）。

1. freedom from「免於…的自由」：介系詞 from 有「遠離」之意，後面接上的是負面的事實，如：

例 **India won freedom from British rule in 1947.**
印度在 1947 年從英國統治中脫離獲得自由。

例 **The villagers have never known freedom from hunger and thirst.**
村民們一直都不知道免於飢荒的自由滋味。

2. freedom to「追求…的自由」：這裡的 to 是不定詞 to，後面需接原形動詞，表達追求該自由，如：

例 **My parents gave me the freedom to do whatever I wanted.**
我的父母讓我自由追求想做的事。

例 **Now that we're retired, we finally have the freedom to travel.**
既然我們都退休了，我們終於可以自由到處旅遊了。

turn one's back on 放棄，拋棄

turn one's back on sb./sth. 可以表示字面上的意思「轉身背對」，也可引申為「背棄」。

A: Did you hear? Robert ran off with his secretary.
你聽說了嗎？羅伯特跟他的祕書私奔了。

B: How could he turn his back on his wife and kids like that?
他怎麼可以就這樣拋妻棄子？

engage in 從事於

engage in 表示「從事、投入」某件事，而當我們說 engage sb. in sth. 就是「讓某人參與」某件事。

A: Have you tried engaging the new guy in conversation?
你有試著和那位新來的人聊天嗎？

B: Yeah, but he's not very talkative.
有啊，但他不是很健談。

as a whole 通盤，整體來說

這個片語用來表示「將好幾部分視為一個整體來考量」。

A: What did you think of the movie?
你覺得那部電影如何？

B: The dialogue was a little silly, but I liked movie as a whole.
對白有點蠢，但整體來說還算不錯。

the rough and tumble of sth. …混亂的情況

rough and tumble 是指「扭打，亂鬥」（當形容詞寫做 rough-and-tumble）。the rough and tumble of sth. 表示鬥來鬥去、相互攻訐的粗暴場面。

A: I hear Oprah's thinking of running for president.
我聽說歐普拉在考慮選總統。

B: I don't think she's ready for the rough and tumble of politics.
我不覺得她準備好去淌政治的混水。

pay tribute to 向…致敬

tribute 是「敬意，讚頌」的意思，pay tribute to sb./sth. 表示公開讚揚某人或某事物。

A: Did you watch the mayor's speech this morning?
你有看市長早上的演講嗎？

B: Yes. He paid tribute to all the firefighters who died in the fire.
有。他向火災當中死亡的打火英雄致敬。

A: What's your secret to success?
你成功的祕訣是什麼？

B: I work hard and never let anything stand in my way.
我認真努力，而且從不讓任何事阻擋我。

曼德拉獲得諾貝爾和平獎之後五個月，南非所有種族首次一起走進投票所，選出曼德拉擔任南非首位黑人總統。他在位期間致力於改善黑人區生活條件、爭取因種族動亂撤離的跨國企業重返南非。1999 年卸任後，他繼續透過基金會教育大眾防範愛滋病的知識。曼德拉於 2013 年逝世。

We Must Always Take Sides

我們一定要選邊站

Elie Wiesel's Nobel Prize Acceptance Speech

埃利維瑟爾諾貝爾獎得獎感言

© lev radin / Shutterstock.com

It is with a ¹⁾**profound** sense of humility that I accept the honor you have chosen to bestow upon me. I know: Your choice ²⁾**transcends** me. This both frightens and pleases me. It frightens me because I wonder: Do I have the right to represent the ³⁾**multitudes** who have ⁴⁾**perished**? Do I have the right to accept this great honor on their behalf? I do not. That would be presumptuous. No one may speak for the dead, no one may interpret their ⁵⁾**mutilated** dreams and visions. It pleases me because I may say that this honor belongs to all the survivors and their children, and through us, to the Jewish people with whose ⁶⁾**destiny** I have always identified.

你們選擇賜予我的榮譽，我懷著深切謙遜之情接受。我知道：你們的選擇超乎我個人的成就。我既惶恐又欣慰。我惶恐是因為我疑惑：我有權利代表那群喪命的人嗎？我有權利代表他們接受這偉大的榮耀嗎？我沒有。這樣太冒昧了。沒人能為死者說話，沒人能詮釋他們殘缺的夢想和願景。我感到欣慰是因為，我可以說這項殊榮屬於所有倖存者和他們的子女，也因此屬於我一直視為命運共同體的猶太人。

VOCABULARY 🎧 36

1) **profound** [prə`faʊnd] (a.) 深刻的，有深度的
The novel shows a profound understanding of human nature

2) **transcend** [træn`sɛnd] (v.) 超越
The band makes music that transcends cultural barriers.

3) **multitude** [`mʌltə‚tud] (n.) 許多（人事物）
A multitude of protesters gathered in the square.

4) **perish** [`pɛrɪʃ] (v.) 死去，消滅
Dozens of people perished in the fire.

5) **mutilate** [`mjutəl‚et] (a.) 毀壞，截除
The body was mutilated by wild animals.

6) **destiny** [`dɛstəni] (n.) 命運，天命
The couple believed it was their destiny to be together.

Can This Be True?
這是真的嗎？

I remember: it happened yesterday or eternities ago. A young Jewish boy discovered the kingdom of night. I remember his [7]**bewilderment**, I remember his [8]**anguish**. It all happened so fast. The ghetto. The [9]**deportation**. The sealed cattle car. The [10]**fiery** altar upon which the history of our people and the future of mankind were meant to be sacrificed. I remember, he asked his father: "Can this be true?" This is the twentieth century, not the Middle Ages. Who would allow such crimes to be committed? How could the world remain silent?

我記得：這一切發生在昨天或永恆之前。一位年輕的猶太男孩發現了暗夜國度（編註：指他所身處且無法逃離的納粹統治）。我記得他的困惑，我記得他的痛苦。一切發生得太快。貧民窟、驅逐出境、被釘死的牲畜車廂（編註：納粹用以載運牲口的火車車廂將一車車的猶太人載往集中營）、用來犧牲我們人民歷史和人類未來的燃燒祭壇（編註：指集中營焚化屍體的火爐）。我記得，他問他的父親：「這是真的嗎？」這是 20 世紀，不是中世紀。誰會容許這種犯罪？這世界怎麼會保持沉默？

And now, the boy is turning to me: "Tell me," he asks. "What have you done with my future?

What have you done with your life?" And I tell him that I have tried. That I have tried to keep memory alive, that I have tried to fight those who would forget. Because if we forget, we are guilty, we are [11]**accomplices**.

現在這男孩轉而問我：「告訴我，你對我的未來做了什麼？你自己的人生是怎麼過的？」我告訴他，我盡力了。我努力維持鮮明的記憶，我努力對抗那些遺忘的人。因為我們若是遺忘，我們就有罪，我們就是幫凶。

LG

ghetto 猶太區

讀作 [ˋgɛto]，指中世紀和近代歐洲各城市因種族歧視劃分出來給猶太人居住的區域。18、19 世紀許多地區已解除猶太人必須居住在猶太區的法律，但二戰時期納粹政權又死灰復燃，並隨後展開猶太人大屠殺。ghetto 在現代英文已不用於指涉猶太區，一般用來表示城市中的「少數民族居住區，貧民窟」。

Eliezer Wiesel 埃利維瑟爾

暱稱 Elie 的埃利瑟維瑟爾（1928~2016）是一位作家及學者，他以自身在波蘭奧斯維辛集中營（Auschwitz concentration camp）和德國布痕瓦爾德集中營（Buchenwald concentration camp）的經歷所寫的作品《夜》 *Night*，同被視為與安妮法蘭克（Anne Frank）的《安妮的日記》 *The Diary of a Young Girl* 記述猶太大屠殺歷史的經典。身為父母、妹妹均死於集中營的猶太大屠殺倖存者，埃利積極投身反種族歧視、推動人權的政治活動，曾任美國大屠殺紀念委員會主席（1980~1986），1986 年獲頒諾貝爾和平獎。

ST. VINCENT & THE GRENADINES 70¢
ELIE WIESEL

© catwalker / Shutterstock.com

> 66 If the only prayer you say throughout your life is "Thank You," then that will be enough.
>
> 如果你終身所說的唯一祈禱詞是「謝謝」，那就夠了。
>
> 埃利維瑟爾談感恩

---

7) **bewilderment** [bɪˋwɪldəmənt] (n.) 迷惑，動詞是**bewilder** [bɪˋwɪldə]
The deer stared at us in bewilderment.

8) **anguish** [ˋæŋgwɪʃ] (n./v.)
（感到）極度的痛苦
The death of her father caused her great anguish.

9) **deportation** [ˌdiporˋteʃən] (n.) 驅逐出境，放逐。動詞為 **deport** [dɪˋport]
If you overstay your visa, you risk deportation.

10) **fiery** [ˋfaɪəri] (a.) 火（一般）的，極熱的，燃燒的
The climbers looked down into the volcano's fiery crater.

11) **accomplice** [əˋkɑmplɪs] (n.) 共犯，幫兇
The murderer's accomplice was given a 10-year sentence.

And then I explained to him how [1)]**naive** we were, that the world did know and remain silent. And that is why I swore never to be silent whenever and wherever human beings endure suffering and [2)]**humiliation**.

然後我向他解釋，我們有多天真，因為這世界明明知道卻保持沉默。所以我發誓，不論任何時候、任何地方，只要有人在忍受痛苦和屈辱，我就永遠不會保持沉默。

Sometimes We Must Interfere
有時我們必須干涉

We must always take sides. [3)]**Neutrality** helps the [4)]**oppressor**, never the victim. Silence encourages the [5)]**tormentor**, never the [6)]**tormented**. Sometimes we must interfere. When human lives are endangered, when human dignity is in [7)]**jeopardy**, national borders and [8)]**sensitivities** become [9)]**irrelevant**. Wherever men or women are [10)]**persecuted** because of their race, religion, or political views, that place must—at that moment—become the center of the universe.

我們一定要選邊站。保持中立就是給壓迫者撐腰，絕對幫不了受害者。沉默是在助長加害者，不是被折磨的人。有時我們必須干涉。當有人的性命受到威脅，當有人的尊嚴陷入危難，國家的邊界和敏感神經就無關緊要。不論在哪裡，不論男女，只要有人因為種族、宗教或政治觀點受到迫害，那個地方——在那一刻——一定要成為最被看重的事。

Of course, since I am a Jew profoundly rooted in my peoples' memory and tradition, my first response is to Jewish fears, Jewish needs, Jewish crises. For I belong to a [11)]**traumatized** generation, one that experienced the [12)]**abandonment** and [13)]**solitude** of our people. It would be unnatural for me not to make Jewish [14)]**priorities** my own: Israel, Soviet Jewry, Jews in Arab lands.

當然，由於我是深植同胞記憶和傳統的猶太人，族人的恐懼、需求和危機是我首先要應付的。我屬於一個受創傷的世代，一個曾經歷過同胞被遺棄和隔離的世代。我若不將猶太人列為優先考量的事，包括以色列、蘇聯猶太人、阿拉伯土地上的猶太人，那就不合理了。

But there are others as important to me. Apartheid is, in my view, as [15)]**abhorrent** as anti-Semitism. To me, Andrei Sakharov's isolation is as much of a [16)]**disgrace** as Iosif Begun's [17)]**imprisonment**. As is the [18)]**denial** of

Andrei Sakharov 沙卡洛夫

1950 年代被譽為蘇聯氫彈之父的沙卡洛夫（1921~1989）因冷戰挑起的軍備競賽、輻射塵污染感到不安，1960 年代開始阻止冷戰雙方地上試爆、與反彈道飛彈，1968 年起被禁止參與與軍事有關的研究。1970 年代，沙卡洛夫轉而積極參與蘇聯人權與民主運動，1975 年獲得諾貝爾和平獎。遭到打壓、賠上所有榮耀與財富的沙卡洛夫不改硬頸態度，1979 年又因公開譴責蘇聯入侵阿富汗，被流放高爾基城。直到 1986 年蘇聯開放才終於返回莫斯科。為了紀念這位人道主義者，歐洲議會將歐洲表揚捍衛人權及思想自由的最高榮譽，命名為沙卡洛夫獎（Sakharov Prize for Freedom of Thought）。

© Olga Popova / Shutterstock.com

VOCABULARY 🎧38

1) **naive** [nɑˋiv] (a.) 天真的
It's naive to believe that all people are good.

2) **humiliation** [hjuˌmɪliˋeʃən] (n.) 羞辱，動詞為**humiliate** [hjuˋmɪliˌet]
My greatest fear is public humiliation.

3) **neutrality** [nuˋtrælətɪ] (n.) 中立
During World War Two, Switzerland adopted a policy of neutrality.

4) **oppressor** [əˋprɛsə] (n.) 壓迫者，壓制者
The people rose up and fought against their oppressors.

5) **tormentor** [tɔrˋmɛntə] (n.) 虐待者，造成痛苦的人
The prisoner swore revenge against his tormenters.

6) **torment** [tɔrˋmɛnt] (v./n.) 折磨，（使）痛苦
Lucy was tormented by nightmares as a child.

7) **jeopardy** [ˋdʒɛpədi] (n.) 危險，風險，危難
I would never put the safety of my family in jeopardy.

8) **sensitivities** [ˌsɛnsɪˋtɪvɪtiz] (n.) 易受傷的感情，易觸動的敏感神經
The sensitivities of the victim's families should be kept in mind.

9) **irrelevant** [ɪˋrɛləvənt] (a.) 不適宜的，不對題的
His comments were irrelevant to the topic of discussion.

10) **persecute** [ˋpɝsɪˌkjut] (v.) 迫害
The Jews have been persecuted for centuries.

11) **traumatized** [ˋtraʊməˌtaɪzd] (a.) 心理受創的
The death of the boy's father left him traumatized.

Solidarity and its leader Lech Walesa's right to [19)]**dissent**. And Nelson Mandela's [20)]**interminable** imprisonment.

但也有其他人同樣對我很重要。在我看來，南非種族隔離跟反猶太人一樣可惡。對我來說，隔離安德烈沙卡洛夫跟監禁約瑟夫比根一樣不能見容。對團結工聯和其領袖萊赫華勒沙發表異議權利的否定也是，對納爾遜曼德拉永無止盡的拘禁亦然。

✡ More People Are Oppressed Than Free
受壓迫者多於自由者

There is so much injustice and suffering crying out for our attention: victims of hunger, of racism, and political persecution, writers and poets, prisoners in so many lands governed by the Left and by the Right. Human rights are being violated on every continent. More people are oppressed than free. And then, too, there are the Palestinians to whose [21)]**plight** I am sensitive but whose methods I deplore. Violence and [22)]**terrorism** are not the answer. Something must be done about their suffering, and soon. I trust Israel, for I have faith in the Jewish people. Let Israel be given a chance, let hatred and danger be removed from her horizons, and there will be peace in and around the Holy Land.

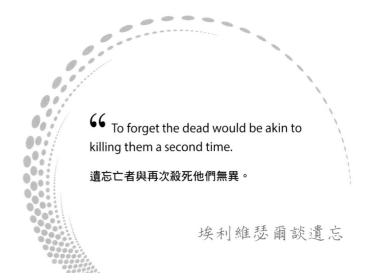

66 To forget the dead would be akin to killing them a second time.

遺忘亡者與再次殺死他們無異。

埃利維瑟爾談遺忘

Iosif Begun 約瑟夫比根

1932 年生於莫斯科的猶太人，這位人權鬥士是一位作家和翻譯家，他因意識形態被囚禁並送往集中營 8 年之久，最後蘇聯在 1987 年迫於猶太政治團體及美國的壓力，將其釋放。

Lech Walesa 萊赫華勒沙與 Solidarity 團結工聯

前波蘭總統華勒沙生於 1943 年，波蘭團結工聯領袖，1983 年獲得諾貝爾和平獎。由他成立（1980 年）、領導的團結工聯主張非暴力反抗，是蘇聯境內第一個獨立工會。波蘭共產黨試圖對該工會迫害未果，最終被迫與其展開談判，並於 1989 年舉行選舉，打破長期由波蘭統一工人黨一黨專政的局面，成立民主國家——波蘭共和國。隔年華勒沙成為波蘭首位民選總統。團結工聯的成功引發模仿，東歐各國社會主義政權相繼垮台，最終促成蘇聯解體。

© catwalker / Shutterstock.com

世上有這麼多不公不義和苦難急需我們關注：挨餓的受害者，遭受種族歧視和政治迫害的受害者，還有作家和詩人，以及在許多由左派和右派統治的國家被監禁的人。每個大陸都在發生違反人權的事。受到壓迫的人比有自由的人還多。此外，我雖有感於巴勒斯坦人的困境，但我要強烈譴責他們的處理方式。暴力和恐怖主義不是答案。他們的苦難應盡快解決。我相信以色列，我對猶太民族有信心。給以色列一個機會，讓仇恨和危險從以色列的地平線上消失，讓和平降臨聖地。

---

12) **abandonment** [əˋbændənmənt] (n.) 遺棄
The couple was charged with attempted child abandonment.

13) **solitude** [ˋsɑləˏtud] (n.) 獨處，孤獨
The lighthouse keeper lived a life of solitude.

14) **priority** [praɪˋɔrətɪ] (n.) 優先（事項），重點，目標
Providing good service to customers is our top priority.

15) **abhorrent** [əbˋhɔrənt] (a.) 可惡的，令人憎惡的
The murderer was given the death sentence for his abhorrent crime.

16) **disgrace** [dɪsˋgres] (n.)
不光彩，丟臉，恥辱
The way those refugees have been treated is a disgrace.

17) **imprisonment** [ɪmˋprɪzənmənt] (n.)
監禁，關押
The robber was sentenced to two years' imprisonment.

18) **denial** [dɪˋnaɪəl] (n.) 拒絕承認，否認
Despite his denial, everyone thinks he's guilty.

19) **dissent** [dɪˋsɛnt] (v./n.) 不同意，（持）異議
Anyone who dissented was asked to raise their hand.

20) **interminable** [ɪnˋtɜmɪnəbel] (a.)
漫長的，冗長的，無止盡的
I always fall asleep during the professor's interminable lectures.

21) **plight** [plaɪt] (n.) 困境，遭遇
The plight of the homeless has worsened over the last decade.

22) **terrorism** [ˋtɛrəˏrɪzəm] (n.) 恐怖行動，恐怖主義
Governments must work together to fight terrorism.

There Is Much to Be Done
還有很多工作要做

Yes, I have faith. Faith in God and even in His creation. Without it no action would be possible. And action is the only remedy to indifference: the most insidious danger of all. Isn't this the meaning of Alfred Nobel's [1]**legacy**? Wasn't his fear of war a [2]**shield** against war?

是的，我有信心。對上帝，甚至對祂所造的人有信心，否則不可能有作為。而有所作為是唯一的解方，能化解冷漠：最狡詐危險的態度。這不就是阿佛烈諾貝爾這項遺澤的意義嗎？他對戰爭的恐懼不正是對抗戰爭的堅實護盾？

There is much to be done, there is much that can be done. One person—a Raoul Wallenberg, an Albert Schweitzer, one person of [3]**integrity**, can make a difference, a difference of life and death. As long as one [4]**dissident** is in prison, our

Raoul Wallenberg 羅爾華倫堡

羅爾華倫堡（1912 年生）是瑞典人，在 1944 年 7 月到 12 月間擔任瑞典駐匈牙利布達佩斯特使，簽發護照給猶太人，並在登記為瑞典領土的建築內庇護猶太人，拯救數萬條生命。華倫堡於 1945 年被蘇聯軍隊逮捕，死期及死因不詳。華倫堡的人道精神廣受讚頌，以色列、美國、加拿大和匈牙利都封他為榮譽公民。

Albert Schweitzer 阿爾伯特史懷哲

被譽為「非洲之父」的史懷哲（1875~1965）是音樂、哲學、神學博士，於 30 歲時發現非洲急需醫療協助，毅然花了七年從頭學起，取得醫學博士，終於以牧師及醫師的身份前往蠻荒，在法屬赤道非洲（現今中非國家加彭 Gabon）建立蘭巴雷內醫院（現稱為史懷哲醫院），行醫長達 35 年。歷經兩次世界大戰，期間史懷哲夫婦成為戰俘，感染疾病，面臨饑荒，還要設法募資，史懷哲為此進出非洲十三次，以他的音樂才能舉辦演奏會，並舉辦數百場演講募款。史懷哲於 1952 年獲得諾貝爾和平獎。

freedom will not be true. As long as one child is hungry, our lives will be filled with anguish and shame. What all these victims need above all is to know that they are not alone, that we are not forgetting them, that when their voices are [5]**stifled**, we shall lend them ours, that while their freedom depends on ours, the quality of our freedom depends on theirs.

還有很多工作要做，還有很多工作可以做。一個人——像羅爾華倫堡那樣、像阿爾伯特史懷哲那樣，一個正直的人，都能發揮影響力，足以改變生死的影響力。只要有一位異議人士身陷囹圄，我們的自由就不是真的。只要有一個孩子挨餓，我們的生活就充滿痛苦和羞愧。這些受害者首先需要的，就是知道自己並不孤單，我們沒有遺忘他們，而且當他們的發言權被扼殺，我們就會替他們發言，他們的自由仰賴我們，而我們自由的品質也仰賴他們。

This is what I say to the young Jewish boy wondering what I have done with his years. It is in his name that I speak to you and that I express to you my deepest gratitude. No one is as capable of gratitude as one who has emerged from the kingdom of night. We know that every moment is a moment of grace, every hour an offering. Not to share them would mean to [6]**betray** them. Our lives no longer belong to us alone, they belong to all those who need us desperately.

那位猶太男孩疑惑我把他的人生弄去哪裡，以上就是我給他的答案。我以他的名義跟你們談話，並向你們表達我最深切的感激。沒有人能像擺脫暗夜國度的人那樣滿懷感激。我們知道每一刻都是感恩的時刻，每一刻都是一份禮物。若不分享它們就意味著背叛它們。我們的人生不再只屬於自己，也屬於所有迫切需要我們的人。

Thank you, Chairman Aarvik. Thank you, members of the Nobel committee. Thank you, people of Norway, for declaring on this singular occasion that our survival has meaning for mankind.

謝謝雅維克主席。謝謝諾貝爾委員會所有成員。謝謝挪威人，感謝你們在這獨特的場合宣稱我們的倖存對人類有意義。

VOCABULARY 40

1) **legacy** [ˋlɛgəsɪ] (n.) 遺產，遺留物
The war left a legacy of death and destruction.

2) **shield** [ʃild] (n.) 盾，防護物，防護罩
The missile system provides a shield against enemy attack.

3) **integrity** [ɪnˋtɛgrətɪ] (n.) 正直，誠實
The principal was a man of great integrity.

4) **dissident** [ˋdɪsɪdənt] (n.) 異議人士，意見不同的人
Many political dissidents were arrested and jailed.

5) **stifle** [ˋstaɪfəl] (v.) 扼殺，掩蓋，讓人窒息
We should be encouraging discussion, not stifling it.

6) **betray** [bɪˋtre] (v.) 背叛，出賣
The spy was executed for betraying his country.

Language Guide

take sides 選擇立場

字面直譯就是「選邊站」，也就是在爭議發生時，表明自己到底支持哪一方。相關的用法有 take sb.'s side。至於不肯選邊站的騎牆派，英文就是 sit on the fence。

A: Whose fault do you think the divorce is, Ron's or Karen's?
你覺得離婚是誰的錯，榮恩還是凱倫？
B: I don't know. I'd rather not take sides.
不知道。我還是不要選邊站。

the center of the universe 宇宙的中心

某事物是 center of sb.'s universe，表示那是某人最重視的事物。因此本文用 the center of the universe 形容一件事，就表現這件事極為要緊，不可等閒視之。用 the center of the universe 形容一個人時，一般用於否定語氣 You're not the center of the universe. 要人「不要太自我中心」。

A: I can't believe how arrogant Elizabeth is.
真不敢相信伊莉莎白會那麼高傲自大。
B: I know. She thinks she's the center of the universe.
對啊。她以為自己是宇宙的中心。

Jew, Soviet Jewry, anti-Semitism
猶太人、蘇聯猶太人與反猶主義

Jew（形容詞為 Jewish）是信奉猶太教（Judaism）的民族，傳統猶太人必需根據猶太律法，學習猶太教義，遵循猶太人的生活、思考方式，才能真正融入猶太社群。

演說中提到猶太人的恐懼等等，最先讓人聯想到的是猶太人大屠殺（The Holocaust）──1930 年代起，德國納粹展開一連串反猶太人活動。猶太人被集中管理或強迫隔離，1941 年起，納粹開始出動部隊大規模殺害猶太人，為了實行「最終解決方案」（Final Solution），猶太人被送至集中營的毒氣室（gas chamber）毒死。據估計，約有 600 萬名猶太人在二次大戰期間遭到屠殺。但猶太人近代歷史上的苦難不止於此。

二次大戰後，蘇聯境內猶太人（Soviet Jewry）歡欣慶賀以色列建國，但以色列親西方的立場引起蘇聯領導者史達林的不滿，他一改戰前拉攏猶太人的做法，實施猶太人清洗，蘇聯境內反猶主義（anti-Semitism）高漲，蘇維埃猶太人遭到殘酷屠殺。直到 1953 年史達林去世，有 100 萬猶太人遇害。

The Holy Land 聖地

對猶太人而言，這個地區是聖城耶路薩冷（Jerusalem）的所在地，位於約旦河與地中海之間，包含約旦河（Jordan River）東岸。不只猶太人，基督徒、穆斯林也都將此地視為聖地。目前在這個地區上的國家有以色列、巴勒斯坦、約旦、黎巴嫩、敘利亞，情勢複雜。

Grammar Master

whatever 用法整理

1. whatever = no matter what：

whatever 當連接副詞時，可以與 no matter what「無論什麼」句型互換，使用時與主要子句之間以逗點相隔。

例 **Whatever you do, don't push that red button.**
不管你做什麼，千萬別按緊急按鈕。

2. whatever ≠ no matter what：

whatever 當複合關係代名詞時，等於 anything that「所有東西」，類似的用法有 whoever = anyone who「任何人」，whichever = any thing that「（同類中）的任何東西」：

例 **You can order whatever you like, as long as you finish it.**
只要你吃的完，點什麼吃都可以。

回頭看看文章的這句話：...I swore never to be silent whenever and wherever human beings endure suffering and humiliation. I swore never to be silent 為主要子句，whenever and wherever 開頭的句子為附屬子句，可以換成 no matter when and where，屬於第一種用法。

德國布痕瓦爾德集中營的猶太勞工，拍攝於 1945 年 4 月 16 日。埃利也在照片中（地上二層左起第七人），當時 16 歲。

©U.S. Defence Visual Information Center/Private H. Miller. (Army)

© Joe Seer / Shutterstock.com

Thank you. Thank you, thank you, thank you, thank you. Thank you to the **LG** [1)]**Academy** for this, all six thousand members. Thank you to the other [2)]**nominees**. All these performances were [3)]**impeccable** in my opinion. I didn't see a **LG** false note anywhere. I want to thank Jean-Marc Vallée, our director. I want to thank **GM** Jared Leto and Jennifer Garner, who I worked with daily.

謝謝各位⋯謝謝學院頒發這項獎,謝謝所有六千位成員。謝謝其他入圍者。我認為所有表演都是無懈可擊,我沒看到任何瑕疵。我要謝謝導演尚馬克瓦利,以及每天跟我共事的傑瑞德雷托和珍妮佛嘉納。

There's a few things—about three things, to my account—that I need each day. One of them is something

Things I Need Each Day

我每天須要的事物

Matthew McConaughey's Oscar Award Speech
馬修麥康納的奧斯卡得獎感言

VOCABULARY 42

1) **academy** [əˋkædəmi] (n.) 學院,藝術院
Pauline is studying at an art academy in France.

2) **nominee** [ˌnɑməˋni] (n.) 被提名人
The nominees for Best Picture will be announced shortly.

3) **impeccable** [ɪmˋpɛkəbəl] (a.) 無缺點的,完美無瑕的
The service at the restaurant was impeccable.

4) **grace** [gres] (v.) 使優美,使增光
The model's face has graced the covers of many magazines.

5) **gratitude** [ˋgrætɪˌtud] (n.) 感恩,感激之意
We gave Kim a present to express our gratitude for her help.

6) **reciprocate** [rɪˋsɪprəˌket] (v.) 報答,交換
They helped us move, so we should reciprocate the favor.

to look up to. Another is something to look forward to. And another is someone to chase.

我認為我每天需要幾件事，大概三件事。其中一件是仰望的對象，另一件是企盼的對象，還有一件是追隨的對象。

Something to Look Up to
仰望的對象

Now, first off, I want to thank God 'cause that's who I look up to. He has [4)]**graced** my life with opportunities that I know are not of my hand or any other human hand. He has shown me that it's a scientific fact that [5)]**gratitude** [6)]**reciprocates**. In the words of the late Charlie Laughton, who said, "When you got God, you got a friend, and that friend is you."

首先我想感謝上帝，因為那是我仰望的對象。他為我的人生增添機會，這不是我或其他人所能給予的。祂向我證明，感恩就會有回報是科學事實。套句已故的查爾斯勞頓說的話：「有了上帝，就有朋友，那個朋友就是你自己。」

Something to Look Forward to
企盼的對象

To my family, that's who and what I look forward to. To my father, who I know is up there right now with a big pot of gumbo. He's got a lemon meringue pie over there. He's probably in his underwear and he's got a cold can of Miller Lite. And he's dancing right now. To you, Dad, you taught me what it means to be a man.

> 66 I love having my hands in the dirt. It is never a science and always an art. There are no rules. And if it comes down to me versus that weed I'm trying to pull out of the ground that doesn't want to come out? I know I'll win.

我喜歡挖挖種種。這絕對無關科學，而是一種藝術。全無規則可循。如果我遇上頑強抵抗，不肯讓我拔起的雜草？我知道我會贏。

馬修麥康納談園藝

謝謝我的家人，那是我引頸企盼的對象。謝謝我的父親，我知道他正在天上吃著一大鍋秋葵濃湯，配一盤檸檬蛋白派，大概只穿著內褲，還喝著一罐冰冷的美樂淡味啤酒，而且還在跳著舞。謝謝你，爸，是你教我做人的意義。

gumbo

美國南方料理，以味道濃重的高湯加肉或蝦，與洋蔥、青椒、芹菜燉煮，並加入秋葵（okra）增稠。

lemon meringue pie

油酥餅乾派皮，內餡是檸檬卡式達醬，上覆以打發蛋白加糖做的蛋白霜烤製而成。

Matthew McConaughey 馬修麥康納

1969 年生於美國德州小鎮，高中畢業時原本計畫要唸法律，但後來改變主意，從德州大學奧斯汀分校取得廣播、電視、電影學位。2000 年代初期，他演出的幾部愛情片都很賣座，成為好萊塢最紅的愛情片男星。到了 2000 年代晚期，他開始挑戰不同戲路，先是在 2011 年演出黑色喜劇《胖尼殺很大》*Bernie*，接著在 2012 年的《舞棍俱樂部》*Magic Mike* 扮演脫衣舞男，終於以 2013 年《藥命俱樂部》*Dallas Buyers Club* 的愛滋病患角色奪下奧斯卡。

簽名上的 jklivin 是他的座右銘 Just keep living，這句話也出現在他的得獎演說中。

Something to Chase
追隨的對象

To my mother who's here tonight, who taught me and my two older brothers—[1)]**demanded**—that we respect ourselves, and what we, in turn, learned was then we were better able to respect others. Thank you for that, Mama.

謝謝我的母親，她今晚也來了，是她教我和我兩位哥哥——要求我們——要自重，我們也因此藉著自重學會尊重他人。媽媽，謝謝妳教我們這點。

Matthew McConaughey 和妻子、小孩於 2014 年共同出席他在好萊塢名人大道（Hollywood Walk of Fame）留下星星的儀式。
© Jaguar PS / Shutterstock.com

To my wife Camila and my kids, Levi, Vida and Mr. Stone, the courage and significance you give me every day I go out the door is [2)]**unparalleled**. You are the four people in my life that I want to make the most proud of me. Thank you.

謝謝我的妻子卡蜜拉，以及我的孩子李維、薇達，還有史東先生（編註：最小的兒子叫 Livingston，Mr. Stone 是他的綽號），你們每天給我的勇氣和意義是無與倫比的。你們四位是我生命中最重要的人，我希望這一生能讓你們以我為榮。謝謝你們。

And to my hero, that's who I chase. Now, when I was 15 years old I had a very important person in my life come to me and say, "Who's your hero?" And I said, I don't know, I [3)]**gotta** think about that. Give me a couple of weeks.

謝謝我的英雄，那是我追隨的對象。我在 15 歲時，我人生中有個重要人物對我說：「誰是你的英雄？」我說，我不知道，給我幾個星期，讓我想一想。

I come back two weeks later, this person comes up and says, "Who's your hero?" I said, "I thought about it. You know who it is?" I said, "It's me in 10 years." So I turned 25. Ten years later, that same person comes to me and goes, "So, are you a hero?" And I was like, " LG Not even close! No, no, no." She said, "Why?" I said, "Because my hero's me at 35."

兩星期後，那人問我：「誰是你的英雄？」我說：「我想過了，你知道是誰嗎？是十年後的我。」於是我 25 歲時，也就是十年後，依然是那個人問我：「你是英雄了嗎？」我說：「差得遠了！不是。」她說：「為什麼？」我說：「因為我現在的英雄是 35 歲的我。」

So you see every day, every week, every month and every year of my life, my hero's always 10 years away. I'm never [4)]**gonna** be my hero. I'm not gonna [5)]**attain** that. I know I'm not. And that's just LG fine with me because that keeps me with somebody to keep on chasing.

所以你看，在我這一生中的每一天、每一星期、每一個月和每一年，我的英雄永遠都是十年後的我。我永遠不會成為自己的英雄，我達不到這目標的。我知道我沒辦法，但沒關係，因為這樣能讓我一直有追隨的對象。

So to any of us, whatever those things are: whatever it is we look up to, whatever it is we look forward to, and whoever it is we're chasing. To that I say: "[6)]**Amen**." To that I say: " LG All right, all right, all right." To that I say: "Just keep living." Thank you.

最後謝謝所有人，不論那些對象是什麼：不論我們仰望的什麼，不論我們企盼的是什麼，不論我們追隨的是誰，我都要對他們說：「阿們。」我要對他們說：「好、沒問題、我一定可以。」我要對他們說：「繼續活在當下。」謝謝各位。

VOCABULARY 🎧 44

1) **demand** [dɪˋmænd] (v.) 要求，需求
   The union is demanding higher pay for workers.

2) **unparalleled** [ʌnˋpærə͵lɛld] (adj.) 無以比擬的，無雙的
   The professor has an unparalleled knowledge of Greek history.

3) **gotta** [ˋgɑtə]（口）即 **got to**
   I'd love to stay longer, but I gotta go now.

4) **gonna** [ˋgɔnə]（口）即 **going to**
   What are you gonna do this weekend?

5) **attain** [əˋten] (v.) 達到，獲得
   You have to work hard if you want to attain your goals.

6) **amen** [ˋeˋmɛn / ˋɑˋmɛn] (int.)（祈禱結束語）阿們
   At the end of the prayer, all the people in the church said, "Amen."

Academy Awards 學院獎

通稱奧斯卡金像獎或奧斯卡獎（Oscars），是每年由美國電影藝術與科學學院（Academy of Motion Picture Arts and Sciences）頒發，設立於 1929 年，於每年的二月下旬舉辦頒獎典禮。奧斯卡獎的評選委員是由學院中的會員和學院邀請的貴賓產生。

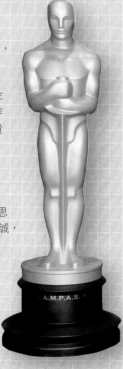

false note 失誤，做錯事

經常會說 strike a false note，字面上的意思是「彈錯一個音」，引申為「虛偽，不真誠，前後矛盾」。

A: What did you think of the mayor's speech?
你對市長的演講看法如何？
B: He said all the right things, but it still struck a false note with me.
他說得頭頭是道，但我還是覺得他言不由衷。

look up to someone 景仰某人

這個片語表示用敬佩、欣賞的態度看某人。

A: Why do you think pro athletes should try to be role models?
你為何認為職業運動員應該為人表率？
B: Because so many young people look up to them.
因為有那麼多年輕人景仰他們。

look forward to 期待，盼望

這個片語後面加上名詞使用，表示對某個人事物非常喜悅而殷切的期待，一般可以在信件結尾加上這個句型，例如 I'm looking forward to your e-mail / reply. 表示「我很期待收到你的電子郵件／回覆／消息」。

A: I'll be arriving in San Francisco on the 25th.
我會在二十五號抵達舊金山。
B: Great! I'm really looking forward to your visit.
太好了，我很期待你的到訪。

Charlie Laughton 查爾斯勞頓

英國演員 Charles Laughton 於 1933 年以《英宮艷史》The Private Life of Henry VIII 獲得奧斯卡最佳男主角。他執導的 1955 年電影《獵人之夜》The Night of the Hunter 被 BBC 選入影史 100 大最佳美國電影。

not even close 差遠了

not even close 的意思其實就是 no，例如有人明明資質平庸，卻自認才華洋溢，是不可多得之才，你就可以告訴他其實他與大師之間「差了十萬八千里」。

A: Do you think my pictures are as good as Ansel Adams?
你覺得我的照片跟攝影大師安瑟亞當斯（1902-1984，美國攝影大師）一樣好嗎？
B: Not even close. You're dreaming if you think you're at that level.
差遠了。如果你真以為有那個水準，那只是妄想。

(that's) fine with me 我無所謂

fine with me 的使用時機是你對於某個事實或意見「無所謂」。更口語的說法有 fine by me、OK by me、OK with me。

A: Do you mind if I smoke?
你介意我抽菸嗎？
B: Fine with me.
我沒差。

「限定」與「非限定」用法整理

關係子句的限定與非限定用法，聽起來很複雜，但其實很簡單！「限定」子句用來修飾不明確的一般名詞，因此需要這個子句來加以「限定」；而「非限定」子句用來修飾特定的名詞，並非必要說明，即使省略也不阻礙理解，因此「不需加以限定」。以下表格整理出兩者的不同與使用時機：

限定用法	非限定用法
所包含的資訊通常是必要訊息	所包含的資訊多半為補充性質
修飾不明確的普通名詞	修飾明確的專有名詞
不需逗點隔開	需逗點隔開
關係代名詞 who, whom, which 可用 that 取代	關係代名詞 who, whom, which 不可用 that 取代，也不能省略
例：People who eat vegetables are likely to be healthy. 吃蔬菜的人比較健康。	例：Carl, who is a Leo, likes to play video games. 那個獅子座的卡蘿，喜歡打電動。

© Featureflash Photo Agency / Shutterstock.com

All right, all right, all right. 是 Matthew McConaughey 的口頭禪，源自他在演出第一部電影《年少輕狂》Dazed and Confused 的演出經驗，他當時第一鏡開拍時非常緊張，他坐在車裡，想著自己跟所飾演的角色有四個相似之處：
一、汽車──Matthew 想：「我現在正在一輛 70 年的雪佛蘭 Chevelle 裡。」
二、吸毒（getting high）──Matthew 想：「Slater（劇中吸大麻的朋友）坐在我的副駕駛座上，我當然有吸毒。」
三、搖滾樂──Matthew 想：「我正在聽 Ted Nugent 的 Stranglehold（Ted Nugent 是知名的硬搖滾歌手）。」

但 Matthew McConaughey 還來不及數到「四、很會把妹」時，電影就開拍了。於是他心裡想，四個中三個。All right! All right! All right! 從此就成了他的口頭禪。

From Razzie to Oscar

從金酸莓到
金像獎

Sandra Bullock's Razzie Award Speech
珊卓布拉克的金酸莓得獎感言

You all better sit down, this is going to be a long night! I think this is an [1)]**extraordinary** award, and I didn't realize that in Hollywood all you had to do was say you'd show up and then you'd get it. 🅖🅜 If I'd known that, I would've said I was appearing at the Oscars a long time ago!

你們最好坐下，這會是漫長的夜晚！我覺得這是非比尋常的獎項，我也沒想到在好萊塢只要表明會出席就有獎可以領。要是早點知道，我早就說了我願意出席奧斯卡頒獎典禮。

No, but this is really wonderful for the most important reasons, because they said no one went to see this film, but I know there's

VOCABULARY 🎧 46

1) **extraordinary** [ɪk`strɔrdən,ɛri] (a.) 非凡的，特別的
Putting men on the moon was an extraordinary achievement.

2) **miraculously** [mə`rækjələsli] (adv.) 出乎意料的，非凡的
(a.) **miraculous** [mə`rækjələs]
The man miraculously survived jumping from the Golden Gate Bridge.

over 700 members here. And that means the majority of the 700 had to have voted, so that means...352, right? But something tells me you all didn't really watch the film, because I wouldn't be here if you really watched it and understood what I was trying to say. So we have Team Bullock here, who's not very happy with you guys. And they brought everyone in the audience tonight a DVD of *All About Steve*.

名製片人 Jeffrey Katzenberg 為夢工廠電影公司 CEO。

back the Razzie and I'll do this again. If you really watched it, you'll remember Brian from our office, who was in the film. Do you remember Brian? What scene was Brian in? Yeah! What was Brian doing in the office scene?

沒有啦，不過這個獎真的很棒最重要的原因是，因為他們說沒人去看這部電影，但我知道這個獎有 700 多位會員。這表示這 700 人中多數都投票了，所以表示有…352 人，對吧？但我覺得你們都沒真正看過這部電影，因為你們若真的看過，也瞭解我想表達什麼，我今天就不會在這裡。所以布拉克粉絲團也來了，他們對你們不是很滿意，今晚他們為各位帶來《求愛女王》的 DVD。（某位觀眾：謝謝！）

對啊，你現在才說謝謝了！大家都會有一份，然後我要跟你們談個條件。我之前說要出席，結果奇蹟般得獎是吧？你們若保證看完這部電影，並認為這真的是，千真萬確，最爛的表演，那我明年會再來。你們若願意看，我明年就會回來，我會退回金酸莓獎，然後再來一次。你們若真的看過，你們會記得我們辦公室的布萊恩，他在這部片中。你們記得布萊恩嗎？布萊恩在哪個場景？（某觀眾：辦公室場景！）對！布萊恩在辦公室那場戲做什麼？（某觀眾：變禿頭！）

🍇 I'll Come Back Next Year
我明年會再回來

Yeah, you say that now! Everyone gets a copy, and this is the deal I'm going to make you. See how when I said I would show up, I [2]**miraculously** won? I'll show up next year if you promise to watch the movie and consider if it was, really and truly, the worst performance. And if you're willing to watch it, then I'll come back next year, I'll give

Sandra Bullock
珊卓布拉克

2010 年奧斯卡影后珊卓布拉克生於 1964 年。她的父親原服務於美軍，母親是德國歌劇歌手，兩人在德國結婚生子，因此珊卓布拉克童年多在德國和奧地利度過，並隨母親巡迴歐洲表演。珊卓布拉克高中時回到美國就學，大學畢業取得戲劇學位，即前往紐約尋求發展機會。

1994 年，珊卓布拉克與基努李維（Keanu Reeves）合演《捍衛戰警》*Speed* 一炮而紅，繼而在《麻辣女王》*Miss Congeniality*、《愛情限時簽》*The Proposal* 展現搞笑功力，2010 年以《攻其不備》*The Blindside* 當中嚴肅的美式足球媽媽黎安（Leigh Anne Tuohy）一角，奪下奧斯卡最佳女主角獎。有趣的是，她得獎前一天，才因《求愛女王》*All about Steve* 獲頒兩座金酸莓獎，還大方出席領獎致詞。

Please, I need Brian's work to be seen! You have this [1]**option** of watching, and we'll leave this here for you guys to take on your way out. Or I brought the final shooting [2]**draft**, and I left a charity event with Jeffrey Katzenberg to come here, and he wasn't happy. But I'm willing to 🔵 go through, page by page, my dialogue.

拜託，希望大家能看看布萊恩的表演！你們有權選擇看或不看，我們會把 DVD 留下，讓你們離開時順手拿一份。或是，我帶來最後的拍攝劇本，我把傑佛瑞凱森柏格拋在一個慈善活動來到這裡，他有點不爽。但我願意在此逐頁讀完我的對白。

So we'll be here for a while. And I'll read the line the way I read it in the film, and then I want anyone who wants to give me a line reading of how I could've done it better to read it back to me. All right? So we can do this till about four o'clock in the morning, or you guys can just watch the movie and [3]**rethink** your decision and have me back next year. And I'll show up and then we can actually go drink afterwards. I've got to

get back to this charity event because it's Jeffrey Katzenberg, and he can prevent me from working again.

所以我們還會在這裡待一陣子。我會像在電影中那樣唸臺詞，然後我希望有人幫我對臺詞，看我該怎麼唸才會更好。好嗎？所以我們可以唸到凌晨四點，或是你們可以自己直接看電影，重新思考你們的決定，明年再請我回來。然後我會出席，結束後我們就能真的去喝一杯。我要回那場慈善活動了，因為那可是傑佛瑞凱森柏格，他可以讓我以後沒頭路。

Thank You for Ruining My Career
謝謝你們毀了我的事業

But I heard over the wire that Bradley Cooper and myself won Best Couple. Again, if you'd seen the film, it's pretty much a film about a woman [4]**stalking** a man. That doesn't really set up the [5]**premise** for a loving couple. So to give us the Worst Couple award is kind of a 🔵 'duh.' I'm just sort of [6]**overstating** the obvious. I just want to help you guys out next year. Just see the movies first and then make your decision. Hope you have a great night. Thank you for ruining my career with a very bad decision!

但我聽說布萊德利庫柏和我贏得最佳情侶獎。再說一次，你們要是有看過電影，這部片子基本上是關於一個女人跟蹤一個男人。那樣的設定不太像一對真心相愛情侶。所以給我們最糟情侶獎根本是「什麼鬼」。我只是在誇大顯而易見的事。我只是想幫你們明年能好好投票。先看完電影，再做決定。祝你們有個美好的夜晚。謝謝你們以非常糟糕的決定毀了我的事業！

But I want you to know that Michael and Brian and Maggie spent so much of their time and their blood trying to 🔵 bring to life how [7]**fucked up** you media people are in *All About Steve*. And that's all we were trying to say. Don't try and 🔵 take us down 'cause we're different, man! You want us to be the same, but we're not. Brian is

> " If you can't pronounce it, you probably shouldn't be putting it in your body or in your environment.
>
> 如果看字念不出來的東西，最好不要放進身體裡，或環境裡。
>
> 珊卓布拉克談污染

VOCABULARY 🎧 48

1) **option** [ˈɑpʃən] (n.) 選項，可選擇的東西
The school counselor can help you explore different career options.

2) **draft** [dræft] (n.) 草稿，草圖
The final draft of my article is due next week.

3) **rethink** [riˈθɪŋk] (v.) 重新考慮，再想
It may be time to rethink our plan.

4) **stalk** [stɔk] (v.) 跟蹤，偷偷靠近
The man was arrested for stalking the famous singer.

5) **premise** [ˈprɛmɪs] (n.) 假設，前提
The conclusion they made was based on a false premise.

6) **overstate** [ˌovɚˈstet] (v.) 誇大，言過其實
Candidates often overstate their ability in job interviews.

always going to be bald. That's what you saw him do in the film, that's who he is in real life. Maggie's tiny, but she's mean! And Michael...Michael doesn't really speak. So just do me a favor, watch it. And then, if you change your mind, I'll be back next year to give back the award. Thank you very much.

但我要你們知道，麥可、布萊恩和瑪姬花了很多時間和心血，在《求愛女王》中把你們媒體人的劣根性演活！那就是我們想說的。不要只因為我們不一樣就來打擊我們，拜託！你們希望我們都一樣，但我們才不一樣。布萊恩會永遠是光頭。就是你們在電影裡看到的，也是他在現實生活中的樣子。瑪姬很嬌小，但她很凶！還有麥可…麥可不太說話。所以幫我個忙，看一下電影。然後你們若是改變主意，我明年就回來退回這個獎。感謝各位。

© Joe Seer / Shutterstock.com

珊卓布拉克並不是第一位奧斯卡／金酸莓雙料影后——2002 年以《擁抱豔陽天》Monster's Ball 得到奧斯卡最佳女主角獎的荷莉貝瑞（Halle Berry），在 2005 年演出《貓女》Catwoman，該片獲得金酸莓獎七項提名，四項得獎，其中一項就是最爛女主角獎——荷莉帶著她的奧斯卡獎座上台領獎，一手握著金像獎，一手握著金酸莓獎，她大方承認自己拍了一部爛片，並把好心幫她卻搞砸的相關人士全部謝了一遍，全場爆笑不斷，歡聲雷動，堪稱是以幽默化解事業災難的典範演出。

荷莉貝瑞於 2002 年以《擁抱豔陽天》一片獲得奧斯卡最佳女主角，是奧斯卡創立 74 年來首位獲此殊榮的非裔女性。以下是她得獎感言的重要片段：

"This moment is so much bigger than me. This moment is for Dorothy Dandridge, Lena Horne, Diahann Carroll. It's for the women that stand beside me: Jada Pinkett, Angela Bassett, Vivica Fox. And it's for every nameless, faceless woman of color that now has a chance because this door tonight has been opened."

「這個時刻的意義遠超過對我個人的意義。這一刻屬於 桃樂絲丹鐔、蓮納荷恩、黛安卡洛（均為早期優秀非裔女星）。這一刻也屬於潔達蘋姬、安琪拉貝瑟、薇薇卡福克斯（均為當時優秀非裔女星）。這一刻也屬於每一位無名的有色人種女性，她們終於也有機會了，因為從現在起，這扇門被打開了。」

© Tinseltown / Shutterstock.com

7) **fucked up** [fʌkt ʌp] (phr.) 糟糕的，搞砸的，精神不正常的
I'll never find a job in this fucked up economy.

2004 年，班艾佛列克（Ben Affleck）以《絕配殺手》Gigli、《夜魔俠》Daredevil、《記憶裂痕》Paycheck 三部電影的演出，獲頒金酸莓獎年度最爛男演員。他隨後在廣播專訪上開玩笑，抱怨根本沒拿到獎，沒想到過幾天他上電視訪談秀「賴瑞金現場」Larry King Live 時，真的收到金酸莓獎座，他當場在節目上把獎座弄壞。後來金酸莓獎主辦單位把獎座放上網拍賣賺了一筆，充作隔年頒獎典禮場地租借費用。

班艾佛列克 2014 年成功雪恥，以《亞果出任務》Argo 與《控制》Gone Girl 兩部佳片奪得金酸莓最佳贖莓獎（Razzie Redeemer Award，頒發給多次入圍金酸莓獎，終於有好表現的影藝人員）。

Sandra Bullock's Oscar Acceptance Speech
珊卓布拉克的奧斯卡得獎感言

Did I really earn this, or did I just [LG] wear you all down? I would like to thank the Academy for allowing me in the last month to have the most [1]**incredible** ride, with rooms full of artists that I see tonight and that I've worked with before and I hope to work with in the future, who inspire me and [LG] blaze trails for us. Four of them, that I've fallen deeply in love with, I share this night with and I share this award with.

我是真的配得上這個獎，還是我把大家累垮了而已？我要謝謝學院讓我能在這個月登上精彩的雲霄飛車（編註：指她才得金酸莓，就獲奧斯卡，一落一起差距非常很大），讓我能跟今晚在座的各位齊聚一堂，大家是我曾合作過的藝人，以及希望未來能合作的藝人，這些人啟發了我、為我們開創新局。其中四位是我深愛的人，我要跟他們分享今晚的榮耀和這個獎。

[LG] Gabby, I love you so much. You are [2]**exquisite**. You are beyond words to me. Carey, your grace and your [3]**elegance** and your beauty and your talent makes me sick. Helen, I feel like we are family, and I don't have the words to express just what I think of you. And Meryl, you know what I think of you, and you are such a good kisser.

蓋比，我非常愛妳。妳很優秀，好到無法用言語形容。凱瑞，妳的溫婉、優雅、美麗和才華實在讓我受不了。海倫，我覺得我們像家人，我無法用言語形容我對妳的感覺。還有梅莉，妳知道我對妳的看法，而且妳真的很會接吻。

So Many People to Thank
太多人要謝

I have so many people to thank for my good fortune in this lifetime, and this is a once-in-a-lifetime experience, I know. To the family that allowed me to play them, the Tuohy family. I know they're in here and

---

[LG] **Sandra Bullock 向對手致意**

2010 年與珊卓布拉克一同入圍最佳女主角的女星包括：

Gabourey Sidibe，美國黑人女星，入圍作品《珍愛人生》*Precious*。
© Everett Collection / Shutterstock.com

Carey Mulligan，英國新生代女星，入圍作品《名媛教育》*An Education*。
© Jaguar PS / Shutterstock.com

Helen Mirren，英國老牌女星，入圍作品《為愛起程》*The Last Station*。
© Jaguar PS / Shutterstock.com

VOCABULARY

1) **incredible** [ɪn`krɛdəbəl] (a.) 極好的，精彩的
The desserts at that restaurant are incredible.

2) **exquisite** [ɪk`skwɪzɪt] (a.) 優美的，完美的，精緻的
The singer's voice is truly exquisite.

3) **elegance** [`ɛləgəns] (n.) 優雅，典雅
The designer's dresses have a timeless elegance.

you'll probably hear from her in a minute...maybe not. Thank you for giving me the opportunity.

在我這幸運的一生中，我有太多人要謝，這也是我人生僅有一次的體驗，我知道。謝謝圖伊家族讓我飾演他們。我知道他們在這裡，你們等一下可能會聽到她講話（黎安妮圖伊）…也許不會。謝謝你們給我這個機會。

To the family that made this film, that gave me the opportunity to do something different, John Lee Hancock, Gil Netter, Alcon, Warner Brothers, the actors, everyone who's shown me kindness when it wasn't fashionable, I thank you. To everyone who was mean to me when it wasn't—like George Clooney threw me in a pool years ago—I'm still holding a grudge.

謝謝拍攝這部電影的大家庭，他們給我機會做不一樣的事，約翰李漢考克、吉爾奈特、愛爾康、華納兄弟、演員們，所有無緣無故親切待我的人，我要謝謝你們。至於那些無緣無故虧待我的人，比如喬治克隆尼多年前把我丟進泳池裡，我到現在還懷恨在心。

> **"** I'm not a fan of reality shows, but I am a fan of people who use their brains and skills and hard work to outsmart people, not to steal someone's man or get drunk on TV.
>
> 我不是實境秀的粉絲，但我很迷用頭腦、用技術努力贏過對手的人，而不是那些在電視上偷人老公或喝個爛醉的人。
>
> 珊卓布拉克談實境秀

珊卓布拉克致詞時說：...George Clooney threw me in a pool 是真有其事。她和喬治克隆尼兩人從年輕未成名前就是好友。有一回兩人都參加一個宴會，克隆尼湊過來邀她牽手一起跳進游泳池，沒想到數到三，克隆尼卻放手讓她一個人跳進去，害她禮服全毀。布拉克在她無比榮耀的時刻，不忘用這種戲謔的方式向老友致意，可見兩人交情匪淺。

© Debby Wong / Shutterstock.com

But there's so many people to thank, not enough time. So I would like to thank what this film was about for me, which is the moms that take care of the babies and the children, no matter where they come from. Those moms and parents never get thanked. I, in particular, failed to thank one.

但是有太多人要謝，時間不夠。所以我要謝謝這部電影對我代表的意義，那就是媽媽會照顧嬰兒和孩子，全天下都一樣。那些媽媽和父母都不會得到感謝。尤其是我，都沒跟媽媽說謝謝。

We Are All Deserving of Love
我們都值得擁有愛

So, if I can take this moment to thank Helga B. for not letting me ride in cars with boys till I was eighteen, 'cause she was right. I would've done what she said I was gonna do. For making me practice every day when I got home—piano, ballet, whatever it is I wanted to be. She said to be an artist you had to practice every day. And for reminding her daughters that there's no race, no religion, no class system, no color, nothing, no sexual [1]**orientation**, that makes us better than anyone else. We are all [2]**deserving** of love.

所以我要藉這一刻謝謝海嘉（編註：珊卓布拉克的媽媽）不讓我在18歲前搭上男孩子的車，因為她是對的。我原本要做的事都被她說中。謝謝她要我每天回到家就

練琴、跳芭蕾等所有我想做的事。她說，要當藝人，就要每天練習。謝謝她教導自己女兒，沒有任何種族、宗教、階級制度、膚色、沒有任何事物、包含性傾向，讓我們優於其他人。我們都值得擁有愛。

So, to that [3]**trailblazer** who allowed me to have that, and this , and this, I thank you so much for this opportunity that I share with these extraordinary women—and my lover, Meryl Streep. Thank you.

所以謝謝這位前輩讓我擁有愛，和這個（編註：她舉起奧斯卡獎座），還有這個，我非常謝謝妳給我這個機會讓我跟一群傑出女性——還有我的愛人，梅莉史翠普分享。謝謝各位。

珊卓布拉克致詞時說：And Meryl, ...you are such a good kisser 是因為同年稍早，她和梅莉史翠普（Meryl Streep）在評論家之選電影獎（Critics' Choice Movie Awards，近年來其權威性及受矚目程度直逼金球獎）同獲最佳女主角獎，兩人在舞台上擁吻，造成轟動，珊卓布拉克隨後致詞時就有說這句：Meryl's a great kisser（梅莉很會接吻）。

© s_bukley / Shutterstock.com

VOCABULARY 🎧 52

1) **orientation** [ˌorɪɛnˈteʃən] (n.) 傾向，態度
The actor refused to discuss his sexual orientation.

2) **deserving (of)** [dɪˈzɜvɪŋ] (a.) 值得的
I think that restaurant is deserving of a Michelin star.

3) **trailblazer** [ˈtrelˌblezɚ] (n.) 開拓者，先驅
Marie Curie was a trailblazer in the fields of physics and chemistry.

Language Guide

something tells me 直覺告訴我

這句話用來表示揣測，而且是憑感覺而非推理所得的看法。

A: Do you believe Roger is really a Harvard graduate?
你相信羅傑真的是哈佛畢業的嗎？

B: Not really. Something tells me he's lying.
不太相信。我覺得他在說謊。

go through 從頭到尾排演一遍

go through 可以表示「仔細審閱」，用在戲劇相關的情況，則表示「排演」

A: Could you help me go through my lines for the play?
你能幫我練習舞台劇的台詞嗎？

B: Sure. Let me take a look at the script.
好啊。讓我看一下劇本。

duh 廢話

這個字也拼寫為 do'h 或 doh，是用來回應無聊、白癡的事。講這個詞的時候，大部分的人都會把手攤開，或是來個翻白眼的表情。

A: You mean penguins can't fly?
你意思是說企鵝不會飛？

B: Duh!
廢話！

Grammar Master

與「現在」及「過去」事實相反的假設語氣

英文的假設語氣是用「說反話」的方式，表達所說的話與事實相反，透過動詞過去式來表達「非事實」。

● 與「現在」事實相反的假設語氣：

使用過去式 V-ed 表達非事實，主要子句也要用過去型態，並在前方加上助動詞 would / could / might... +V 表示：

例 If I lived in Taipei, I could see you anytime.
如果我住台北的話，我就能隨時跟你碰面。

● 與「過去」事實相反的假設：

珊卓在本篇說的 If I'd known that, I would've said I was appearing at the Oscars a long time ago!（我要是知道的話，我會說我早就出席奧斯卡了。）本句的時間發生在過去，因此，在過去的時間使用過去型態表達，就會用到過去完成式 had + pp，同樣地，主要子句也會使用過去完成式，並在前方加上助動詞而形成：would / could / might... + have + pp。

例 If I were smarter, I would get better grades.
如果我再聰明一點的話，我的成績會更好。

例 If you'd been born rich, you wouldn't have to work a day in your life.
如果你是含金湯匙出生的話，你就不用這樣辛苦工作了。

bring to life 把…演活

bring to life 字面上的意思是「讓…活過來」，引申為幫事物注入生命，使其如真實般呈現。

A: What did you think of Tom's performance as Hamlet?
你覺得湯姆的哈姆雷特演得如何？

B: It was great. He really brought the role to life.
很棒。他真的演活那個角色了。

take sb. down 嫌棄，貶低

take down 有讓東西倒下的意思，在此表示打擊一個人的自信，讓人覺得自己被貶低，遭到撻伐。

A: Did you see the review of Batman v. Superman in the paper?
你有看到報上對《蝙蝠俠對超人：正義曙光》的評論嗎？

B: Yeah. That movie critic really took Ben Affleck down.
有啊。那個影評人把班艾弗列克嫌到臭頭。

wear sb. down 把人累壞，讓人屈服

這個片語是指讓人覺得很累，也可以表示消磨他人意志，使人屈服。

A: I thought you said you weren't getting Billy a new bike for Christmas.
我以為你說你不會幫比利買新腳踏車當耶誕禮物。

B: I wasn't going to, but he eventually wore me down.
我原本不要，但他最後讓我屈服了。

blaze (the/a) trail 開疆闢土

blaze 當名詞是「（刻在樹皮上的）記號」，當動詞就是「在（樹）上刻記號」，blaze (the/a) trail 就像走入樹林探路，在沿途的樹皮上做記號，讓後面的人跟著前進。引申為開創新局、成為典範，讓後來的人依循跟隨。

A: Why is Le Corbusier your favorite architect?
柯比意為什麼是你最喜愛的建築師？

B: Because he blazed a trail in the field of architecture.
因為他為建築界開創新局。

hold a grudge 記恨，心裡有疙瘩

grudge 是「怨恨」，hold a grudge 表示被人得罪之後耿耿於懷，一直對那個人心懷怨恨。

A: Has Alice forgiven you for forgetting her birthday yet?
愛麗絲原諒你忘記她的生日沒？

B: No. She can really hold a grudge.
還沒。她很會記仇的。

珊卓布拉克得到奧斯卡上台第一句話，就讓人見識到她的機智：Did I really earn this, or did I just wear you all down? 她借用得獎電影《攻其不備》當中的台詞，成功化解與競爭對手間的緊張與尷尬。

珊卓布拉克在演出本片之前，大都演出浪漫喜劇，這是她第一次入圍就得獎。有人或許會懷疑評審的判斷，但布拉克善用自己的搞笑形象，短短幾分鐘內把全場逗樂，卻又能適切的讚揚對手，還讓大家感念起天下父母心，讓人不得不佩服她亦莊亦諧、收放自如的巨星丰采。

Wisdom from a Former Teen

前青少年的智慧

Justin Timberlake's Teen Choice Decade Award Speech
賈斯汀提姆布萊克的青少年票選十年成就獎得獎感言

The Value of Respect
尊重的價值

Thank you, Teen Choice. As a former teen, a while ago, who's made a few choices along the way, I'm here to tell you that you and your choices matter. In my case, I grew up in Millington, Tennessee, just outside of Memphis, where I was blessed to be raised by parents and a family who taught me some big lessons. They taught me to respect them. They taught me to respect myself and to respect all people on the basis of their character—not where they live, not what they did for a living or the color of their skin. My parents did their best to fill my young mind not with ¹⁾**prejudice** or hate but with ²⁾**compassion** and love.

謝謝青少年票選獎，已經脫離青少年有一陣子的我，這一路走來做了一些選擇，我想告訴各位，你們和你們的選擇很重要。以我來說，我在田納西州米靈頓長大，就在曼非斯外。我有幸由父母撫養長大，生長在教會我人生大道裡的家庭。他們教會我尊重他們。他們教我尊重自己，尊重所有人的性格，而不是因為他們的背景，不是他們的職業或膚色。我父母竭盡全力不用偏見或仇恨灌溉我的心靈，而是用慈悲和愛。

I think it's part of the reason why to this day I try to live my life working closely with, making music with and spending so much of my time

VOCABULARY 🎧 54

1) **prejudice** [ˈprɛdʒədɪs] (a.) 偏見，歧視
We must continue to fight against racial prejudice.

2) **compassion** [kəmˈpæʃən] (n.) 同情，憐憫
The doctor had great compassion for his patients.

3) **straight** [stret] (a.) 異性戀的；(n.) 異性戀
I'm not sure whether Allen is gay or straight.

4) **gay** [ge] (a.) 同性戀的；(n.) 同性戀
Do you have any gay friends?

5) **legend** [ˈlɛdʒənd] (n.) 傳奇人物，傳奇故事
Warren Buffett is an investing legend.

6) **reverend** [ˈrɛvərənd] (n.) 牧師（字首大寫作為對教士的尊稱）
Reverend Martin Luther King, Jr. was a great civil rights leader.

7) **resonate** [ˈrɛzəˌnet] (v.) 使⋯產生共鳴，引起回響
The candidate's message resonated with voters.

8) **onstage** [ɑnˈstedʒ] (adv.) 上（舞）臺；(a.) 臺上的
The audience cheered as the singer walked onstage.

with an amazing group of people: male, female, ³⁾**straight**, ⁴⁾**gay**, every walk of life—people who help each other and find a common ground. I was drawn to all these people not because they look like me, but because they think and feel like me. The truth is we are all different, but that does not mean we all don't want the same thing.

我想這也是為什麼我這一輩子到今天都盡可能和一群多采多姿的人努力做音樂、花時間相處，不論他們是男是女、異性戀或同性戀、各種生活背景——能互相幫助和找到共同點的人。我被這些人吸引，不是因為他們看起來像我，而是因為他們的思想和感受與我相似。事實上我們都不一樣，但這不表示我們想要的東西不一樣。

Learning from the Greats
向大人物學習

So, message: To all you teens out there, I ask you to not learn from my example, but from the example of all the greats that have come before me. For me, a big moment growing up was when I discovered that there was a music ⁵⁾**legend** living right down the street from me, the ⁶⁾**Reverend** Al Green, who taught the world a lesson that ⁷⁾**resonates** now, I think, more than ever: Let's stay together. I learned from so many music greats: Michael Jackson, Aretha Franklin, Elton John, Garth Brooks, Stevie Wonder. I even learned a lot from the guy standing next to me ⁸⁾**onstage** [points to Kobe Bryant] on how to arrive early and stay late—because that's how you become a champion.

所以我給各位的訊息是：所有青少年們，請你們不要以我為榜樣，而是拿我之前的大人物為榜樣。對我來說，我成長中的重要時刻，是當我發現我家附近就住著一位音樂傳奇人物，阿爾格林牧師，我認為他教給世界的啟示，至今仍能引起共鳴，且尤甚以往：大家一起來。我從許多音樂大人物獲益良多：麥可傑克森、艾瑞莎弗蘭克、艾爾頓強、葛斯布魯克、史提夫汪達，甚至從站在我身旁的人學到如何早到不早退（指著柯比布萊恩），因為這是成為冠軍的關鍵。

Justin Timberlake 賈斯汀提姆布萊克

1981 年生。1995 年參與少男團體 NSYNC 出道，2002 年解散後，賈斯汀推出的每張唱片都大賣，至今已獲得 9 座葛萊美獎、3 座全英音樂獎（Brit Award）、10 座告示牌排行榜音樂獎（Billboard Music Award），以及 4 座艾美獎。

賈斯汀提姆布萊克 2000 年參加 Teen Choice Awards 的造型，當時他還是少男團體 NSYNC 的成員。

Ali's Undying Wisdom
阿里的不朽智慧

Speaking of great ⁹⁾**champs**, I believe we can all learn from the greatest of all time: Muhammad Ali. Muhammad Ali fought in the ring, but he fought for peace, too. And he became the ¹⁰⁾**heavyweight** champion of the world because, as we all know, he could float like a butterfly and sting like a bee. Our world lost that champ this year, so tonight, I want to share three pieces of his ¹¹⁾**undying** wisdom that have helped me and may help you along your journey.

說到偉大的冠軍，我相信我們都能從古往今來最偉大的人物學習：穆罕默德阿里。阿里是拳擊手，但他也為和平戰鬥。他成為世界重量級冠軍，因為我們都知道，他能像蝴蝶一樣飛舞，像蜜蜂一樣螫人。今年這位冠軍離開人世，所以今晚，我要分享他三樣不朽的智慧，這些智慧幫助了我，也可能對你們的人生旅程有幫助。

Teen Choice Awards 青少年票選獎

1999 年創辦的 Teen Choice Awards，是美國福斯廣播公司所主辦的年度頒獎典禮，旨在表彰音樂、電影、體育、電視、時尚相關領域的傑出貢獻，得獎者是由 13~19 歲青少年票選出（因此稱為 Teen Choice），得獎者會獲得一個實際大小的衝浪板。

泰勒絲（Taylor Swift）與 2012 年度衝浪板；麥莉希拉（Miley Cyrus）與 2013 年衝浪板。

9) **champ** [tʃæmp] (n.)（口）冠軍，優勝者（**champion** 的簡稱）
Do you think the champ will be able to defend his title?

10) **heavyweight** [ˋhɛviˏwet] (a.)（拳擊）重量級的；(n.) 重量級拳擊手
Did you watch the heavyweight title fight last night?

11) **undying** [ʌnˋdaɪɪŋ] (a.) 不朽的，永恆的
The groom swore his undying love to the bride.

Number one: Don't count the days, make the days count. Now you are young, as I once was, but do not think for a moment that what you do doesn't count. It does. Not just to you, but also to the world and your [1)]**generation** who will someday [2)]**inherit** this world from [3)]**old-timers** like me and Kobe.

第一：不要虛度光陰，而是認真過每一天。你們現在還年輕，跟我以前一樣，但不要有任何一刻認為自己所做的事不算什麼。任何事都有意義。不只對你自己有意義，也對這個世界，對你們的世代都有意義，你們這一代總有一天會從像我和柯比這些老一輩的人手中繼承這世界。

Be Part of the Solution
投身參與解決問題

Number two: Service to others is the rent you pay for your room here on earth, so be generous, be kind, be fair. I think we all can agree that with all the [4)]**tension** in the world today that can divide us, we should be part of the solution and not part of the problem. You don't have to make a difference on a global stage. You can [5)]**volunteer** in your neighborhood or in another neighborhood nearby where people might look a little different from you, and they might teach you a thing or two.

第二：為他人服務是你在這世上生存所付的租金，所以要慷慨、要善良、要公正。我想我們都同意，現今這世界的緊張局勢會分裂我們，所以我們應該想辦法解決，而不是製造問題。你們不用站在全球舞台上發揮影響力，可以在自己的社區當義工，或到附近的社區為一些跟你長得不一樣的人服務，他們也可能教你不少東西。

Do the Impossible
做不可能的事

Third, here's maybe the greatest thing a teen can learn from the champ. These are words to remember when anyone tries to tell you to give up, tell you to [6)]**give in** because whatever you're trying to do is impossible. The champ said this: Impossible is just a word thrown around by small men who find it easier to live in the world they've been given than to explore the power they have to change it. Impossible is not a fact. It's an opinion. Impossible is [7)]**potential**. Impossible is temporary. Impossible is nothing. So go out, do the impossible and just go on and become the greatest generation yet.

第三，這可能是青少年能從拳王阿里身上學到最棒的事。當有人叫你放棄或投降，只因為你正在努力做的是不可能的事，那麼你可以記住這句話。拳王說的這句話是：「不可能」只是一群卑微的人隨口說說，他們寧可滿足於現狀，而不願探索本身的力量去改變這世界。「不可能」不是事實，只是一種意見。「不可能」是有潛力的，「不可能」是暫時的，沒有什麼是不可能的。所以放手去吧，去做不可能的事，去吧，成為史上最偉大的世代。

LG
Muhammad Ali 拳王阿里
穆罕默德阿里生於 1942 年，原名小卡修斯馬塞勒斯克萊（Cassius Marcellus Clay, Jr.），美國拳擊手。他於 1960 年羅馬奧運奪得輕量級金牌，之後轉入職業拳賽，60~63 年間累積了 19 勝 0 敗，全球拳擊高手都是他的手下敗將。66 年到67 年初，七次衛冕拳王寶座，紀錄至今無人能敵。他不但被公認為最偉大拳擊手，更被評為 20 世紀最偉大運動員。

阿里的鬥志不只表現在拳擊場上，他無所畏懼的公開自己的穆斯林信仰，並改名穆罕默德。越戰期間表明自己為良知拒絕服役者（conscientious objector，因個人信念或宗教信仰，拒絕履行兵役義務者），因而遭到判刑（最後並未入獄）。當激進民權組織遊行時，阿里不懼輿論壓力，與伊斯蘭國民大會（Nation of Islam）領袖站在一起。晚年的阿里罹患帕金森氏症，他仍不改拳王本色，與之搏鬥 32 年，終於在 2016 年過世。

© Featureflash Photo Agency / Shutterstock.com

VOCABULARY 56)

1) **generation** [ˌdʒɛnəˋreʃən] (n.) 代，世代
We should all do our part to preserve the planet for future generations.

2) **inherit** [ɪnˋhɛrɪt] (v.) 遺傳，繼承
Michelle inherited her mother's light blue eyes.

3) **old-timer** [ˋoldˋtaɪmə] (n.) 老人，守舊的人
The old-timers sat in the park playing checkers.

4) **tension** [ˋtɛnʃən] (n.) 緊張，張力
The courtroom was full of tension as the verdict was read.

5) **volunteer** [ˌvɑlənˋtɪr] (v.) 志願服務
John volunteered to join the army because he loved his country.

6) **give in** [gɪv ɪn] (phr.) 放棄，讓步，投降
The government refused to give in to the terrorists' demands.

7) **potential** [pəˋtɛnʃəl] (n.) 潛力，可能性；(a.) 潛在的，可能的
Going to university will help you reach your full potential.

walk of life 社會階層

這個片語是指一個人的社經地位及社會背景，也可以用來表示「職業」。

A: Did you send your kids to an exclusive school?
你是送孩子念貴族學校嗎？

B: No. The school they went to had students from every walk of life.
沒有。他們念的學校學生來自各個階層。

raise vs. rise vs. arise

這三個單字在形或義上相近，但仔細比較，用法差很多喔！

1. **raise**：為及物動詞，後方需加上受詞，常見的意思有「舉起、抬起、升高」、本句中的意思為「養育；種植、飼養」，另外還有其他定義，如：「募集」、「提出（意見）」、「提高（數量、價錢）」，其過去式為規則變化：raise, raised, raised。

例 **Please raise your hand if you have a question.**
有問題的請舉手。

例 **I'm trying to raise money to start a business.**
我正在努力集資創業。

例 **You should raise that question at tomorrow's meeting.**
你應該在明天的會議上提出這個問題。

例 **The government plans to raise taxes next year.**
政府打算在明年漲稅。

2. **rise**：是不及物動詞，有「上升、上漲、增加、起身」的意思，過去式為不規則變化：rise, rose, risen。

例 **The sun rises in the east and sets in the west.**
太陽從東邊升起、西邊落下。

例 **Early to bed and early to rise makes a man healthy, wealthy and wise.**
早睡早起讓人健康、富裕、有智慧。

例 **Don't you dare raise your voice at me!**
不准對我大聲講話！

3. **arise**：是不及物動詞，指「（事情）發生、產生」，過去式也是不規則變化：arise, arose, arisen。片語 arise from 則是指「起因於」，後方接上事件發生的原因，等同 result from：

例 **Singlish arose in the mid-20th century.**
新加坡英語在二十世紀中期出現。

例 **Most conflicts arise from fear or ignorance.**
多數衝突都是因恐懼或無知而產生。

common ground 共識，共通點

要注意作「共通點」解釋時的用法，只能用來形容「事件、狀況」的共通點，若要說「他們兩個有許多共通點」，英文則是 They have a lot in common。

A: These negotiations are going nowhere.
這些談判毫無結果。

B: Yeah. If we can't find common ground, we'll never reach an agreement.
是啊，如果我們再沒有共識，我們永遠也別想達成協議。

Al Green 阿爾格林

Albert "Al" Green 生於 1946 年，是 70 年代初期著名的靈魂樂、節奏藍調歌手，被稱作 The Reverend Al Green（阿爾格林牧師）是因為他後來真的成為牧師。賈斯汀致詞中說的 Let's Stay Together 是阿爾格林的 1972 年推出的代表作；1980 年首次推出宗教意味濃厚的福音歌曲專輯，得到第一座葛萊美獎；1988 年重回流行曲風至今。阿爾格林歷年來唱紅許多歌曲，被譽為「最後一位偉大的靈魂歌手」。1955 年入選搖滾名人堂，2002 年獲得葛萊美終身成就獎，他到目前共獲得 8 座葛萊美獎。

© s_bukley / Shutterstock.com

know a thing or two 很有一手

這個片語是對某件事情非常瞭解，可別誤解為「略知一二」，只懂一點點囉。

A: I'm thinking of buying a PC. Do you have any suggestions?
我想買一台電腦。可以推薦我一台嗎？

B: You should ask Bob—he knows a thing or two about computers.
你應該問鮑伯——他對電腦很有一套。

賈斯汀出道至今，已贏得 22 座 Teen Choice Award，是男性藝人紀錄保持者。拳王阿里於 2016 年 6 月 3 日去世，賈斯汀在同年 7 月 31 日獲頒的 Teen Choice Decade Award 是 Teen Choice Award 的最高榮譽，是為了表彰他過去 10 年不斷創新進步。賈斯汀藉此機會向阿里致敬，既顯示他的謙遜，也展現他的高度，表現非常得體。如此智慧圓融，難怪能長期受到評審和青少年的愛戴。

Being an [1]**ally** means a great deal to me and so I am gonna say some stuff and I might be [2] **LG** **preaching** to the choir but I'm gonna say it, not just for us, because on Monday morning, people are gonna click a link to hear what that woman from **LG** [3] *Scandal* said on that awards show. So I think some stuff needs to be said.

身為盟友對我來說意義重大，所以我要說點東西，或許有相互取暖的意味，但我還是要說，這不只是為了我們，因為到星期一早上，大家會點開網頁，聽這個出演《醜聞風暴》的女人在頒獎典禮上說了什麼。所以我想我還是要說點東西。

Fighting the Good Fight

為正義而戰

Kerry Washington's GLAAD Media Award Speech

凱莉華盛頓同性戀者反詆毀聯盟獎得獎感言

© Kathy Hutchins / Shutterstock.com

VOCABULARY 🎧 58

1) **ally** [ˈælaɪ] (n.) 盟友，同盟國
Who is the president's closest political ally?

2) **preach** [pritʃ] (v.) 講道，說教
The priest preached for over an hour last Sunday.

3) **scandal** [ˈskændəl] (n.) 醜聞
The scandal ruined the politician's reputation.

4) **citizenship** [ˈsɪtɪzənˌʃɪp] (n.) 公民身分，公民權
Maria is thinking of applying for American citizenship.

5) **disability** [ˌdɪsəˈbɪləti] (n.) 殘疾，殘障
The school has a class for children with learning disabilities.

6) **lesbian** [ˈlɛzbiən] (n./a.) 女同性戀（的）
More and more lesbians are coming out of the closet.

7) **bisexual** [ˌbaɪˈsɛkʃuəl] (n./a.) 雙性戀（的）
Famous bisexuals include David Bowie and Lady Gaga.

There are people in this world who have the full rights of [4]**citizenship**, in our communities, our countries, around the world, and then there are those of us who, to varying degrees, do not. We don't have equal access to education, to health care and some other basic liberties like marriage, a fair voting process, fair hiring practices. Now, you would think that those kept from our full rights of citizenship would band together and 🔳 fight the good fight. But history tells us that no, often, we don't.

這世上有人擁有完整的公民權利，包括我們的社區、我們的國家、世界各地，但其中有些人在某些程度上的權利卻不完整。我們在教育、醫療和一些其他基本權利方面沒有平等的管道，比如婚姻、公

正的投票程序、公平的徵聘常規。你們會認為，那些沒有完整公民權利的人會團結對抗，為正義而戰。但歷史告訴我們，不會，我們往往不會。

Women, poor people, people of color, people with [5]**disabilities**, immigrants, gay men, [6]**lesbians**, [7]**bisexuals**, [8]**trans** people, [9]**intersex** people, we have been 🔳 pitted against each other and made to feel like there are limited seats at the table for those of us that fall into the [10]**category** of "other." As a result, we have become afraid of one another. We compete with one another, we judge one another, sometimes we betray one another. Sometimes even within our own communities, we designate who among us is best suited to represent us and who, really, shouldn't even really be invited to the party. As "others," we are taught that to be successful, we must reject those other "others" or we will never belong.

女性、窮人、有色人種、殘障人士、移民、男同性戀、女同性戀、雙性戀、跨性別、雙性別，我們一直在互相較量，彼此以為我們被歸類為「異己」這個種類的代表席位有限。於是我們害怕彼此、互相競爭、互相批判，有時互相背叛。我們有時甚至在自己的群體中指定誰才是最能代表我們全體的人，以及誰根本不應該受邀加入群體。身為「異己」，我們被告誡為了成功，一定要排斥其他的「異己」，否則我們永遠不會有歸屬。

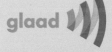

Scandal 《醜聞風暴》
美國廣播公司製作的《醜聞風暴》，是關於華府「危機處理專家」奧利維亞波普（Olivia Pope，由凱莉華盛頓飾演）的政治驚險影集，根據前白宮新聞助理茱蒂史密斯的真實生活改編，她後來自己成立危機管理公司。在《醜聞風暴》中，茱蒂的虛構版在費茲傑羅格蘭特總統的政府中任職，後來離職，成立奧利維亞波普事務所，專門為有錢有勢的公眾人物維護形象。

GLAAD Media Awards
同志媒體獎
GLAAD（Gay & Lesbian Alliance Against Defamation，同性戀者反詆毀聯盟）是一個美國非官方組織，旨在監督媒體、影視等行業以公正、包容、客觀的角度報導及表現同性戀者，並提供媒體與性別認同、性傾向相關的正確資訊及數據。在他們的努力下，美國大多重要媒體都已修正態度，更包容客觀的報導同性戀及相關政策。GLAADMedia Awards 是 GLAAD 舉辦的年度媒體獎，授與媒體、影視業對促進同志平權有所貢獻的名人。

Kerry Washington 凱莉華盛頓

1977 年生。2012 年接演《醜聞風暴》後闖出一片天，以此劇獲得艾美獎及金球獎提名。2013 年，凱莉華盛頓獲母校喬治華盛頓大學（George Washington University）授與榮譽學位；2014 年入選《時代雜誌》「最具影響力百大人物」Time 100。

© By www.GlynLowe.com, via Wikimedia Commons

凱莉華盛頓在 2013 年喬治華盛頓大學畢業典禮致詞。

---

8) **trans** [træns] (a.) 即 **transgender** [ˌtrænsˋdʒɛndɚ] 跨性別的，指不認同自己生理性別的人，許多有變裝或變性的行為，但並不是所有跨性別者都是同性戀
The group supports equal rights for the trans community.

9) **intersex** [ˋɪntɚˌsɛks] (a.) 具備兩種生理特徵的， (n.) 陰陽人
Have you ever met an intersex person?

10) **category** [ˋkætəˌgɔrɪ] (n.) 種類，範疇
The light truck category includes SUVs, minivans and pickup trucks.

> You may not be thinking about politics, but politics is thinking about you.
>
> 你或許不太考慮政治，但政客正算計著你。

凱莉華盛頓談政治

LGBT 多元性別

LGBT（或 GLBT）是由女同性戀者（lesbian）、男同性戀者（gay）、雙性戀者（bisexual）、跨性別者（transgender）這四個字的第一個字母組成。其他常見的相關縮寫有 LGBTQ，當中的 Q，代表酷兒（queer，反對界定何謂正常、區分性別、追求家庭契約的自由性別者）或是性別認同障礙者。LGBTI 的 I 代表同時具備兩種生理特徵的陰陽人（intersex）。

但一般來説，目前 LGBT 這個縮寫的含意已超過字面上的四種族群，也涵蓋所有非異性戀者（non-heterosexual），以及支持多元性別的異性戀者（heterosexual）。

Defense of Marriage Act 婚姻保護法

簡稱為 DOMA 的婚姻保護法，是美國國會於 1996 年通過、柯林頓總統簽屬的法案，將婚姻定義為「一男一女」的結合，限制了同性婚姻及配偶的法律權利。2013 年，美國最高法院宣判 DOMA 違憲，讓原本在同性婚姻合法州登記及婚的同性伴侶，從此擁有與異性戀夫妻相同的權利。

civil union 同性婚姻

也被稱作「公民結合」，是指由法律（民事法）確立並保護的結合關係，其效力等同或類似婚姻。主要用在讓同性伴侶得到婚姻保障的情況，但也適用於不想結婚但同居的異性伴侶。

I know part of why I'm getting this award is because I play characters that belong to [1]**segments** of society that are often pushed to the margins. Now, as a woman and a person of color, I don't always have a choice about that. But I've also made the choice to participate in the storytelling about the members of the LG LGBT community. I've made the choice to play a lot of different kinds of people, in a lot of different kinds of situations. In my career, I've not been afraid of inhabiting characters who are judged and who are misunderstood and who have not been granted full rights of citizenship as human beings.

我知道我得這個獎的部分原因，是因為我飾演的角色，都屬於在社會中被推到邊緣的群體。身為女性和有色人種，我對此一直是別無選擇。但我一直選擇參與為 LGBT 群體成員說故事的角色。我選擇扮演許多處於各種不同情況的不同人物。在我的職涯中，我不怕飾演遭受非議和誤解、且一直未被賦予完整公民權利的角色。

> When you buy into the cultural idea of what's acceptable and unacceptable, you reinforce negative stereotypes and prejudices. That wouldn't work for me. I don't love to give advice to anyone, because we all have to make our own choices, but I'd want to live my life in truth.
>
> 當你接受什麼可以做，什麼又不可以做的文化觀念，就是在助長負面的刻板印象及偏見。我可不幹。我不喜歡給人建議，因為我們都必須自己做選擇，但我想要誠實地過生活。

凱莉華盛頓談刻板印象

VOCABULARY 🎧 60

1) **segment** [ˋsɛɡmənt] (n.) 部分，部門
Which market segment is this product targeted at?

2) **irony** [ˋaɪrəni] (n.) 諷刺，反語
Mark Twain is famous for his clever use of irony.

3) **disenfranchised** [ˏdɪsɪnˋfræntʃaɪzd] (a.) 被剝奪公民權的
Thousands of disenfranchised voters protested the election results.

4) **radical** [ˋrædɪkəl] (a.) 激進的，極端的
The government took radical steps to deal with the energy crisis.

5) **inclusive** [ɪnˋklusɪv] (a.) 包容多元的（特指不同族群的）
Our aim is to create a fairer, more inclusive society.

6) **diverse** [dɪˋvɝs] (a.) 多元的，不同的
San Francisco is a culturally diverse city.

The Power of Inclusive Storytelling
包容多元故事呈現的力量

But here's the great [2)]**irony**: I don't decide to play the characters I play as a political choice. Yet the characters I play often do become political statements. Because having your story told as a woman, as a person of color, as a lesbian, or as a trans person or as any member of any [3)]**disenfranchised** community is sadly often still a [4)]**radical** idea. There is so much power in storytelling and there is enormous power in [5)]**inclusive** storytelling and inclusive representations.

但有一大諷刺是：我並非因為政治考量而選擇我所飾演的角色，但我飾演的角色往往確實變成政治立場的體現。因為悲哀的是，身為女性、有色人種、女同性戀或跨性別者，或任何權益被剝奪的人，所呈現的故事往往仍是激進的主題。說故事的力量是很強大的，包容多元的故事呈現和表現，其力量更是巨大

That is why the work of GLAAD is so important. We need more LGBT representation in the media. We need more LGBT characters and more LGBT storytelling. We need more [6)]**diverse** LGBT representation and by that, I mean lots of kinds of different kinds of LGBT people, living all kinds of lives, and this is big—we need more employment of LGBT people in front of and behind the camera!

所以同性戀者反詆毀聯盟的工作才會如此重要。我們需要更多 LGBT 代表出現在媒體上。我們需要更多 LGBT 的角色和故事呈現。我們需要更多樣化的 LGBT 代表，這表示需要更多來自各種不同背景的各種不同類型的 LGBT 人士，而且更重要的是——我們的幕前幕後都需要更多 LGBT 的媒體工作者！

So in 1997, when Ellen made her famous declaration, it took place in an America where the [LG] Defense of Marriage Act had just passed months earlier and [LG] civil unions were not yet legal in any state. But also remember, just 30 years before that, the Supreme Court was deciding that the ban against [7)]**interracial** marriages was [8)]**unconstitutional**. [GM] Up until then, [9)]**heterosexual** people of different races couldn't marry who they wanted to marry either.

所以在 1997 年，艾倫做出她著名的出櫃宣言時，當時的美國才剛通過婚姻保護法幾個月，而且任何一州的同性婚姻都尚未合法化。但請記住，只比當時更早三十年，最高法院也才剛裁定跨種族婚姻禁令是違憲的。在那之前，不同族裔的異性戀也不能結婚。

---

7) **interracial** [ˌɪntɚˋreʃəl] (a.) 跨人種的
The number of interracial couples is growing rapidly in the United States.

8) **unconstitutional** [ˌʌnkɑnstəˋtuʃənəl] (a.) 違反憲法的
Constitution [kɑnstəˋtuʃən] (n.)（大寫）美國憲法
New York's death penalty law was ruled unconstitutional.

9) **heterosexual** [ˌhɛtərəˋsɛkʃuəl] (a./n.)
異性戀者（的）
In many countries, only heterosexual couples are allowed to marry.

So when black people today tell me that they don't believe in gay marriage, the first thing that I say is "Please don't let anybody try to get you to vote against your own best interest by feeding you messages of hate." And then I say, "You know people used to say that stuff about you and your love and if we let the government start to [LG] **legislate** love in our lifetime, who do you think is next?"

所以當今天黑人同胞告訴我，他們不認同同性婚姻，我回答的第一句是：「請不要任人擺佈投票反對自身最大利益，當他灌輸給你的是仇恨。」然後我還會說：「你知道以前有人針對你和你所愛的人說同樣的話，如果我們這一代讓政府開始立法管制愛情，你覺得下一位會是誰？」

We Must Be Allies
我們一定要結盟

We can't say that we believe in each other's [LG] **fundamental** [LG] **humanity** and then [LG] turn a blind eye to the reality of each other's existence and the truth of each other's hearts. We must be allies and we must be allies in this business because to be represented is to be [LG] **humanized** and as long as anyone, anywhere is made to feel less human, our very definition of humanity is [LG] at stake and we are all vulnerable.

我們不能說我們相信彼此的基本人性，卻對彼此存在的現實和真心視而不見。我們一定要結盟，在這個行業上成為同盟，因為有人出來代表我們，我們才會被當人看待，而且只要在任何地方、有人覺得自己不被當人看待，我們對人性的定義就陷入危機，我們就都有危險。

We must see each other, all of us and we must see ourselves, all of us and we have to continue to be bold and [LG] break new ground until this is how it is, until we are no longer "firsts" and "[5] **exceptions**" and "rare" and "[6] **unique**." In the real world, being an "other" is the [7] **norm**. In the real world, the only norm is [6] **uniqueness** and our media must [8] **reflect** that. Thank you GLAAD for fighting the good fight. God bless you.

我們一定要看見彼此，我們所有人，我們也要看見自己，我們所有人，我們要繼續勇敢，開創新局面，直到這一切變成理所當然，直到我們不再成為「先鋒」、「例外」、「罕見」和「獨特」。在真實世界中，身為「異己」是正常的。在真實世界中，唯一正常的是獨一無二，而我們的媒體必須反映這點。謝謝同性戀者反詆毀聯盟為正義而奮鬥。上帝保佑你們。

   I like how people will post pictures of me with other women that I adore, hugging on red carpets, and say, "See?" Are we so uncomfortable with love between two people of the same gender that we immediately label it as sexual? But I've never been bothered by the lesbian rumor. There's nothing offensive about it, so there's no reason to be offended.

我喜歡人們拿著我跟我喜愛的女性在紅毯上相擁的照片，然後說「你看吧？」我們真的一看到同性相愛就不舒服，要馬上聯想到性關係嗎？但我對同性戀的謠言完全無所謂。同性戀根本無傷大雅，沒有理由覺得被冒犯。

凱莉華盛頓談同志傳言

VOCABULARY 62

1) **legislate** [ˈlɛdʒɪsˌlet] (v.) 立法，制定法律
The committee was formed to legislate against child marriage.

2) **fundamental** [ˌfʌndəˈmɛntəl] (a.) 基礎的，根本的
There was a fundamental flaw in his argument.

3) **humanity** [hjuˈmænəti] (n.) 人類，人道
What are the biggest issues facing humanity today?

4) **humanize** [ˈhjumənˌaɪz] (v.) 使具有人性
The company hired a PR firm to help humanize its image.

5) **exception** [ɪkˈsɛpʃən] (n.) 例外
Every rule has an exception.

6) **unique** [juˈnik] (a.) 獨特的，獨一無二的。名詞是 **uniqueness** [juˈnɪknɪs] 獨特性
The singer has a unique singing style.

7) **norm** [nɔrm] (n.) 常態，常規
These days, smaller families have become the norm.

8) **reflect** [rɪˈflɛkt] (v.) 反射，反映
A mirror reflects light.

preach to the choir 相互取暖，同病相憐

也可以說 preach to the converted。preach 是「講道」，choir 是教堂裡的「唱詩班」，converted 是「已經改信、皈依宗教的（人）」，對著唱詩班和已經信教的人講道，意思就是聽者與自己心意相通，完全能了解自己的意思。

A: Why would anyone want to get married? It's all responsibility and no fun.
為什麼會有人想結婚？只有一大堆責任，全無樂趣可言。

B: Hey, you're preaching to the choir. I'm staying single for life.
嘿，你不用說服我。我打算一輩子打光棍。

band together 團結，一致對外

band together 跟上一篇的 stay together 一樣，都表示團結合作，以對抗敵人或度過困境。

A: The wages and working conditions here are awful.
這裡的薪資和工作環境很糟。

B: I know. We should all band together and form a union.
對啊。我們應該團結起來組織工會。

fight the good fight 為正義而戰

源自於《聖經》〈提摩太前書 6:12〉：Fight the good fight of faith, lay hold on eternal life. （你要為真道打那美好的仗，持定永生。）用來表示為了高貴美好的信念奮鬥。

A: I'm volunteering at a charity that prepares meals for the homeless.
我在一個慈善機構當志工，幫遊民做飯。

B: I'm glad to hear that you're fighting the good fight.
很高興聽到你為公益奮鬥。

pit...against... 使⋯與⋯對抗

pit 當名詞時表「鬥雞場」，當動詞時有「使⋯與⋯相鬥」之意。

A: What do you think made the Civil War so horrible?
你覺得美國內戰最糟的是什麼？

B: The fact that it pitted brother against brother.
就是挑起兄弟鬩牆。

turn a blind eye 對不想知道的事視若無睹

這個片語源自英國十九世紀海軍名將納爾遜（Admiral Horatio Nelson），他的右眼受傷失明，後來在一次戰役中，他明知指揮旗號下令暫停攻勢，但納爾遜故意把望遠鏡對著右眼，說他沒看到什麼旗號，繼續進攻。因此這個片語就表示故意迴避不想知道的事，假裝視若無睹。

A: Why do you think there's so much bullying in schools these days?
你覺得為什麼現在有那麼多校園霸凌事件？

B: I think a lot of teachers turn a blind eye to it.
我覺得很多老師假裝視若無睹。

at stake 處於危急關頭，吉凶未卜

stake 有「危險，風險」的意思，某樣人事物處於 at stake 的狀況，就代表前途不明，有遭逢厄運的危險。

A: The town should be evacuated before the hurricane hits.
這個鎮應該在颶風侵襲前撤離居民。

B: I know. Thousands of lives are at stake.
對啊。成千上萬的生命遭受威脅。

break new ground 有所突破

當有人獲得前所未有的突破，或是在某個領域有新發現，就可以說他 break new ground，他的成就也就可以用形容詞 groundbreaking 來形容。

A: Did you see that show about new cancer treatments?
你有看到那個介紹癌症新療法的節目嗎？

B: Yeah. Those researchers are really breaking new ground.
有啊。那些研究人員真的大有突破。

GM

Grammar Master　　　　**not until vs. until**

1. until 指一個動作持續「直到（某時間點）為止」。

例 **I was up until three in the morning writing my report.**
我起床寫報告寫到凌晨三點。

2. not (...) until 強調某行為「在（某時間點）之前尚未發生」，也就是「直到（某時間點）之後才開始進行」，等於 **not (...) before**。本句 Up until then, heterosexual people of different races couldn't marry who they wanted to marry either. 「在當時之前，不同種族的異性戀不能結婚。」，亦即「不同種族的異性戀通婚直到當時才合法。」後者翻譯較不能顯現出英文原句中的 not，但較符合中文說法。

例 **Not until our daughter called us did we stop worrying.**
直到女兒打電話來，我們才停止擔心。

例 **I didn't start studying until the night before the exam.**
我一直讀書讀到考試前一天晚上。

凱莉華盛頓儘管出身優渥的書香家庭，集美貌與聰明於一身，又嫁給曾是國家美式足球聯盟（National Football League，NFL）球員的演員兼製作人 Nnamdi Asomugha，家庭事業都得意，但她從未忘記自己的同胞與同性，也不曾失去對弱勢的同理。凱莉華盛頓走紅前參與多部電影的演出，但都是某某人的另一半（《雷之心靈傳奇》雷查爾斯的妻子、《最後的蘇格蘭王》伊迪阿敏的妻子、《驚奇四超人》石頭人的女朋友、《決殺令》姜戈的妻子），成名後積極為消除種族、性別歧視及同志平權發聲，證明了自己絕非花瓶。

I stand before you as a ¹⁾**doormat**. Oh, I mean as a female entertainer. Thank you for ²⁾**acknowledging** my ability to continue my career for 34 years in the face of ³⁾**blatant** sexism and 🔠 misogyny and constant bullying and relentless abuse. It's ⁴⁾**mind-blowing** to be honored like this after the very public year I've had. I feel stuck, and I feel sad. And quite frankly, today I feel ⁵⁾**bloated**. I didn't really feel like standing up and getting an award—I didn't feel worthy of that. But I knew I had to drag myself out of my bed, put on my boots and walk up here and say thank you to you guys.

站在你們面前的我是塊踩腳墊。噢,我是說女藝人。感謝你們認可我這 34 年來在面對公然的性別歧視和厭女主義,以及不間斷的霸凌和無情的凌虐下,還能繼續留在演藝界的能力。經過媒體曝光如此多的一年,我能獲得這個獎真是令人驚訝。我覺得不知所措,也覺得悲哀。坦白說,今天我覺得腫腫的。我原本不太想爬起來領獎,我覺得我不值得。但我知道我要把自己拖下床,穿上靴子,走到這裡來向各位說謝謝。

A Difficult Beginning
艱難的開始

I started off in a difficult time. People were dying of AIDS everywhere. It wasn't safe to be gay. It wasn't cool to be associated with the gay community. It was 1979 and New York was a very scary place. In the first year I was held at ⁶⁾**gunpoint**, ⁷⁾**raped** on a rooftop with a knife digging into my throat. And I had my apartment broken into and robbed so many

I'm Still Standing

我依然屹立不搖

Madonna's Billboard Woman of the Year Award Speech
瑪丹娜的告示牌女性年度獎得獎感言

© Kathy Hutchins / Shutterstock.com

VOCABULARY 🎧 64

1) **doormat** [ˋdor͵mæt] (n.) 踩腳墊,常用來形容任人踐踏的人
I'm tired of being my wife's doormat.

2) **acknowledge** [əkˋnɑlɪdʒ] (v.) 認可,承認
The historian is acknowledged as an expert in his field.

3) **blatant** [ˋbletənt] (a.) 公然的,露骨的
People were shocked by the president's blatant lies.

4) **mind-blowing** [ˋmaɪnd͵bloɪŋ] (a.) 令人驚奇的
Skydiving is a mind-blowing experience.

5) **bloated** [ˋblotɪd] (a.) 水腫的,腫脹的
I woke up feeling tired and bloated this morning.

6) **gunpoint** [ˋgʌn͵pɔɪnt] (n.) 槍口下;**at gunpoint** 即「在槍口的威脅下」
The storekeeper was robbed at gunpoint.

times I just stopped locking the door. In the years that followed, I lost almost every friend I had to AIDS or drugs or gunshot.

我出道時正歷經艱難時期。當時到處有人死於愛滋病，身為同性戀並不安全，跟同性戀族群往來不是一件很酷的事。**1979** 年的紐約是很可怕的地方。在紐約的第一年，我遭持槍劫持、喉嚨被刀子頂著，在屋頂被強暴。我的公寓多次遭破門搶劫，後來我索性不鎖門。接下來幾年，我幾乎失去所有朋友，他們不是因為感染愛滋病，就是因為吸毒或遭槍殺。

A Different Kind of Feminist
另類的女性主義者

I remember feeling [8)]**paralyzed**. It took me a while to pull myself together and get on with my creative life—to get on with my life. I took comfort in the poetry of Maya Angelou, and the writings of James Baldwin, and in the music of Nina Simone. I remember wishing I had a female peer I could look to for support. Camille Paglia, the famous [9)]**feminist** writer, said I set women back by [10)]**objectifying** myself sexually. So I thought, "Oh, if you're a feminist, you don't have sexuality, you deny it." So I said, "Fuck it. I'm a different kind of feminist. I'm a bad feminist."

我記得當時感到萎靡不振。我花了一段時間振作起來，繼續我的創作生活——繼續過我的生活。我在馬婭安傑盧的詩詞、詹姆斯鮑德溫的作品和妮娜西蒙的音樂中尋找慰藉。我記得當時希望自己能有位女性同輩的支持。知名女性主義作家卡米拉帕格里亞卻說我以性感方式物化自己，讓女性開倒車。所以我想她的意思是：「噢，如果要當女性主義者，就不能有性慾，要假裝沒有。」所以我說：「我不管，我就是另類的女性主義者。我是不良女性主義者。」

Madonna 瑪丹娜

1958 年出生於密西根州，20 歲到紐約追求舞者夢。她於 1983 年獲得唱片合約，推出暢銷專輯《瑪丹娜》，開始以挑戰主流尺度的歌詞、MV 影帶及大膽言行闖蕩演藝界。
根據《金氏世界紀錄》統計，瑪丹娜的唱片銷售紀錄僅次於披頭四、貓王，以及麥可傑克森，同時擁有最多告示牌排行榜冠軍單曲（12 首）及最多冠軍專輯（8 張），並被告示牌排行榜評為流行音樂最成功藝人第二名（僅次於音樂團體披頭四）。

©Stamptastic / Shutterstock.com

瑪丹娜的心靈導師
Maya Angelou 馬婭安傑盧

1928~2014，美國作家、詩人，六本激勵人心的系列自傳是最重要作品。馬婭前半生極為坎坷，後來成為成功的舞者，也參與歌劇演出，巡迴歐洲並廣泛學習語言。三十歲前後開始寫作，結交許多非裔美國作家，進而積極投入民權運動。馬婭安傑盧一生創作不輟，獲獎無數，2011 年獲頒美國總統自由勳章。

© Oleg Anisimov / Shutterstock.com

Nina Simone 妮娜西蒙

1933~2003 年，美國著名爵士歌手、作曲家、鋼琴家。創作類型包括藍調、R&B（節奏藍調）、靈魂樂。妮娜西蒙生長在具有反抗種族歧視的家庭，就學時又因家貧和膚色無法進入優秀的音樂學院，讓她在 1960 年代開始積極參與種族平權運動，演唱許多抗議歌曲。

妮娜西蒙帶有氣音的變音唱腔極為獨特，她的歌曲經常被翻唱及收做廣告、電影配樂，因而受到年輕世代的喜愛。

By Gerrit de Bruin, via Wikimedia Commons

James Baldwin 詹姆斯鮑德溫

1924~1987 年，美國作家、詩人、劇作家，一生關注同志及黑人平權運動。其半自傳體小說《向蒼天呼籲》 *Go Tell It on the Mountain* 曾獲《時代雜誌》選為 1923-2005 年 100 部最佳英語小說。

By Allan warren, via Wikimedia Commons

7) **rape** [rep] (v./n.) 強姦
The girl was raped on her way home from school.

8) **paralyzed** [ˋpærəˏlaɪzd] (a.) 麻痺的，驚呆的，氣餒的
Gary felt paralyzed after his divorce.

9) **feminist** [ˋfɛmənɪst] (a.) 女性主義的；(n.)女性主義者
I took a class on feminist theory in college.

10) **objectify** [əbˋdʒɛktəˏfaɪ] (v.) 物化
The author was accused of objectifying women.

No Safety Net
沒有安全網

I realized that I could not be a victim any longer, that everything happened for a reason. And my job was to learn from every shitstorm I wandered into. As you can imagine, all these unexpected events not only helped me become the [1]**daring** woman that stands before you, but also reminded me that I am vulnerable. And in life, there is no real safety except for self-belief. And, an understanding that I am not the owner of my talents.

我明白我不能再當受害者，所有事出必有因。我的任務就是從我碰到的爛事中學習。大家可以想見，這些不期而至的事件，不僅讓我變成站在你們眼前的勇敢女性，也讓我明瞭，我是脆弱的。生命中，沒有真正的安穩，只能相信自己。也讓我瞭解到，我不是自己的才華的主宰。

I was of course inspired by Debbie Harry and Chrissie Hynde and Aretha Franklin, but my real [2]**muse** was David Bowie. He [3]**embodied** male and female spirit, and that suited me just fine. He made me think there were no rules. But I was wrong. There are no rules— if you're a boy. If you're a girl, you have to play the game. What is that game? You are allowed to be pretty and cute and sexy. But don't act too smart. Don't have an opinion. Don't have an opinion that is out of line with the [4]**status quo**, at least. You are allowed to be objectified by men and dress like a [5]**slut**, but don't own your [5]**sluttiness**.

我當然也受到黛比哈里、克里西海特和艾瑞莎弗蘭克林的啟發，但我真正的靈感來源是大衛鮑伊。他體現了男性和女性的精神，正好適合我。他讓我覺得，世上沒有規則。但我錯了。世上是沒有規則——如果你是男生的話。你若是女生，就得遵守遊戲規則。什麼遊戲呢？妳可以展現漂亮、可愛和性感，但別表現得太聰明。不能有意見，至少不能有離經叛道的意見。可以讓男人物化妳，可以打扮得像個蕩婦，但妳的放蕩不能只為了讓自己爽。

You Will Be Criticized
你會被批判

And do not, I repeat, do not share your own sexual fantasies with the world. Be what men want you to be. But more importantly, be what women feel comfortable with you being around other men. And finally, do not age. Because to age is a sin. You will be criticized, you will be [6]**vilified**, and you will definitely not be played on the radio.

LG

Debbie Harry 黛比哈里
1945 年生，70、80 年代紅極一時新浪潮（new wave）樂團 Blondie 的主唱，亦參與大量電影、電視演出。Debbie Harry 前衛的雙色金髮造型、結合性感和龐克的打扮，成為後世搖滾女歌手模仿的對象。

© JStone / Shutterstock.com

Aretha Franklin
艾瑞莎弗蘭克林
1942 年生，美國歌手，橫跨靈魂樂及流行音樂，有 Lady Soul（靈魂歌后）的稱號，得過 19 座葛萊美獎，其中 11 座是最佳節奏藍調女藝人獎，更是首位進入搖滾音樂名人堂（Rock & Roll Hall of Fame）的女性藝人。

Chrissie Hynde
克里西海特
1951 年生，美國創作歌手、吉他手，搖滾樂團 The Pretenders（偽裝者樂團）主唱兼吉他手，成功結合龐克音樂、吉他手的陽剛，與她自身女性的特質，將優美的流行曲風融入狂野的音樂，形成特殊的搖滾風格。

© 3 song photography / Shutterstock.com

VOCABULARY 66

1) **daring** [ˈdɛrɪŋ] (a.) 大膽的，敢於冒險的
Critics praised the artist's daring use of color.

2) **muse** [mjuz] (n.) 繆思，（帶來靈感的）女神、人
The artist's lover was his muse for many years.

3) **embody** [ɪmˈbɑdi] (v.) 具體呈現，將…具體化
Parents should embody the values they want to teach their children.

4) **status quo** [ˈstætəs kwo] (phr.) 現狀。這個字是拉丁文，尤指社會結構、價值觀、政治局勢
Most people seem happy with the status quo.

5) **slut** [slʌt] (n.) 蕩婦。**sluttiness** [ˈslʌtɪnəs] 是指「蕩婦般的行為舉止」，形容詞為 **slutty** [ˈslʌti]「放蕩的」
I hit him because he called my girlfriend a slut.

6) **vilify** [ˈvɪləˌfaɪ] (v.) 毀謗，詆毀
Michael Jackson was often vilified by the media.

西恩潘（Sean Penn）年輕時以脾氣火爆著稱。

而且不能，我再說一次，不能跟世界分享你的性幻想。只能當男人心目中的女人。但更重要的是，你在男人身旁的樣子要讓其他女人覺得自在。最後，不能變老。因為變老是一種罪惡。你會被批判、被詆毀，而且廣播絕對不會再放你的歌。

When I first became famous, there were [7]**nude** photos of me in *Penthouse* and *Playboy* magazine. Photos that were taken from art schools that I posed for back in the day to make money. They weren't very sexy.

Eventually I was left alone because I married Sean Penn, and not only would he 🆖 bust a cap in your ass, but I was 🆖 off the market. For a while I was not considered a threat.

我剛開始走紅時，我的裸照出現在《閣樓》和《花花公子》雜誌上。那些照片是我之前在藝術學校當人體模特兒賺錢時拍的。那不是很性感的照片。後來大家放過我，是因為我嫁給西恩潘，不只是因為他會做掉你，也因為我死會了。有段時間我不被視為構成威脅。

Years later, divorced and single—sorry Sean—I made my *Erotica* album and my *Sex* book was released. I remember being the headline of every newspaper and magazine. Everything I read about myself was [8]**damning**. I was called a [9]**whore** and a witch. One headline compared me to [10]**Satan**.

幾年後，我離婚、恢復單身——抱歉，西恩——我錄製了《情慾》專輯，發行《性》寫真書。我記得當時我登上每份報紙和雜誌頭條。我看到所有關於我的報導都在咒罵。大家說我是妓女和巫婆。有個新聞標題把我比作撒旦。

 瑪丹娜的繆思

David Bowie 大衛鮑伊

1947~2016 年，英國搖滾樂手、音樂製作人、演員。大衛鮑伊有「搖滾變色龍」的稱號，他第一個受到廣泛矚目的造型，是 1972 年專輯當中雌雄同體的 Ziggy Stardust。但他不只在造型服裝上勇於嘗試，在音樂風格上也變化多端，堅持自己的理想與創意，對 70 年代的搖滾樂影響尤其深厚。大衛鮑伊一生持續音樂創作實驗，直到因肝癌過世前兩天還發行最後專輯 Blackstar。

大衛鮑伊曾在百大搖滾樂手票選中名列第七，唱片總銷量一億三千六百萬張。他亦長期關注人權及自由，他的歌曲 *Heroes*，在冷戰時期被視為東、西德的地下國歌。

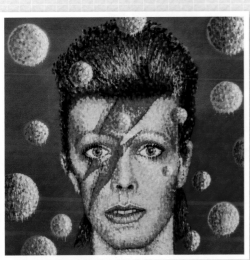

美國知名音樂家王子（Prince Rogers Nelson，1958~2016）以跨性別的妖豔裝扮著稱。

7) **nude** [nud] (a.) 裸體的
The movie has several nude scenes.

8) **damning** [ˋdæmɪŋ] (a.) 咒罵的，譴責性的
The paper published a damning report about government corruption.

9) **whore** [hor] (n.) 妓女，淫婦
Can you believe my boss told me not to dress like a whore?

10) **Satan** [ˋsetən] (n.) 魔鬼，撒旦
Many Christians today don't believe in Satan.

I said, "Wait a minute. Isn't Prince running around with [1]**fishnets** and high heels and lipstick with his butt hanging out?" Yes, he was. But he was a man. This was the first time I truly understood women do not have the same freedom as men. People say I'm [2]**controversial**. But I think the most controversial thing I have ever done is to [3]**stick around**. Michael is gone. Tupac is gone. Prince is gone. Whitney is gone. Amy Winehouse is gone. David Bowie is gone. But I'm still standing. I'm one of the lucky ones, and every day I 🄛🄖 count my blessings.

我說：「等一下，王子不就是穿著網襪、高跟鞋、塗口紅、露出屁股到處晃嗎？」沒錯，他是，但他是男人。這是我第一次真正瞭解到，女人沒有跟男人一樣的自由。大家都說我是爭議性人物，但我認為我自己做過最有爭議的事，就是打死不退。麥可離開了，吐派克離開了，王子離開了，惠妮離開了，艾美懷恩豪斯離開了，大衛鮑伊離開了，但我仍屹立不搖。我算是幸運的一個，而且每天珍惜我的福份。

Appreciating Our Own Worth
欣賞我們自己的價值

What I would like to say to all women here today is this: Women have been so [4]**oppressed** for so long. They believe what men have to say about them. They believe they have to back a man to get the job done. And there are some very good men worth backing, but not because they're men—because they're worthy. As women, we have to start appreciating our own worth and each other's worth. Seek out strong women to [5]**befriend**, to [6]**align** yourself with, to learn from, to [7]**collaborate** with, to be inspired by, to support, and [8]**enlightened** by.

今天我想對在場所有女性說的是：女性受到壓抑太久，以致於男人說女人該怎麼做就照單全收。她們相信自己必須支持男人完成工作。有些好男人是值得支持，但不是因為他們是男人——而是因為他們值得。身為女人，我們要開始欣賞自己的價值和彼此的價值。找堅強的女性做朋友、跟她們結盟、向她們學習、跟她們合作、受她們鼓舞、支持她們，並受她們啟發。

It's not so much about receiving this award as it is having this opportunity to stand before you and say thank you. Not only to the people who have loved and supported me along the way—you have no idea how much your support means—but to the doubters and [9]**naysayers** and everyone who 🄛🄖 gave me hell and said I could not, that I would not or I must not. 🄖🄜 Your resistance made me stronger, made me push harder, made me the fighter that I am today. It made me the woman that I am today. So, thank you.

與其說我是來接受這個獎，不如說是利用這個機會，站在各位面前表達感謝。我不只要感謝這一路以來愛我和支持我的人——你們不知道你們的支持對我有多重要——也要感謝那些質疑我、反對我的人，所有找我麻煩、說我做不到、不能或不應該去做的人。你們的阻力讓我變得更堅強、讓我更努力、造就我成為今天的戰士，讓我變成現在這樣的女性。所以，謝謝你們。

1) **fishnet** [ˈfɪʃ.nɛt] (n.) 漁網，漁網狀物
I think fishnet stockings are sexy.

2) **controversial** [ˌkɑntrəˈvɝʃəl] (a.) 有爭議的
Gun control is a very controversial subject.

3) **stick around** [stɪk əˈraʊnd] (phr.) 逗留，停留，待上一陣子
Tim stuck around after dinner to help with the dishes.

4) **oppress** [əˈprɛs] (v.) 壓迫
The dictator has opressed his people for decades.

5) **befriend** [bɪˈfrɛnd] (v.) 結交（朋友）
The new student was befriended by several of his classmates.

6) **align (with)** [əˈlaɪn] (v.)（與人）合作、結盟
The candidate won the election by aligning himself with the conservatives.

7) **collaborate** [kəˈlæbəˌret] (v.) 共同合作
The two companies collaborated on the project.

8) **enlighten** [ɪnˈlaɪtən] (v.) 啟發，教導
The goal of the show is to both entertain and enlighten viewers.

9) **naysayer** [ˈneˌseə] (n.) 唱反調者，反對者
If the author had listened to the naysayers, he never would have written his book.

misogyny 厭惡女性

misogyny 讀作 [mɪˋsɑdʒəni]，表示厭惡女性的表現，如憎恨女性、貶抑女性、物化女性、對女性施暴，甚至一切與女性相關的意象。厭女普遍存在於古今中外，不論是歷史傳說、文化藝術、宗教教義，都常見將災禍歸罪於女性、把女性歸做次等、視女性為不潔的例子。近代心理學及女性主義理論，認為這是父權主義（patriarchy）的一種表現，藉此維持男尊女卑、女性附屬於男性的從屬關係。

lose sth. to sb. 被…奪走…

lose 是「輸，被打敗」的意思，lose to sb. 就是「輸給（某人）」。而 lose sth. to sb. 則是因…而失去…。

A: I didn't know Patricia was a widow.
　 我不知道派翠莎喪偶了。
B: Yes. She lost her husband to cancer last year.
　 沒錯。她的丈夫去年因癌症去世。

Camille Paglia 卡米拉帕格里亞

1947 年生，美國著名社會學者及女性主義評論家，熱衷發表與美國流行文化及政治相關評論。她主張女性要靠展現實力得到性別平等，反對任何偏袒、優待女性的政策與措施，因為如此只會讓女性更弱，並強化女性不足堪大任的形象，進而損害能與男性平起平坐女性的機會。這種與目前主流女性主義相違背的言論，讓她得到「反女性主義的女性主義者（anti-feminist feminist）」的封號。

set back 拖累

這個片語表示「調回以前的水準」，用在具體的事物，可以表示如「錢花掉，積蓄變少」、「把時鐘調回冬令時間（調晚一小時）」。也可以用在抽象的事物，如文中表示女性追求不被物化的進程被抵銷，也就是「開倒車，退步」。

make 用法總整理

1. make + 受詞 + 原形動詞：make 在這裡當使役動詞，有「讓、允許、命令」之意。

例 **I really wish somebody would make that guy shut up.**
　 我真的好希望有人能讓那傢伙閉嘴。

2. make + 受詞 + 形容詞 / 名詞 / pp：受詞後方的所接的形容詞（名詞或 pp）用來補充說明受詞的狀態，make 在這裡表「成為、變成」之意。

例 **Listening to music makes me happy.** [接形容詞]
　 聽音樂讓我開心。

例 **Joining the military made him a man.** [接名詞]
　 從軍讓他成為一個男人。

現在你知道娜姊說的 Your resistance made me stronger, made me push harder, made me the fighter that I am today. 三個 make，各代表上面的哪個用法嗎？

A: Why did the new subway line take so long to complete?
　 新的地鐵線怎麼拖這麼久才完工？
B: Government budget cuts set the project back several years.
　 政府預算縮減讓計畫延誤幾年。

shitstorm 大災難

這個字是 shit（屎）＋ storm（風暴）組成，是指大災難、大混亂，也被借用來形容公眾人物突然間被輿論罵爆，成為眾矢之的慘況。後者這種用法是在社交網站普及之後出現的，因為透過網路散佈，才能在短時間內激起巨大的不滿能量，如風暴般向特定人士潑灑。

bust a cap (in sb.'s ass) 開槍（殺人）

cap 是槍彈藥筒底部的「底火」。bust a cap 原為軍事用語「開槍」的意思，後來被黑幫及饒舌高手借用，bust a cap in sb.'s ass 就是「開槍殺人」。

A: What are you gonna do if Ray doesn't give you your money?
　 老雷要是不還你錢，你有什麼打算？
B: I'm gonna bust a cap in his ass.
　 我就宰了他。

off the market 死會

字面上的意思是「從市場上消失」，引申為已經有男、女朋友或已婚。

A: Do you think I should ask Pam out on a date?
　 你覺得我該邀阿潘出來約會嗎？
B: Don't bother. She's off the market.
　 不必費事了。她已經有男朋友了。

count one's blessings 感謝老天保佑

blessing 是「（上帝）賜福，值得慶幸的事」，count one's blessings 直譯為「細數發生在自己身上的好事」，也就是知道自己有多幸運，心懷感恩的意思。

A: How do you stay optimistic when the economy is so bad?
　 經濟情況這麼差，你為什麼能這麼樂觀？
B: I make a point of counting my blessings every day.
　 我每天都提醒自己要心懷感恩。

give sb. hell 找（某人）麻煩

hell（地獄）就是會讓人生不如死，give sb. hell 不只是讓人日子難過，而且是在形容處處找碴，故意跟人過不去的難搞行徑。

A: Why are you so afraid of being late?
　 你怎麼這麼怕遲到啊？
B: If I'm even a minute late, the boss will give me hell.
　 就算只遲到一分鐘，我的老闆就會讓我吃不完兜著走。

這是瑪丹娜獲頒告示牌 2016 年度女性（Billboard's 2016 Woman of the Year）的演說。她的演說不堆砌難字，即使是粗話也照說不誤；不人云亦云，就算會引人側目還是要說；不虛偽矯情，哪怕要揭自己的瘡疤也不畏縮——就像她的音樂。瑪丹娜從出道時的壞女孩模樣、後來的離經叛道性感形象，到最後成為流行音樂女皇，都很難讓人與「知性」、「典範」聯想在一起，但只要聽過她演說的人，很難不對她肅然起敬，也很難不受到煽動——想成為跟她一樣真誠的自己。

Nobody Ever Has to Say "Me Too" Again

活出女性的時代

Oprah Winfrey's Golden Globe Award Acceptance Speech
歐普拉溫芙蕾金球獎得獎感言

#metoo **The Most Elegant Man**
最優雅的男子

In 1964, I was a little girl sitting on the [1]**linoleum** floor of my mother's house in Milwaukee watching Anne Bancroft present the Oscar for best actor at the 36th Academy Awards. She opened the envelope and said five words that [2]**literally** made history: "The winner is Sidney Poitier. " Up to the stage came the most elegant man I had ever seen. I remember his tie was white, and of course his skin was black, and I'd never seen a black man being celebrated like

© Kathy Hutchins / Shutterstock.com

VOCABULARY 70

1) **linoleum** [lɪˋnoliəm] (n.) 亞麻油地板（以亞麻仁油、樹脂、木粉、石灰烘烤壓製而成的室內地板鋪材）
We have an old linoleum floor in our kitchen.

2) **literally** [ˋlɪtərəli] (adv.) 照字面意思地，毫不誇張地，簡直
We saw literally thousands of animals on the safari.

3) **bone-tired** [ˋbonˋtaɪrd] (a.) 精疲力竭的
Bob was bone-tired after a day at the factory.

4) **privilege** [ˋprɪvəlɪdʒ] (n.) 恩典，殊榮，特權
It's been a privilege to teach so many excellent students.

5) **sustain** [səˋsten] (v.) 維持，支撐，支援
Very few planets are capable of sustaining life.

that. I've tried many, many, many times to explain what a moment like that means to a little girl, a kid watching from the cheap seats, as my mom came through the door [3]**bone-tired** from cleaning other people's houses.

1964 年，我還是小女孩時，在密爾瓦基的母親家裡，我坐在亞麻地板上，等著安妮班克勞馥頒發第 36 屆奧斯卡金像獎最佳男主角獎。她打開信封，說出了真正名留青史的五個字：「得獎的是薛尼鮑迪。」走上台的，是我所見過最優雅的男子。我記得他當時繫著白色領帶，當然膚色是黑色，我當時從未見過黑人能受到如此頌揚。我曾多次努力解釋像這樣的一刻，看在一位處境相對懸殊的小女孩眼中，意義有多重大，而我的母親當時剛幫別人家打掃完，正拖著疲憊不堪的身軀走進家門。

But all I can do is quote and say that the explanation's in Sidney's performance in *Lilies of the Field*: "Amen, amen, amen, amen."

但我所能做的，就是引用薛尼在《野百合》中所演唱來解釋：「阿們⋯」

An Honor and a Privilege
是榮譽，也是恩典

In 1982, Sidney received the Cecil B. DeMille award right here at the Golden Globes, and it is not lost on me that at this moment, there are some little girls watching as I become the first black woman to be given this same award. It is an honor—it is an honor and it is a [4]**privilege** to share the evening with all of them, and also with

the incredible men and women who've inspired me, who've challenged me, who've [5]**sustained** me and made my journey to this stage possible. Dennis Swanson, who took a chance on me for *A.M. Chicago*; Quincy Jones, who saw me on that show and said to Steven Spielberg, "Yes, she is Sophia in *The Color Purple*; Gayle, who's been the definition of what a friend is; and Stedman, who's been my rock—just a few to name.

1982 年，薛尼獲得金球獎西席地密爾獎，我明白此刻也有一些小女孩正看著我以首位非裔女性的身分獲得這項同樣的獎。這是份榮譽——是榮譽也是恩典，能夠與她們以及曾激勵我、挑戰我、支持我、助我踏上這座舞台的的偉大男女共度今晚的典禮。是丹尼斯斯萬森給我機會主持《早晨芝加哥》；然後昆西瓊斯在那個節目看到我，並告訴史蒂芬史匹柏：「對，她就是《紫色姊妹花》的蘇菲亞。」蓋爾絕對是夠格的朋友；還有斯特德曼，他一直是我的靠山——這些是其中幾位。

Oprah Winfrey
歐普拉溫芙蕾

1954 年生，美國電視談話節目主持人、製作人，曾獲時代雜誌百大影響力人物，參與演出 1985 年史匹柏電影《紫色姊妹花》*The Color Purple*，曾獲奧斯卡及金球獎最佳女配角提名。

歐普拉早年生活困頓，多次遭性侵並意外懷孕，14 歲產下死嬰。19 歲展開廣播生涯，1985 年成為晨間脱口秀 *AM Chicago* 主持人，快速成功，後以歐普拉溫芙蕾秀（*The Oprah Winfrey Show*）成為全國聯播電視主持人，透過節目長期關切貧困人士，對美國大眾極具影響力。歐普拉跨足出版、影藝事業，投入慈善工作，在美國媒體界呼風喚雨。

© Tinseltown / Shutterstock.com

Sidney Poitier 薛尼鮑迪
生於 1927 年，1964 年以《野百合》*Lilies of the Field* 一片，成為第一位獲得奧斯卡金像獎及金球獎的黑人。《野百合》講述一個到處打零工的美國黑人幫助一群東歐修女蓋教堂的故事。Amen 是他在劇中的角色 Homer Smith 教修女們唱的福音歌曲。

薛尼鮑迪於 2002 年獲得奧斯卡終身成就獎。

© Featureflash Photo Agency / Shutterstock.com

#metoo Speaking Your Truth
道出真相

I want to thank the Hollywood Foreign Press Association because we all know that the press is under [1]**siege** these days. But we also know that it is the [2]**insatiable** [3]**dedication** to uncovering the absolute truth that keeps us from turning a blind eye to [4]**corruption** and to injustice, to [5]**tyrants** and victims, and secrets and lies. I want to say that I value the press more than ever before as we try to [6]**navigate** these [7]**complicated** times, which brings me to this: what I know for sure is that speaking your truth is the most powerful tool we all have. And I'm especially proud and inspired by all the women who have felt strong enough and [8]**empowered** enough to speak up and share their personal stories. Each of us in this room are celebrated because of the stories that we tell, and this year we became the story.

我要謝謝好萊塢外國記者協會，因為我們都知道媒體已陷入四面楚歌。但我們也知道，是揭露真相的奉獻精神永遠不滅，讓我們能在面對腐敗和不公義、暴君和受害者，以及祕密和謊言時不會視而不見。我想說，在我們努力駕馭這複雜的時代時，我比以往更重視媒體，這讓我明白：我確信，說出真相，是我們所擁有的最強大工具。對於所有鼓起勇氣和賦予自身力量，大聲說出並分享自己個人遭遇的女性，我尤其引以為傲，並深受鼓舞。我們在場的每一個人都曾因為呈現他人的故事而受到表揚，而今年，我們成了故事的主角。

But it's not just a story affecting the entertainment industry. It's one that transcends any culture, geography, race, religion, politics, or workplace. So I want tonight to express gratitude to all the women who have endured years of abuse and [9]**assault** because they, like my mother, had children to feed and bills to pay and dreams to pursue. They're the women whose names we'll never know. They are domestic workers and farm workers. They are working in factories and they work in restaurants and they're in [10]**academia**, and engineering and medicine and science. They're part of the world of tech and politics and business. They're our athletes in the Olympics and they're our soldiers in the military.

但這不只是影響娛樂界的故事，這是超越任何文化、地理、種族、宗教、政治或職場的故事。所以今晚我要對那些忍受多年虐待和侵犯的女性表達感謝，因為她們就跟我的母親一樣，有孩子要養、有帳單要付、有夢想要追求。她們的名字是我們永遠無法得知的。她們有的是家庭幫傭，有的是農場工人，有的在工廠和餐廳工作，有的在學術界、工程界、醫藥界和科學界工作。她們有人是科技、政治和商業界的一份子，也有參加奧運的運動員，還有軍隊的軍人。

#metoo Recy Taylor's Story
雷西泰勒的故事

And there's someone else, Recy Taylor, a name I know and I think you should know too. In 1944, Recy Taylor was a young wife and a mother. She was just walking home from a church service

> 66 Every time you state what you want or believe, you're the first to hear it. It's a message to both you and others about what you think is possible. Don't put a ceiling on yourself.

每當你說想要或相信什麼，第一個聽到的人是自己。這是你給自己和他人的訊息，透露你認為什麼是可能的。不要給自己設限。

歐普拉談自我設限

VOCABULARY 72

1) **siege** [sidʒ] (n.) 圍攻
The siege of the city lasted for eight months.

2) **insatiable** [ɪnˋseʃəbl̩] (a.) 永不滿足的，貪得無厭的
The young man had an insatiable hunger for success.

3) **dedication** [ˏdɛdɪˋkeʃən] (n.) 投入，專注
Thanks to your dedication, we were able to finish the project on time.

4) **corruption** [kəˋrʌpʃən] (n.) 腐敗，貪污
Many political leaders have been tried for corruption.

5) **tyrant** [ˋtaɪrənt] (n.) 暴君，專制蠻橫的人
Iraq was ruled by a brutal tyrant.

6) **navigate** [ˋnævəˏget] (v.) 應付、處理（複雜情況）
The diplomat was skilled at navigating difficult political situations.

7) **complicated** [ˋkɑmpləˏketɪd] (a.) 複雜的，難懂的
The instructions were too complicated for me to understand.

she'd attended in Abbeville, Alabama, when she was [11)]**abducted** by six armed white men, raped and left [12)]**blindfolded** by the side of the road coming home from church. They threatened to kill her if she ever told anyone, but her story was reported to the [LG] NAACP, where a young worker by the name of Rosa Parks became the lead [13)]**investigator** on her case, and together they sought justice.

還有一位，雷西泰勒，是我知道的名字，我覺得你們也應該要知道。1944 年時，雷西泰勒是年輕的人妻和母親。她在阿拉巴馬州阿比維爾市上完教堂走路回家時，遭到六名持槍白人男子劫持、強暴，她被蒙住雙眼，被丟棄在從教堂返家的路旁。他們威脅她若告訴別人，他們會殺了她，但美國全國有色人種協進會接獲報案，一位名叫羅莎帕克斯的年輕工作人員帶領調查此案，她們一起討公道。

66 Excellence is the best deterrent to racism or sexism.

登峰造極是遏止種族歧視和性別歧視的最佳方法。

歐普拉談傑出

But justice wasn't an option in the era of [LG] Jim Crow. The men who tried to destroy her were never [14)]**prosecuted**. Recy Taylor died ten days ago, just [LG] shy of her 98th birthday. She lived, as we all have lived, too many years in a culture broken by brutally powerful men.

但在種族隔離法實行的年代，正義無法獲得伸張，傷害她的那群男人從未遭到起訴。雷西泰勒十天前剛過世，差幾天就要過 98 歲生日了。跟我們所有人一樣，她多年來活在一個被殘暴男權破壞的文化中。

8) **empower** [ɪm`pauə] (v.) 准許，使人能夠
The charity's goal is to empower poor women.

9) **assault** [ə`sɔlt] (n.) 施暴，侵害
The athlete was found guilty of sexual assault.

10) **academia** [ˌækə`dimiə] (n.) 學術界
My father spent most of his career in academia.

11) **abduct** [æb`dʌkt] (v.) 挾持，綁架
The millionaire's child was abducted by a criminal gang.

12) **blindfold** [`blaɪndˌfold] (v.) 矇住眼睛
The reporter was blindfolded and taken to the rebels' secret base.

13) **investigator** [ɪn`vɛstəˌgetə] (n.) 調查員
Investigators are seeking the cause of the plane crash.

14) **prosecute** [`prɑsɪˌkjut] (v.) 起訴（某人）
The boy was caught stealing, but the store owner decided not to prosecute.

#metoo Their Time Is Up
他們的時代結束了

For too long, women have not been heard or believed if they dared to speak their truth to the power of those men. But their time is up. Their time is up. Their time is up. And I just hope that Recy Taylor died knowing that her truth, like the truth of so many other women who were tormented in those years, and even now tormented, goes marching on. It was somewhere in Rosa Parks' heart almost 11 years later, when she made the decision to stay seated on that bus in Montgomery, and it's here with every woman who chooses to say, LG "Me too." And every man—every man who chooses to listen.

長久以來，若有女性敢勇於說出遭男權壓迫的真相，也從未有人願意傾聽或相信她們。但他們的時代結束了。他們的時代結束了。他們的時代結束了。我只希望雷西泰勒過世時能明白，她所遭遇的真相，就像多年來許多其他女性曾經或正受到凌虐的真相一樣，能繼續被記住。如同那件事發生約 11 年後，羅莎帕克斯在蒙哥馬利的公車上堅持不讓坐給白人時（編註：詳見本書「馬丁路德金恩的諾貝爾獎得獎感言」補充說明），她的心中仍記著這個真相，以及選擇說出「我也是」的每位女性，心中也記著這個真相。還有每位男人——每位選擇聆聽的男人。

#metoo Hope for a Brighter Morning
期盼更光明的早晨

In my career, what I've always tried my best to do, whether on television or through film, is to say something about how men and women really behave. To say how we experience shame, how we love and how we rage, how we fail, how we retreat, [1]**persevere** and how we overcome. I've interviewed and portrayed people who've [2]**withstood** some of the ugliest things life can throw at you, but the one quality all of them seem to share is an ability to maintain hope for a brighter morning, even during our darkest nights.

在我的職涯中，不論是在電視上或透過電影，我一直盡我所能談論男男女女真實生活上的行為。談論我們怎麼經歷羞恥、怎麼去愛、怎麼憤怒、怎麼失敗、怎麼退縮、堅持，以及怎麼克服。我採訪和扮演過的人物曾在人生中承受過一些最醜陋的事，但他們都有一個共同的特質，就是能懷抱著明早會更光明的希望，就算他們正處於最黑暗的夜晚。

So I want all the girls watching here now to know that a new day is on the horizon! And when that new day finally dawns, it will be because of a lot of magnificent women, many of whom are right here in this room tonight, and some pretty [3]**phenomenal** men, fighting hard to make sure that they become the leaders who take us to the time when nobody ever has to say "Me too" again.

所以我希望正在看這一幕的女孩們，要知道新的一天即將到來！當這新的一天終於到來時，原因是因為有許多偉大的女性，而且其中有許多人今晚就在現場，還有一些非常出色的男人，他們正努力奮鬥著，好確保能帶領大家走向永遠沒人再需要說「我也是」的時代。

VOCABULARY 74

1) **persevere** [ˌpɝsəˋvɪr] (v.) 不屈不撓，堅持不懈
If you persevere in your studies, I'm sure you can get into a good college.

2) **withstand** [wɪθˋstænd] (v.) 抵擋，承受住，過去式與pp為**withstood** [wɪθˋstʊd]
The dam has withstood many earthquakes.

3) **phenomenal** [fəˋnɑmənəl] (a.) 傑出的，極好的，驚人的
The movie was a phenomenal success.

Language Guide

cheap seats 廉價座位區

在表演場館裡，離表演場地越遠、視野越差的座位，售價越便宜，這樣的座位區段，就是 cheap seats。由於巨蛋場地的 cheap seats 位置不但很遠，還非常高，因此也被戲稱為 nosebleed section（流鼻血區，海拔高氣壓低，容易流鼻血）。文中歐普拉坐在家中看電視，卻說她是在 cheap seats，以此表示她是從很遠的地方遙望偶像。

Cecil B. DeMille Award 西席地密爾獎

這是金球獎的終身成就獎，以第一屆得獎者 Cecil B. DeMille（美國電影導演，美國影藝學院創辦元老）為名。這個獎表彰終身致力於電影、娛樂事業的人士，從 1952 年開始頒發，製片家華特迪士尼（Walt Disney）、導演史蒂芬史匹柏（Steven Spielberg）、馬丁史柯西斯（Martin Scorsese）、黑人導演及演員摩根費里曼（Morgan Freeman）、丹佐華盛頓（Denzel Washington）等都曾獲獎，上一年度（2017 年）得獎者為梅莉史翠普（Meryl Streep）。

Grammar Master
強調用的分裂句

分裂句 It is...(that/who/where/when)... ，就是將欲強調的部分從句子中分裂出來，放在 It is 後面，用來加強語氣或是強調用。強調的部份可以是句中的主詞、受詞、地點、時間，或片語等，如本句 It's not just a story that is affecting the entertainment industry. 當中的 not a story 就是要強調的部分，將本句還原為一般的句子，就是 A story is affecting the entertainment industry.（一個故事正在改變娛樂圈。）跟一般句比較起來，本句特別強調出以下事實：「正在影響娛樂圈的，並非那個故事」。

• 一般句
Alex saw Rebecca at the café yesterday.
艾力克斯昨天在咖啡廳看到蕾貝卡。

• 分裂句：

1. 強調主詞
It was Alex who saw Rebecca at the café yesterday.
看到蕾貝卡在咖啡廳的人是艾力克斯。

2. 強調受詞
It was Rebecca who/whom Alex saw at the café yesterday.
艾力克斯在咖啡廳看到的人是蕾貝卡。

3. 強調地點
It was at the café where Alex saw Rebecca yesterday.
昨天艾力克斯是在咖啡廳看到蕾貝卡的。

4. 強調時間
It was yesterday when Alex saw Rebecca at the café.
艾力克斯在咖啡廳看到蕾貝卡的時間是昨天。

NAACP 美國全國有色人種協進會

全名 **National Association for the Advancement of Colored People**，創立於 1909 年，是一個非裔美國人的民權組織，旨在修除種族仇恨及種族歧視，確保所有人的政治、社會、教育和經濟權利。NAACP 最初成立，是為了對抗 1876~1965 年間，美國南方各州施行的種族隔離法（**Jim Crow Laws**）。

shy of (sth.) 數量上差一點就…

shy 在口語中可表示「缺乏」、「不夠」，因此 shy of... 就是「不足」的意思。

A: Are apartments in your building expensive to rent?
你住的那棟房子的公寓房租貴嗎？
B: We pay just shy of 1,200 dollars.
我們要付將近 1200 元。

Jim Crow laws 吉姆克勞法

美國南部各州以及邊境各州對有色人種實行種族隔離制度的法律，於 1876~1965 年間實施。此法律規定公共設施必須依照種族的不同而隔離使用。吉姆·克勞這個名字來自於《蹦跳的吉姆·克勞》這首歌，這是當中黑人角色的名字，1833 年吉姆·克勞成為「黑人」的貶義詞，故 19 世紀的種族隔離法案也以它命名。

Me too 我也是

或寫做 #MeToo。Me too. 這個短語是社運人士 Tarana Bruke 首先使用，幫助性受害者說出受害經過，以平復傷痛。2017 年底，多位女性勇敢出面指控美國影業大亨 Harvey Weinstein 長期對女星施以性侵、騷擾，女星 Alyssa Milano 提議大家在推特上寫下 #MeToo 作為聲援，引發巨大迴響，許多人在寫下 #MeToo 的同時，也說出隱藏多年的遇害秘密，不再視為羞恥。

#MeToo 激起的社會能量，進而推動了 2018 年初的 Time's Up 反性騷擾運動，美國影藝界 300 位女性工作者加入並捐款，成立一個法律辯護基金，提供各界無權無勢的婦女所需的法律支援，以停止所有產業性別歧視。

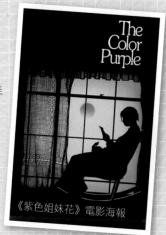

《紫色姐妹花》電影海報

和前一篇同為女性前鋒的主講者瑪丹娜相較，歐普拉溫芙蕾和她一樣有出身貧困、遭受性侵的悲慘境遇，而瑪丹娜較專注於女性自覺的大膽追求，歐普拉的形象則很溫暖，她長期濟弱扶傾、致力慈善事業，說起同理無權無勢婦女的困境很具說服力。這種差異或許反映出美國黑人希望成為主流的期望，也或許是歐普拉作為一個媒體人的敏感度所致。同樣都是光芒萬丈的女性強人，瑪丹娜靠叛逆使壞登上大位，歐普拉則選擇政治正確，難怪這場演說之後，會被拱出馬、角逐下屆美國總統了。

Meryl Streep's Golden Globe Award Speech
梅莉史翠普金球獎得獎感言

Thank you. I love you all. You'll have to forgive me. I've lost my voice in screaming and [1)]**lamentation** this weekend. And I lost my mind sometime earlier this year. So I have to read.

謝謝大家，我愛你們。你們要原諒我。我的嗓子因為這週末的叫喊與哀慟而啞了，而且我今年稍早已經失魂落魄了，所以我要看演講稿。

A Bunch of People from Other Places
一群外地來的人

Thank you, 🔤 Hollywood Foreign Press. Just to 🔤 pick up on what Hugh Laurie said, you and all of us in this room, really, belong to the most vilified segments in American society right now. Think about it. Hollywood, foreigners, and the press. But who are we? And, you know, what is Hollywood anyway? It's just a bunch of people from other places.

Hollywood, Foreigners, and the Press

好萊塢、外國人和媒體

休羅利是英國演員，在美國以 2004~2012 年影集《流氓醫生》 *House* 中的格瑞利豪斯醫生 Dr. Gregory House 聞名。

謝謝好萊塢外國記者協會。套一句休羅利的話，大家和在場所有人，真的，現在都屬於美國社會最受到污衊的一群人。想想看，好萊塢、外國人和記者媒體。但我們是什麼人？還有，說實在的，好萊塢到底是什麼？就是一群外地來的人。

I was born and raised and created in the public schools of New Jersey. Viola was born in a [2)]**sharecropper**'s cabin in South Carolina, and grew up in Central Falls, Rhode Island. Sarah Paulson was raised by a single mom in Brooklyn. Sarah Jessica Parker was one of seven or eight kids from Ohio. Amy Adams was born in Italy. Natalie Portman was born in Jerusalem. Where are their birth [3)]**certificates**? And the beautiful Ruth Negga was born in Ethiopia, raised in Ireland. And

---

VOCABULARY 🎧 76

1) **lamentation** [ˌlæmənˈteʃən] (n.) 哀悼，痛哭。動詞為 **lament** [ləˈmɛnt]
A song of lamentation was sung at the funeral.

2) **sharecropper** [ˈʃɛrˌkrapə] (n.) 佃農
The famous blues musician was the son of poor sharecroppers.

3) **certificate** [səˈtɪfɪkɪt] (n.) 證書，憑證
You can use this gift certificate at any of our stores.

4) **nominate** [ˈnamə.net] (v.) 提名
12 Years a Slave was nominated for nine Oscars.

5) **crawl (with)** [krɔl] (v.) 充斥著（常用於進行式）
The jungle was crawling with insects.

6) **martial** [ˈmarʃəl] (a.) 好戰的，尚武的，**martial arts** 即「武術」，須用複數型
Taekwondo is the most popular martial art in the world.

7) **breathtaking** [ˈbrɛθˌtekɪŋ] (a.) 令人驚嘆的，驚人的
The scenery in Yosemite is breathtaking.

she's here [4)]**nominated** for playing a small town girl from Virginia. Ryan Gosling, like all the nicest people, is Canadian. And Dev Patel, born in Kenya, raised in London, is here for playing an Indian raised in Tasmania.

我是在紐澤西州長大，在當地公立學校受教育。薇拉是在南卡羅萊納州的農家出生，在羅德島州中央瀑布長大。莎拉保羅森是在布魯克林由單親媽媽撫養長大。莎拉潔西卡帕克在俄亥俄州長大的老家有七、八個小孩，她是其中之一。艾美亞當斯生於義大利。娜塔莉波曼在耶路撒冷出生。他們的出生證明在哪裡？美麗的蘿絲奈格在衣索比亞出生，在愛爾蘭長大。而她現在因飾演維吉尼亞州小鎮女孩而獲得提名。雷恩葛斯林跟所有最友好的人一樣，來自加拿大。出生於肯亞的戴夫帕托在倫敦長大，來這裡飾演在澳洲塔斯馬尼亞長大的印度人。

Hollywood is [5)]**crawling** with outsiders and foreigners. If you kick them all out, you'll have nothing to watch but football and 🅛🅖 mixed [6)]**martial** arts, which are not the arts. They gave me three seconds to say this. An actor's only job is to enter the lives of people who are different from us and let you feel what that feels like. And there were many, many, many powerful performances this year that did exactly that—[7)]**breathtaking**, [8)]**passionate** work.

好萊塢到處都是外地人和外國人。若是將他們都踢出去，大家就沒東西可看了，除了美式足球和混合武術，但這根本不是藝術。他們給我三秒鐘說這些，演員唯一的工作是詮釋各式各樣不同的人生，讓大家體會他們的感受。今年有數不清的強大表演確實做到這點，而且都是令人嘆為觀止、熱情洋溢的作品。

A Stunning Performance
驚人的表演

There was one performance this year that [9)]**stunned** me. It sank its hooks in my heart. Not because it was good. There was nothing good about it. But it was effective and it did its job. It

Meryl Streep
梅莉史翠普

1949 年生，高中加入戲劇社團，大學主修戲劇，最後取得耶魯大學藝術碩士。1975 年畢業後首登百老匯，兩年後登上大銀幕。她因百老匯演出受到影星勞伯狄尼洛（Robert De Niro）注意，得到 1978 年金獎電影《越戰獵鹿人》*The Deer Hunter* 的演出機會，首度獲奧斯卡最佳女配角提名；1979 年以《克拉瑪對克拉瑪》*Kramer vs. Kramer* 得到第一座奧斯卡最佳女配角獎；主演 1982 年電影《蘇菲亞的選擇》*Sophie's Choice*，獲得第一座奧斯卡最佳女主角獎。

梅莉史翠普是奧斯卡及金球獎提名紀錄保持者，被公認為當今最傑出女演員。2011 年，美國總統歐巴馬頒給她國家藝術勳章（National Medal of Arts），是美國授與藝術工作者的最高榮耀。

made its intended audience laugh and show their teeth. It was that moment when the person asking to sit in the most respected seat in our country imitated a [10)]**disabled** reporter, someone he [11)]**outranked** in privilege, power, and the capacity to fight back. It kind of broke my heart when I saw it. I still can't get it out of my head because it wasn't in a movie. It was real life.

今年有個驚人的表演，讓我目瞪口呆，令我揪心。不是因為表演得好，根本一點都不好，卻很有效果，也達到了目的。那場表演讓預期的觀眾露齒而笑了。那一刻，那個正在尋求坐上我們國家最備受尊崇位置的人，卻在模仿身障記者，一個在特權階級、權力和反擊能力各方面都不如他的人。看到那一刻，我心碎了。我到現在還無法忘懷，因為那不是在拍電影，而是發生在現實生活的事。

圖片來源：網路圖片

川普 2015 年競選美國總統期間，曾以言語攻擊患有先天關節萎縮症的記者 Serge Kovaleski，並公開模仿他甩動殘肢的動作。

8) **passionate** [ˈpæʃənɪt] (a.) 有熱忱的，熱情的
Brazilians are passionate about soccer.

9) **stun** [stʌn] (v.) 使人大吃一驚
The singer was stunned when she found out she'd won the competition.

10) **disabled** [dɪsˈebəld] (a.) 殘障的，殘廢的；(n.) 殘障者
The school has a special program for disabled children.

11) **outrank** [aʊtˈræŋk] (v.) 地位高於
A general outranks a colonel.

And this instinct to humiliate, when it's modeled by someone in the public platform, by someone powerful, it [1)]**filters** down into everybody's life, because it kind of gives permission for other people to do the same thing. [2)]**Disrespect** invites disrespect. Violence [3)]**incites** violence. When the powerful use their position to [4)]**bully** others, we all lose.

這種羞辱別人的本能一旦由權勢強大的人在公共平臺上做出壞榜樣，這將滲透每個人的生活，因為這等於是允許他人做同樣的事。不敬引來不敬，暴力招來暴力。一旦當權者利用職權霸凌他人，我們就都輸了。

 ### Holding Power to Account
監督當權者

This brings me to the press. We need the principled press to 🇱🇬 hold power to account, to 🇱🇬 call them on the carpet for every outrage. That's why our founders [5)]**enshrined** the press and its freedoms in our constitution. So I only ask the famously 🅶🅼 [6)]**well-heeled** Hollywood Foreign Press and all of us in our community to join me in supporting the Committee to Protect [7)]**Journalists**. Because we're going to need them going forward. And they'll need us to [8)]**safeguard** the truth.

這讓我想到媒體，我們需要有原則的媒體監督當權者，批判他們所做的每件惡行。所以我們的國父們才會在憲法中尊崇新聞媒體和其自由。所以我請極為富有的好萊塢外國記者協會和我們在演藝圈的所有人，跟我一起支持保護記者委員會。因為我們往後的日子會很需要他們，他們也需要我們守護真相。

One more thing. Once when I was standing around on the set one day whining about something—we were going to work through supper, or the long hours or whatever—Tommy Lee Jones said to me, "Isn't it such a privilege, Meryl, just to be an actor?" Yeah, it is. And we have to remind each other of the privilege and the responsibility of the act of [9)]**empathy**. We should all be very proud of the work Hollywood honors here tonight. As my friend, the dear [10)]**departed** Princess Leia, said to me once, "Take your broken heart, make it into art." Thank you.

還有一件事，有一次我在拍攝現場抱怨某件事時——因為我們拍到無法吃晚餐，或是要超時拍攝之類的——湯米李瓊斯跟我說：「梅莉，當演員不就是一種恩典嗎？」對，沒錯。而且我們要互相提醒，同理心也是一種恩典和責任。好萊塢今晚在此表揚的成果，我們應該要引以為傲。如同我的朋友，親愛的已故莉亞公主（編註：為《星際大戰》的角色，由 **Carrie Fisher** 飾演，2016 年去世。）曾跟我說的：「把妳破碎的心化為藝術。」謝謝各位。

> **"** I think that you find your own way. In the end, it's what feels right to you. Not what your mother told you. Not what some actress told you. Not what anybody else told you but the still, small voice

你會找到自己的路，到頭來，那會是你感覺對的事。不是你媽媽跟你說的，不是哪個女演員跟你說的，不是任何人，而是那平靜的、小小的聲音。

梅莉史翠普談人生方向

VOCABULARY 78

1) **filter** [ˋfɪltə] (v.) 滲透，過濾
   The noise of traffic filtered through the curtains.

2) **disrespect** [ˌdɪsrɪˋspɛkt] (n./v.) 不敬，無禮，輕蔑
   The student treated his teacher with disrespect.

3) **incite** [ɪnˋsaɪt] (v.) 煽動，激起
   The protester was charged with inciting a riot.

4) **bully** [ˋbʊlɪ] (v.) 霸凌，欺負
   The skinny boy was often bullied by his classmates.

5) **enshrine** [ɪnˋʃraɪn] (v.) 珍藏，將…奉為神聖不可侵犯
   Freedom of speech is enshrined in the Bill of Rights.

6) **well-heeled** [ˋwɛlˋhild] (a.) 富有的
   The resort is popular with well-heeled tourists.

7) **journalist** [ˋdʒɝnəlɪst] (n.) 新聞工作者，新聞記者
   The journalist has won many awards for his reporting.

8) **safeguard** [ˋsef͵gɑrd] (v.) 保護，防衛
   This software can safeguard your computer against viruses.

9) **empathy** [ˋɛmpəθɪ] (n.) 共鳴，同理心
   The man's empathy for the poor led him to start a charity.

10) **departed** [dɪˋpɑrtɪd] (a.) 已故的，去世的
    We'll always remember our departed loved ones.

Hollywood Foreign Press Association
好萊塢外國記者協會

簡稱 HFPA，由近百位外籍娛樂記者組成，美國一年一度的電視及電影盛會金球獎，就是由 HFPA 舉辦，並由協會成員投票選出得獎者。與電影奧斯卡金像獎（Academy Awards）和電視艾美獎（Emmy Awards）不同的是，金球獎因受限於缺乏專業投票團，故略過技術方面的獎項，只頒發普通獎項。頒獎日為每年的一月中旬，距離三月的奧斯卡頒獎典禮頗近，故被稱為「奧斯卡的風向球」。

pick up on 深入探討，回應

這個片語表示更深入討論某人所說的話，或是對某件事做出回應。

A: I'd like to pick up on a couple of the points you made.
我想針對你的幾個論點做些回應。

B: OK. I'm all ears.
好。我洗耳恭聽。

這個片語有另一個意思，一是「察覺，領會學習」：

A: Did you notice that Haley was in a bad mood?
你有發現海莉心情不好嗎？

B: No. I didn't pick up on that at all.
沒有，我完全沒察覺。

mixed martial arts 混合武術

縮寫為 MMA，又稱為綜合格鬥，是一種不限套路的搏擊運動，選手可以自由發揮，任意選擇擊敗對手最有效率的武術。這項運動最早期興起於巴西，稱作 vale tudo（無限制格鬥），幾乎沒有規則，選手亦不戴護具，比賽極為血腥暴力，後來改稱 mixed martial arts 以強調競技形象。但梅莉史翠普還是挖苦說這雖名為 arts，卻不是藝術（art）。

© Vladimir Vasiltvich / Shutterstock.com

hold sb. to account 叫人出來面對

這個片語是要犯錯的人出來解釋，或是出來面對應負的責任或懲罰。

A: Do you think the president was right to pardon that minister?
你覺得總統赦免那個部長是對的嗎？

B: No. I think he should have been held to account for his crimes.
不。我認為他應該對自己的罪行擔起應負的責任。

call on the carpet 斥罵

on the carpet 是在形容一個人因犯錯遭殃，call sb. on the carpet 就是「訓斥責罵某人」。

A: What's wrong? You look like your dog just died.
怎麼了？你看起來垂頭喪氣。

B: I just got called on the carpet by the boss.
我剛剛被老闆臭罵一頓。

由 well- 組成的複合形容詞

本處的 well-heeled「衣食無虞的、富裕的」為複合形容詞，在 well 之後以連字號（-）連接過去分詞 pp 所形成的複合形容詞相當常見，更多的例子如下：

a well-behaved boy 守規矩的男孩

a well-known guitarist 有名的吉他手

a well-done steak 一客全熟牛排

a well-trained doctor 受過良好訓練的醫師

這類形容詞除了可以放在名詞前修飾之外，也可放在 be 動詞之後作為補語。

本篇跟前一篇同為金球獎西席地密爾獎（Cecil B. DeMille Award）的得獎演說，梅莉史翠普是歐普拉的前任得獎者。金球獎於每年一月初頒獎，梅莉史翠普上台領獎的 2017 年 1 月 9 日，距川普前一年 11 月 8 日當選也才短短兩個月，離川普即將上任又只剩 12 天，因此與媒體關係極差的川普，自然成為整場頒獎典禮嘲諷揶揄的對象。不過相較於滿場笑鬧，梅姨畢竟是去領終身成就獎的，致詞態度莊重、言之有物是必須的。

Emma Thompson's Golden Globe Award Speech
艾瑪湯普遜金球獎得獎感言

I can't thank you enough, Hollywood Foreign Press, for honoring me in this capacity. I don't wish to burden you with my debts, which are heavy and numerous, but I think that everybody involved in the making of this film knows that we owe all our pride and all our joy to the genius of Jane Austen. It occurred to me to wonder how she would react to an evening like this. This is what I came up with:

對於好萊塢外國記者協會如此的肯定，我不勝感激。我不希望讓你們承擔我沉重的人情債，但我想參與製作這部電影的人都知道，我們應該要將所有榮耀和喜樂歸給珍奧斯汀的才華。我突然想知道換做是她，在今晚這樣的場合會有什麼反應。以下是我的想像：

Notes from Jane Austen
珍奧斯汀的筆記

Four A.M. Having just returned from an evening at the Golden ¹⁾**Spheres**, which despite the ²⁾**inconveniences** of heat, noise and ³⁾**overcrowding**, was not without its pleasures. Thankfully, there were no dogs and no children. The gowns were ⁴⁾**middling**. There was a good deal of shouting and behavior ⁵⁾**verging** on the ⁶⁾**profligate**. However, people were very free

The Genius of Jane Austen
珍奧斯丁的才華

© Featureflash Photo Agency / Shutterstock.com

with their ⁷⁾**compliments** and I made several new acquaintances:

凌晨四點，剛剛從金球體獎晚會回來（編註：艾瑪湯普遜假裝珍奧斯汀對現代世界的金球獎不熟），雖然有悶熱、噪音和擁擠等不便，但並非沒有樂趣。幸好沒有狗，也沒有小孩。禮服都很普通。聽到不少尖叫聲，看到不少幾近放蕩的行為。不過，大家都不吝讚美，

VOCABULARY 🎧 80

1) **sphere** [sfɪr] (n.) 球體
All points on a sphere are an equal distance from the center.

2) **inconvenience** [ˌɪnkənˈvinjəns] (n.) 不便之處，麻煩
The blackout at our hotel was a major inconvenience.

3) **overcrowding** [ˌovɚˈkraʊdɪŋ] (n.) 過度擁擠
New prisons must be built to solve the problem of overcrowding.

4) **middling** [ˈmɪdəlɪŋ] (a.) 中等的，平凡的
Michael was a man of middling height.

5) **verge (on)** [vɝdʒ] (v.) 接近，瀕臨
The waiter who served us was verging on rude.

6) **profligate** [ˈprɑfləgɪt] (a.) 浪費的，揮霍的，放肆的
The millionaire's wife is a profligate spender.

7) **compliment** [ˈkɑmpləmənt] (n./v.) 讚美，恭維
Carol often receives compliments from her teachers.

8) **enchanting** [ɪnˈtʃæntɪŋ] (a.) 迷人的
The young girl had an enchanting smile.

9) **extraction** [ɪkˈstrækʃən] (n.) 血統，出身
His mother's family is of German extraction.

10) **copiously** [ˈkopiəsli] (adv.) 充裕地，大量地。形容詞為 **copious** [ˈkopiəs]
The soup was copiously seasoned with garlic and spices.

11) **erudite** [ˈɛruˌdaɪt] (a.) 博學的
Several erudite scholars will be speaking at the conference.

12) **countenance** [ˈkaʊntənəns] (n.) 面容，表情
The lady was of noble countenance.

13) **unconscionable** [ʌnˈkɑnʃənəbəl] (a.) 過度的，無理的
We were kept waiting for an unconscionable amount of time.

14) **hoyden** [ˈhɔɪdən] (n.) 野丫頭，頑皮姑娘
The actress plays a charming hoyden in the film.

15) **purloin** [pɝˈlɔɪn] (v.) 盜取，盜用
Did you purloin that pen from the office?

16) **nefarious** [nəˈfɛriəs] (a.) 邪惡的，惡毒的
The police uncovered a nefarious plot to overthrow the government.

我也結識了幾個新朋友：

Miss Lindsay Doran, of Mirage, wherever that might be, who is largely responsible for my presence here, an [8)]**enchanting** companion about whom too much good cannot be said; Mr. Ang Lee, of foreign [9)]**extraction**, who most unexpectedly LG appeared to understand me better than I understand myself; GM Mr. James Schamus, a [10)]**copiously** [11)]**erudite** gentleman; Miss Kate Winslet, beautiful in both [12)]**countenance** and spirit; Mr. Pat Doyle, a composer and a Scot, who displayed the kind of wild behavior one has learned to expect from that race.

幻影（沒聽過這個地方）的琳賽鐸朗小姐（編註：本片製作人，Mirage 是幻影製片公司），多虧了她我才能出現在這裡，她是迷人的同伴，她的好處多到說不完；來自國外的李安先生，最出乎意料的是，他似乎比我更瞭解我自己；詹姆斯夏慕斯先生（共同製作人），他是博學多聞的紳士；凱特溫斯蕾小姐內外兼修；派翠克道爾先生，他是作曲家，一個蘇格蘭人，他展現的熱情奔放相信是民族天性。

I attempted to converse with Mr. Sydney Pollack, but his charms and wisdom are so generally

© Andy Lidstone / Shutterstock.com

pleasing that it proved impossible to get within ten feet of him. The room was full of interesting activity until 11:00 p.m., when it emptied rather suddenly. The lateness of the hour is due therefore not to the dance, but to the waiting in a long line for a horseless carriage of [13)]**unconscionable** size. The modern world has clearly done nothing for transport.

我想跟薛尼波勒（編註：執行製作人）交談，但他的魅力和智慧太討人喜歡，以致於我擠不進他十英尺內。現場的活動很有意思，直到晚上 11 點，人突然就散了。時間之所以拖太晚，不是因為舞會，而是大排長龍等著搭巨大的無馬四輪車。摩登世界的交通工具顯然毫無長進。

P.S. Managed to avoid the [14)]**hoyden** Emily Tomkins who has [15)]**purloined** my creation and added things of her own. [16)]**Nefarious** creature.

附註：我成功避開了淘氣的艾蜜莉湯金斯（編註：艾瑪湯普遜假裝珍奧斯汀把她的名字記錯了），她偷了我的作品，還添加了自己的東西。惡毒的傢伙。

With gratitude and apologies to Miss Austen, thank you.

向奧斯汀小姐致上謝意和歉意，謝謝各位。

Emma Thompson
艾瑪湯普遜

1959 年生，英國著名演員及劇作家，是史上唯一獲得最佳女主角及編劇雙料榮銜的奧斯卡得主。這並不是艾瑪湯普遜唯一的雙料紀錄：她以《長日將盡》 The Remains of the Day 和《以父之名》 In the Name of the Father 於 1994 年雙料入圍奧斯卡最佳女主角及女配角；並因李安導演電影《理性與感性》 Sense and Sensibility 雙料入圍多個獎項的最佳改編劇本及最佳女配角，並獲得 1996 年奧斯卡最佳改編劇本獎。本篇演說是同年金球獎的最佳改編劇本得獎致詞。改編珍奧斯汀小說得獎的女演員，以模擬珍奧斯汀語氣所寫的稿子致詞，完全顯示出她雙料提名的實至名歸。

© Kathy Hutchins / Shutterstock.com

Why Did It Take So Long?

為何拖這麼久？

Will Farrell's Mark Twain Prize for American Humor Speech
威爾法洛的馬克吐溫美國幽默獎得獎感言

Thank you so much for that warm [1]**ovation**. As I stare at this magnificent [2]**bust** of 🔲 Mark Twain, I'm reminded of how humbled I am to receive such an honor and how I [3]**vow** to take very special care of it. I will never let it out of my sight. I will find a place of honor in my house for this magnificent bust. If my children try to touch it or even look at it, I'll beat them. It means that much to me. In fact, I told my wife that maybe I should buy it its own seat for the plane ride home. And no, I'm not done. I just started the speech. Why would you think I'm done?

威謝各位熱情的掌聲。看著這偉大的馬克吐溫半身像，讓我想到獲得如此榮耀的我是多麼謙遜，以及我發誓會如何特別保管它。

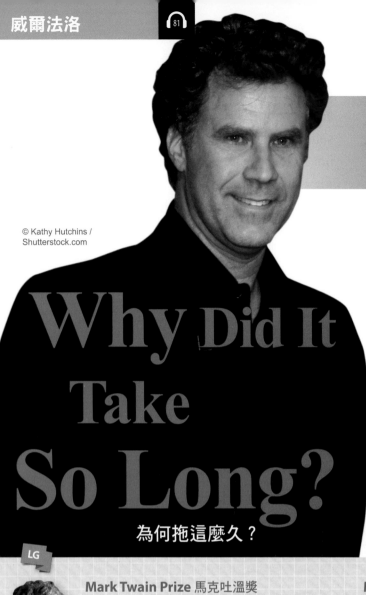

Mark Twain Prize 馬克吐溫獎

Airstream 是一個高級休閒旅行拖車的品牌，以閃亮的鋁製渾馬克吐溫美國幽默獎（Mark Twain Prize for American Humor）是約翰甘迺迪表演藝術中心（John F. Kennedy Center for the Performing Arts）於 1998 年設立的年度獎項，頒獎地點在華府的甘迺迪中心音樂廳（Kennedy Center Concert Hall），由美國公共電視網（Public Broadcasting Service，PBS）錄影轉播。

馬克吐溫美國幽默獎的獎座為大作家的半身像。
Photographer: Robert Fulton, 1967.

© Deatonphotos / Shutterstock.com
約翰甘迺迪表演藝術中心。

Mark Twain 筆名的由來

mark twain 意思是標記二噚深（也就是 mark number two）。噚（fathom）在古英文中的本意是「兩臂之長」，後引申用為長度單位，大約 370 公分。mark twain 是水運領航員的專業術語，表示水深二噚寬，這是輪船可以安全通過的最淺水深。

這個筆名源自克萊門斯（Samuel Langhorne Clemens，作家馬克吐溫的本名）早年的水手生涯。在 1883 年的作品——《密西西比河上的生活》Life on the Mississippi 裡頭，克萊門斯提到這個筆名其實並不是出自於他的原創，而是從密西西比河上的老船長艾賽亞賽勒斯（Isaiah Sellers）而來，老船長喜歡將他熟知的水文知識和船舶生活發表在報章雜誌上，並在文章最後簽上 Mark Twain。得知這位老船長的死訊時，克萊門斯才剛開始在報社工作，需要一個筆名，於是便將這個筆名繼承下來，終身所用。

VOCABULARY 🎧 82

1) **ovation** [oˋveʃən] (n.) 熱烈鼓掌
The crowd gave the singer a standing ovation at the end of the concert.

2) **bust** [bʌst] (n.) 半身像
The writer keeps a bust of Shakespeare on his desk.

3) **vow** [vaʊ] (v.) 發誓
Al's wife made him vow to never gamble again.

4) **recipient** [rɪˋsɪpiənt] (n.) 獲得者
Scholarship recipients will be informed by mail.

5) **consecutive** [kənˋsɛkjʊtɪv] (a.) 連續的，連貫的
It rained for six consecutive days.

6) **emphatically** [ɪmˋfætɪkli] (adv.) 斷然，堅決的。形容詞為 **emphatic** [ɪmˋfæˌtɪk]
The suspect emphatically denied being at the scene of the crime.

我絕不會讓它離開我的視線，我會在家裡給這座偉大的半身像弄個貴賓席。我的小孩要是想碰它或甚至看著它，我會揍他們。它對我的意義就是如此重大。事實上，我跟老婆說搭機回去時，也許該為它買個位子。（此時後面的樂隊開始演奏下台音樂）不行，我還沒說完。我的演講才剛開始，你們怎麼會以為我說完了？

Who Is Mark Twain?
馬克吐溫是誰？

I want to sincerely thank the Kennedy Center for this prize and the fine folks at PBS for airing this special. I'm the 14th [4]**recipient** of the LG Mark Twain prize. You're probably asking yourself, "Why did it take so long?" Well, for 13 [5]**consecutive** years, I've been begged by the Kennedy Center to accept this award, and for 13 consecutive years, I've [6]**emphatically** said no. For years, I had many questions about this Mark Twain, the first being, "Who is he?" It's been LG dawning on me that since I was a small boy I've thoroughly enjoyed his delicious fried chicken.

我想要誠摯威謝甘迺迪中心頒發這個獎，也謝謝公共電視台優秀的工作人員轉播這場特別典禮。我是第 14 位馬克吐溫獎得主。你們心裡可能在問：「怎麼會拖到現在？」哎，連續這 13 年來，甘迺迪中心一直哀求我接受這個獎，而 13 年來一而再、再而三的，我都斬釘截鐵地拒絕。多年來，我對這位馬克吐溫一直有諸多疑問，首先是，「他是誰啊？」然後突然間我明白了，我從小就很愛吃他的美味炸雞。

Colonel Sanders 肯德基爺爺
1890~1980 年，1952 年逾美國猶他州創設著名炸雞連鎖肯德基（Kentucky Fried Chicken，KFC），並擔任品牌代言人。1964 年高齡 73 歲時將公司出售，但繼續擔任 KFC 的形象大使。

Then my wife informed me that I was thinking of LG [7]**Colonel** Sanders, not Mark Twain. It turns out that GM he's considered America's finest

author and [8]**humorist**, but that his real name isn't Mark Twain, it's Jerry Goldman. Before that, it was Judy Blume, and before that, of course, Samuel Langhorne Clemens. Despite my failing to grasp the importance of Mark Twain and what exactly he did, I decided to accept this award because of the prize money—one billion dollars, paid out over the next 10,000 years. To say that I'm [9]**thrilled** to be here is a complete [10]**understatement**. And to make this evening even more thrilling, I've just been informed that I'm only the 11th[11]Caucasian to receive this prestigious award.

然後我老婆告訴我，我想到的是肯德基爺爺，不是馬克吐溫。原來他是公認美國最優秀的作家和幽默大師，但他的本名不是馬克吐溫，是傑瑞高德曼。在那之前，是茱莉布盧姆（編註：Jerry Goldman、Judy Blume 都是現場來賓），再之前，當然，是塞姆朗赫恩克萊門斯。雖然我未掌握住馬克吐溫的重要性，以及他到底是做什麼的，但我決定接受這個獎，因為獎金——有十億美元，在未來一萬年分期付款。興奮無比仍不足以形容此刻的心情，今晚更讓我激動的，是我剛得知，我是第 11 位白人獲得這個聲譽卓著的獎。

PBS/Scott Suchman

Will Farrell
威爾法洛

1967 年生，美國知名喜劇演員，1995 年加入 NBC 電視台綜藝節目《週末夜現場》的演出，因模仿美國總統小布希（George W. Bush）等多位名人受到歡迎，是少數在這個節目演出超過七年的成員。威爾法洛事業擴及電影、配音、百老匯，甚至打過美國職棒大聯盟（為新戲宣傳，並為癌症慈善機構募款）！他曾在 2007 年被選為「簽名最糟的名人」，問題不出在他字的美醜，而是因為他會一邊簽名一邊慫恿索取簽名的人：「你說你是我最忠實的粉絲，證明啊。」威爾法洛於 2011 年獲得馬克吐溫美國幽默獎。

---

7) **colonel** [ˈkɝnəl] (n.) 陸軍上校
By the end of the war, Johnson had been promoted to colonel.

8) **humorist** [ˈhjumərɪst] (n.) 幽默作家
That column is written by a famous humorist.

9) **thrilled** [θrɪld] (a.) 非常興奮的，極為激動的
We were thrilled to meet our idol in person.

10) **understatement** [ˈʌndɚˌstetmənt] (n.) 保守的說法
Calling Kobe a good player is an understatement.

11) **Caucasian** [kɔˈkeʒən] (n./a.) 白種人（的）
Police are looking for a Caucasian male driving a blue van.

I Had One Dream
我曾有個夢想

I can't tell you enough how special it is to stand here on this stage at the Kennedy Center, in front of this amazing audience, while being watched on PBS by hundreds of people. It's very [1)]**surreal**. You have to understand, as a kid growing up in Irvine, California—where I would sit in my room and listen to records of Steve Martin and the original 🔳 *Saturday Night Live* cast, or stay up late and watch 🔳 Johnny Carson on *The Tonight Show* to see what [2)]**comedians** he would have on—I had one dream, one singular focus. Even at the earliest stage, I can remember wanting to do one thing and one thing only: sell insurance.

這種特別的感覺是我無法形容的，能站在甘迺迪中心的臺上，在這群美妙的觀眾面前，還有在公共電視的數百名觀眾在看（編註：在虧 PBS 根本沒人看）。感覺很超現實。你們要明白，對一個生長在加州爾灣的孩子來說，我會在我房間裡聽史提夫馬丁和最早《週六夜現場》班底的錄音，或熬夜觀賞強尼卡森的《今夜秀》，看他會請來哪些喜劇演員——我曾有個夢想，唯一明確的目標。就算是在早年階段，我記得我只想做一件事，唯一的一件事：賣保險。

> 66 When going on a roller coaster bring nuts and bolts with you, lean to the person in front and say: "Woah dude, these came out of your seat!"
>
> 去搭雲霄飛車要帶一些螺帽和螺栓，然後靠向前面的人說：「哇老兄，這些東西從你的椅子下掉出來了！」

威爾法洛惡作劇教學

> 66 I just read that last year 4,213,257 people got married. I don't want to start any trouble, but shouldn't that be an even number?
>
> 我剛讀到資料說去年有 4,213,257 人結婚。我不想找麻煩，但不是應該要是個偶數嗎？

威爾法洛談結婚人口

So to be standing here feels somewhat odd. Whether it was auto, home or life, fire, flood or earthquake, I just wanted to make people feel safe. Do you have enough 🔳 [3)]**inland** [4)]**marine** insurance or busines 🔳 [5)]**overhead** expense disability insurance? These are the things I thought when I was a kid. But the insurance game didn't happen for me. So I 🔳 fell back on comedy, and here I am now. There are so many people I need to thank for helping me make tonight possible.

所以站在這裡感覺有點奇怪。不論是汽車險、房屋險或壽險、火災、水災或地震險，我只希望讓大家有安全感。你們有足夠的內陸運輸險，或事業經常費用傷殘保險嗎？這些都是我小時候在想的事。但我最後沒能從事保險業。所以我退而求其次，進了喜劇圈，然後我就在這裡了。今晚能來這裡領獎，要感謝很多人幫我。

First off, I'd like to thank all the wonderful people who spoke or performed tonight 🔳 on my behalf, an amazing [6)]**lineup**. All of you taking time out of your busy personal and professional schedules to be here 🔳 means the world to me, and if any of you ever need me to speak on your behalf, for any reason, just know that I sincerely

---

VOCABULARY 🎧 84

1) **surreal** [sə`riəl] (a.) 超現實的，夢幻般的，離奇的
Running into Madonna at the supermarket was a surreal experience.

2) **comedian** [kə`midiən] (n.) 諧星，喜劇演員
Jim Carrey is my favorite comedian.

3) **inland** [`ɪn.lænd] (a.) 內陸的；(adv.) 往內地
The Black Sea is a large inland sea.

4) **marine** [mə`rin] (a.) 航運的，船舶的
There's a marine supply store near the harbor.

5) **overhead** [`ovɚ`hɛd] (a./n.) 經常費用 (的)
Their high overhead costs forced them to raise prices.

6) **lineup** [`laɪn.ʌp] (n.) 表演者名單，(球賽) 選手陣容。也可做 **line-up**
Our team has a strong lineup this season.

mean this—I'm probably unavailable. But thank you and I'm sorry ahead of time.

首先，我要謝謝今晚所有為我發言或表演的人，真是很美妙的陣容。你們在百忙中抽空過來，對我來說意義重大。你們若有人將來需要我為你們發言，事無分大小，我在此很認真的說，我可能沒空。但謝謝你們，我提前說抱歉了。

A Huge Debt of Gratitude
巨大的恩情債

One of the people you saw tonight to whom I owe a huge debt of gratitude is Mr. Adam McKay. Together, Adam and I have created [7]*Anchorman*, *Talladega Nights*, *Stepbrothers* and *The Other Guys*, a Broadway show and a comedy website. I would also not be standing here if it weren't for *Saturday Night Live* [8]**executive** producer Lorne Michaels.

各位今晚看到的其中一位是亞當麥凱先生，我對他感激不盡。亞當和我一起做過《銀幕大角頭》、《王牌飆風》、《爛兄爛弟》、《B咖戰警》和一檔百老匯秀，以及一個喜劇網站。若沒有《週六夜現場》的執行製作洛恩麥可斯，我也不會站在這裡。

Thank you, Lorne, for taking a chance on me and giving me the opportunity to be on *Saturday*

> " When you're stressed you eat ice cream, cake, chocolate and sweets. Why?
> Because stressed spelled backwards is desserts.
> Mind = Blown.
>
> 壓力很大時會吃冰淇淋、蛋糕、巧克力和糖果。為什麼？
> 因為有壓力的（stressed）這個字反過來拼就是點心（desserts）。
> 沒想到吧。

威爾法洛談壓力

Night Live, the show I always dreamed of being on. And finally, what makes tonight truly special is that I can share it with my family. I'm so grateful to all of you guys for your continued support and love for the things I do. But mostly I'd like to thank my lovely wife, Viveca.

謝謝你，洛恩，押寶在我身上，讓我有機會出演《週六夜現場》，那是我一直夢想出演的節目。最後，今晚真正特別的，是我能跟家人分享這個獎。我非常感謝你們一直以來對我所作所為的支持與愛護。但我最要感謝的是我的愛妻薇薇卡。

Saturday Night Live《週六夜現場》

簡稱 SNL 的《週六夜現場》於每週六深夜在美國 NBC 頻道現場直播，是美國電視史上獲艾美獎提名最多的節目，節目長度 90 分鐘，內容包羅萬象，從模仿秀、短劇到專訪，每週都會邀請不同的來賓加入，與節目固定班底一同演出。因內容輕鬆逗趣，經常惡搞政治人物、諷刺社會現象，在美國大受歡迎。從 1975 年開播至今，已經孕育出不少優秀的喜劇演員，像是艾迪墨菲（Eddie Murphy）、班史提勒（Ben Stiller）、麥克邁爾斯（Mike Myers）等，本篇主講人就是以固定演出 SNL 成名。

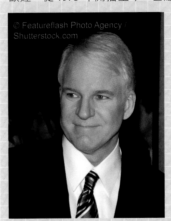

© Featureflash Photo Agency / Shutterstock.com

史提夫馬丁（Steve Martin）從 SNL 最早時期就開始參與演出，只要有他出的那集收視率就大暴增。他也是 SNL 最受歡迎的客串主持人，前後共被邀請 15 次，這個紀錄到近期才被亞歷克鮑德溫（Alec Baldwin，17 次）打破。

The Tonight Show《今夜秀》

這個 1954 年開播的深夜廣播／電視節目，是史上最長壽的脫口秀。主持期間最長的紀錄保持人，是從廣播橫跨電視的 Johnny Carson（1962-1992），然而拜電視普及所賜，目前大眾最熟悉的主持人應為傑雷諾（Jay Leno，主持期間為 1992-2009 及 2010-2014）。這個節目在美國電視界的地位極高，喜劇演員無不以坐上該節目主持椅為至高榮譽，大衛賴特曼（David Letterman）、傑雷諾、傑利賽菲爾德（Jerry Seinfeld）、艾倫狄珍妮（Ellen DeGeneres）及本書另一位主講者康南歐布萊恩（Conan O'Brien）均名列其中。

© Wikimedia Commons（NBC Television）

導演伍迪艾倫（Woody Allen）於 1964 年在強尼卡森的《今夜秀》接受訪問。

7) **anchorman** [ˈæŋkəˌmæn] (n.)（電視、廣播）新聞男主播
The reporter was promoted to anchorman after several years on the job.

8) **executive** [ɪɡˈzɛkjətɪv] (a.) 執行的，主管級的；(n.) 高階主管
Roberta works as an executive secretary.

位於華盛頓特區的林肯紀念堂、華盛頓紀念碑（高度近 170 公尺）、國會大廈（左至右），都在甘迺迪表演藝術中心附近。

Before I do that, however, I should really thank my first and second wives, Donna and Julie. Donna, what can I say? We were just too young when we got married. I mean literally too young, we were 13. Ah, [1]**heck**, you were 13, I was nine. I was in the third grade, and it wasn't right—or legal—but I hope you're well and I thank you for your support. As for Julie, you left me for Gary Busey, and I will never blame you for that, ever.

不過，在這之前，我應該好好威謝我的第一任和第二任妻子，唐娜和茱莉。唐娜，我能說什麼呢？我們當年結婚時都太年輕。我說年紀小是真的很小，我們只有 13 歲。哎，其實妳 13 歲，我 9 歲。我當時才三年級，這是不對的——也不合法——但我希望妳過得好，也謝謝妳的支持。還有茱莉，你為了蓋瑞布希（編註：美國性格男星。Donna 和 Julie 這兩位前妻都不存在，是威爾法洛胡謅的）離開我，我永遠不會為此怪妳。

 You Got a Big Mouth
你有個大嘴巴

Finally, Viveca, all I can say is thank you, and thank God I found you. You've given us three beautiful boys, and we have a wonderful life together. But I do have to say, sometimes you get a little [2]**lippy**, OK? You got a big LG mouth, and you like to run it. Now I'll tell you one thing, and one thing only, OK? Tonight is my night, all right? I love you, but I'm really sick of that big mouth of yours, OK? And I won't stand it, OK? Do you hear me? You look at me when I talk to you.

最後，薇薇卡，我能說的只有謝謝妳，感謝上帝讓我遇到妳。妳幫我們生了三個漂亮的兒子，我們一起過著美好的生活。但我不得不說，有時妳有一點愛頂嘴，好嗎？妳有個大嘴巴，喜歡我講一句妳回十句。現在我要告訴妳一件事，只有一件事，好嗎？今晚是我的大日子，好嗎？我愛妳，但我真的厭倦了妳的大嘴巴，好嗎？我不會再忍受，好嗎？妳聽到了嗎？我跟妳說話時，妳要看著我。（編註：威爾法洛開始咆哮，變得非常激動。是在故意模仿灑狗血的表演方式）

After the show, if I want to go on a [3]**bender** with Gwen Ifill and buy a couple of [4]**spearguns** and try to [5]**scale** the Washington Monument, I'm going to do it, OK? And there's nothing you can say to stop me. I love you.

節目結束後，我要是想跟格溫艾菲爾去喝個痛快，買魚矛槍爬到華盛頓紀念碑的尖頂上，我一定會去，好嗎？妳說什麼都阻止不了我，我愛妳。

魚矛槍 (speargun)

So once again, I thank you for this magnificent night and this amazing honor. And I want to thank the Kennedy Center for being one of the few places that [6]**upholds** comedy as what it truly is, an art form. Thank you and good night. Now you can play the music.

所以再次威謝各位，讓我擁有這美好的夜晚和無上的榮耀，我也要謝謝甘迺迪中心，這是少數推崇喜劇真正的價值，視其為藝術形式的地方。謝謝各位，晚安。可以放音樂了。

Official White House Photo by Pete Souza

2011 年 10 月 21 日，歐巴馬總統在白宮橢圓形辦公室向威爾法洛致賀，右邊是威爾法洛的夫人 Viveca Paulin。

1) **heck** [hɛk] (interj.) 感嘆語，表示驚訝、討厭或加強語氣，為 **hell** 的委婉語
Where the heck have you been?

2) **lippy** [ˈlɪpi] (a.) 愛頂嘴的
Don't get lippy with me, young lady!

3) **bender** [ˈbɛndə] (n.)（俚）飲酒作樂，喝得爛醉
Bill decided to quit drinking after his last bender.

4) **speargun** [ˈspɪrˌɡʌn] (n.)（水下用）魚矛槍
Have you ever been speargun fishing?

5) **scale** [skel] (v.) 攀登到頂點
The prisoners escaped by scaling the prison wall.

6) **uphold** [ʌpˈhold] (v.) 支持，維護
It's the duty of police officers to uphold the law.

Language Guide

dawn on sb. 赫然發現

dawn 當動詞有「破曉」的意思，後接介系詞 on 或 upon 再接人，就表示一個人「突然發現」、「終於明白了」、「第一次得知」。

A: I hear David recently started dating again.
我聽說大衛最近又開始跟人約會了。

B: Yeah. It finally dawned on him that his wife wasn't coming back.
是啊。他終於明白他太太不會回心轉意了。

inland marine insurance 內陸運輸險

主講人致詞時故意講些保險專業名詞來搞笑。marine insurance 是保障海運損失「海上運輸險」，inland marine insurance 雖然名字裡有 marine，但是只保障陸上及內陸航空一切事變及災害所致之毀損、滅失及費用的「內陸運輸險」。因為在過去只有保障海上運輸損失的 marine insurance，後來就成為「運輸險」的代名詞了。

Grammar Master

consider 用法

動詞 consider 有兩種意思，一是「考慮、細想」，另一個是「認為、當做」，用法不太一樣。consider 在本句 ...he's considered America's finest author and humorist.（…他被認為是美國最偉大的作家與幽默家。）中當「認為、當做」的意思，為被動用法，由 consider + O. + adj./N. 變化而來。

1. consider 當「認為」：

● consider + 受詞 + 受詞補語「把…認為是…」，受詞補語可以是形容詞或名詞，此句型常以被動式出現：

例 **Talking with your mouth full is considered rude.**
講話時嘴裡有食物是不禮貌的。[加形容詞]

後方接名詞時，等於 think of/refer to/regard/view...as...：

例 **I consider him a good friend.**
我把他視為好朋友。[加名詞]

注意：consider 不可以與 as 連用，這裡的 consider A B 其實是 consider A (to be) B 省略了 to be 而來。

● consider + it + adj. + that 子句 / to V「認為某事是…」：虛主詞 it 用來代替後面的 that 子句或 to V 所帶出的事件。

例 **I considered it odd that he always wore a hat.**
他老是戴一頂帽子讓我覺得很怪。

2. consider 當「考慮、細想」：

● consider + N/Ving：後方只能接名詞和動名詞 Ving 形式。

例 **Are you considering college?**
你考慮上大學嗎？[加名詞]

例 **We should consider buying a new car.**
我們應該考慮買一輛新車。[加 Ving]

overhead (expense) 經常費用

overhead (expense) 也叫「行政管理費」，是指開辦企業的固定經常費用，如水電、房租及行政管理人員的薪資…這類無法歸入特定部門或產品的支出。講稿中提到的 business overhead expense disability insurance（事業經常費用傷殘保險）是專給依賴少數幾人營運的小規模企業投保，以防這些人傷殘期間企業無法正常營運。

fall back on 回來依靠

fall back 是「後退，撤退」，fall back on 這個片語表示工作受挫之後，轉往另一種專長發展事業。

A: Why did your dad insist that you study accounting?
你爸爸為什麼堅持要你學會計？

B: So I have something to fall back on if I don't make it in Hollywood.
以防萬一我在好萊塢發展不順，能有個退路。

on one's behalf 為了某人 (做某事)

也可以說 in one's behalf、in / on behalf of sb.、in one's name。這個片語有兩種意思，本文的用法是「為了某人做某件事」、「為了某人的緣故」。

A: Are you sure it's safe to take a bus home this late?
你確定這麼晚搭公車回家安全嗎？

B: Yes. Don't worry on my behalf. It's perfectly safe.
確定。別為我擔心。絕對安全。

另一個意思是「做某人的代表」，請參見「小馬丁路德金恩博士演說」補充頁。

mean the world to (sb.) 對…意義重大

這個片語表示一樣東西（對某人）非常重要，經常用來感念別人施予的恩情。

A: Have you ever regretted having children?
你曾經後悔生小孩嗎？

B: No. My kids mean the world to me.
沒有。孩子是我的一切。

run (one's) mouth 頂撞

用來形容人喋喋不休，尤指不斷用言語頂撞他人。

A: I wish Eddie would stop running his mouth.
真希望艾迪不要再一直嗆別人了。

B: I know. If he keeps it up, he's gonna start a fight.
對呀。他再繼續這樣，有人要跟他打架了。

何謂美式幽默（American humor）？其實很難有明確定義，但看看馬克吐溫獎得獎人在台上的表演，就算還是不清楚美式幽默的定義，至少可以知道什麼是幽默了：威爾法洛演說一開頭大言不慚、自吹自擂，接著馬上幫自己漏氣，說自己根本分不清馬克吐溫跟肯德基爺爺；睜眼說瞎話也是重要的特色，像是說獎金有十億美金，以及自己有三任太太。捉弄聽眾是本篇最好笑的部分，法洛鋪陳一段從小熬夜看《今夜秀》的哏，最後破哏竟是夢想賣保險。諧仿八點檔誇張演技及最後對妻子說的那段話，膽敢把玩笑開到枕邊人身上去，還真是算他狠了。

Creating a Sense of Purpose

打造使命感

© Harvard University

Mark Zuckerberg's Harvard University Commencement Speech
馬克祖伯格哈佛大學畢業典禮演說

I'm honored to be with you today because, let's face it, you accomplished something I never could. If I LG get through this speech, it'll be the first time I actually finish something at Harvard. Class of 2017, congratulations!

今天很榮幸來參加你們的畢業典禮，因為，面對現實吧，你們達到了我從未達到的成就。我若熬過這場演講，這就是我第一次真正在哈佛完成一件事。**2017 年畢業班，恭喜！**

I'm an [1]**unlikely** speaker, not just because I LG dropped out, but because we're [2]**technically** in the same generation. We walked this yard less than a decade apart, studied the same ideas and slept through the same LG Ec10 lectures. We

may have taken different paths to get here, but today I want to share what I've learned about our generation and the world we're building together.

我是個出人意表的畢業典禮演講者，不只是因為我輟學，也因為嚴格來說，我跟你們是同輩。我進校園的時間跟你們相距不到十年，學習過同樣的概念，在同樣的經濟學概論課堂上呼呼大睡。我們可能經由不同的途徑來到這裡，但今天我想分享我在我們這一代、以及在我們一起打造的世界所學到的東西。

位於美國麻州查爾斯河畔的哈佛大學，是全世界最具威望的研究型大學之一，其法律及商業課程最為出名。

VOCABULARY 88

1) **unlikely** [ʌnˋlaɪklɪ] (a.) 意想不到的，不太可能的
Steve and Cindy make an unlikely couple.

2) **technically** [ˋtɛknɪklɪ] (adv.) 嚴格說來
Technically, nuts are a type of fruit.

3) **prank** [præŋk] (n.) 惡作劇
Billie likes playing pranks on his friends.

4) **going-away party** [ˋgoɪŋəˋwe ˋpɑrtɪ] (phr.) 歡送會
We threw Rob a going-away party before he left for France.

A Lot of Good Memories
許多美好的回憶

But first, the last couple of days have brought back a lot of good memories. How many of you remember exactly what you were doing when you got that e-mail telling you that you got into Harvard? I was playing Civilization and I ran downstairs, got my dad, and for some reason, his reaction was to video me opening the e-mail. That could've been a really sad video. I swear getting into Harvard is still the thing my parents are most proud of me for.

但首先，這幾天我想起許多美好的回憶。你們有多少人記得當你們收到哈佛的錄取通知電郵時，你們在做什麼？我當時在玩《文明帝國》，然後我跑下樓找我爸爸，不知為何，他的反應是拍攝我點開電郵的過程。那原本可能是令人難過的影片。我敢說，能被哈佛錄取，至今仍是我父母最引以為傲的事。

What about your first lecture at Harvard? Mine was Computer Science 121 with the incredible Harry Lewis. I was late so I threw on a T-shirt and didn't realize until afterwards it was inside out and backwards with my tag sticking out the front. I couldn't figure out why no one would talk to me—except one guy, KX Jin, he just went with it. We ended up doing our problem sets together, and now he runs a big part of Facebook. And that, Class of 2017, is why you should be nice to people.

你們在哈佛的第一堂課是哪個課程呢？我的是電資 121，教授是了不起的哈瑞路易斯（編註：電腦科學家、數學家，哈佛大學知名教授）。我當時遲到了，穿了一件 T 恤，後來才發現我的衣服不但內外穿反，前後也穿反，所以標籤在前面露出來。我不知道為什麼沒

人跟我講話，除了 KX 金，他並不介意。後來我們一起做分組作業，他現在臉書擔當大任。2017 年畢業班，這就是你該善待他人的原因。

But my best memory from Harvard was meeting Priscilla. I had just launched this [3]**prank** website Facemash, and the ad board wanted to "see me." Everyone thought I was going to get kicked out. My friends threw me a [4]**going-away** party. As luck would have it, Priscilla was at that party with her friend.

但我在哈佛最美好的回憶，就是認識普莉希拉。我當時架設惡作劇網站 Facemash，然後行政委員會表示想「見我」。大家都以為我要被踢出校門了。我的朋友還幫我辦了歡送派對。幸好當時普莉希拉（編註：後來成為他的妻子）跟她朋友出席了派對。

美國大學的課程代號

演講中提到的 Ec10 可解釋為 Economy 初級課程，也就是經濟學概論、經濟學原理之類的課程，因美國大學的「初級課程」會以 1 字頭編號，隨著年級（首位數字從 1 變到 2、3、4）及程度提升，數字會越大。也因此引申為某領域「最基礎的知識」，英文會稱之為…101。

Facemash

Zuckerberg 大二時入侵哈佛宿舍的門禁系統，取得學生大頭照，然後將照片兩兩並列，要大家票選哪一位比較有吸引力，軟體一上線反應還算熱烈，但很快就被學校關閉，Zuckerberg 被控以破壞學校資訊安全、侵犯隱私權、侵犯著作權，面臨退學處分，後來被撤銷。Zuckerberg 以 Facemash 為基礎繼續發展，後來成為 thefacebook.com。

problem set 分組討論

美國的大學生對 problem set 都不會陌生，教授每學期都會發兩三次分組討論作業，題目會有相當難度，要學生以一到兩週的時間討論解題，目的在於訓練學生運用課堂所學。最常出現在理工、數學、經濟、電腦等科目。

Mark Zuckerberg
馬克祖伯格

生於 1984 年，現為社群網站 Facebook 的董事長兼執行長。Mark Zuckerberg 從小即展現程式設計的天才，尤其擅長創作溝通工具及遊戲，高中時就被微軟高薪招攬，但他選擇進入哈佛，隨後於大二輟學，2004 年與哈佛大學同學 Dustin Moskovitz、Eduardo Saverin、Chris Hughes 共同創立 Facebook。2010 年被《時代雜誌》選為年度風雲人物，2016 年以 516 億美元打入富比世全球富豪榜第五名（打破最年輕前五大富豪紀錄），2017 年獲頒哈佛大學榮譽博士。

© Frederic Legrand - COMEO / Shutterstock.com

Savings 101

We met in line for the bathroom in the PfoHo Belltower, and in what must be one of the all-time romantic lines, I said: "I'm going to get kicked out in three days, so we need to go on a date quickly." Actually, any of you graduating can use that line. We've all started [1]**lifelong** friendships here, and some of us even families. That's why I'm so grateful to this place.

我們是在普福爾茨海默舍堂鐘塔排隊等上廁所時認識，然後我說了肯定是史上最浪漫的搭訕詞：「我三天後要被踢出校門了，所以我們要盡快約會。」其實你們畢業生都可以借用這句話。我們一輩子的友誼都是從這裡開始，有些甚至成為家人。所以我對這地方充滿感恩。

Finding Your Purpose Isn't Enough
尋找使命仍不夠

Today I want to talk about purpose. But I'm not here to give you the standard [2]**commencement** about finding your purpose. We're [3]**millennials**.

> Facebook was not originally created to be a company. It was built to accomplish a social mission—to make the world more open and connected.
>
> 臉書原本不是為了成立一家公司而設立。當初設立是為了達成一個社會使命——讓世界更加開放，更加彼此連結。
>
> 馬克祖伯格談臉書

> I think a lot of the time there isn't such a black-and-white difference between what's a platform and what's an app. It's really just like the most important apps become platforms.
>
> 我認為網路平台和應用軟體往往沒有非常大的差別。其實很像是最有用的應用軟體就會變成網路平台。
>
> 馬克祖伯格談網路平台和應用軟體

We'll try to do that [4]**instinctively**. Instead, I'm here to tell you finding your purpose isn't enough. The challenge for our generation is creating a world where everyone has a sense of purpose.

今天我想談談使命。但我不是來這裡講一場關於尋找使命的制式畢業演講。我們是千禧世代，我們憑本能就會尋找使命。我反而是來這裡告訴你們，尋找使命仍不夠。我們這一世代的挑戰，是打造一個大家都有使命感的世界。

One of my favorite stories is when John F. Kennedy visited the NASA space center, he saw a [5]**janitor** carrying a broom and he walked over and asked what he was doing. The janitor responded: "Mr. President, I'm helping put a man on the moon." Purpose is that sense that we are part of something bigger than ourselves, that we are needed, that we have something better ahead to work for. Purpose is what creates true happiness.

VOCABULARY 🎧 90

1) **lifelong** [ˈlaɪfˌlɔŋ] (a.) 一生的
The designer had a lifelong love of fashion.

2) **commencement** [kəˈmɛnsmənt] (n.) 畢業典禮
Do you know who's giving the commencement address?

3) **millennial** [mɪˈlɛnɪəl] (n.) 千禧世代的人；(a.) 千禧年的，一千年的
Millennials have a reputation for being lazy and spoiled.

4) **instinctively** [ɪnˈstɪŋktɪvli] (adv.) 憑直覺地，本能地。
形容詞為 **instinctive** [ɪnˈstɪŋktɪv]
Martha instinctively clutched her purse as the young men approached.

5) **janitor** [ˈdʒænɪtə] (n.) 工友
Does your apartment building have a janitor?

6) **automation** [ˌɔtəˈmeʃən] (n.) 機械自動化
Plant automation will result in the loss of hundreds of jobs.

7) **decline** [dɪˈklaɪn] (v./n.) 下跌，衰退
Wages have declined over the past several years.

8) **disconnected** [ˌdɪskəˈnɛktɪd] (a.) 與社會、現實脫節的
Ironically, too much time on social media makes people feel disconnected.

我最喜歡的故事之一，是約翰甘迺迪造訪太空總署太空中心時，看到一名工友拿著掃帚，於是走上前問他在做什麼。那位工友說：「總統先生，我在幫人類登上月球。」使命感就是我們都在參與比自己更重要的事、我們被需要、還有更好的事要去做的感覺。使命是真正幸福的來源。

You're graduating at a time when this is especially important. When our parents graduated, purpose reliably came from your job, your church, your community. But today, technology and [6]**automation** are eliminating many jobs. Membership in communities is [7]**declining**. Many people feel [8]**disconnected** and depressed, and are trying to 🛡 fill a void.

你們畢業的此時此刻使命尤其重要。我們的父母畢業時，使命主要來自工作、教會、社區。但現在，科技和自動化已經取代許多工作。參與社區事務的人數也在下降。許多人感到孤單和沮喪，都在努力填補心靈空虛。

Pforzheimer House 普福爾茨海默舍堂

被暱稱為 PfoHo [ˈfo͵ho] 的 Pforzheimer House 屬於哈佛大學（Harvard University）大學部哈佛學院（Harvard College）的 12 所學生舍堂（文中提到的 **Kirkland House** 也是其中之一），供大二以上學生住宿。舍堂除了提供住宿，也有師生休息室、宴會廳，以促進師生間的交流。PfoHo Belltower 是 Pforzheimer House 最大最豪華的區域之一，這裡的宴會廳有大酒吧，是學生狂歡的所在。

> " I'm interested to go deeper and study the positive and negative aspects of these technologies, and how best to use them in our services.
>
> 我想更深入研究這些科技所帶來的正向影響與反面效果，進而將科技更好地運用在臉書服務中。
>
> 馬克祖伯格談 2018 年新目標

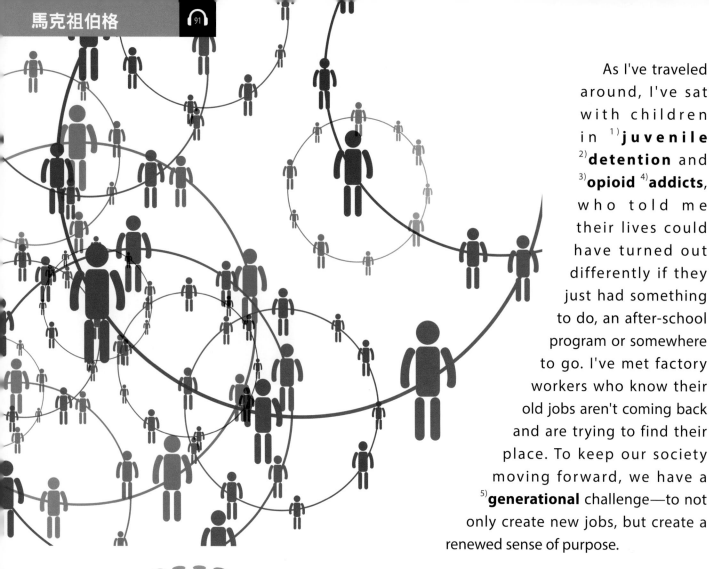

As I've traveled around, I've sat with children in ¹⁾**juvenile** ²⁾**detention** and ³⁾**opioid** ⁴⁾**addicts**, who told me their lives could have turned out differently if they just had something to do, an after-school program or somewhere to go. I've met factory workers who know their old jobs aren't coming back and are trying to find their place. To keep our society moving forward, we have a ⁵⁾**generational** challenge—to not only create new jobs, but create a renewed sense of purpose.

我四處旅行時，曾和少年拘留所裡的孩子以及毒癮者聊，他們告訴我，他們當初若有事做，比如課後活動或有地方可去，生命會變得不一樣。我認識了工廠工人，他們知道原先的工作回不來了，正努力找屬於自己的工作。為了推動社會前進，我們這一代正面臨挑戰，不僅要創造工作機會，還要重新打造使命感。

 All People Want to Connect
所有人都想建立關係

I remember the night I launched Facebook from my little dorm in 🄻🄶 Kirkland House. I went to Noch's with my friend K.X. I remember telling him I was excited to connect the Harvard community, but one day someone would connect the whole

❝ The question isn't, "What do we want to know about people?," It's, "What do people want to tell about themselves?"

問題不在於「我們想探知人們的哪些面向？」而是「人們想透露他們的哪些面向？」

馬克祖伯格談社群

VOCABULARY 🎧 92

1) **juvenile** [ˋdʒuvə͵naɪl] (a.) 少年的，幼稚的
The young offender was sent to juvenile hall.

2) **detention** [dɪˋtɛnʃən] (n.) 拘留，扣留
Several prisoners escaped from the detention center last night.

3) **opioid** [ˋopɪ͵ɔɪd] (n./a.) 鴉片類藥物（的）
The country is faced with a growing opioid crisis.

4) **addict** [ˋædɪkt] (n.) 有癮的人，癮蟲
Many drug addicts turn to crime to support their habits.

5) **generational** [͵dʒɛnəˋreʃənəl] (a.) 一個世代的
Family conflicts are often caused by generational differences.

6) **impact** [ˋɪmpækt] (n./v.) 影響，衝擊
The book had a huge impact on my thinking.

world. **The thing is**, it never even occurred to me that someone might be us. We were just college kids. We didn't know anything about that. There were all these big technology companies with resources. I just assumed one of them would do it. But this idea was so clear to us—that all people want to connect. So we just kept moving forward, day by day.

我記得我在柯克蘭宿舍的小房間創辦臉書的那晚。我跟朋友 **K.X.** 到皮諾丘披薩店（編註：**Noch's** 是當地人對 **Pinocchio's Pizza & Subs** 的簡稱），我記得我當時告訴他，我很興奮能讓哈佛社群互相建立關係，但有一天，有人會讓全世界互相建立關係。重點是，我完全沒想那會是我們。我們當時只是大學生，對於該怎麼做一無所知。當時有很多財力雄厚的大型科技公司，我只是以為其中一家公司會做。但我們當時的想法很清楚——所有人都想建立關係。於是我們一直不斷朝這目標邁進，每天往前邁進一點。

I know a lot of you will have your own stories just like this. A change in the world that seems so clear you're sure someone else will do it. But they won't. You will. But it's not enough to have purpose yourself. You have to create a sense of purpose for others. I found that out the hard way. You see, my hope was never to build a company, but to make an [6]**impact**. And as all these people started joining us, I just assumed that's what they cared about too, so I never explained what I hoped we'd build.

我知道你們許多人都有類似這種屬於自己的故事。這世界顯然該做某種改變，你們相信會有人去做。但其實沒有，是你們要去做。但自己有使命仍然不夠。你們要為其他人打造使命感。我是吃了些苦頭才領會的。要知道，我的願望本來不是要開公司，而是發揮影響力。然後有人陸續加入我們，我以為那也是他們關心的事，所以我從沒解釋我希望能發展出什麼。

A couple years in, some big companies wanted to buy us. I didn't want to sell. I wanted to see if we could connect more people. We were building the first News Feed, and I thought if we could just launch this, it could change how we learn about the world.

幾年後，一些大公司想要買下我們的網站，但我不想賣。我想看看我們能否讓更多人建立關係。我們當時正在建立第一個動態時報，我認為我們若能推出這功能，可以改變我們瞭解這世界的方式。

Nearly everyone else wanted to sell. Without a sense of higher purpose, this was the [7]**startup** dream come true. It tore our company apart. After one tense argument, an advisor told me if I didn't agree to sell, I would regret the decision for the rest of my life. Relationships were so [8]**frayed** that within a year or so every single person on the management team was gone.

當時幾乎其他每個人都想賣。在沒有更高的使命感下，那是新創企業夢想成真。我們的公司因此分裂。經過一場激烈爭論，一位顧問告訴我，我若不同意出售，我下半輩子都會後悔這個決定。因為人際關係太緊張，一年左右，管理團隊每個人都離開了。

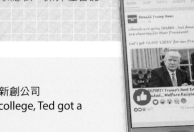

7) **startup** [ˈstɑrtˌʌp] (n.) 新創公司
After graduating from college, Ted got a job at a tech startup.

8) **frayed** [fred] (a.) 神經緊張的，快要崩潰的
My nerves were frayed after taking care of the kids all day.

> **❝** All of my friends who have younger siblings who are going to college or high school—my number one piece of advice is: You should learn how to program.
>
> 給每一個有弟弟、妹妹要上大學或高中的朋友——我的頭號建議就是：一定要學會程式設計。
>
> *馬克祖伯格談必要技能*

That was my hardest time leading Facebook. I believed in what we were doing, but I felt alone. And worse, it was my fault. I wondered if I was just wrong, an [1]**imposter**, a 22 year-old kid who had no idea how the world worked. Now, years later, I understand that is how things work with no sense of higher purpose. It's up to us to create it so we can all keep moving forward together.

那是我帶領臉書最艱難的時期。我當時相信我們在做的事，但我覺得孤單。更糟的是，那都是因為我的錯。我懷疑自己是不是錯了，一個冒牌貨，一個22歲、不知道天高地厚的小屁孩。但幾年下來，現在我懂了，要是沒有更高的使命感，就會是這種情況。我們要打造使命感，這樣才能一起向前邁進。

Every Generation Has Its Defining Works
每個世代都有屬於自己的偉業

Our generation will have to deal with tens of millions of jobs replaced by automation like self-driving cars and trucks. But we have the potential to do so much more together. Every generation has its defining works. More than 300,000 people worked to put a man on the moon—including

that janitor. Millions of volunteers [2]**immunized** children around the world against [3]**polio**. Millions of more people built the Hoover Dam and other great projects.

我們的世代要應付數千萬個工作機會被自動化取代，比如自動駕駛汽車和貨車。但我們有潛力一起做更多事。每一個世代都有屬於自己的偉業。一人登陸月球，背後有三十萬人的努力，包括那位工友。有數百萬義工為世界各地幼童施打小兒麻痺症疫苗。更有數百萬人建造胡佛水壩等其他偉大工程。

These projects didn't just provide purpose for the people doing those jobs, they gave our whole country a sense of pride that we could do great things. Now it's our turn to do great things. I know, you're probably thinking: I don't know how to build a dam, or get a million people involved in anything. But let me tell you a secret: No one does when they begin. Ideas don't come out fully formed. They only become clear as you work on them. You just have to get started.

這些計畫不只為做這些工作的人提供使命，也帶給我們整個國家榮耀感，讓我們知道自己能做偉大的事。現在輪到我們去做偉大的事

> **❝** People can be really smart or have skills that are directly applicable, but if they don't really believe in it, then they are not going to really work hard.
>
> 有些人絕頂聰明或擁有一技之才，但如果他們不相信自己在做的事，就不會太努力工作。
>
> *馬克祖伯格談工作*

---

1) **imposter** [ɪmˋpɑstə] (n.) 冒充者，騙子。也拼做**impostor**
The imposter was arrested for pretending to be a police officer.

2) **immunize** [ˋɪmjəˏnaɪz] (v.) （預防接種）使免疫
Have you been immunized for yellow fever?

3) **polio** [ˋpolɪo] (n.) 小兒麻痺
Polio is still a common disease in Africa.

4) **inadequate** [ɪnˋædəkwɪt] (a.) 不夠格的，不能勝任的
Dan's successful older brother makes him feel inadequate.

5) **idealistic** [aɪˏdiəˋlɪstɪk] (a.) 滿懷理想的，理想主義的
People tend to be more idealistic when they are younger.

6) **misunderstand** [ˏmɪsʌndəˋstænd] (v.) 誤解。名詞為 **misunderstanding** [ˏmɪsʌndəˋstændɪŋ]
I told him the meeting was today, but I think he misunderstood.

了。我知道，你們大概在想：我不會建造水壩，也不知如何動員一百萬人參與任何事。但讓我告訴你們一個祕密：沒有人在開始做的時候就有先見之明。想法一開始都不太成形，只有付諸行動才會越來越清晰。你只需要開始。

If I had to understand everything about connecting people before I began, I never would have started Facebook. Movies and pop culture get this all wrong. The idea of a single eureka moment is a dangerous lie. It makes us feel 4)**inadequate** since we haven't had ours. It prevents people with seeds of good ideas from getting started.

如果我必須先瞭解關於建立社群的一切才能創業，那我就永遠不會創辦臉書了。不論是電影或流行文化都搞錯了。靈光一現是危險的謊言。那讓我們覺得自己不夠格，因為我們沒有靈光一現的感覺，這會阻礙醞釀著創意種子的人開始付諸行動。

It's good to be 5)**idealistic**. But be prepared to be 6)**misunderstood**. Anyone working on a big vision will get called crazy, even if you end up right. Anyone working on a complex problem will get blamed for not fully understanding the challenge, even though it's impossible to know everything 7)**up front**. Anyone taking 8)**initiative** will get criticized for moving too fast, because there's always someone who wants to slow you down.

理想主義是好的，但要做好被誤解的心理準備。努力實踐遠大願景的人都會被稱為瘋子，就算最後證明你是對的。努力解決複雜問題

的人都會被責怪未充分瞭解其中的困難，就算不可能事先知道每件事。開創先河的人都會被批評太過躁進，因為總是有人想拖慢你的腳步。

In our society, we often don't do big things because we're so afraid of making mistakes that we ignore all the things wrong today if we do nothing. The reality is, anything we do will have issues in the future. But that can't keep us from starting.

在這個社會，我們往往不做大事，因為我們害怕犯錯，只要我們什麼都不做，就能忽略今天所有的問題。但事實上，我們現在做任何事，未來都會衍生問題。但我們不能因此原地踏步。

66 We look for people who are passionate about something. In a way, it almost doesn't matter what you're passionate about.

我們找的是對事物有熱情的人。可以說，幾乎是不論對什麼有熱情都好。

馬克祖伯格談人才

LG

Eureka! 我發現了！

讓 Eureka! 這個希臘文感嘆詞名流青史的人，就是偉大數學家阿基米德（Archimedes，西元前 287-212 年）。話說有一天他在泡澡時，看到浴缸裡的水位因他浸入而上升，突然靈光一現理解到「浮體原理」，解決了他正在苦惱的問題：如何幫國王測定王冠的黃金純度。他實在太興奮了，跳出浴缸光著身子就跑到街上大喊 Eureka! Eureka!

7) **up front** [ʌp frʌnt] (phr.) 一開始，預先
The full cost of treatment must be paid up front.

8) **initiative** [ɪˋnɪʃətɪv] (n.) 進取心，首創精神
Employees who show leadership and initiative will be promoted to management.

Let's Do Big Things
我們來做大事

So what are we waiting for? It's time for our generation-defining public works. How about stopping climate change before we destroy the planet, and getting millions of people involved manufacturing and installing solar panels? How about curing all diseases and asking volunteers to track their health data and share their **LG** genomes? Today we spend 50 times more treating people who are sick than we spend finding cures so people don't get sick in the first place. That makes no sense. We can fix this. How about [1)]**modernizing** democracy so everyone can vote online, and [2)]**personalizing** education so everyone can learn?

那我們還等什麼？我們這個世代該找出屬於自己的公共事務了。我們何不在毀滅地球前阻止氣候變遷，讓數百萬人開始製造並安裝太陽能板？何不治癒所有疾病，並請志願者追蹤自己的健康數據和分享基因組？比起尋找處方讓大家打一開始就不要生病，我們現在投入五十倍的資金在治療病患。這根本不合理。我們可以改正這個問題。何不將民主制度現代化，讓大家都能上網投票，並將教育個人化，好讓大家都能學習？

These achievements are within our reach. Let's do them all in a way that gives everyone in our society a role. Let's do big things, not only to create progress, but to create purpose. So taking on big meaningful projects is the first thing we can do to create a world where everyone has a sense of purpose.

LG

genome 基因組

指一個生物體的染色體當中完整的 DNA 序列。分享基因組協助建立詳盡的人類遺傳變異目錄的意義，在於醫界能據此研究為何有些人較易罹患某種疾病，有助於最終找出預防及治療的方法。

這些成就是我們能做到的。讓我們社會中的每人都參與這些任務。讓我們做大事，不但要創造進步，也要打造使命。所以，挑戰有意義的重大任務是我們首先要做的事，這樣才能打造大家都有使命感的世界。

Change starts local. Even global changes start small—with people like us. In our generation, the struggle of whether we connect more, whether we achieve our biggest opportunities, **LG** comes down to this—your ability to build communities and create a world where every single person has a sense of purpose. Class of 2017, you are graduating into a world that needs purpose. It's up to you to create it. Congratulations, Class of '17! Good luck out there.

改變是從在地開始，就算全球性的改變也是從小地方開始，由你我開始。在我們這個世代，我們是否能跟更多人建立關係、是否能把握最大的機會，這些努力歸根究底要看的就是──你建立社群的能力，以及打造每個人都有使命感的世界的能力。**2017 年畢業班**，你們畢業後將進入一個需要使命的世界。創造使命就看你們的了。恭喜，**2017 年畢業班**！祝入社會後一切好運。

VOCABULARY 96

1) **modernize** [ˈmɑdən͵aɪz] (v.)
（使）現代化
The government has announced plans to modernize the army.

2) **personalize** [ˈpɝsnəl͵aɪz] (v.) 使個人化
Are employees allowed to personalize their cubicles?

get through 熬過

這裡表示自己（或是陪伴別人）度過一個艱難的過程。

A: What's your secret to getting through final exams?
你熬過期末考的秘訣是什麼？

B: Lots and lots of coffee!
喝很多很多咖啡！

drop out 退學，退出

drop 這個字有很多用法，除了 drop out 外，常見使用 drop 的片語有：drop by（非正式的拜訪，順路拜訪）、drop a line（寫信）、drop dead（突然死亡，口語上也用來詛咒人去死）、drop off（入睡；減少，下降）。

A: So how was the marathon?
馬拉松比賽跑得怎麼樣？

B: Not so great—I dropped out halfway through.
不太好，我跑到一半就退出了。

bring back 勾起回憶

這個片語的用法很多，演講中意指讓人「回想起過去的事情」。

A: I thought you'd totally forgotten about your ex-boyfriend.
我以為妳已經完全忘了妳那前男友。

B: So did I, but seeing him again brought it all back.
我自己也以為，但再次見到他，之前的回憶都回來了。

關係副詞 when

關係副詞共有四個：when, where, why 與 how，皆是由「介系詞 + 關係代名詞 which」而來，本句 You're graduating at a time when this is especially important. 關係副詞 when 就相當於 at which（in which 或 on which），是用來修飾前方表時間的名詞 a time。這裡的 time 是可數名詞，指「某個時刻」。

- when = in which

例 **The author doesn't mention the year in which the story takes place.**
作者沒提到故事發生的年份。

- when = on which

例 **Good Friday is the day on which Jesus died on the cross.**
聖週五是耶穌被釘死於十字架上的那一天。

- when = at which

例 **Did you record the time at which the sample was taken?**
你有記錄採集樣本是在哪一天嗎？

go with it 順其自然，不在意

可以表示不論好壞全部接受。也可以說 go with the flow。

A: I'm really nervous about my date with Jason.
要跟傑森約會讓我好緊張。

B: My advice is just relax and go with it.
我的建議是順其自然。

as luck would have it 運氣就是這麼好

這個片語可用於正面語氣，表示「就是這麼好運」。

A: What did you do when you ran out of gas?
你汽車沒油那時是怎麼處理的？

B: As luck would have it, there was a gas station nearby.
運氣有夠好，附近剛好有加油站。

也可用反諷的語氣表示「真是有夠歹運」。

A: Your husband caught you cheating on him?
妳老公抓到你劈腿？

B: Yeah. As luck would have it, he came home from work early.
對啊。真是有夠倒霉，他提早下班回家。

fill a void 填補心靈空虛

也會說 fill the void。void 是「空缺，空間」，也有「空虛，寂寞」的意思。因此 fill a/the void 可以表示「遞補空缺」，也可以表示「填補心靈空虛」。

A: How did Christopher become an alcoholic?
克里斯多福怎麼會變成酒鬼？

B: After his wife died, he started drinking to fill the void.
妻子過世後，他就開始借酒澆愁。

The thing is... 問題是…

後面接藉口或是解釋，為口語用法；也可強調後接的事物。

A: Can you pick me up after work tonight?
今晚下班可以來接我嗎？

B: The thing is, my car's in the shop.
問題是，我的車子送修。

come down to... （關鍵）在於…，歸結於…

慣用語 come down to sth. 表示「體認到最關鍵、最重要的事是…」。

A: I can't decide which TV to buy—I really like both of them.
我沒辦法決定要買哪一台電視，兩台我都很喜歡。

B: Well, I guess it comes down to which is the best value for the money.
嗯，我想最終要看哪一台比較物超所值吧。

Mark Zuckerberg 從唸大學時小試身手差點被退學，到草創 Facebook 被人控告剽竊創意（後來和解），到堅持不賣公司搞到眾叛親離，年紀輕輕的他浪裡來火裡去都沒在怕。他曾說過一段話：Move fast and break things. Unless you are breaking stuff, you are not moving fast enough.（快速移動，搞點破壞。若沒有鬧出亂子，就是移動不夠快速。）就是他創業過程的最佳註腳。

Your Dream Will Change

夢想會改變

Conan O'Brien's Dartmouth Commencement Speech
康納歐布萊恩的達特茅斯學院畢業演說

Before I begin, I must point out that behind me sits a highly admired president of the United States and [1]**decorated** war hero while I, a cable television talk show host, has been chosen to stand here and [2]**impart** wisdom. I pray I never witness a more damning example of what is wrong with America today.

在我開始前，我必須點出，坐在我後面的是備受尊崇的美國總統兼受勳戰爭英雄（編註：老布希），而我，只是有線電視台的脫口秀主持人，被選中站在這裡傳授智慧。我祈禱關於美國不太正常一事，我永遠不要看到比這更明顯的範例。

© lev radin / Shutterstock.com

The Value of a College Diploma
大學文憑的價值

Graduates, [3]**faculty**, parents, relatives, [4]**undergraduates**, and old people that just come to these things: Good morning and congratulations to the Dartmouth Class of 2011. Today, you have achieved something special, something only 92 percent of Americans your age will ever know: a college diploma. That's right, with your college diploma you now have a [5]**crushing** advantage over eight percent of the [6]**workforce**. I'm talking about [7]**dropout** losers like Bill Gates, Steve Jobs, and Mark Zuckerberg. [8]**Incidentally**, speaking of Mr. Zuckerberg, only

VOCABULARY 98

1) **decorated** [ˋdɛkəˏretɪd] (a.) 功勳彪炳的，得到很多勳章的
The highly decorated pilot died on a combat mission.

2) **impart** [ɪmˋpɑrt] (v.) 傳授，透露
Parents have a duty to impart morals to their children.

3) **faculty** [ˋfækəltɪ] (n.)（高等院校、學系）全體教師（和行政人員）
Students and faculty are invited to attend the lecture.

4) **undergraduate** [ˏʌndɚˋgrædʒuɪt] (n./a.) 大學生（的），**graduate** 即「畢業生」
All undergraduates are required to take at least one science course.

5) **crushing** [ˋkrʌʃɪŋ] (a.) 嚴厲的，壓倒的
The death of their son was a crushing blow.

6) **workforce** [ˋwɝkˏfɔrs] (n.) 勞動力，勞動人口
Millions left the workforce during the recession.

at Harvard would someone have to invent a [9]**massive** social network just to talk with someone in the next room.

畢業生、教職員、家長、親戚、大學生，和就愛出席這類場合的老人家：早安並恭喜達特茅斯學院的 2011 年畢業班。今天，你們達成特殊成就，只有 92% 的同齡美國人擁有：大學文憑。沒錯，有了大學文憑，你們相較 8% 的勞動人口，有決定性優勢。我說的是輟學的魯蛇，例如比爾蓋茲、史提夫賈伯斯和馬克祖克柏。順帶說一下，說到祖克柏先生，只有在哈佛才會有人為了跟隔壁房間的人講話發明一個鋪天蓋地的社群網站。

Life Is Not Fair
人生不公平

My first job as your commencement speaker is to illustrate that life is not fair. For example, you have worked tirelessly for four years to earn the diploma you'll be receiving this weekend. And Dartmouth is giving me the same degree for interviewing the fourth lead in *Twilight*. Another example that life is not fair: If it does rain, the powerful rich people on stage get the tent. Deal with it.

身為你們的畢業典禮演講者，我第一件事要說明的，就是人生是不公平的。比如說，你們孜孜不倦努力四年才能取得本週末會收到的文憑。但我只是採訪了《暮光之城》排名第四的主角（編註：第一主角是演高中女孩 Bella 的 Kristen Stewart，第二主角是演吸血鬼 Edward 的 Robert Pattinson，第三主角是演狼人 Jacob 的 Taylor Lautner，第四主角是誰就沒人說得清了），達特茅斯學院就給我相同的學位。另一個人生不公平的例子是，現在若是下雨，只有臺上有錢有勢的人有棚子。面對現實吧。

Though some of you may see me as a [10]**celebrity**, you should know that I once sat where you sit. Literally. Late last night I [11]**snuck** out here and sat in every seat. I did it to prove a point: I am not bright and I have a lot of free time. But this is a wonderful occasion and it is great to be here in New Hampshire, where I am getting an

[12]**honorary** degree and all the legal fireworks I can fit in the trunk of my car.

You know, New Hampshire is such a special place. When I arrived I took a deep breath of this crisp New England air and thought, "Wow, I'm in the state that's next to the state where Ben and Jerry's ice cream is made."

你們其中或許有些視我為名人，但你們要知道我也曾坐在你的位子。我說真的，我昨晚偷偷溜來這裡，坐了每個座位。我這麼做是為了證明：我不聰明，而且很閒。但這是很美妙的場合，能來到新罕布夏州真的很棒，我在此獲得榮譽學位，還有滿滿一整個後車廂的合法鞭炮（編註：鞭炮在美國大多地區都為非法，在新罕布夏州則為合法）。你們知道，新罕布夏州真是很特別的地方。我到這裡時，深深吸了一口新英格蘭冷冽清新的空氣，心想：「哇，我所在的這州，正是班傑利冰淇淋公司發源地的隔壁州。」

© Keith Homan / Shutterstock.com

班傑利冰淇淋（Ben and Jerry's）1978 年創立於佛蒙特州（Vermont），當地以乳製品和楓糖漿聞名。

© Kathy Hutchins / Shutterstock.com

Conan O'Brien
康納歐布萊恩

生於 1963 年，美國脫口秀主持人。就讀哈佛大學時曾擔任《哈佛諷刺家》*The Harvard Lampoon* 雜誌社長，畢業後前往好萊塢，從事喜劇影集編劇。後遷往紐約，為《周末夜現場》*Saturday Night Live* 和卡通《辛普森家庭》*The Simpsons* 編劇，1993 ～ 2009 年在 NBC 電視台主持脫口秀《康南歐布萊恩深夜秀》*Late Night with Conan O'Brien*，進而成為《康南歐布萊恩今夜秀》*The Tonight Show with Conan O'Brien* 主持人，卻只主持了 7 個月就被傑雷諾（Jay Leno）搶走飯碗。康南歐布萊恩本篇演講，就是在講這段失意的經歷。

---

7) **dropout** [ˋdrɑpˏaʊt] (n.) 中輟生
It's hard for high school dropouts to find good jobs.

8) **incidentally** [ˏɪnsəˋdɛntəlɪ] (adv.) 順帶一提
Incidentally, I know another good Thai restaurant you should try.

9) **massive** [ˋmæsɪv] (a.) 巨大的，龐大的
The bus was crushed by a massive boulder.

10) **celebrity** [səˋlɛbrɪtɪ] (n.) 名人，名流
Have you heard the latest gossip about that celebrity?

11) **sneak** [snik] (v.) 偷偷地走，溜
動詞三態：**sneak, snuck** [snʌk]**, snuck**
The boys snuck into the movie theater without paying.

12) **honorary** [ˋɑnəˏrɛrɪ] (a.) 名譽的（學位、職位，稱號等）
The author was awarded an honorary degree.

> *Starbucks says they are going to start putting religious quotes on cups. The very first one will say, Jesus! This cup is expensive!*
>
> 星巴克說打算開始在杯子上印宗教語錄。第一句要印的就是：「耶穌啊！這杯還真貴！」

康納歐布萊恩笑談星巴克

註：Jesus! 為表示驚訝的語助詞，同「天哪！」

But ^{LG} don't get me wrong, I take my task today very seriously. When I got the call two months ago to be your speaker, I decided to prepare with the same intensity many of you have devoted to an important term paper. So late last night, I began. I drank two cans of Red Bull, ¹⁾**snorted** some ^{LG} Adderall, played a few hours of *Call of Duty*, and then opened my ²⁾**browser**. I think Wikipedia ^{LG} put it best when they said "Dartmouth College is a private ^{LG} Ivy League University in Hanover, New Hampshire, United States." Thank you and good luck.

紅牛（Red Bull）是源自泰國的澳洲品牌，是全球銷量最大的能量飲料。
© Baranov E / Shutterstock.com

但請別誤會，我今天是很認真對待我的任務。兩個月前我接到請我演講的電話時，我決定認真準備講稿，就像你們準備重要的期末報告一樣。所以我昨天深夜，開始臨時抱佛腳。我喝了兩罐紅牛，吸了一些阿得拉興奮劑，玩了幾小時《決勝時刻》，然後才打開瀏覽器。我想維基百科寫的已經是最好的了：「達特茅斯學院是位在美國新罕布夏州漢諾瓦的私立常春藤大學。」謝謝大家，祝福各位。

Fear of Failure
失敗的恐懼

Eleven years ago, I gave an address to a graduating class at Harvard. I haven't spoken at a graduation since because I thought I had nothing left to say. But then 2010 came. And now I'm here, 3,000 miles from my home, because I learned a hard but profound lesson last year and I'd like to share it with you. In 2000, I told graduates," Don't be afraid to fail." Well now I'm here to tell you that, though you should not fear failure, you should do your very best to avoid it. ^{LG} Nietzsche famously said "Whatever doesn't kill you makes you stronger." But what he failed to stress is that it almost kills you. Disappointment stings, and for ³⁾**driven**, successful people like yourselves it is ⁴⁾**disorienting**. What Nietzsche should have said is "Whatever doesn't kill you makes you watch a lot of Cartoon Network and drink mid-price ^{LG} Chardonnay at 11 in the morning."

> *Today I interviewed a squirrel in my backyard and then threw to commercial. Somebody help me.*
>
> 我今天在後院訪問了一隻松鼠，然後說要進廣告。誰來救救我。

康納歐布萊恩的第一條推文

VOCABULARY 🎧100

1) **snort** [snɔrt] (v.)（俚）（用鼻子）吸食（毒品）
The rapper was caught snorting cocaine in his car.

2) **browser** [ˈbraʊzɚ] (n.) 瀏覽器
Which browser do you prefer using?

3) **driven** [ˈdrɪvən] (a.) 奮發圖強的，積極進取的
You have to be driven to succeed in business.

4) **disorienting** [dɪsˈɔriəntɪŋ] (a.) 讓人暈頭轉向的。動詞為 **disorient** [dɪsˈɔriənt]
I found the movie's lack of plot disorienting.

5) **nurture** [ˈnɝtʃɚ] (v.) 栽培，養育
Parents have a duty to nurture and protect their children.

> According to a new survey, 40 percent of adults in Mexico say they would move to the United States if they got a chance. The number would have been higher, but the other 60 percent already live here.

根據一則新調查，四成的墨西哥成年人表示如果有機會，會想移居美國。數字原本應該更高，但其他六成已經住這裡了。

康納歐布萊恩笑談墨西哥移民

Friedrich Nietzsche
尼采

1844~1900，德國哲學家，存在主義（existentialism）大師，存在主義是一種貶抑理性的哲學思想，認為人生在世的意義並非理性可以推知闡明，強調個人的主觀經驗才是一切的最高準則，同時也認為人擁有絕對的選擇自由，沒有義務要遵守某個道德標準或宗教信仰，尼采就提出過「上帝已死」的言論，一語道盡存在主義者對有神論的反對態度。

Chardonnay 夏多內葡萄

原產自法國勃根地，因這個品種的葡萄易於栽種、產量豐富，被廣泛種植於美國加州」澳中智利、中國各地，而且隨著不同的風土能釀出多變風味，成為全球最受歡迎的白葡萄酒種類，是白葡萄酒愛好者高貴不貴的選擇。

11 年前，我在哈佛為一個畢業班發表演說。從那時候起我從未在畢業典禮上演講，因為我覺得該說的都說了。但過了 2010 年。我現在來到這裡，距離我家三千英里，因為我去年得到慘重但深刻的教訓，我想跟各位分享。2000 年時，我告訴畢業生：「不要害怕失敗。」現在我在此告訴你們，雖然不該害怕失敗，但應該努力避免失敗。尼采說過很有名的一句話：「毀滅不了你的事會讓你更強大。」但他沒強調的是，這種事會差點要你的命。失望的感覺刺痛人心，對於像你們這樣發奮圖強的成功人士來說，會讓人迷失方向。尼采應該要說：「毀滅不了你的事會讓你一直看卡通頻道，早上 11 點就開始喝不太貴的夏多內白酒。」

Now, by definition, commencement speakers at an Ivy League college are considered successful. But a little over a year ago, I experienced a profound and very public disappointment. I did not get what I wanted, and I left a system that had [5] **nurtured** and helped define me for the better part of 17 years.

常春藤盟校畢業典禮的演講者理所當然被視為成功人士。但一年多前，我經歷深刻的失意且眾所皆知。我沒得到所想要的，反而離開了培育我，幫助我成名的體系，這是我待了快 17 年的地方。

My Most Satisfying Year
我最滿意的一年

But then something [1]**spectacular** happened. I started trying things. I grew a strange, [2]**cinnamon** beard. I dove into the world of social media. I started [3]**tweeting** my comedy. I **LG** threw together a national tour. I played the guitar. I did [4]**stand-up**, wore a skin-tight blue leather suit, recorded an album, made a [5]**documentary**, and frightened my friends and family. Ultimately, I abandoned all [6]**preconceived** [7]**perceptions** of my career path and took a job on **LG** basic cable with a network most famous for showing [8]**reruns**. I did a lot of silly, [9]**unconventional**, [10]**spontaneous** and seemingly [11]**irrational** things and guess what: With the exception of the blue leather suit, it was the most satisfying year of my professional life. To this day I still don't understand exactly what happened, but I have never had more fun, been more challenged—and this is important— had more [12]**conviction** about what I was doing.

但接下來發生了令人驚奇的事，我開始嘗試一些東西。我開始留奇怪的肉桂色鬍子。我深入社群媒體的世界，用推特發表我的笑話，展開全國巡迴，我彈吉他，單人上台表演，穿著緊身藍皮西裝，錄專輯，拍紀錄片，把我的朋友和家人都嚇壞了。最後，我放棄了所有對我職涯之路先入為主的認知，接下基本有線電視台的工作，其所屬聯播網以重播節目聞名。我做了很多愚蠢、不合傳統、隨性，看起來極為荒謬的事，猜猜看怎麼樣：除了藍色皮西裝之外，這是我專業生涯中最令人滿意的一年。到現

在我仍不懂到底發生什麼事，但我從未比這時候更開心、更覺得具有挑戰──重要的是──我更相信自己在做的事。

How could this be true? Well, it's simple: There are few things more [13]**liberating** in this life than having your worst fear realized. I went to college with many people who prided themselves on knowing exactly who they were and exactly where they were going. At Harvard, five different guys in my class told me that they would one day be president of the United States. Four of them were later killed in motel shoot-outs. Your path at 22 will not necessarily be your path at 32 or 42. One's dream is constantly evolving, rising and falling, changing course. This happens in every

> " The Canadian government continues to say they will not help us if we go to war with Iraq. However, the prime minister of Canada said he'd like to help, but he's pretty sure that last time he checked, Canada had no army.

加拿大政府仍說如果我們（美國）出兵伊拉克，他們不會支援。然而，加國總理說他很想幫忙，但他很確定他上次確認時，加拿大沒有軍隊。

康納歐布萊恩笑談加拿大

VOCABULARY 102

1) **spectacular** [spɛkˋtækjələ] (a.) 精彩的，壯觀的
The sunsets on the island were spectacular.

2) **cinnamon** [ˋsɪnəmən] (a.) 肉桂（色）的，（毛髮）紅色的
I'm thinking of dying my hair cinnamon.

3) **tweet** [twit] (v.) 用推特發出短訊；(n.) 推特短訊
President Trump likes tweeting to the American public.

4) **stand-up** [ˋstænd.ʌp] (n.) 單口相聲，單人脫口秀
Many actors started their careers doing stand-up.

5) **documentary** [.dɑkjəˋmɛntəri] (n.) 紀錄片
Can you recommend a good documentary on the Vietnam War?

6) **preconceived** [.prikənˋsivd] (a.) 已先入為主的，既有成見的
You shouldn't let preconceived ideas affect your judgment.

7) **perception** [pəˋsɛpʃən] (n.) 認知，看法
There is a public perception that the government is incompetent.

8) **rerun** [ˋri.rʌn] (n.) 重播（節目）
There's nothing but reruns on TV tonight.

> **"** I just want to say to the kids out there watching: you can do anything you want in life, unless Jay Leno wants to do it too.
>
> 我想對電視機前的孩子們說：你這輩子想做什麼都可以，只要不是傑雷諾也想要的就可以。

康納歐布萊恩笑談人生目標

沉迷於追逐夢想 **25** 年後，我的夢想在 **47** 歲改變了。幾十年來在演藝界，每位喜劇演員最終的目標都是主持《今夜秀》。那就像聖杯，跟許多人一樣，我以為達到那個目標就代表我成功了。但事實並非如此，沒有特定的工作或職業目標能界定我，也不該用那些來界定你。

In 2000, I told graduates to not be afraid to fail, and I still believe that. But today I tell you that whether you fear it or not, disappointment will come. The beauty is that through disappointment you can gain [15]**clarity**, and with clarity comes conviction and true [16]**originality**.

在 **2000** 年，我告訴畢業生不要怕失敗，我現在仍相信這點。但今天我要告訴各位，不論你怕不怕，人生難免會失意。其中的妙處是，透過失意你的頭腦會更清晰，藉此獲得信念和真正的創造力。

job, but because I have worked in comedy for 25 years, I can probably speak best about my own profession.

這怎麼可能是真的？嗯，很簡單：在人生中，沒幾件事比起最大的恐懼成真，更令人感到解脫了。我在大學時，許多同學清楚知道自己是什麼樣的人，有明確的目標，也引以為傲。在哈佛，我班上有五人告訴我，他們有一天會當上美國總統。其中四人後來在汽車旅館的槍戰中被殺害。你們 22 歲時走的道路，未必是 32 歲或 42 歲時會走的道路。人的夢想是一段不斷起伏變化的過程。每樣工作都是如此，但因為我在喜劇界 25 年了，我或許用自己的專業說明最好。

At the age of 47, after 25 years of [14]**obsessively** pursuing my dream, that dream changed. For decades, in show business, the ultimate goal of every comedian was to host *The Tonight Show*. It was the LG Holy Grail, and like many people I thought that achieving that goal would define me as successful. But that is not true. No specific job or career goal defines me, and it should not define you.

9) **unconventional** [ˌʌnkənˈvɛnʃənəl] (a.) 不依慣例的，不合常規的
Drew Barrymore had a very unconventional upbringing.

10) **spontaneous** [spɑnˈtenɪəs] (a.) 隨興的，順其自然的
Jerry likes girls who are fun and spontaneous.

11) **irrational** [ɪˈræʃənəl] (a.) 不理性的，不明事理的
Don's parents are worried about his increasingly irrational behavior.

12) **conviction** [kənˈvɪkʃən] (n.) 信念，堅信
His conviction that the death was a murder proved correct.

13) **liberating** [ˈlɪbəretɪŋ] (a.) 讓人感到解脫的
Arthur says he finds retirement very liberating.

14) **obsessively** [əbˈsɛsɪvli] (adv.) 過分關心地，執念地，過分地
Why are so many people obsessively taking selfies these days?

15) **clarity** [ˈklærəti] (n.)（思路）清晰，明了
The philosopher was known for his clarity of thought.

16) **originality** [əˌrɪdʒəˈnæləti] (n.) 獨創性，創見
The artist's paintings showed great originality.

 GM Different Than You Imagined
與你想像的不同

Many of you here today are getting your diploma at this Ivy League school because you have committed yourself to a dream and worked hard to achieve it. And there is no greater [1]**cliché** in a commencement address than "follow your dream." Well I am here to tell you that whatever you think your dream is now, it will probably change. And that's OK. Four years ago, many of you had a specific vision of what your college experience was going to be and who you were going to become. And I bet, today, most of you would admit that your time here was very GM different from what you imagined. Your roommates changed, your major changed, for some of you your sexual orientation changed. I bet some of you have changed your sexual orientation since I began this speech. I know I have. But through the good and especially the bad, the person you are now is someone you could never have [2]**conjured** in the fall of 2007.

你們今天許多人會拿到常春藤聯盟學校的畢業證書，是因為你們為夢想付出，且努力去實現。在畢業典禮致詞中，沒有什麼比說「去追隨你的夢想」更陳腔濫調了。我要告訴你們，不管你們現在的夢想是什麼，未來也可能會變。但沒關係。四年前，你們許多人對於大學體驗和未來想成為什麼人都有特定的願景。我打賭，現在你們大部分人會承認，你們實際的大學生活跟原本的想像很不一樣。你們的室友換了、主修科系換了，有些人的性傾向也改了。我打賭，你們有些人的性傾向在我開始演講後就改了。我知道我改了。但經

過種種好事和壞事，尤其是壞事，現在的你，是你在 2007 年秋季想像不到的。

 Amazing Things Will Happen
精彩可期

I have told you many things today, most of it foolish but some of it true. I'd like to end my address by breaking a [3]**taboo** and quoting myself from 17 months ago. At the end of my final program with NBC, just before LG signing off, I said "Work hard, be kind, and [4]**amazing** things will happen." Today, receiving this honor and speaking to the Dartmouth Class of 2011 from behind a LG tree trunk, I have never believed that more. Thank you very much, and congratulations.

今天我告訴你們很多事，大部分都很蠢，但有些是真話。我要打破一個禁忌並引述我自己在 17 個月前說的話來結束這場演講。我在國家廣播公司最後一個節目收尾時，就在結束前，我說：「努力工作、善待他人，未來就精彩可期。」現在，在我接受這份榮譽，並在這塊樹幹後面為達特茅斯學院 2011 年畢業班演講之際，我更加相信那句話。感謝大家，恭喜各位。

LG

The Lone Pine 達特茅斯老樹樁

達特茅斯學院（Dartmouth College）是美國長春藤盟校最小型的一所，位於新罕布夏州。該校周圍松樹林立，The Lone Pine 是達特茅斯的象徵物之一，是一棵在創校之初（1769 年）就有的老松樹，於 19 世紀末遭雷擊、暴風摧折，殘樁目前安放在校園一座小山丘上，畢業生在樹樁周圍的松林舉辦班級日（class day，畢業前一天最後的班級聚會）是達特茅斯的傳統，而畢業典禮的講台，就是 The Lone Pine 的造型。

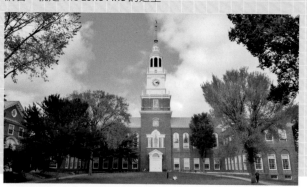

VOCABULARY 104

1) **cliché** [kliˋʃe] (n.) 陳腔濫調
The author's writing is filled with clichés.

2) **conjure (up)** [ˋkʌndʒɚ] (v.)（用魔法）變出，令人想起
The chef conjured up a delicious meal out of a few basic ingredients.

3) **taboo** [tæˋbu] (n.) 禁忌，戒律
Marrying a relative is a taboo in many cultures.

4) **amazing** [əˋmezɪŋ] (a.) 令人驚嘆的
Wow, you look amazing in that dress!

Don't get me wrong. 請別誤會。

get 在這邊是「理解」的意思。

A: How come you're breaking up with Cindy? I thought you really liked her.
你怎麼會跟辛蒂分手？我以為你很喜歡她。

B: Don't get me wrong. I do like her. It's just that I like Michelle better!
不要誤會了，我是很喜歡她，只是我更喜歡蜜雪兒！

Adderall 安非他命緩釋劑

Adderall 是一種安非他命緩釋劑的註冊品牌，這類治療注意力不足過動症（ADHD，Attention Deficit Hyperactivity Disorder，一種神經生理疾病，患者容易分心、衝動）的藥物在美國可以透過處方取得，雖有副作用，但可增強注意力，提高智能表現，被視為一種「聰明藥」，許多美國大學生在準備重要考試前會使用。

put it 表達

put 在這邊是「說」的意思，總是與 it 連用。

A: So what does Kevin's new girlfriend look like?
凱文的新女友長相如何？

B: Let me put it this way—he's gone out with better looking girls.
我就這麼說吧一他跟更漂亮的女孩交往過。

Ivy League 常春藤聯盟

Ivy League 是美國東北部八所大學（布朗、哥倫比亞、康乃爾、達特茅斯、哈佛、賓州、普林斯頓、耶魯）組成的名校聯盟，是全球接受捐款最多的學校，擁有優秀的學生與師資。

different + from, than, 還是 to ?

表達「與…不同」時，different from, different than, different to 都有人使用，最正確也最普遍的用法是different from：

例 **Jack looks very different from his brothers.**
傑克長得跟他的兄弟們很不一樣。

本文中出現的different than普遍在北美地區使用，英式英文的使用率也有增加的傾向，但different than與different from在用法上有一個不同之處：different than後面可以加上子句，在以下狀況使用時，會比different from更精確：

例 **Things are different than they were a year ago.**
事情跟一年前相比都變了。

比起Things are different from the way they were a year ago.上一句更簡單明瞭。

至於 different to 則在英式英文中最常見，但就正確性上多有爭議，應避免使用。書寫時，最保險的方式還是使用 different from 就好。

the better part of (sth.) 大半，大多數

這個片語是指「佔掉大多數」，也可以說 the best part of (sth.)。

A: How long ago did Frank lose his job?
法蘭克多久以前失業的？

B: He's been out of work the better part of a year.
他已經失業快一年了。

throw sth. together 急就章

也可以說 slap something together，不論是 throw together 或是 slap together，都是隨便丟一丟、弄兩下就出去的意思。

A: That house doesn't seem very well constructed.
那棟房子看起來蓋得不太堅固。

B: Yeah. It looks like they just threw it together.
是啊。看來是偷工減料蓋出來的。

basic cable 基本有線電視

美國有線電視業者通常都會提供許多套裝方案，最便宜的基本方案大約有 50 ～ 100 個頻道可供選擇。相較於高資費的方案有上千台及可收看到最新電影，基本有線電視的頻道數相當有限，內容也較陳舊，優點是只要付最基本的費用就可以收看。

Holy Grail 最重要的東西

Holy Grail 是指基督教中的「聖杯」，也就是耶穌受難時，用來裝盛耶穌聖血的杯子。所以當我們用 The Holy Grail of...（也可以小寫 holy grail）形容某個東西，說它是某領域的聖杯，代表這東西的重要性非同小可，是大家都在追尋的終極目標。

A: Is Wimbledon an important competition?
溫布頓是一項重要的比賽嗎？

B: Yeah. It's the Holy Grail of tennis.
沒錯。那可是網球界的聖杯。

sign off 節目收播

在廣播節目接近尾聲時，主持人會開始說結語，這樣的動作就是 sign off。引申為結束工作告退，或是結束一天上床睡覺。

A: Is your favorite DJ still on?
你最喜歡的 DJ 還在廣播上嗎？

B: No. He signs off at midnight.
不。他午夜十二點收播。

" I've dreamed of being a talk show host on basic cable ever since I was 46.

我夢想要成為基本有線電視台脫口秀主持人，打從我 46 歲開始的。

康納歐布萊恩笑談夢想

Rik Mayall's Exeter University Graduation Speech
里克馬亞爾的艾希特大學畢業演說

Five Mantras 五個箴言

©Featureflash Photo Agency / Shutterstock.com

Ladies and gentlemen, 28 years ago that man [points], Paul Jackson, walked in to a ²⁾**fledgling** nightclub up in London called the Comedy Store, and asked me if I'd like to be on television. Now that was a very big deal in those days. There were only three channels, so if you went on ³⁾**telly** you'd be famous for life overnight. So I said "Yes, please. I would like to be on television." So I went along to the BBC and there in the makeup department I saw the most beautiful woman on the planet. She quickly became my friend, and then my best friend, and then my

VOCABULARY 106

1) **mantra** ［ˈmʌntrə]（n.）（印度教，佛教）箴言，老生常談
My mantra is "work hard, play hard."

2) **fledgling** ［ˈflɛdʒlɪŋ]（a.）剛開始的，缺乏經驗的
Lots of fledgling companies go out of business in their first year.

3) **telly** ［ˈtɛli]（n.）即 **television**，「電視」的英國口語說法
There's nothing good on the telly tonight.

4) **mistress** ［ˈmɪstrɪs]（n.）情婦
Many wealthy men have mistresses.

5) **doctorate** ［ˈdɑktərɪt]（n.）博士學位
How long did it take to complete your doctorate?

6) **disgusting** [dɪsˈgʌstɪŋ]（a.）令人噁心的，令人討厭的
The food at that restaurant is disgusting.

⁴⁾**mistress**, and then pregnant, and then my wife, and then the mother of my three children. So, Paul, I want to take this rare opportunity to thank you formally and publically for my life.

各位女士先生，28 年前那個人（指），保羅傑克遜走進倫敦一家剛開的夜總會，叫做喜劇俱樂部，問我想不想上電視。這在當年是件大事。當時只有三家電視台，所以你當時要是上電視，就能一夜間成名。所以我說：「好，願意，我要上電視。」所以我到了英國廣播公司，在化妝間我看到世上最美的女人。她很快成了我的朋友、最好的朋友、情人，然後懷孕，然後是我的妻子，和我三個孩子的媽。所以，保羅，我要藉著這少有的機會正式公開謝謝你對我人生的影響。

Never in My Wildest Dreams
作夢都沒想到

Right, now to business—Rik Mayall's ⁵⁾**doctorate**. Well, ladies and gentlemen, what can I say? This is extraordinary. This is such an honor, such a joy, such a treat, such a terrible mistake. Now, I have done most things in my long and ⁶⁾**disgusting** life and I thought I'd done pretty much everything available to me, but I never in my [LG] wildest dreams imagined anything like this could ever happen to me.

對，現在說正事，里克馬亞爾的博士學位。呃，各位女士先生，我能說什麼？這真是了不得，如此榮幸、如此喜悅、如此樂事、如此可怕的錯誤。到現在，我已在這漫長、令人討厭的人生完成大部分的事，而且能做的事也差不多都做了，但我作夢都沒想到這種事會發生在我身上。

I am not a clever person, and I've [LG] got away with it for a very long time, but now you lot have all caught me. Here I am with all you ⁷⁾**brainy** people, and I'm the man without a brain cell to mention. Yes, I passed my [LG] 11 Plus exam in 1967, but everything [LG] went downhill from there. I failed seven [LG] O Levels. Yes, I failed my maths O Level three times [holds two fingers up]. I went on from there to get two F's and a U for my [LG] A Levels. "F" means fail—you guys wouldn't know. The U was for [LG] uffensive ⁸⁾**drivel**. No, it's true. But then Manchester University let me in on an interview. I mean, they're not up to your standards, obviously. They'll take anything up there. But me! I mean…⁹⁾**ugh**!

我不聰明，也僥倖得過且過這麼久了，但現在又被你們這些人抓到了。現在跟你們這群有腦筋的人在一起，我卻沒有腦細胞可言。對，我是在 1967 年通過初中入學預試，但從那時候起一切都在走下坡。我七次沒通過 O 水準。對，我考了三次都沒通過數學 O 水準（舉起兩根手指）。接下來的 A 水準拿了兩次 F 和一次 U。「F」是不及格，你們不會知道的。U 是討厭的胡扯。不是，這是真的。但後來曼徹斯特大學在一次面試後讓我入學。我是說，顯然他們的標準沒有你們高。他們願意接受任何人。但我耶！還真是…呃！

Book Report

Rik Mayall 里克馬亞爾

1958 ～ 2014 年，英國著名喜劇演員，是 80 年代另類喜劇先驅，英國國家廣播公司（BBC）的影集《年輕人》The Young Ones 和《黑爵士》Blackadder 是他的成名作。里克馬亞爾曾參與演出無數電視影集和喜劇表演，包括《哈利波特》電影的皮皮鬼（Peeves The Poltergeist）——但他的鏡頭都被剪光了！

©Featureflash Photo Agency / Shutterstock.com

7) **brainy** [ˋbreni] (a.)（口）腦筋好的，聰明的
Eating fish can make kids more brainy.

8) **drivel** [ˋdrɪvəl] (n./v.) 廢話，胡說
Don't waste your time reading such drivel.

9) **ugh** [ʌg] (int.) 表示輕蔑、厭惡的感嘆聲
Ugh! This coffee is terrible.

F Time to Start Enjoying Your Life
該開始享受人生

I didn't exactly fail my drama degree from Manchester. I just failed to turn up for the exams. It's not that I was too stupid. I was just too drunk, and I was too in-bed-with-girls-from-the-English-department. So here I am now, Rik Mayall, one 11 Plus, three O Levels [holds up four fingers], and a doctorate. Doctor Rik Mayall—unbelievable. Thank you all so much for your imagination and charity. But the celebrations today aren't for me, they're for you lot. You are the guys who did all the work, and now, my young friends, is the time to start enjoying your life. Forget about academia. You've done your work. Start celebrating your success, start ¹⁾**reaping** your rewards, start living your lives to the full in the real, ²⁾**nasty**, sexy world out there.

我在曼徹斯特修的戲劇學位也不算是不及格。我只是考試時沒出席。不是因為我太笨，而是我當時喝太醉了，當時跟英語系的女同學睡太多了。所以現在的我，里克馬亞爾，一次初中入學預試、三次O水準（舉起四根手指）和一個博士學位。里克馬亞爾博士，真不敢相信。感謝你們的想像力和善行。但今天的典禮不是為我辦的，是為你們。是你們完成所有工作，年輕朋友們，該是時候開始享受們的人生了。別管學術界了。你們已經完成學業。開始慶祝你們的成功，開始回收你們的報酬，開始在真實、險惡和迷人的世界盡情過你們的日子。

F Time to Start Enjoying Your Life
該開始享受人生

Wait! In return for Exeter's ³⁾**astonishing** generosity in making me a "doctor," let me give you youngsters a present. Five mantras [holds up four fingers] to carry with you through your lives. These are mine. These are what have helped me not only to survive, but to be happy, yeah? Now remember these.

等等！為了回報艾希特大學慷慨無比地讓我當上「博士」，我要給你們年輕人一個禮物。讓你們終生受用的五個箴言（舉起四隻手指）。也是讓我受用的箴言，不但幫助我生存，也讓我保持喜樂，好嗎？所以請記住這五個箴言。

Number one: All men are equal, therefore no one can ever be your genuine ⁴⁾**superior**. Number two: It's your future. It's yours to create. Your future is as bright as you make it. Number three: Change is a constant of life, so you must never ever lose your wisdom—your wisdom that you nurtured and ⁵⁾**enriched** here at Exeter University. Number four: If you want to live a full and complete human life you have to be free. Freedom is ⁶⁾**paramount**. And number five: Love is the answer.

第一：人人平等，所以沒人能真正比你高級。第二：自己的未來自己創造。自己的未來有多光明就看你自己了。第三：改變是生活的常態，所以永遠不要失去智慧，就是你在艾希特大學培養和充實的智慧。第四：若想過完整的人生，你要不受束縛。自由是至高無上的。第五：愛是答案。

So, my friends, there's my present to you. You just make sure that you've always got those five things—equality, opportunity, wisdom, freedom and love—and you'll be all right. You'll be all right with that and a bit of good luck. So good luck. Congratulations and good luck, my young friends. You go out there and have yourselves a fucking good life. ⁷⁾**Bon voyage** my young friends.

所以，我的朋友們，這是我送給各位的禮物。你們只要確保做到這五件事——平等、機會、智慧、自由和愛——你們就能安然無恙。只要能夠做到，再加上一點好運就能順利。所以，祝大家好運，恭喜並祝福各位，我的年輕朋友們。你們出去以後要讓自己過美好的生活。一路順風，我的年輕朋友們。

VOCABULARY 108

1) **reap** [rip] (v.) 獲得，得到，收穫
   If you study hard, you'll reap the benefit at exam time.

2) **nasty** [ˋnæstɪ] (a.) 難處理、忍受的，惡劣的，惡意的
   The nasty weather kept us indoors all day.

3) **astonishing** [əˋstɑnɪʃɪŋ] (a.) 令人驚嘆的
   The magician performed astonishing tricks.

4) **superior** [suˋpɪrɪə] (n.) 位階比自己高的人
   We were taught not to question our superiors.

5) **enrich** [ɪnˋrɪtʃ] (v.) 讓東西增長，提升事物的價值
   Doing volunteer work has enriched my life.

6) **paramount** [ˋpærəˏmaunt] (a.) 至高無上的，最重要的
   The economy was the paramount issue in the election.

7) **bon voyage** [bɑn vɔɪˋɑʒ] (phr.) （法）一路平安
   Our parents wished us bon voyage.

wildest dreams 所有想像得到的可能性

字面上是「最狂野的夢想」，表示一個人能想像得到、能懷抱夢想的所有可能性，只會用在 in one's wildest dreams、never / not in one's wildest dreams 這兩種情況。

A: Did you ever think you'd be able to retire at such a young age?
你以前有想過自己能這麼年輕就退休嗎？

B: No, not in my wildest dreams.
沒有，完全料想不到。

get away with sth. 得逞，不因某事受懲罰

get away 是「逃離」的意思，get away with sth. 表示做錯事沒有得到處罰，不必承擔後果。

A: I'm thinking of cheating on the test tomorrow.
我明天考試想要作弊。

B: Don't. You won't get away with it.
別這樣。你不會得逞的。

11 Plus 初中入學預試

這是英國針對初中入學前（11~12 歲）學童所做的測驗，主要考語言推理（verbal reasoning）如英文，及非語言推理（non-verbal reasoning）如數學，做為未來應往文科或理科發展的參考。在過去，全英格蘭、威爾斯地區學童都會受測，目前只剩英格蘭部分地區及北愛爾蘭還在考 11 Plus。

插入語法

當說話者想在一句話中同時表達多樣、細微的敘述時，即可使用插入語，亦即將一個獨立單字、片語、子句或句子插入原本那句話，用來修飾、說明、強調或連接句子。再說得直接一點，文章中用括號、破折號及逗點補充說明的地方，就是插入語。附帶一提，若一個插入語與主詞屬於同等關係時，即為「同位語」。

例 If you listen carefully, **boys**, you just may learn something.〔單字當插入語〕
如果你仔細聽的話，你會學到東西。

例 The food at that restaurant, **to be honest**, isn't very good.〔片語當插入語〕
老實說，那間餐廳的餐點不是很好吃。

例 The idea that pandas only eat bamboo **(though not exactly correct)** isn't too far from the truth.〔省略語當插入語〕
熊貓只吃竹子這件事（雖然不是百分百正確）並不算是偏離事實太遠。

例 **Mr. Patterson**, our math teacher, is retiring at the end of the year.〔同位語〕
我們的數學老師派特森先生在今年底即將退休。

go downhill 同走下坡

這個片語是在形容急速惡化。

A: Is that sushi place across the street any good?
對街那間壽司店好嗎？

B: It used to be, but it's been going downhill lately.
以前不錯，但最近退步了。

O Levels 普通程度、A Levels 高級程度

O Levels 是指英國的中學生畢業時取得普通教育證書（General Certificate of Education，簡稱 GCE）要通過的考試，16 歲高中畢業通過可取得 GCE O-Level 證書。而 A Levels 是普通教育高級程度證書（General Certificate of Education Advanced Level，18 歲大學預科畢業通過可取得 GCE A-Level。演講中提到的這些都是較早期的考試，英國教育制度已經歷許多變革，不再全部適用。

至於演講中提到的 F 是指 fail（不及格），而 U 其實是 ungraded（未達最低分標準），**uffensive** 跟 offensive（有夠討厭的）諧音，是主講者開玩笑胡謅的字。

turn up 出現（在某處）

這個片語是指在某個地方現身。

A: Were there a lot of people at the party?
有很多人參加派對嗎？

B: No. Only about a dozen people turned up.
沒。只有十來個人到場。

to the full 到最大極限

這個片語是指達到最好的程度、最高極限，完完全全毫不保留。

A: Did you like the play last night?
你喜歡昨晚的戲嗎？

B: Yes. I enjoyed it to the full.
喜歡。我看得非常開心。

-ster 字尾組成的名詞

演講中出現的 youngster 這個字，是「年輕朋友」的意思。-ster 這個字尾是用來表示跟某事物有關的人，如 prankster（prank 惡作劇）是「愛胡鬧的人」，mobster（mob 暴民）是「暴徒」。

本篇和上篇都是喜劇演員獲頒榮譽學位的演說。發表演說時，Conan O'Brien 是跌落事業谷底的哈佛畢業生，Rik Mayall 則是成績一塌糊塗的劣等生攀上人生高峰。儘管兩人從頭到尾插科打諢，大開自己玩笑，然而到最後不約而同都提到人生無常，只要運用智慧、保持頭腦清明就不必害怕，閃現出喜劇演員嬉笑背後的人生歷練。

Rik Mayall
1958 - 2014

Preserving the Beauty Around Us
保護周圍環境的美

科米蛙的南安普敦大學畢業演説
Kermit the Frog's Southampton College Commencement Speech

LG President Steinberg, Chancellor Sillerman, distinguished guests and my fellow [1)]**amphibians**, I stand here before you a happy and humble frog.

史汀堡校長、席勒曼校監、貴賓和兩棲類伙伴,在你們面前的我是個快樂謙卑的青蛙。

Growing Up in the Swamps
在沼澤出生長大

GM When I was a [2)]**tadpole** growing up back in the [3)]**swamps**, I never imagined that I would one day address such an outstanding group of scholars. And I am sure that when you were children growing up back in your own particular swamps or suburbs, you never imagined you would sit here on one of the most important days of your life listening to a short, green talking frog deliver your commencement address. All of us should feel very proud of ourselves...and just a little bit silly.

我還是蝌蚪時是在沼澤長大,從未想像過有一天能在一群傑出的學者面前演講。相信你們小時候在自己的沼澤或郊區長大時,也從未想過在你們人生中最重要的日子,會坐在這裡聽著一隻能講話的短小綠青蛙為你們發表畢業感言。我們都應該為自己感到驕傲…又覺得有點傻。

VOCABULARY 🎧110

1) **amphibian** [æmˋfɪbɪən] (n.) 兩棲動物,形容詞為 **amphibious** [æmˋfɪbɪəs]
Frogs are the most common amphibian in the world.

2) **tadpole** [ˋtæd͵pol] (n.) 蝌蚪
It takes months for tadpoles to develop into frogs.

4) **swamp** [swɑmp] (n.) 沼澤
Thousands of alligators live in the swamp.

4) **muck** [mʌk] (n.) 淤泥
Scrape the muck off your boots before you come in.

5) **colonial** [kəˋlonɪəl] (n./a.) 殖民地居民;殖民(地)的
The colonials fought many years for independence.

6) **spindly** [ˋspɪndlɪ] (a.) 細瘦的
Jake is self-conscious about his spindly legs.

7) **slam dunk** [slæm dʌnk] (phr.) (籃球)灌籃
All our players are too short to slam dunk the ball.

In any case, congratulations to all of you graduates. As we say in the wetlands, "Ribbit, ribbit, knee-deep, ribbit," which means "May success and a smile always be yours, even when you're knee-deep in the sticky [4)]**muck** of life."

總之，恭喜各位畢業生。如同我們在濕地所說的：「呱呱，深及膝蓋，呱呱」，意思是：「祝你成功，並永保微笑，就算人生陷入及膝爛泥中。」

Now, I know that there are some people out there who wonder what brought me here today. Was it the incoming tide on Shinnecock Bay? Was it the all-you-can-eat midnight buffet aboard the Paumanok? Or was it the promise that I'd get to play basketball with Sidney Green and the Runnin' [5)]**Colonials**? Don't let my [6)]**spindly** little arms fool you. I can [7)]**slam dunk** one mean basketball. While those are all very good reasons for coming to this beautiful campus, today I am here for an even more important reason—to thank each and every one of you at Southampton College.

我知道有人覺得奇怪，我今天怎麼會出現在這裡。是因為辛納克灣（編註：該校位於辛納克灣）漲潮了嗎？還是為了保馬尼克號船上的吃到飽午夜自助餐？或是有人邀我來跟西德尼格林和奔跑殖民者隊一起打籃球？別被我細小的手臂騙了，我可是灌籃高手。以上都是來到這所美麗校園的好理由，但今天我是為了一個更重要的原因來這裡——感謝南安普敦大學在座的各位。

Teaching an Old Frog New Tricks
教老青蛙新把戲

First, of course, I want to thank you for bestowing upon me this Honorary Doctorate of Amphibious Letters. To tell you the truth, I never even knew there was such a thing as amphibious letters. After all those years on *Sesame Street*, you'd think I'd know my alphabet. It just goes to show that you can teach an old frog new tricks.

首先，當然，我要謝謝你們授予我兩棲類文學榮譽博士學位。說實話，我從不知道有兩棲類文學這個學科。在芝麻街這麼長一段日子，你會以為我精通文字。常言說得好：老青蛙也能學新把戲。

Pamanok 保馬尼克號
是紐約曼哈頓鄰近地區長島（Long Island）的舊稱。Paumanok 是美國原住民語，意思是納貢之島（the island that pays tribute），因為在殖民初期，當地居民必須付錢才不會被原住民攻擊。而演講中的 Paumanok 是南安普敦大學所有的一艘船，上面有吃到飽餐廳。

Sidney Green 西尼格林
1961 年生，前美國職籃芝加哥公牛隊（Chicago Bulls）選手，1996 年退休轉任南安普敦大學奔跑殖民者隊（Runnin' Colonials）的教練，跟本篇演說發表時間同年。

Kermit the Frog 科米蛙
溫和膽小的布青蛙 Kermit the Frog 是美國布偶師吉姆亨森（Jim Henson，1936 ～ 1990 年）創作的布偶秀《布偶歷險記》*The Muppets* 當中最有名的角色，同時也是兒童教育節目《芝麻街》*Sesame Street* 的主要角色。

科米蛙和豬小姐（Miss Piggy）。

© catwalker / Shutterstock.com

It's great to have an honorary doctorate. I have spoken with my fellow ¹⁾**honorees**— Professor Merton, ²⁾**Ms.** Meaker, Mr. Gambling— and as honorary doctors we promise to have regular office hours, put new magazines in our waiting room, and to make late night house calls ³⁾**regardless** of your health plan ⁴⁾**coverage**. On behalf of all of us, thank you sincerely.

能獲得榮譽博士學位感覺很棒。我已經跟其他受獎者談過──莫頓教授、米克女士、甘柏林先生──身為榮譽醫生，我們保證有正常的營業時間，會在候診室放新雜誌，且不論你們的醫療保險範圍如何，都會接受深夜出診。我代表我們衷心感謝各位。（編註：醫生和博士都是 doctor，Kermit 因此開玩笑說自己是榮譽醫生）

But I'm also here at Southampton to thank you for something even more important. I am here to thank you for the great work that you have done, and for the great work that you will be doing with your lives. You have dedicated yourselves to preserving the beauty that is all around us. While some might look out at this great ocean and just see a magnificent view, you and I know that this ocean—and every ⁵⁾**ecosystem**—is home to an ⁶⁾**indefinable** number of my fellow animals.

但我來到南安普敦，還要為更重要的事表示感謝。我要謝謝各位過去和未來的卓越付出。你們竭力保護周遭環境的美。雖然有些人會把這片浩瀚的海洋看成壯麗的景致而已，你我都知道，這片海洋，以及每個生態系統，都是我們這群數不清動物的家。

Saving Our World and Our Home
拯救我們的世界和家園

As you go out into the world, never LG lose sight of the fact that you are not just saving the environment, you are saving the homes and lives of so many of my relatives. On behalf of frogs, fish, pigs, bears and all of the other species who are lower than you on the food chain, thank you for dedicating your lives to saving our world and our home. In the words of my cousin, LG Newt— no, not that Newt, this is another Newt—we appreciate what you are doing more than you can even imagine.

當你們走向世界時，不要忘記你們不只是在拯救環境，也在拯救我們同類的家園和生命。我代表青蛙、魚、豬、熊等所有在食物鏈中比你們低層的物種，感謝你們奉獻生命拯救我們的世界和家園。套句我表哥紐特說的──不是那個紐特，是另一個蠑螈紐特──我們對你們作為的感激之情是你們無法想像的。

And so I say to you, the 1996 graduates of Southampton College, you are no longer tadpoles. The time has come for you to drop your tails and leave this swamp. But I am sure that wherever I go as I travel around the world, I will find each and every one of you LG working your tails off to save other swamps and give those of us who live there a chance to survive. We love you for it. Enjoy life! And thank you very much.

所以我想對你們說，南安普敦大學 1996 年畢業班，你們不再是蝌蚪了。現在該是扔掉尾巴，離開這片沼澤的時候。但我相信不論我到世界哪個角落，我都會看到你們每個人盡心竭力，拯救其他沼澤，給住在沼澤的我們一個生存機會。為此我們愛你們。享受生活！感謝各位。

此 newt 非彼 Newt

newt 是兩棲動物「蠑螈」，因此 Kermit 說這是他表哥。但其實他是在開紐特金瑞契（Newt Gingrich）的玩笑。這篇演說的時間是 1996 年夏天，而當時美國的政治風雲人物是共和黨領袖 Newt Gingrich，他於 1994 年底帶領共和黨終結民主黨在國會長達 40 年的多數黨局面，擔任眾議院議長，展開與執政民主黨柯林頓政府的鬥爭，1995 年底更因未通過預算，造成美國政府關閉 21 天，是美國歷史上最長的政府停擺。

© Christopher Halloran / Shutterstock.com

VOCABULARY 🎧 112

1) **honoree** [ˌɑnəˋri] (n.) 領獎人，（宴會的）主要來賓
Will today's honorees please come to the stage?

2) **Ms.** [mɪz] (n.) 女士，可用於每位女士，不區分婚姻狀況
Many women insist on being called Ms.

3) **regardless** [rɪˋgɑrdlɪs] (adv.) 不管，不顧
The job is open to anyone, regardless of experience.

4) **coverage** [ˋkʌvərɪdʒ] (n.) 保險（涵蓋範圍）
I have medical coverage through my employer.

5) **ecosystem** [ˋiko͵sɪstəm] (n.) 生態系統，是由代表「生態的，環境的」字首 eco- 加上 system（系統）組成
Pollution has caused great damage to the ecosystem.

6) **indefinable** [͵ɪndɪˋfaɪnəbəl] (a.) 難以形容的，難以說明的
The Northern Lights have an indefinable beauty.

President 和 Chancellor 的差別

在美國，一所大學會有一個校長，稱為 President，而該大學不同校區或是所屬學院的最高行政長官，則稱為 Chancellor。

What brings you here? 什麼風把你吹來的？

就像中文的「什麼風把你吹來的？」表示對方的造訪令人意外。

A: Hey, Mark. What brings you here? I thought you hated shopping.
嗨，馬克。你怎麼會來這裡？我還以為你討厭逛街。

B: I do. My wife dragged me here.
我是討厭啊。我老婆拖我來的。

know (one's) stuff 精通

這個片語是指一個人對自己所屬的領域很專精。《芝麻街》Sesame Street 是美國著名的兒童節目，教導英文字母（alphabet）、生活字彙及兒童英文，所以 Kermit the Frog 才說 know my alphabet。

A: Are you sure your computer guy can fix my PC?
你確定你那個修電腦的能修好我的電腦嗎？

B: Yeah. He really knows his stuff.
是呀。他技術很好的。

it (just/only) goes to show (that...) 常言道…

go to show 表示「證明，看得很明顯」，it (just/only) goes to show (that...) 這個句型總與格言、諺語連用，來講一些基本的道理，或是指出故事的道德訓示。

A: That paper got caught publishing another fake story.
那家報紙又被抓到刊登一篇假新聞。

B: It just goes to show you can never trust the news.
所以說啦，絕對不能相信新聞。

lose sight of sth. 忘記，忽略…

sight 是名詞「看見，目睹」，當我們說一個人 lose sight of sth.，字面上是他沒看見某物，但其實是他「忘記」、「忽略」某件事的意思。

A: We can't let ourselves lose sight of our goals.
我們不能忘記我們的目標。

B: You're right. We need to focus on what's important.
說得對。我們必須專注在重要的事上。

work one's tail off 非常努力

也可以說 work one's ass / buns / butt off，都是在形容非常辛勤工作。一般都用在負面語氣，表示為工作賣命，把自己累個半死的樣子。

A: The boss says he wants the report on his desk by Friday.
老闆說星期五之前要交報告。

B: We're gonna have to work our tails off to get it done on time.
我們得卯起來做才能趕上了。

形容詞片語的用法

形容詞片語是由形容詞子句簡化而來的，形容詞子句中的關係代名詞 who、which、that 為形容詞子句的主詞時，就可以與 be 動詞一起簡化，形成形容詞片語。這樣的簡化只能用在「限定用法」的形容詞子句。形容詞片語可分成以下兩種：

1. Ving 開頭的形容詞片語：本例句就是此類，tadpole 主動執行 grow up（長大）這個動作，因此將動詞改成 Ving 形式：

例 **I was a tadpole growing up back in the swamps.**
= I was a tadpole **that was growing** up back in the swamps.
= I was a tadpole **(that was) growing** up back in the swamps.

最後將關係代名詞 that 與 be 動詞 was 一起省略，後方的 growing up in the swamps 就成為形容前方名詞的形容詞片語。

例 **Who is the lady (that is) standing over there?**
站在那裡的女士是誰？

2. pp 開頭的形容詞片語：句中的先行詞是被動完成後方的動作時，就將該動詞變成分詞 pp 形式。

例 **Sammy likes the dresses (that are) sold in the store**
珊米喜歡那間店裡的洋裝。

《布偶歷險記》The Muppets 的布偶。
©Featureflash Photo Agency / Shutterstock.com

芝麻街布偶。
©Lester Balajadia / Shutterstock.com

在《布偶歷險記》The Muppets 當中，科米蛙說話總是小小聲的，努力在瘋瘋癲癲的布偶群中維持秩序，負責招呼每一集的真人來賓。讓這樣一個謹小慎微的的聲音來對萬物之靈的人類呼求，請我們保護環境，不要忘了他們這些無助的動物，怎不令人揪心？

巴拉克歐巴馬甘迺迪勇氣獎得獎感言
Barack Obama's JFK Profile in Courage Award Speech

Lessons in Courage

勇氣的啟示

 ## An Attractive Calling
令人嚮往的感召

To those of us of a certain age, the Kennedys [1]**symbolized** a set of values and attitudes about [2]**civic** life that made it such an attractive calling. The idea that politics in fact could be a noble and [3]**worthwhile** pursuit. The notion that our problems, while significant, are never [4]**insurmountable**.

對於我們有一定年紀的人來說，甘迺迪家族象徵一套公民生活的價值觀和態度，是令人嚮往的感召。其概念是政治可以是高尚且有價值的追求。其觀念是我們的問題雖然重大，但絕非無法克服。

The belief that America's promise might [5]**embrace** those who had once been locked out or left behind and that opportunity and dignity would no longer be restricted to the few but extended to the many.

 LG

Profile in Courage Award

這個獎項的名稱來自甘迺迪 1957 年獲得普立茲獎的著作《當仁不讓》*Profile in Courage*，內容描述多位美國參議員不畏政治風險、不惜賭上前途、擇善固執的故事。Profile in Courage Award 就是在表彰最能符合書中人物精神的人物。這個獎項從 1990 年開始頒發，遴選單位為甘迺迪家族成員及跨黨派菁英組成的約翰甘迺迪圖書館基金會（John F. Kennedy Library Foundation），每年在 JFK 生日（5 月 29 日）前後頒發。

VOCABULARY 114

1) **symbolize** [ˋsɪmbə͵laɪz] (v.) 象徵
The stars on the American flag symbolize the 50 states.

2) **civic** [ˋsɪvɪk] (a.) 公民（資格）的，市民（資格）的
Voting is your civic duty.

3) **worthwhile** [ˋwɝθˋwaɪl] (a.) 值得花時間、金錢、精神等的，有價值的
Did you find the course worthwhile?

4) **insurmountable** [͵ɪnsɚˋmaʊntəbəl] (a.) 不能超越的，不能克服的
The company was faced with insurmountable debt.

5) **embrace** [ɪmˋbres] (v.) 全心接納，信奉
It's difficult for old people to embrace new ideas.

6) **scope (of)** [skop] (n.)（行動、思想等）眼界，範圍
Your question is beyond the scope of this discussion.

其信念是美國的承諾會接納那些曾被拒之門外或落後的人，且機會和尊嚴不再受限於少數人，而是提供給大眾。

The responsibility that each of us has to play a part in our nation's destiny, and by virtue of being Americans, play a part in the destiny of the world. I can see truthfully that the example of Jack and Bobby Kennedy helped guide me into politics, and that the guidance of Teddy Kennedy made me a better public servant once I arrived in Washington.

其責任是我們每個人對我們國家的命運都扮演好角色，且由於身為美國人，對這世界的命運也都扮演好角色。我深深理解約翰甘迺迪和巴比甘迺迪的榜樣引領我參與政治，泰德甘迺迪的指導在我到華府上任後，使我成為更好的公僕。

Perilous Times
危險時期

For whatever reasons I receive this award, whatever the scale, the challenges that we overcame, and the ⁶⁾**scope** of progress we made over my presidency, it is worth pointing out that in many ways the times that President Kennedy ⁷⁾**confronted** were far more ⁸⁾**perilous** than the ones that we confront today.

我不論是出於什麼原因和標準，或因為克服什麼挑戰，或在總統任期內取得多少進展而獲得這個獎，值得指出的是，甘迺迪總統面臨的時代在許多方面都比我們今天所面臨的更危險。

He entered the Oval Office at just 43, only a few years after Khrushchev had threatened to bury America. Wars raged around the world. Large ⁹⁾**swaths** of the country knew poverty far deeper and more ¹⁰⁾**widespread** than we see today. A young ¹¹⁾**preacher's** cause was just gaining ¹²⁾**traction** across a land ¹³⁾**segregated** not only by custom but by law.

他年僅 43 歲就入主白宮的橢圓形辦公室，就在赫魯雪夫威脅要埋葬美國後幾年。當時的世界戰爭四起。全國各地的貧困程度比我們今日所見的更深遠廣泛。有位年輕牧師（編註：指金恩博士）的理想，在這片因不同習俗和法律仍施行種族隔離的土地上，才剛日漸引人注目。

LG

Oval Office 橢圓形辦公室

白宮（White House）是美國總統的官邸及辦公處，而 Oval Office 就是美國總統在白宮的辦公室。白宮坐落於華盛頓哥倫比亞特區（Washington, D.C.），為新古典主義建築。第一位進駐的元首為第二任總統約翰亞當斯（John Adams），他也是美國第一任副總統。以前白宮也有 President's Palace、President's House 及 Executive Mansion 等稱號，直到第二十六任總統羅斯福（Theodore Roosevelt）任內，「白宮」才成為官方代名詞。白宮不但是國家歷史地標之一，也在 2007 年被美國建築師協會（American Institute of Architects）評選為美國最受喜愛建築第二名。現今 White House 一詞也用來泛稱美國政府，而 Oval Office 更代表美國最高權力核心。

©Wikimedia Commons

白宮中間的圓弧位置，即橢圓形辦公室所在。

Barack Obama 巴拉克歐巴馬

1961 年生。美國民主黨籍政治家，第 44 任美國總統，為第一位非裔美國總統，於 2008 年初次當選美國總統，並於 2012 年成功連任。

他就任總統後，對內全面實施恢復美國經濟的計劃，對移民、公民醫療保健、教育等領域進行變革；對外主張從阿富汗和伊拉克撤軍，並向伊斯蘭世界表示友善，還和核武大國俄羅斯簽署削減核武器的《布拉格條約》。2009 年獲頒諾貝爾和平獎。歐巴馬於 2017 年 1 月以 60% 的民意支持率卸任，由共和黨的唐納川普接任。

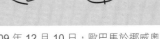

2009 年 12 月 10 日，歐巴馬於挪威奧斯陸獲頒諾貝爾和平獎證書與獎章。

---

7) **confront** [kənˋfrʌnt] (v.) 面對，面臨
It takes courage to confront our fears.

8) **perilous** [ˋpɛrələs] (a.) 危險的，險惡的
We're living in perilous economic times.

9) **swath** [swɑθ] (n.) 大片，大面積，大量
Large swaths of forest are being cleared for farming.

10) **widespread** [ˋwaɪd͵sprɛd] (a.) 普遍的，廣泛的
The tornado caused widespread destruction.

11) **preacher** [ˋpritʃɚ] (n.) 講道者，牧師
The religious leader started out as a street preacher.

12) **traction** [ˋtrækʃən] (n.) （進步、成功所需的）支持、注意、接受度
The product is starting to gain traction in the marketplace.

13) **segregated** [ˋsɛgrɪ͵getɪd] (a.) 施行種族隔離的
My grandfather went to segregated schools as a child.

Nikita Khrushchev 赫魯雪夫

1894～1971 年。赫魯雪夫在史達林死後，於 1956 年成為蘇聯最高領導人，他在內政上，推行文藝自由化、進行農業改革。外交上，他與美國和西歐針鋒相對，成為冷戰代表人物。1961 年 6 月，赫魯雪夫與甘迺迪會議，討論柏林問題，他再度要求英美法撤出西柏林（第一次提出是在 1958 年），遭甘迺迪斷然拒絕，同年 8 月，蘇聯與東德築起柏林圍牆。1962 年，他策劃的古巴飛彈危機使美俄幾近發動核子戰爭。1964 年因政變下台，赫魯雪夫從此淡出政壇。

© fifg / Shutterstock.com

It's worth remembering the times in which President Kennedy led us, because for many Americans I know that this feels like an uncertain and even perilous time. The forces of 1)**globalization** and technology have upended many of our established 2)**assumptions** about the economy. They have provided a great opportunity and also great inequality and uncertainty for far too many.

甘迺迪總統領導我們的時代是值得銘記的，因為我知道許多美國人覺得當今是個不穩定、甚至危險的時代。全球化和科技的力量顛覆了我們對經濟的許多既定觀念。它們提供了無限的機會，也為許多人帶來了不少不平等和不確定性。

The Necessity of Courage
勇氣的必要性

And at such moments, courage is necessary. At such moments, we need courage to stand up to hate not just in others but in ourselves. At such moments, we need the courage to stand up to 3)**dogma** not just in others but in ourselves. At such moments, we need courage to believe

that together we can 4)**tackle** big challenges like inequality and climate change.

在這樣的時刻，勇氣是必要的。在這樣的時刻，我們需要勇氣對抗仇恨，不只是別人的仇恨，同時也是我們自己的仇恨。在這樣的時刻，我們需要勇氣挺身對抗，不僅僅是對抗他人盲目的信念，同時還有自己盲目的信念。在這樣的時刻，我們需要勇氣去相信我們可以一起對抗不平等和氣候變遷之類的重大挑戰。

Courage, President Kennedy knew, requires something more than just the absence of fear. Any fool can be fearless. Courage, true courage, 5)**derives** from that sense of who we are, what are our best selves, what are our most important 6)**commitments**, and the belief that we can dig deep and do hard things for the enduring benefit of others.

甘迺迪總統知道勇氣不只需要無畏。任何匹夫都能無畏。勇氣，真正的勇氣，是源自對自我的了解、發掘出自身的優點、知道自己所能做出的重要承諾，以及相信自己能盡最大力量為他人的長久利益而努力的信念。

Because of the tragedies that 7)**befell** each of them, sometimes we forget how fundamentally the story they told us about ourselves changed the 8)**trajectory** of America. And that's often where courage begins, with the story we tell ourselves about who we are and what's important and about our own capacity to make a difference.

由於發生在他們每個人身上的悲劇，我們有時會忘記他們告訴我們的故事是如何從根本上改變了美國的發展方向。而這也往往是勇氣開始的地方，包括那些我們告訴自己的故事：關於自己的本質、什麼才是真正重要的，以及我們的影響力究竟有多大。

I hope that current members of Congress recall that it actually doesn't take a lot of courage to aid those who are already powerful, already comfortable, already influential. But it does require

VOCABULARY 116

1) **globalization** [ˌglobəlɪˋzeʃən] (n.) 全球化
Globalization is an inevitable trend.

2) **assumption** [əˋsʌmpʃən] (n.) 假設，假定
Your argument is based on false assumptions.

3) **dogma** [ˋdɔgmə] (n.) 教條，既定的信念
Don't let yourself be blinded by political dogma.

4) **tackle** [ˋtækəl] (v.) 著手處理，對付
The government has promised to tackle inflation.

5) **derive (from)** [dɪˋraɪv] (v.) 起源，來自
Many French words are derived from Latin.

6) **commitment** [kəˋmɪtmənt] (n.) 承諾，承擔的義務
Stacy wants to get married, but her boyfriend is afraid of commitment.

some courage to [9]**champion** the vulnerable and the sick and the [10]**infirm**, those who often have no access to the [11]**corridors** of power.

我希望現在的國會議員能回想一下，協助那些已經有權勢、生活舒適且已經有影響力的人，其實不需要太多勇氣。但支持弱勢和老弱病殘的人，確實需要一些勇氣，他們往往沒有通往權利核心的管道。

Our Responsibility as Citizens
我們身為公民的責任

We lose sight sometimes of our own [12]**obligations**, all the quiet acts of courage that unfold around us every single day, ordinary Americans who give something of themselves not for personal gain but for the enduring benefit of another. The courage of a single mom who is working two jobs to make sure her kid can go to college. The courage of somebody who volunteers to help some kids who need help.

我們有時忽視自己的義務，每一天我們周遭都有人在安靜地表現勇氣，平凡的美國人付出一點自己的力量，不為自身利益，而是為了他人的長久利益。單親媽媽的勇氣就是兼兩份工作，以確保孩子能上大學。其他人的勇氣還包括擔任義工，幫助其他需要幫助的孩子。

When we recognize these acts of courage, we then necessarily recognize our own responsibility as citizens and as part of the human family to get involved and take a stand, to vote, to pay attention.

當我們認可這些勇氣的行為，我們也必然認可自己身為公民的責任，以及身為人類大家庭一份子該擔起參與並表達立場、去投票、去表達關注的責任。

LG

Jack, Bobby, and Teddy Kennedy 政治世家甘迺迪

被美國人暱稱為 JFK 及 Jack Kennedy 的約翰甘迺迪（John F. Kennedy），1917 年生，1961 年就任美國總統時年僅 43 歲，是美國歷史上當選總統最年輕的一位。甘迺迪被許多美國人視為史上最偉大，也是口才最好的總統之一，Ask not what your country can do for you, ask what you can do for your country.（不要問國家能為你做什麼，要問你能為國家做些什麼。）是他最常被人引用的一句話。

他任內歷經古巴飛彈危機、柏林圍牆建立、黑人民權運動，並繼續支持越戰，以及與蘇聯的太空競賽，還成立和平工作團（Peace Corps）。1963 年 11 月 22 日，甘迺迪於德州達拉斯市遭到暗殺身亡，得年 46 歲。

Bobby Kennedy 是對羅伯甘迺迪（Robert F. Kennedy，RFK）的暱稱，1925 年生，律師出身的他很受擔任總統的哥哥 JFK 倚重，被任命為司法部長。他嚴打黑手黨，並對黑人民權運動非常支持，後來金恩博士遇刺，就是由他發表演說公開消息。1968 年，就在金恩博士遇刺後數月，羅伯甘迺迪遭伊斯蘭激進份子暗殺身亡，得年 42 歲。

Teddy Kennedy 是對愛德華甘迺迪（Edward Moore "Ted" Kennedy）的暱稱，1932 年生，是甘迺迪家的小弟，在兩位哥哥遭暗殺後獨撐整個政治家族，並擔任參議員超過 40 年。他延續兩位兄長的自由主義信念，在參議院推動一系列改善勞工、移民權益、消弭階級種族差異的立法不遺餘力，2008 年更是第一個支持歐巴馬代表民主黨參選總統的大老，當時的他已罹患腦癌病情沉重。愛德華甘迺迪於 2009 年病逝，享年 77 歲。

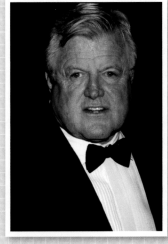
© Everett Collection / Shutterstock.com

美國民權運動檯面上的要角：金恩博士（左）、約翰甘迺迪總統（中）、司法部長羅伯甘迺迪（右）。
© IgorGolovniov / Shutterstock.com

$1
MARTIN LUTHER KING
JOHN FITZGERALD KENNEDY
ROBERT FITZGERALD KENNEDY
ST. VINCENT AND THE GRENADINES

---

7) **befall** [bɪˋfɔl] (v.)（不幸）降臨於，發生
The drought that befell the country caused thousands to starve.

8) **trajectory** [trəˋdʒɛktəri] (n.)（歷史、事情等的）發展方向
The accident changed the trajectory of Dan's life.

9) **champion** [ˋtʃæmpiən] (v.) 支持，擁護
The lawyer has championed women's rights for years.

10) **infirm** [ɪnˋfɜm] (a.) 體弱的，衰弱的
The virus mostly attacks the old and infirm.

11) **corridor** [ˋkɔrɪdɚ] (n.) 走廊，迴廊
My office is at the end of the corridor.

12) **obligation** [ˏɑbləˋgeʃən] (n.)（道義或法律上的）義務，責任
You can try our product with no obligation to buy.

121

That's what the ordinary courage of everyday people can inspire when you're paying attention, the quiet [1)]**sturdy** courage of ordinary people doing the right thing 🄛🄖 day in and day out. They don't get attention for it. They don't seek it. They don't get awards for it. But that's what's defined America.

只要你注意，這就是一般老百姓的平凡勇氣所能發揮的力量，是一般人日復一日每天盡本分所表現出安靜堅定的勇氣。他們不會受到注意，這並非他們所求。他們沒因此得到獎賞。但就是這些讓美國成為美國。

The People I Think Of
我想到的人

I think of women like my grandmother and so many like her who 🄛🄖 worked their way up from a secretarial pool to management and in the process pushed the 🄛🄖 glass ceiling just a little bit higher.

我想到像我祖母和許多像她那樣的女性，她們從秘書室一路晉升到管理階層，在這過程中逐漸將玻璃天花板推高一些。

I think of the troops and the cops and the [2)]**first responders** that I've met who have put themselves at risk for strangers they will never know. And business owners who make every kind of sacrifice they can to make sure that their workers 🄛🄖 have a shot. And workers who take the risk of starting a new career, retraining at my age.

我想到我見過的軍隊、警察和第一線急救人員，為了從不認識的陌生人，他們讓自己置身於險境。以及業主做出各種犧牲，好確保員工有機會。以及在我這個年齡冒險開啟事業第二春和重新接受訓練的員工。

I think of Dreamers who [3)]**suppress** their fears to keep working and striving in the only country they've ever called home. And every American who stands up for immigrants because they know that their parents or grandparents or great grandparents were immigrants too, and they know that America is an idea that only grows stronger with each new person who adopts our common [4)]**creed**.

我想到夢想家（在兒童時期由父母等人帶領，非法入境美國，現為無證移民），他們抑制自己的恐懼，在這可稱為家的唯一一國家不斷努力和奮鬥。我也想到每個支持移民的美國，因為他們知道自己的父母、或祖父母、或曾祖父母也都是移民，他們也知道美國其實是一種信念，而且每位接受共同信條的新移民會讓美國更茁壯。

I think of every young [5)]**activist** who answers the injustices still [6)]**embedded** in our criminal justice system not with violence, not with despair, but with peaceful protests and analysis and constructive recommendations for change.

我想到每個年輕的維權人士，對於我們刑事司法體制仍體現出的不公不義，他們以非暴力、不絕望的方式做出回應，而是以和平示威和分析，以及建設性的建議方式尋求改變。

That very [7)]**Kennedyesque** idea that America is not the project of any one person and that each

 VOCABULARY 118

1) **sturdy** [ˋstɜdɪ] (a.) 堅強的，剛毅的
We must remain sturdy in the face of tragedy.

2) **first responder** [fɜst rɪˋspɑndɚ] (n.)
（需第一時間趕赴現場的）緊急救護人員等
It took first responders 20 minutes to arrive at the scene of the accident.

3) **suppress** [səˋprɛs] (v.) 抑制，忍住
It's not healthy to suppress your feelings.

4) **creed** [krid] (n.) 信條，信念，主義
The U.S. is home to people of every race and creed.

5) **activist** [ˋæktəvɪst] (n.) 運動人士，活躍人士
Dozens of human rights activists were arrested at the march.

6) **embed** [ɪmˋbɛd] (v.) 埋入，深植
A people's culture is embedded in its language.

of us can make a difference and all of us ought to try.

這種甘迺迪式的觀念是，美國不是只屬於一個人的任務，而是我們每個人都能發揮影響力，而且我們所有人都應該嘗試。

I know that the values and the progress that we cherish are not [8]**inevitable**, that they are [9]**fragile**, in need of constant renewal.

我知道我們珍惜的價值觀和進步不是必然的，它們是脆弱的，需要不斷更新。

I've said before that I believe what Dr. King said, that "the [10]**arc** of the moral universe is long but it bends toward justice," but I've also said it does not bend on its own. It bends because we bend it, because we put our hand on that arc, and we move it in the direction of justice and freedom and equality and kindness and generosity. It doesn't happen on its own.

我曾說過，我相信金恩博士說的，「道德世界的發展雖漫長，但終歸正義」，但我也說過，它不會自己調整方向。是我們要去調整它，因為我們著手去調整，將它移往正義、自由、平等、慈悲和寬宏的方向。這不會自己發生。

© ChameleonsEye / Shutterstock.com

7) **-esque** [sk] (suf.) 表「…式的、般的」形容詞字尾
The artist is known for his Dalí-esque paintings.

8) **inevitable** [ɪnˋɛvɪtəbəl] (a.) 必然（發生）的，不可避免的
Death and taxes are inevitable.

9) **fragile** [ˋfrædʒəl] (a.) 易碎的，脆弱的
Be careful with that glass bowl — it's very fragile.

10) **arc** [ɑrk] (n.)（故事等的）劇情、發展
The movie doesn't follow a conventional story arc.

A Choice We Must Make
我們必須做的選擇

And so we are constantly having to make a choice because progress is fragile. And it's [1)]**precisely** that fragility, that [2)]**impermanence**, that is a [3)]**precondition** of the quality of character that we celebrate tonight.

所以我必須不斷做出選擇，因為進步是脆弱的。也正是這種脆弱、無常，是這種品格的先決條件，我們今晚在此頌揚它。

If the [4)]**vitality** of our democracy, if the gains of our long journey to freedom were [5)]**assured**, none of us would ever have to be courageous. None of us would have to risk anything to protect them. But it's in its very [6)]**precariousness** that courage becomes possible and absolutely necessary.

如果我們民主的生命力、漫長的自由之路保證能得到，我們就不需要勇敢。我們就不需要冒險保護它們。但就是因為民主如此脆弱，我們才有可能勇敢且必須勇敢。

John F. Kennedy knew that our best hope and our most powerful answer to our doubts and to our fears lies inside each of us, in our willingness to joyfully embrace our responsibility as citizens, to stay true to our [7)]**allegiance**, to our highest and best ideals, to maintain our regard and concern for the poor and the aging and the [8)]**marginalized**, to put our personal or party interest aside when LG duty to our country calls or when conscience demands.

約翰甘迺迪知道，對於我們內心的疑惑和恐懼，我們最大的希望和最強而有力的答案就在我們每人心中，是我們身為公民心甘情願接

受的責任，堅持忠誠，堅定於我們最高與最好的理想，保持我們對窮人、老人和弱勢族群的關心和關懷，需要為國家盡義務時、或良心召喚時，把我們個人或黨派利益放一邊。

That's the spirit that has brought America so far and that's the spirit that will always carry us to better days.

這就是帶領美國走到現在的精神，也是會一直帶領我們邁向更美好日子的精神。

And I take this honor that you have bestowed on me here tonight as a [9)]**reminder** that, even out of office, I must do all that I can to advance the spirit of service that John F. Kennedy represents.

我視你們今晚賜予我的榮譽為一種提醒，就算已經卸任，我必須竭盡所能促進約翰甘迺迪所代表的服務精神。

> Change is the law of life. And those who look only to the past or present are certain to miss the future.
>
> 改變是生命的法則。只看過去或現在的人，必定會錯過未來。
>
> *JFK 談改變*

VOCABULARY 120

1) **precisely** [prɪˋsaɪslɪ] (adv.) 正好，恰好
That's precisely what I mean!

2) **impermanence** [ɪmˋpɝmənəns] (n.) 無常，暫時性
Buddhists believe in the impermanence of all things.

3) **precondition** [ˌprikənˋdɪʃən] (n.) 先決條件，前提
Israel says it has no preconditions for peace talks.

4) **vitality** [vaɪˋtælətɪ] (n.) 活力，生氣
Manufacturing is important to the region's economic vitality.

5) **assured** [əˋʃʊrd] (a.) 確定的，有保障的
The success of the project is far from assured.

6) **precariousness** [prɪˋkɛriəsnɪs] (n.) 不穩定，有危險。
形容詞為**precarious** [prɪˋkɛriəs]
Many workers are concerned with the precariousness of their jobs.

7) **allegiance** [əˋlidʒəns] (n.)（對國家、工作、人）忠誠
The soldiers swore allegiance to the emperor.

8) **marginalized** [ˋmardʒɪnəlˌaɪzd] (a.) 被排擠到社會邊緣的，忽視的
Women have long been marginalized in Muslim countries.

9) **reminder** [rɪˋmaɪndə] (n.) 提示，提醒
The cooling temperatures are a reminder that winter is coming.

by virtue of (something) 因為，由於

也可以說 by reason of...，就是「基於（某種原因）」。

A: Do you think Al was given the position because of his family's influence?
你覺得艾爾獲得那個職位，是因為他的家族影響力嗎？

B: No. I think he was hired by virtue of his talent and experience.
不是。我認為他是因為才能和經驗獲聘。

dig deep 用盡力量

dig deep 字面上是「深入挖掘」，引申為用盡心智、身體的力量。

A: You looked really tired at the end of the race.
你比賽跑到最後時看起來超累的。

B: I was. I really had to dig deep to make it across the finish line.
我是啊。我真的必須使盡最後一絲力氣才能越過終點線。

the corridors of power 權力中心

corridor 為「走廊」的意思。在許多跟政府秘辛、政治黑幕的電影裡，都會出現陰暗大廈走廊的畫面，象徵不為人知的事情在此發生。像白宮或是美國首都華府（Washington D.C.）都可稱為 the corridors of power。

take a stand 採取某立場

stand 當名詞有「立場，態度」的意思，要求人 take a stand 就表示「選邊站」，表明自己的立場。

A: Why are you voting for Hillary?
你為什麼要投給希拉蕊？

B: Because she's taken a stand on women's rights.
因為她採取女權主義的立場。"

day in and day out 日復一日的

這個片語用來形容每天都固定要發生的事，都置於句首或句尾。

A: I'm tired of doing the same boring tasks day in and day out.
我受夠了日復一日做同樣無聊的工作。

B: Maybe it's time to start looking for a new job.
或許到了開始找新工作的時候。

work one's way up 晉升

表示一個人在工作上獲得提拔，爬上更高的位置。

A: How long did it take Steve to work his way up to head chef?
史蒂夫花了多久爬上主廚的位子？

B: Nearly a decade.
將近十年。

glass ceiling 隱形的天花板

指企業對女性職員晉升的障礙，以透明的 glass（玻璃）來形容一種外面看似男女平等，但就是阻擋女性向上晉升的障礙，像 ceiling（天花板）一樣讓女性無法突破。

have a shot (at) 有機會，放手一試

shot 這個字有許多意思，在此指做某事的機會，

A: Do you think our team has a shot at winning the title?
你覺得我們球隊有機會贏得冠軍嗎？

B: I doubt it, but you never know.
我很懷疑，但世事難料啊。

duty calls 責無旁貸

duty 是「責任」，duty calls 字面上的意思是「責任在召喚」，表示義不容辭，此事非做不可。

A: How about seeing a movie tonight?
今晚一起看電影如何？

B: I'd like to, but duty calls. I have to finish my paper.
我很想，但有任務在身。我必須把我的報告寫完。

關係子句中，關係代名詞 who, which 多半可以用關係代名詞 that 代換，但還是有些例外。在前面章節已經介紹只能使用關係代名詞 that 的時機，本文介紹不可使用關代 that 的兩個時間點：

A. 介系詞之後不可使用關代 that，本句即屬此例：

例 **This is the building in which he works.**
那就是他上班的大樓。

　This is the building in that he works. (X)

B. 逗點之後，即「非限定子句」，不可使用關代 that：

例 **This morning I talked to Ms. Chang, who lives next to us.**
今天早上我和住在隔壁的張小姐聊天。

歐巴馬卸任之後鮮少公開露面，面對繼任者川普多次批評他的重要政績，如「歐記健保」（歐巴馬於 2010 年簽署的「平價醫療法案」）、DACA（歐巴馬於 2012 年成立的《延緩遣返無證入境兒童》計畫），並威脅要撤銷，他做何感想？2017 年 5 月，我們在歐巴馬領取甘迺迪勇氣獎的致詞上，聽到了他的心聲。儘管從頭到尾都沒聽到川普、共和黨等字眼，但他沉痛且一再的呼籲，就是在要求執政者及美國大眾「將政策至於政治之上」——這正是甘迺迪勇氣獎頒發給他的理由。

Duty, Honor, Country

義務、榮譽、國家

Douglas MacArthur's Sylvanus Thayer Award Speech
道格拉斯麥克阿瑟席凡尼斯賽爾獎獲獎感言

© Yeongsik Im / Shutterstock.com

As I was leaving the hotel this morning, a doorman asked me, "Where are you 🔤 bound for, General?" and when I replied, "West Point," he remarked, "Beautiful place. Have you ever been there before?"

我今天早上離開旅館時，門房問我：「將軍，你要去哪裡？」我回答：「西點。」他說：「很漂亮的地方。你去過那裡嗎？」

No human being could fail to be deeply moved by such a [1]**tribute** as this award. Coming from a profession I have served so long and a people I have loved so well, it fills me with an emotion I cannot express. But this award is not intended primarily to honor a personality, but to symbolize a great moral code—a code of [2]**conduct** and [3]**chivalry** of those who guard this [4]**beloved** land. For all eyes and for all time, it is an expression of the [5]**ethics** of the American soldier.

沒有人在獲得這個獎項時不會深受感動。這個獎來自我長久以來從事的職業，以及我所熱愛的同袍，所以我此刻心情難以言表。但這個獎的主旨不在推崇人格，而是象徵偉大的道德規範——守護這片心愛土地之人的行為準則和騎士精神。古往今來，這都是美國軍人的道德表現。

VOCABULARY 🎧122

1) **tribute** [ˈtrɪbjut] (n.) 稱頌，致敬
The painting is a tribute to the artist's genius.

2) **conduct** [ˈkɑn.dʌkt] (n.) 行為，品行
The employee was fired because of his unprofessional conduct.

3) **chivalry** [ˈʃɪvəlri] (n.)（中世紀）騎士精神，紳士風度
The age of chivalry is long gone.

4) **beloved** [bɪˈlʌvɪd / bɪˈlʌvd] (a.) 深受喜愛的
Terry's beloved aunt passed away recently.

5) **ethics** [ˈɛθɪks] (n.) 道德標準，倫理觀
The company was known for its poor business ethics.

6) **hallowed** [ˈhælod] (a.) 神聖的，受人崇敬的
Oxford is a hallowed institution of higher learning.

7) **dictate** [ˈdɪk.tet] (v.) 決定，命令，規定，要求
The weather will dictate how long we stay.

Three Hallowed Words
三個神聖的詞

Duty, honor, country. Those three [6)]**hallowed** words [7)]**dictate** 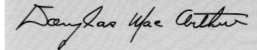 what you ought to be, what you can be, what you will be. They are your [8)]**rallying** point to build courage when courage seems to fail, to regain faith when there seems to be little cause for faith, to create hope when hope becomes [9)]**forlorn**. They build your basic character. They [10)]**mold** you for your future roles as the [11)]**custodians** of the nation's defense. They make you strong enough to know when you are weak, and brave enough to face yourself when you are afraid.

義務、榮譽、國家，這三個神聖的詞決定了你應該成為什麼人、可以成為什麼人、將會成為什麼人。這些詞是你快要喪失勇氣時，用來鼓起勇氣的凝聚力，在理念的信念渺茫時重拾信念，在絕望時創造希望。這些詞能塑造你的基本性格，形塑你未來的角色，使你成為捍衛國家的守護者。這些詞能在你虛弱時堅強地認清事實，在你恐懼時勇敢面對自己。

They teach you to be proud and [12)]**unbending** in honest failure, but humble and gentle in success; not to [13)]**substitute** words for action, nor to seek the path of comfort, but to face the stress of difficulty and challenge; to learn to stand up in the storm, but to have compassion on those who fall; to master yourself before you seek to master others; to have a heart that is clean, a goal that is high; to learn to laugh, yet never forget how to weep; to reach into the future, yet never neglect the past; to be serious, yet never to

Sylvanus Thayer Award
席凡尼斯賽爾獎

這個獎項創於 1958 年，是為了表彰「西點軍校之父」席凡尼斯賽爾上校（Sylvanus Thayer）所設立。他擔任西點軍校校長期間（1817~1833年），除了引進軍事教育理論，提高西點學術水準，更將土木工程設為該校的主要課程，使西點軍校成為優秀的工程學校。美國建國之初的鐵路、公路、橋樑、港口等基本建設，大部由該時期的西點軍校畢業生修建。席凡尼斯賽爾獎每年頒發給對美國有貢獻，能代表西點校訓 Duty, Honor, Country（義務、榮譽、國家），堪為西點學生模範的美國公民。

席凡尼斯賽爾上校畫像，Robert Walter Weir 繪。

take yourself too seriously. They teach you in this way to be an officer and a gentleman.

這些詞教導你在真正失敗時保持自尊且不屈不撓，但在成功時保持謙虛仁厚；勿紙上談兵，勿求安逸，而是要面對困境和挑戰的壓力；學習在暴風雨中屹立不搖，但也要對倒下的人懷抱悲憫；想掌控別人之前，先掌控自己；心靈要純淨，目標要崇高；學會歡笑，但不能忘記怎麼哭泣；展望未來，但不要忘記過去；處事慎重，但不要把自己看得太重。這些詞以這種方式教導你成為軍官和紳士。

Douglas MacArthur
道格拉斯麥克阿瑟

麥克阿瑟將軍（1880~1965 年）是美國著名的軍事將領。麥帥本身就是西點軍校畢業生，1903 年以創校百年來的最佳成績畢業，之後參加第一次世界大戰，戰後（1919 年）擔任西點軍校校長，是史上最年輕校長，他除了增加學術課程、奠定嚴格的軍事紀律，更強調體育運動表現，以符合現代戰爭體能要求。

第一次世界大戰時的麥帥。

---

8) **rally** [ˋræli] (v.)（重新）整合，重振（精神）。**rallying point** 即「號召力，凝聚點」
The commander rallied the troops and led the charge.

9) **forlorn** [fɚˋlɔrn] (a.) 幾乎無望的，被遺棄的，孤獨的
The orphans had forlorn looks on their faces.

10) **mold** [mold] (v.) 塑造
The coach hopes to mold his players into a winning team.

11) **custodian** [kʌsˋtodiən] (n.) 監護人，保管人
Teachers are the custodians of knowledge.

12) **unbending** [ʌnˋbɛndɪŋ] (a.) 不屈不撓的，堅定的，不妥協的
The union was unbending in its demands for higher pay.

13) **substitute** [ˋsʌbstəˌtut] (v.) 替代
You can substitute honey for sugar in the recipe.

© Joseph Sohm / Shutterstock.com

West Point 西點軍校

The United States Military Academy（USMA， 美國軍事學院），簡稱為 West Point, Army（西點陸軍學校），位於紐約哈德遜河西岸。創立於 1802 年，西點是美國最早的軍事學院，為世界四大軍校之一，創校 200 年來畢業的軍事人才中，出了 3700 為將軍。西點軍校治學非常嚴格，新生必須學業、體能及領導能力優異（1976 年開始招收女生），還要有被淘汰的心理準備──西點軍校第一年的開除率為 23%，最後平均只有七成的入學生能夠畢業。畢業生取得學士學位，必須入伍服役至少 5 年。

西點軍校校徽

The American Soldier
美國士兵

And what sort of soldiers are those you are to lead? Are they reliable? Are they brave? Are they capable of victory? Their story is known to all of you. It is the story of the American soldier. My estimate of him was formed on the battlefield many, many years ago, and has never changed. I regarded him then as I regard him now, as one of the world's noblest figures, not only as one of the finest military characters, but also as one of the most [1]**stainless**. His name and fame are the [2]**birthright** of every American citizen. In his youth and strength, his love and loyalty, he gave all that [3]**mortality** can give. He needs no [4]**eulogy** from me or from any other man. He has written his own history and has written it in red on his enemy's breast.

你帶領哪種士兵？他們可靠嗎？勇敢嗎？有能力打勝仗嗎？他們的故事各位都耳熟能詳。這是美國士兵的故事。我對美國士兵的評價多年前就已在戰場上建立，且從未改變。他當時在我心目中的印象跟現在一樣，是世上最高尚的人，不僅是最優秀的軍事人物，也是最完美無瑕的。他的名譽和聲望是每個美國公民與生俱來的權利。他以青春和毅力、愛與忠誠，付出所有人類所能給予的。他不需要我或其他人的頌揚。他已自行寫下自己的歷史，而且是用敵人胸膛上的鮮血所寫。

But when I think of his patience under [5]**adversity**, of his courage under fire, and of his modesty in victory, I am filled with an emotion of admiration I cannot put into words. He belongs to history as furnishing one of the greatest examples of successful [6]**patriotism**. He belongs to [7]**posterity** as the instructor of future generations in the principles of liberty and freedom. He

VOCABULARY 🎧124

1) **stainless** [ˋstenlɪs] (a.) 無瑕疵的，未被玷汙的
   Few politicians have stainless reputations.

2) **birthright** [ˋbɝθ͵raɪt] (n) 與生俱來的權力，基本人權
   Education is the birthright of every citizen.

3) **mortality** [mɔrˋtælətɪ] (n.) 人類，必死性
   His father's death made him more aware of his own mortality.

4) **eulogy** [ˋjulədʒɪ] (n.) 悼詞，讚頌
   Stanley's son delivered the eulogy at his funeral.

5) **adversity** [ædˋvɝsətɪ] (n.) 逆境，厄運
   We must remain strong in the face of adversity.

6) **patriotism** [ˋpetrɪə͵tɪzəm] (n.) 愛國精神，愛國主義
   No one can question the politician's patriotism.

7) **posterity** [pɑsˋtɛrətɪ] (n.) 後世，後代子孫
   Historic sites should be preserved for posterity.

belongs to the present, to us, by his virtues and by his achievements.

但我一想到他在逆境中的耐心、在火場中的勇氣，以及戰勝時的謙遜，都讓我充滿無法言喻的敬佩之情。他屬於歷史，為最成功的愛國主義範例增添一筆。他屬於後代子孫，是後世自由和自主信條的指導者。他和他的美德與成就都屬於現在、屬於我們。

Enduring Fortitude
堅韌不拔

In 20 campaigns, on a hundred battlefields, around a thousand campfires, I have witnessed that enduring [8)]**fortitude** and that [9)]**invincible** determination which have carved his statue in the hearts of his people. From one end of the world to the other, he has drained deep the [10)]**chalice** of courage.

在二十場戰役中、在一百座戰場上、在一千堆營火旁，我見證過他堅韌不拔和不屈不撓的決心，這種形象已烙印在人民心中。從天涯到海角，他已深深乾下勇氣之杯。

> "We are not retreating — we are advancing in another direction.
>
> 我們並非撤退——我們是朝另一個方向前進。

絕不撤退的麥克阿瑟將軍

The soldier, above all other men, is required to practice the greatest act of religious training—sacrifice. In battle, and in the face of danger and death, he [11)]**discloses** those divine [12)]**attributes** which his 🔲 Maker gave when he created man in his own image. No physical courage and no [13)]**brute** instinct can take the place of the divine help which alone can sustain him.

士兵必須超越所有人來實踐終極宗教訓練的行為——犧牲。在戰爭中，在面臨危險和死亡時，他要顯露出造物主在按自己形象創造人類時所賦予他的屬靈。沒有不怕死的勇氣和殘暴本能可代替神性的幫助，唯有神性能支撐他。

However horrible the incidents of war may be, the soldier who is 🔲 called upon to offer and to give his life for his country is the noblest development of mankind. You now face a new world, a world of change. The thrust into outer space of the satellite and missiles marked the beginning of another [14)]**epoch** in the long story of mankind—the chapter of the space age.

無論戰爭的狀況有多可怕，被要求為國家犧牲性命的士兵是人類最高尚的產物。你們正面臨新的世界、變動的世界。在衛星和飛彈推進外太空時，就已翻開另一段漫長人類史的時代——太空時代的篇章。

---

8) **fortitude** [ˋfɔrtəˌtud] (n.) 堅忍，剛毅
Richard bore his long illness with great fortitude.

9) **invincible** [ɪnˋvɪnsəbel] (a.) 無敵的
Yesterday's loss proved that the team isn't invincible.

10) **chalice** [ˋtʃælɪs] (n.)（天主教）聖餐杯，高教酒杯
The priest placed the golden chalice on the altar.

11) **disclose** [dɪsˋkloz] (v.) 顯露，透漏，公開
The reporter refused to disclose the identity of his source.

12) **attribute** [ˋætrəˌbjut] (n.) 特質
The interviewer asked me what I consider my best attribute.

13) **brute** [brut] (a.) 畜生（般）的，野蠻的，粗暴的
The dictator ruled his country with brute force.

14) **epoch** [ˋɛpək] (n.)（新）紀元，（重要）時期
The 19th century was an epoch of great change.

> Age wrinkles the body. Quitting wrinkles the soul.
>
> 年老讓身體變皺。放棄讓靈魂生皺紋。

麥克阿瑟將軍談放棄

Winning Wars
贏得戰爭

And through all this change and development, your mission remains fixed, determined, [1)]**inviolable**—it is to win our wars. All other public purposes, all other public projects, all public needs, great or small, will find others for their accomplishment; but you are the ones who are trained to fight. Yours is the profession of arms, the will to win, the sure knowledge that in war there is no substitute for victory, that if you lose, the nation will be destroyed, that the very [2)]**obsession** of your public service must be duty, honor, country.

歷經所有改變和發展，你們的任務依然堅定不變、不容違背，就是贏得戰爭。所有其他公共目標、公共計畫、公共需求，不論大小，都有其他人會去完成；但你們是為了打仗而受訓的一群。你們是以戰鬥為職業，以戰勝為意志，你們當然都知道，在戰爭中，勝利是

無可替代的，你們若打敗仗，國家會被毀滅，所以你們最該執著的公共服務必定是義務、榮譽和國家。

Others will debate the controversial issues, national and international, which divide men's minds. But [3)]**serene**, calm, [4)]**aloof**, you stand as the nation's war guardians, as its lifeguards from the raging tides of international conflict, as its [5)]**gladiators** in the [6)]**arena** of battle.

有人會辯論具爭議性的全國和國際議題，這會導致人民意見分裂。但你們身為國家的戰爭守護者，身為國際紛爭怒潮的救生員，身為戰場上的鬥士，你們要穩重、冷靜、保持超然。

For a century and a half you have defended, guarded and protected its hallowed traditions of liberty and freedom, of right and justice. Let civilian voices argue the merits or [7)]**demerits** of our processes of government. Whether our strength is being [8)]**sapped** by politics grown too [9)]**corrupt**, by crime grown too [10)]**rampant**, by

> Never give an order that can't be obeyed.
>
> 絕不要發出無法被遵守的命令。

麥克阿瑟將軍談領導統御

VOCABULARY　126

1) **inviolable** [ɪnˋvaɪələbəl] (a.) 不可侵犯的
All citizens have the inviolable right to a fair trial.

2) **obsession** [əbˋsɛʃən] (n.) 執著，著迷
Our company is proud of its obsession with quality.

3) **serene** [səˋrin] (a.) 安詳的，平靜的，穩重的
The Buddha statue wore a serene smile.

4) **aloof** [əˋluf] (a.) 超然的，冷漠的
I try to remain aloof from office politics.

5) **gladiator** [ˋglædɪˌetə] (n.)（古羅馬）鬥士
I loved Russell Crowe's performance as the gladiator.

6) **arena** [əˋrinə] (n.) 競技場，競爭場所
Today's businesses must be able to compete in the international arena.

7) **demerit** [diˋmɛrɪt] (n.) 缺點，過失，記過
The plan has both merits and demerits.

8) **sap** [sæp] (v.) 削弱，大傷元氣
Exercising in the heat really saps my strength.

9) **corrupt** [kəˋrʌpt] (a.) 貪污的，腐敗的
The corrupt official was sentenced to life in prison.

10) **rampant** [ˋræmpənt] (a.) 猖獗的，蔓延的
The government fought to bring the rampant inflation under control.

11) **guidepost** [ˋgaɪdˌpost] (n.) 指導原則，路標
God's word serves as our guidepost.

morals grown too low, by taxes grown too high; whether our personal liberties are as firm and complete as they should be. These great national problems are not for your professional participation or military solution. Your [11]**guidepost** stands out in the night: duty, honor, country.

一個世紀半以來，你們已守護、保衛和保護自由自主與公平正義的神聖傳統。至於我們政府程序的優點或缺點，就由平民去發聲辯論，不論我們的力量因為政治過於腐敗而耗盡，或因犯罪過於猖獗、或道德過於敗壞、或課稅過高；不論我們的個人自由是否如情理之中的堅定和完整。這些重大的國家問題不是我們的職責，也不適合用軍力解決。在暗夜裡指引你們道路的原則就是：義務、榮譽和國家。

66 Preparedness is the key to success and victory.

萬全準備是通往成功與勝利之路。

麥克阿瑟將軍談成功之道

66 The best luck of all is the luck you make for yourself.

最棒的運氣是自己創造的。

麥克阿瑟將軍談運氣

The Long Gray Line
西點軍魂

You are the 1)**leaven** which binds together the entire 2)**fabric** of our national system of defense. From your ranks come the great captains who hold the nation's destiny in their hands the moment the war bell sounds. The Long Gray Line has never failed us. Were you to do so, a million ghosts in brown 3)**khaki**, in blue and gray, would rise from their white crosses thundering those magic words: duty, honor, country.

你們是結合整個國家防衛系統結構的媒介。在戰爭鐘響的那一刻，國家的命運就掌握在你們隊伍中偉大的領導手上。西點軍魂從不讓我們失望。你們若讓我們失望，身穿卡其色、藍色和灰色制服的百萬軍魂，會從插著白色十字架的墳墓中站起來，怒吼著神奇的口號：義務、榮譽和國家。

This does not mean that you are 4)**warmongers**. On the contrary, the soldier, above all other people, prays for peace, for he must suffer and bear the deepest wounds and 5)**scars** of war. But always in our ears ring the 6)**ominous** words of Plato, that wisest of all philosophers: "Only the dead have seen the end of war."

這不表示我們是好戰份子。反之，士兵會比所有人更祈求和平，因為他必須承受最深的戰爭創傷和傷疤。但我們耳邊總是會響起最有智慧的哲學家，柏拉圖的不祥預言：「唯有死者能看到戰爭結束。」

The shadows are lengthening for me. The 7)**twilight** is here. My days of old have vanished. They have gone 8)**glimmering** through the dreams of things that were. Their memory is one of beauty, watered by tears and 9)**caressed** by the smiles of yesterday.

我的影子逐漸拉長，暮色將至，我的遲暮之年消逝了。歲月隨著往日夢境閃爍而逝。昔日美麗的記憶有淚水滋潤、有歡笑撫慰。

I listen then, but with thirsty ear, for the melody of faint 10)**bugles** blowing 11)**reveille**, of far drums beating the long roll. In my dreams, I hear again the crash of guns, the strange, 12)**mournful** 13)**mutter** of the battlefield. But in the evening of my memory, always I come back to West Point. Always there echoes and re-echoes: duty, honor, country.

我渴望的耳朵留神聽著當年吹著起床號的軍號，聽著遠方的擊鼓聲隆隆作響。在睡夢中，我再次聽到槍響、戰場上怪異的悲悽低語聲。但在午夜夢迴的記憶中，我總是回到西點。總是有個聲音在耳邊一再迴盪：義務、榮譽、國家。

Today marks my final roll call with you, but I want you to know that when I cross the river, my last conscious thoughts will be of the Corps, and the Corps, and the Corps. I 14)**bid** you farewell.

今天是我最後一次為大家點名，但我希望你們知道，待我渡過冥河時，我最後一絲意識會是軍隊，除了軍隊還是軍隊。珍重再見。

VOCABULARY 128

1) **leaven** [ˋlɛvən] (n.) 酵素，潛移默化的力量
Love is the leaven that transforms our lives.

2) **fabric** [ˋfæbrɪk] (n.) 結構，構造，組織
Laws help hold the fabric of society together.

3) **khaki** [ˋkæki] (n.) 卡其布（軍服）
Khaki is a very durable material.

4) **warmonger** [ˋwɔrˌmʌŋgə] (n.) 主戰者，好戰份子
Churchill was called a warmonger by his critics.

5) **scar** [skɑr] (n.) 疤，傷痕，創傷
The conflict left deeps scars on the country.

6) **ominous** [ˋɑmɪnəs] (a.) 不祥的，預兆的
The ominous sound of approaching warplanes filled the air.

7) **twilight** [ˋtwaɪˌlaɪt] (n.) 黃昏，晚期
The singer is in the twilight of her musical career.

8) **glimmer** [ˋglɪmə] (v.) 發出微光，閃爍不定
The lights of the city glimmered in the distance.

9) **caress** [kəˋrɛs] (v./n.) 撫慰，擁抱
She caressed his shoulder and whispered in his ear.

10) **bugle** [ˋbjugəl] (n.) 號角，軍號
The soldiers awoke at sunrise to the sound of the bugle.

11) **reveille** [ˋrɛvəli] (n.) 起床號，早晨集合點名
Reveille was played at 6 a.m. every morning.

12) **mournful** [ˋmornfəl] (a.) 悲傷的，憂傷的
The musicians at the funeral played a mournful tune.

13) **mutter** [ˋmʌtə] (n./v.) 嘀咕，咕噥，抱怨
The old man muttered to himself as he walked down the street.

14) **bid** [bɪd] (v.) （舊）祝，向（人）表示
I must now bid you goodbye.

bound for 前往（目的）

表示朝一個特定的目標前進。bound for 後面接的可以是地方（即「目的地」），也可以是事物（即「目標」）。

A: Excuse me. Is this the New York train?
不好意思，請問這是到紐約的火車嗎？
B: No. It's bound for Boston.
不。這是開往波士頓。

Maker 造物者

即 God（上帝），演講中麥帥接著說的話即出自《聖經》〈創世紀 1:27〉：God created man in his own image。英文片語 meet (one's) maker 直譯為「去見上帝」，也就是蒙主寵召，死了。

A: This is the third time Steve's been caught drunk driving.
這是史蒂夫第三次被抓到酒駕了。
B: Wow. He's gonna meet his maker one of these days.
哇。他遲早要蒙主寵召了。

「門當戶對」的平行結構

此篇演講運用大量的平行結構，讀起來順暢並令人印象深刻。平行結構運用標點符號或連接詞，將相同的文法結構做連結，以表達相似的概念，這種簡單的結構能讓句子更簡潔有力，其標題「Duty, Honor, Country」就是平行結構。注意，平行結構講求門當戶對，逗點或連接詞前後所接的結構要一樣才行。

1. 形容詞的平行結構

例 **Early to bed and early to rise makes a man healthy, wealthy and wise.**
早睡早起讓人身體健康、富裕、且聰明。

2. 動詞的平行結構

例 **To be, or not to be, that is the question.**
做與不做都是問題。

例 **Surfing, skiing and skateboarding are my favorite sports.**
衝浪、滑雪和溜滑板是我最喜歡的運動。

3. 介系詞的平行結構

例 **I promise to be true to you in good times and in bad, in sickness and in health.**
我承諾，無論順境或逆境、疾病或健康，我都會對你忠誠。

call upon 號召，要求

call 有「召集」的意思，call upon (sb.) 表示一個人受到召集。也可以說 call on。

A: What are those people marching about?
這些人是為何遊行？
B: They're calling on the government to end the death penalty.
他們在要求政府廢除死刑。

The Long Gray Line 西點軍魂

這個詞是指西點軍校的學生及畢業生，因為西點的制服是灰色的。一部 1955 年的美國軍教片就叫《西點軍魂》The Long Gray Line，這部真人實事改編的電影透過校內老士官長的故事，讓人窺見西點軍校的精神。

© imdb.com

1955 年電影《西點軍魂》金獎導演約翰福特（John Ford）作品。

on the contrary 正好相反

contrary 是指「對立的一方，反面」，on the contrary「在相反那一方」，就是正好相反的意思了。

A: Was the professor's lecture boring?
教授的演講無聊嗎？
B: No. On the contrary, it was quite interesting.
沒有，而且正好相反，他講得相當有趣。

long roll 戰鼓聲

在古代，士兵聽到一長串連續擊鼓聲，就代表敵軍來襲，必須趕緊整隊，準備作戰。

roll call 點名

這裡的 roll 是「名冊」的意思，roll call 表示照名冊呼喊，有就是課堂上或軍隊「點名」的意思。

第二次世界大戰，麥帥受召到菲律賓擔任美國遠東軍總司令，並受委任指揮澳洲軍隊，1944 年晉升五星上將（five-star general，歷史上只有 9 位）。戰後參與日本重建、韓戰，奠定美國與台灣的軍事合作。1951 年因意見不合被杜魯門總統解職，回到美國受到全國民眾英雄式歡迎，著名的《老兵不死》Old Soldiers Never Die 演說即在此時發表，聲望如日中天時出馬角逐共和黨總統候選人失利，之後告老還鄉。本篇演說發表於 1962 年 5 月 12 日，是麥克阿瑟將軍最後一次造訪西點軍校。

© catwalker / Shutterstock.com

© Route66 / Shutterstock.com

The Source of My Songs

我歌曲的來源

Leonard Cohen's Prince of Asturias Award Speech
李歐納柯恩阿斯圖里亞斯親王獎得獎感言

It's a great honor to stand here before you tonight. Perhaps, like the great [1)]**maestro**, [LG] Riccardo Muti, [GM] I'm not used to standing in front of an audience without an orchestra behind me, but I'll do my best as a [2)]**solo** artist tonight.

今晚能站在這裡是一大榮耀。或許就像大師里卡多穆蒂一樣，我不習慣在背後沒有管弦樂隊時站在觀眾前面，但我今晚會盡力演好獨角戲。

 An Expression of Gratitude
表達感激之情

I stayed up all night last night wondering what I might say to this [3)]**august** assembly. And after I'd eaten all the chocolate bars and peanuts in the [4)]**minibar**, I [5)]**scribbled** a few words. I don't think I have to [LG] refer to them. Obviously, I'm deeply

VOCABULARY 🎧130

1) **maestro** [ˈmaɪstro] (n.) 大音樂家，知名指揮家
   Toscanini was the greatest maestro of his day.

2) **solo** [ˈsolo] (a.) 單獨的，單獨表演的
   The explorer made a solo trip to the South Pole.

3) **august** [ɔˈgʌst] (a.) 尊榮的，令人敬畏的
   We found ourselves in august company at the royal ball.

4) **minibar** [ˈmɪnɪˌbɑr] (n.)
   （旅館客房內的）冰箱，經常備有水酒、零食
   Do we have to pay for the drinks in the minibar?

5) **scribble** [ˈskrɪbəl] (v.) 潦草地書寫，隨意亂畫
   Kelly got in trouble for scribbling in her textbook.

6) **dimension** [dɪˈmɛnʃən] (n.) 方面，層面
   Becoming a volunteer has added a whole new dimension to my life.

7) **unease** [ʌnˈiz] (n.) 心神不寧，不安，不自在
   North Korea's missile tests have caused growing unease among its neighbors.

8) **charlatan** [ˈʃɑrlətən] (n.) 江湖術士，不懂裝懂的人，騙子
   The famous healer turned out to be a charlatan.

touched to be recognized by the Foundation. But I've come here tonight to express another [6)]**dimension** of gratitude. I think I can do it in three or four minutes, and I will try.

我昨晚整夜沒睡，想著要對這麼尊貴的來賓說什麼。我吃光房間小冰箱裡的巧克力棒和花生後，草草寫了幾個字，但我想不必再參考筆記。很顯然，能受到基金會肯定讓我深受感動。但我今晚到此是要表達另一層面的感激。我想我可以在三、四分鐘內說完，我儘量。

When I was packing in Los Angeles to come here, I had a sense of [7)]**unease** because I've always felt some ambiguity about an award for poetry. Poetry comes from a place that no one commands and no one conquers. So I feel somewhat like a [8)]**charlatan** to accept an award for an activity which I don't command. In other words, if I knew where the good songs came from I'd go there more often.

我在洛杉磯打包行李準備來這裡時，我感到一絲不安，因為一直以來，我對辦給詩詞的獎感覺有點複雜。詩詞屬於無人稱王、未被征服的領域。所以在一個未能掌控的領域得獎，讓我感覺有點像江湖騙子。換句話說，要是知道好歌來自哪裡，我會更常去那裡。

Leonard Cohen 李歐納柯恩

1934 ～ 2016 年，加拿大詩人、歌手、音樂家。作品經常關切宗教、社會、政治議題，愛與恨、孤單與疏離也是常見的主題。原本是詩人及小説家的柯恩自小受愛唱歌的母親音樂薰陶，但他一直到 33 歲才展開音樂事業。他是藝文界難得的通才，創作形式多元（詩、小説、流行音樂、宗教音樂、爵士樂），含括領域也廣（出書、音樂、電視、電影）。1984 年專輯 *Various Positions* 當中的歌曲 Hallelujah（哈雷路亞）算是他最為人知的作品，至今已被約 200 位藝人以各種語言翻唱，為美國音樂史上最常被改編、改編形式最多變的歌曲之一。

© john dory / Shutterstock.com

Prince of Asturias Award
阿斯圖里亞斯親王獎

創立於 1981 年，由阿斯圖里亞斯親王基金會發起，獎勵對象為藝術、文學、社會科學、科學技術、交流與人文、國際合作各界的傑出貢獻者，1986 年增設和平獎，1987 年增設體育獎。儘管這個獎的得主至目前為止大半為西班牙及西班牙語系國籍，但並不以此為限，有助於讓世界看到西語界對全球的貢獻。

由於創立初期的阿斯圖里亞斯親王已於 2014 年登基成為西班牙國王費利佩六世，基金會及獎項均已改為符合新繼承人萊昂諾爾公主性別的阿斯圖里亞斯女親王獎（Princess of Asturias Award）。

©Wikimedia Commons（Creator:FPA）

Love is a fire
It burns everyone
It disfigures everyone
It is the world's excuse
for being ugly

愛是一把火
燒傷人
摧毀人
愛是世界變得醜惡的藉口

李歐納柯恩談愛

琴格 (fret)

A Beautiful Instrument
漂亮的樂器

I was ¹⁾**compelled** in the ²⁾**midst** of that ³⁾**ordeal** of packing to go and open my guitar. I have a **LG** Conde guitar, which was made in Spain in the great ⁴⁾**workshop** at No. 7 Gravina Street—a beautiful instrument that I acquired over 40 years ago. I took it out of the case and I lifted it. It seemed to be filled with helium—it was so light. And I brought it to my face. I put my face close to the beautifully designed **LG** rosette, and I ⁵⁾**inhaled** the fragrance of the living wood. You know that wood never dies.

我在打包行李時感到很煩，不得不打開吉他盒。我有一把 Conde 吉他，西班牙格拉維納街 7 號一間很棒的工作室製造的，是我在 40 年前購得的漂亮樂器。我把吉他拿出硬盒，舉起來。它像是灌了氫氣，真的好輕。我把吉他拿到面前，把臉湊近設計精美的玫瑰花飾，吸入實木的芳香。你知道木頭永遠不會死。

I inhaled the fragrance of ⁶⁾**cedar** as fresh as the first day that I acquired the guitar. And a voice seemed to say to me, "You are an old man and you have not said thank you. You have not brought your gratitude back to the soil from which this fragrance ⁷⁾**arose**." And so I come here tonight

1) **compel** [kəm`pɛl] (v.) 強迫，使不得不
The court compelled the man to appear as a witness.

2) **midst** [midst] (n.) 當中，中間
The country is in the midst of a severe recession.

3) **ordeal** [ɔr`diəl] (n.) 折磨，嚴峻考驗
Taking the civil service exam was quite an ordeal.

4) **workshop** [`wɜk.ʃɑp] (n.) 工作室，小工廠
The wooden toys are made at a small workshop.

5) **inhale** [ɪn`hel] (v.) 吸入（氣體），吸氣
Several people were taken to the hospital after inhaling the fumes.

6) **cedar** [`sidɚ] (n.) 西洋杉，雪松
Lebanon is famous for its cedar forests.

rosette 玫瑰花飾

文中是指木吉他中央孔外圈的環狀花紋。rosette 是法文的 rose（玫瑰），用來指各種圓形或環形的花樣設計，如 rosette window（玫瑰花窗）。

to thank the soil and the soul of this people that has given me so much—because I know just as an identity card is not a man, a credit [8]**rating** is not a country.

我吸聞著那西洋杉的芳香，就跟買到吉他的第一天一樣清新。有個聲音似乎在對我說：「你年事已高，而且你沒有說過謝謝。你沒有把你的感激之情帶回蘊育出這種香氣的土壤。」所以今晚我來這裡感謝這塊土地，和這個民族靈魂豐盛的恩賜，因為我知道一紙身份證不代表一個人，信用評級不代表一個國家。

 ## Finding a Voice
尋找自己的聲音

Now, you know of my deep association and [9]**fraternity** with the poet Federico Garcia Lorca. I could say that when I was a young man, an [10]**adolescent**, and I hungered for a voice, I studied

---

LG

西班牙傑出作家 Federico Garcia Lorca

1898 ～ 1936 年。被視為西班牙最傑出作家的佛多里柯賈西亞羅卡是一位詩人及劇作家，以作品批判資本主義及強權欺壓，1936 年西班牙內戰時期因反對法西斯主義叛軍，遭叛軍殺害。他的作品在佛朗哥將軍當權期間一直被禁，直到 70 年代才解禁。

© rook76 / Shutterstock.com

---

the English poets and I knew their work well, and I copied their styles, but I couldn't find a voice. It was only when I read, even in translation, the works of Lorca that I understood that there was a voice. It's not that I copied his voice. I wouldn't dare. But he gave me permission to find a voice, to locate a voice; that is, to locate a self, a self that is not fixed, a self that struggles for its own existence.

大家都知道我和詩人佛多里柯賈西亞羅卡的淵源及孺慕之情。我可以說，我年輕時，還是個青少年，我渴望屬於自己的聲音，我研究了英國詩人，我很熟悉他們的作品，我模仿他們的風格，但我找不到屬於我的聲音。只有在我讀到羅卡的作品，即便是翻譯版，我才明白就是那種聲音。不是我模仿他的聲音。我不敢。但是他允許我去找出自己的聲音，鎖定自己的聲音；也就是找到自我，一個不被定型的自我，一個為自己的存在而奮鬥的自我。

And as I grew older, I understood that instructions came with this voice. What were these instructions? The instructions were never to [11]**lament** casually. And if one is to express the great inevitable defeat that awaits us all, it must be done within the strict [12]**confines** of dignity and beauty.

隨著年紀增長，我明白這個聲音伴隨著指引。是什麼指引？這些指引叫我不能無病呻吟。一個人若要表達出我們終將面對的失敗，一定要用尊嚴和美麗來詮釋。

And so I had a voice, but I didn't have an instrument. I didn't have a song. And now I'm going to tell you very briefly a story of how I got my song.

所以我有自己的聲音，但我沒有樂器。我沒有歌。現在我要告訴各位一個小故事，我是怎麼找到我的歌。

---

7) **arise** [əˋraɪz] (v.) 產生，出現，形成。
三態為：**arise**，**arose**，**arisen**
If any problems arise, just let me know.

8) **rating** [ˋretɪŋ] (n.) 評分，評價
That hotel has a two-star rating.

9) **fraternity** [frəˋtɜnəti] (n.) 友愛，手足之情
The Olympic Games help promote fraternity among nations.

10) **adolescent** [͵ædəlˋɛsnt] (n.) 青少年
Many adolescents are bullied online.

11) **lament** [ləˋmɛnt] (v.) 悲嘆，痛惜
Local residents lamented the loss of the park.

12) **confines** [ˋkɑnfaɪns] (n.)
（固定用複數）範圍，界限
The criminal was ordered to remain in the confines of his home.

I was an [1]**indifferent** guitar player. I banged the [2]**chords**. I only knew a few of them. I **LG** sat around with my college friends, drinking and singing the folk songs, or the popular songs of the day, but I never **LG** in a thousand years thought of myself as a musician or as a singer.

我本來是個平庸的吉他手，我會彈幾個和弦，只是略懂皮毛。我跟大學朋友坐在一起殺時間，喝酒唱民歌，或是唱點當時的流行歌，但我從來沒有想過自己是音樂家或是歌手。

Finding a Teacher
尋找老師

One day in the early '60s, I was visiting my mother's house in Montreal. The house is beside a park, and in the park there's a tennis

" When you've fallen on the highway
and you're lying in the rain,
and they ask you how you're doing
of course you'll say you can't complain...

你已經跌在路上
躺在雨中
大家問你還好吧
當然你會說「還過得去」…

李歐納柯恩談低落

© Route66 / Shutterstock.com

court where many people come to watch the beautiful young tennis players enjoy their sport. I wandered back to this park, which I'd known since my childhood, and there was a young man playing a guitar. He was playing a [3]**flamenco** guitar, and he was surrounded by two or three girls and boys who were listening to him. I loved the way he played. There was something about the way he played that captured me.

60 年代初某一天，我回蒙特婁看我的母親。我母親的房子在一處公園旁，公園裡有一座網球場，許多人會來看青春美麗的網球員打球。我漫步回到這座兒時常來的公園，有個年輕人在那裡彈吉他。他彈著佛朗明哥吉他，周圍有兩、三個女孩和男孩在欣賞他的彈奏。我喜歡他彈吉他的方式。他彈吉他的方式吸引了我。

It was the way I wanted to play—and knew that I would never be able to play. And I sat there with the other listeners for a few

---

VOCABULARY 134

1) **indifferent** [ɪnˋdɪfrənt] (a.) 平庸的，漠不關心的
Fans were angered by the team's indifferent performance.

2) **chord** [kɔrd] (n.) （音樂）和弦
I can only play a few simple chords.

3) **flamenco** [fləˋmɛŋko] (n.) 佛朗明哥舞，佛朗明哥音樂
We saw an amazing flamenco performance in Madrid.

4) **appropriate** [əˋproprɪət] (a.) 適當的，恰當的
Is this movie appropriate for small children?

5) **broken** [ˋbrokən] (a.) （語言）不流利的，爛的
The waiter couldn't understand our broken Spanish.

6) **appointment** [əˋpɔɪntmənt] (n.) 預約，約會
That salon is always busy, so you should make an appointment.

7) **sequence** [ˋsikwəns] (n.) 一連串，連續，順序
The witness described the sequence of events that led to the murder.

8) **tremolo** [ˋtrɛmə͵lo] (n.) 顫音
I'm learning how to play tremolo on the violin.

9) **fret** [frɛt] (n.) 琴格，是琴頸上用銅條劃分出來的格子，手指按在不同位置能決定高低音
The frets on my guitar were so worn I had to replace them.

moments and when there was a silence, an 4)**appropriate** silence, I asked him if he would give me guitar lessons. He was a young man from Spain, and we could only communicate in my 5)**broken** French and his broken French. He didn't speak English. And he agreed to give me guitar lessons. I pointed to my mother's house, which you could see from the tennis court, and we made an 6)**appointment**; we settled the price.

那就是我想彈吉他的方式，而且我知道我永遠無法彈成這樣。我跟其他人坐在一起聽了一會兒，現場一度安靜下來，不讓人覺得突兀的片刻安靜，趁這時候我問他是不是願意教我彈吉他。他是來自西班牙的年輕人，我們只能用破法語彼此溝通。他不會說英語。他同意教我彈吉他。我指了指母親的房子，從網球場就可以看到，然後我們約好時間，也談好價錢。

And he came to my mother's house the next day and he said, "Let me hear you play something." I tried to play something. He said, "You don't know how to play, do you?" I said, "No, I really don't know how to play." He said, "First of all, let me tune your guitar. It's all  out of tune." So he took the guitar and he tuned it. He said, "It's not a bad guitar." It wasn't the Conde, but it wasn't a bad guitar. So he handed it back to me. He said, "Now play." I couldn't play any better.

隔天他來到我母親家，他說：「讓我聽聽你彈的。」我試著彈了一下。他說：「你不會彈，對吧？」我說：「不會，我真的不會彈。」他說：「首先，我要幫你的吉他調音。這些音調全不對。」於是他拿起吉他調音。他說：「這吉他不錯。」這不是 Conde 牌，但還不錯。他把吉他還給我。他說：「彈吧。」我彈得沒有比較好。

He said "Let me show you some chords." And he took the guitar and he produced a sound from that guitar that I'd never heard. And he played a 7)**sequence** of chords with a 8)**tremolo**, and he said, "Now you do it." I said, "It's out of the question. I can't possibly do it." He said, "Let me put your fingers on the 9)**frets**." And he put my fingers on the frets. And he said, "Now play." It was a mess. He said, "I'll come back tomorrow."

他說：「我教你彈幾個和弦。」然後他拿起吉他，彈了幾個音，是我的吉他從未發出過的樂音。然後他用顫音彈一連串和弦，然後說：「換你。」我說：「不可能，我彈不出來。」他說：「我幫你把手指放在琴格上。」然後他把我的手指放在琴格上。然後他說：「彈吧。」彈得亂七八糟。他說：「我明天再來。」

> There is a crack in everything. That's how the light gets in.
>
> 一切皆有殘缺。
> 這樣光才進得來。
>
> 李歐納柯恩談希望

He came back tomorrow. He put my hands on the guitar. He placed it on my lap in the way that was appropriate, and I began again with those six chords—a six chord [1)]**progression** that many flamenco songs are based on. I was a little better that day.

他明天回來，把我的手放在吉他上，把吉他放在我腿上正確的位置，我開始彈六個和弦進行，許多佛拉明哥歌曲都是根據這六個和弦進行編曲的。我那天彈得好一點了。

The third day—improved, somewhat improved. But I knew the chords now. And I knew that although I couldn't [2)]**coordinate** my fingers with my thumb to produce the correct tremolo pattern, I knew the chords. I knew them very well by this point.

第三天，有進步了，多少有點進步。至少我會彈和弦了。我知道我的手指和拇指雖然還不協調，無法彈出正確的顫音，但我會彈和弦了。這時我已經彈得很熟了。

Losing a Teacher
失去老師

The next day, he didn't come. I had the number of his [3)]**boarding house** in Montreal. I phoned to find out why he'd missed the appointment, and they told me that he'd taken his life—that he'd committed suicide. I knew nothing about the man. I didn't know what part of Spain he came from. I didn't know why he came to Montreal. I didn't know why he stayed there. I didn't know why he appeared there in that tennis court. I didn't know why he took his life. I was deeply [4)]**saddened**, of course.

隔天，他沒來。我有他在蒙特婁寄宿家庭的電話號碼。我打電話過去，想知道他為何沒依約前來，他們告訴我，他自殺了。我不認識那個人，我不知道他來自西班牙哪裡。我不知道他為何來蒙特婁。我不知道他為何留在那裡。我不知道他為何那天出現在網球場。我不知道他為何自殺。當然，我很難過。

But now I disclose something that I've never spoken about in public. It was those six chords—it was that guitar pattern that has been the basis of all my songs and all my music.

但我現在把這件從未公開的事說出來了。那六個和弦的吉他指型，是我所有歌曲和音樂的基礎。

Dimensions of Gratitude
各方面的感激

So now you will begin to understand the dimensions of the gratitude I have for this country. Everything that you have found [5)]**favorable** in my work comes from this place. Everything that you have found favorable in my songs and my poetry is inspired by this soil.

所以你們現在會開始瞭解我對這國家各個層面的感激。你們若喜歡我的作品，一切都是來自這地方。你們若是喜歡我的歌和詩，一切靈感都來自這片土地。

So I thank you so much for the warm [6)]**hospitality** that you have shown my work because it is really yours, and you have allowed me to [7)]**affix** my signature to the bottom of the page. Thank you so much, ladies and gentlemen.

所以我要感謝你們對我的作品表現出慷慨的熱情，因為這其實來自你們，是你們允許我在頁底簽署我的名字（編註：隱喻「雖然說是我的音樂，但真正的來源是西班牙這塊土地及其人民」）。感謝各位女士先生。

© Rama

---

1) **progression** [prə`grɛʃən] (n.) 連續（和音）
Could you teach me that chord progression?

2) **coordinate** [ko`ɔrdə,net] (v.) 協調
The dancers practiced coordinating their moves.

3) **boarding house** [`bordɪŋ haus] (n.) 有供餐的宿舍，寄宿公寓
Several residents died in the boarding house fire.

4) **sadden** [`sædən] (v.) 哀痛，讓人難過
It saddened Henry to hear of his friend's death.

5) **favorable** [`fevərəbəl] (a.) 稱讚的，喜歡的
Response to the proposal has been mainly favorable.

6) **hospitality** [ˌhɑspɪ`tælətɪ] (n.) 好客，殷勤招待
Hawaiians are famous for their hospitality.

7) **affix** [ə`fɪks] (v.) 附上（簽名等），貼上（郵票等）
Please affix your signature to the document.

Language Guide

Riccardo Muti 交響樂指揮大師穆蒂

1941 年生,義大利指揮家,現任芝加哥交響樂團(Chicago Symphony Orchestra)音樂總監。與李歐納柯恩同年獲得阿斯圖里亞斯親王獎,穆蒂獲得藝術獎,李歐納柯恩獲得文學獎。

© flickr.com/photos/hansthijs/

refer to... 參考…

這個片語可以表示多種意思,像是「參閱(資料)」、「與…有關」、「…指的是」。

A: Did you have to refer to your notes during your speech?
你演講時有看小抄嗎?

B: No. I was able to memorize the whole thing.
沒有。我把整篇背起來了。

Grammar Master

表達現在習慣的 be used to + Ving / N

本句 I am used to standing in front of an audience without an orchestra behind me. 「我不習慣在後面沒有管弦樂隊的狀況下站在觀眾面前。」句中 be used to 之後加上動名詞 Ving 或名詞,表達「現在的習慣」,表示演講者到現在依然持續此習慣。

如果要表達「過去的習慣」,則使用 used to + V,指過去曾經作過某事,但現在已經不再這樣做。否定:didn't use to V。疑問句則是:Did 主詞 use to V...?

例 **I used to exercise every day, but now I hardly ever exercise.**
我以前每天運動,但是現在很少運動了。

例 **I'm used to living in Taipei.**
我習慣住在台北。

例 **I used to live in Taipei.**
我以前住在台北。

sit around 閒坐

表示無所事事,坐著殺時間。

A: Did you do anything fun on the weekend?
你週末有做什麼有趣的事嗎?

B: No. I just sat around watching TV.
沒。就只有坐著看電視。

in a thousand years 絕對不會

會用否定語氣 not / never in a hundred / thousand / million years 表示強調「從來沒有,絕對不會」。

A: You must have been surprised when you won the lottery.
你中大樂透時一定超驚喜吧。

B: Yeah. Never in a million years did I think I'd win.
對啊。我想都沒想過會中獎。

out of tune 走音

tune 是「音調」,這個片語在演說中所指,就是字面上的意思「走音」的意思。

A: How come you never sing karaoke with us?
你為什麼都不跟我們去唱卡拉OK?

B: It's too embarrassing. I always sing out of tune.
太丟臉了。我都會走音。

chord progression 和絃進行

旋律其實就是一連串和弦的進行,一組不斷重複的和弦進行,或是從一組和弦進行轉為另一組和弦進行,決定音樂的流動,而一個文化地區或音樂類型中不斷出現的和弦進行模式,形成了該種音樂的特殊韻味。而文末的 guitar pattern 就是彈奏合弦的「指型」,即彈奏吉他時手指在琴格上按壓的位置組合。

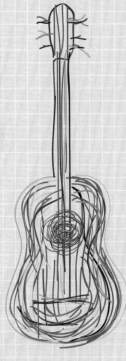

take one's (own) life 自殺

字面上的意思是「取走自己的生命」,也就是自殺。若是殺死別人,就是 take sb.'s life。

A: How did Robin Williams die?
羅賓威廉斯是怎麼死的?

B: He took his own life.
他結束自己的生命。

本書最後一篇的主講者,與本書第一篇主講者巴布狄倫,是常被相提並論的兩位音樂詩人,也是前後期的阿斯圖里亞斯親王獎得主(巴布狄倫 2007 年藝術獎,李歐納柯恩 2011 年文學獎)。觀察兩位演講的內容,巴布狄倫淡淡的訴說著音樂家盛名光環之外的日常,李歐納柯恩則說出一個神秘久遠的故事。兩篇讀完都沒有慷慨激昂,只留低迴的詩意。

最啟發人心的英文得獎感言：EZ TALK 總編嚴選特刊 / EZ
叢書館編輯部作 . -- 初版 . -- 臺北市：日月文化 , 2018.03
　面；　公分 . -- (EZ 叢書館；30)
ISBN 978-986-248-705-1(平裝附光碟片)
1. 英語 2. 演說 3. 讀本
805.18　　　　　　　　　　　　　　　107000491

EZ 叢書館 30

最啟發人心的英文得獎感言
EZ TALK 總編嚴選特刊

總　編　審：Judd Piggott
專案企劃執行：陳思容
主　　　編：潘亭軒
資　深　編　輯：鄭莉璇
文　法　撰　寫：鄭莉璇
校　　　對：潘亭軒、鄭莉璇
封　面　設　計：謝捲子
版　型　設　計：蕭彥伶
內　頁　排　版：蕭彥伶、黃宥辰
錄　音　後　製：純粹錄音後製有限公司
錄　音　人　員：Jacob Roth、Stephanie Buckley

發　行　人：洪祺祥
副　總　經　理：洪偉傑
副　總　編　輯：曹仲堯
法　律　顧　問：建大法律事務所
財　務　顧　問：高威會計師事務所
出　　　版：日月文化出版股份有限公司
製　　　作：EZ 叢書館
地　　　址：臺北市大安區信義路三段151號8樓
電　　　話：(02)2708-5509
傳　　　真：(02)2708-6157
網　　　址：www.ezbooks.com.tw
郵　撥　帳　號：19716071日月文化出版有限公司

總　經　銷：聯合發行股份有限公司
電　　　話：(02)2917-8022
傳　　　真：(02)2915-7212
印　　　刷：中原造像事業股份有限公司
初　版　一　刷：2018 年 3 月
初　版　四　刷：2020 年 4 月
定　　　價：350 元
I　S　B　N：978-986-248-705-1

日月文化集團
HELIOPOLIS
CULTURE GROUP

客服專線 02-2708-5509
客服傳真 02-2708-6157
客服信箱 service@heliopolis.com.tw

廣告回函
台灣北區郵政管理局登記證
北台字第 000370 號
免貼郵票

日月文化集團 讀者服務部 收

10658 台北市信義路三段151號8樓

對折黏貼後，即可直接郵寄

日月文化網址：**www.heliopolis.com.tw**

最新消息、活動，請參考 FB 粉絲團

大量訂購，另有折扣優惠，請洽客服中心（詳見本頁上方所示連絡方式）。

| 日月文化 | EZ TALK | EZ Japan | EZ Korea |

大好書屋・寶鼎出版・山岳文化・洪圖出版　EZ 叢書館　EZ TALK　EZ Japan　EZ Korea

感謝您購買 最啟發人心的英文得獎感言 EZ TALK 總編嚴選特刊

為提供完整服務與快速資訊，請詳細填寫以下資料，傳真至02-2708-6157或免貼郵票寄回，我們將不定期提供您最新資訊及最新優惠。

1. 姓名：＿＿＿＿＿＿＿＿＿＿＿＿＿＿＿　性別：□男　　□女

2. 生日：＿＿＿＿年＿＿＿＿月＿＿＿＿日　職業：＿＿＿＿＿

3. 電話：（請務必填寫一種聯絡方式）

　　（日）＿＿＿＿＿＿＿＿＿（夜）＿＿＿＿＿＿＿＿＿（手機）＿＿＿＿＿＿＿＿

4. 地址：□□□＿＿＿＿＿＿＿＿＿＿＿＿＿＿＿＿＿＿＿＿＿＿＿

5. 電子信箱：＿＿＿＿＿＿＿＿＿＿＿＿＿＿＿＿＿＿＿＿＿＿＿

6. 您從何處購買此書？□＿＿＿＿＿＿＿縣/市＿＿＿＿＿＿＿書店/量販超商

　　□＿＿＿＿＿＿＿網路書店　□書展　□郵購　□其他

7. 您何時購買此書？　　年　　月　　日

8. 您購買此書的原因：（可複選）

　　□對書的主題有興趣　□作者　□出版社　□工作所需　□生活所需

　　□資訊豐富　　□價格合理（若不合理，您覺得合理價格應為＿＿＿＿＿）

　　□封面/版面編排　□其他＿＿＿＿＿＿＿＿＿＿＿＿＿＿＿＿＿

9. 您從何處得知這本書的消息：　□書店　□網路／電子報　□量販超商　□報紙

　　□雜誌　□廣播　□電視　□他人推薦　□其他

10. 您對本書的評價：（1.非常滿意 2.滿意 3.普通 4.不滿意 5.非常不滿意）

　　書名＿＿＿＿　內容＿＿＿＿　封面設計＿＿＿＿　版面編排＿＿＿＿　文/譯筆＿＿＿＿

11. 您通常以何種方式購書？□書店　□網路　□傳真訂購　□郵政劃撥　□其他

12. 您最喜歡在何處買書？

　　□＿＿＿＿＿＿＿縣/市＿＿＿＿＿＿＿書店/量販超商　□網路書店

13. 您希望我們未來出版何種主題的書？＿＿＿＿＿＿＿＿＿＿＿＿＿＿

14. 您認為本書還須改進的地方？提供我們的建議？

＿＿＿＿＿＿＿＿＿＿＿＿＿＿＿＿＿＿＿＿＿＿＿＿＿＿＿＿＿＿＿＿＿

＿＿＿＿＿＿＿＿＿＿＿＿＿＿＿＿＿＿＿＿＿＿＿＿＿＿＿＿＿＿＿＿＿

＿＿＿＿＿＿＿＿＿＿＿＿＿＿＿＿＿＿＿＿＿＿＿＿＿＿＿＿＿＿＿＿＿

＿＿＿＿＿＿＿＿＿＿＿＿＿＿＿＿＿＿＿＿＿＿＿＿＿＿＿＿＿＿＿＿＿